A GOOD DAY TO DIE

OTHER NOVELS BY STEPHEN SOLOMITA

A Piece of the Action
Bad to the Bone
Forced Entry
Force of Nature
A Twist of the Knife

A GOOD DAY TO DIE

STEPHEN SOLOMITA

OTTO
PENZLER
BOOKS

Otto Penzler Books
129 W. 56th Street
New York, NY 10019
(Editorial Offices only)

Macmillan Publishing Company
866 Third Avenue
New York, NY 10022

Maxwell Macmillan Canada, Inc.
1200 Eglinton Avenue East
Suite 200
Don Mills, Ontario M3C 3N1

Macmillan Publishing Company is part of the Maxwell Communication Group of Companies.

Library of Congress Cataloging-in-Publication Data
Solomita, Stephen.
A good day to die/by Stephen Solomita.
p.   cm.
ISBN 1-883402-03-4
I. Title.
PS3569.0587G66   1993
813'.54—dc20   93-19400
CIP

Otto Penzler Books are available at special discounts for bulk purchases for sales promotions, premiums, fund-raising, or educational use. For details, contact:
Special Sales Director, Macmillan Publishing Company
866 Third Avenue, New York, NY 10022

10   9   8   7   6   5   4   3   2   1

Printed in the United States of America

for Paul Goldstein
traveling still

ACKNOWLEDGMENTS

Gotta thank two friends of mine. Jim Appello for his hunting insights and Dake Cassen for dredging up memories of Vietnam firefights. Their help and their patience provided many of the crucial details that (hopefully) make A *Good Day to Die* authentic.

ONE

Lorraine Cho knew it was five o'clock when Melissa Williams switched off the radio in the middle of Andy Williams' version of *Moon River*. Leaving poor Andy to come off sounding like a sick cow.

Mooooooooooooooo . . . click.

Melissa always turned the radio off at five o'clock. Even if the waiting room was crowded with patients who'd been given three o'clock appointments to see one or another of the doctors who owned and staffed the Downtown Brooklyn Medical Center. The clinic's official hours were 9:00 A.M. to 5:00 P.M. and *that*, as Melissa had told Lorraine on more than one occasion, was *that*.

Lorraine Cho had always considered Melissa's abrupt termination of Lite FM's afternoon programming a clear case of blaming the victim. The doctors allotted twenty-three minutes to each patient. They'd reached that figure after a weekend conference on *The Modern Medical Practice*, given in Vail, Colorado, by a manufacturer of business software systems. The simple fact that they, the doctors, were usually out making rounds in one of the affiliated hospitals until nine-thirty or ten didn't enter into their calculations. Nor the fact that, two or three times a week, hospital emergencies had the staff scurrying to reschedule appointments. The conference had shown the partners how to maximize their profit by increasing efficiency. To, for instance, have patient number three get undressed in an examining room while patient number two was being asked to cough and patient number one urinated into a plastic cup.

Lorraine paused for a moment. She removed her earphones and let her fingers drop from the typewriter to her lap.

"The natives are restless," Melissa whispered.

1

"As usual," Lorraine replied without raising her head. She could hear the low buzz of the patients in the waiting room, but she couldn't see them. Nor could she see Melissa Williams. Lorraine Cho was blind.

"You ready to leave?"

Lorraine smiled. Melissa had already pulled on her jacket. "I've got a few more reports to do. I'll be fine."

"I don't like you going home by yourself."

"It's only a few blocks."

Lorraine sighed. They went through this little ritual whenever she had to work late, despite the fact that she lived in a group home on Lawrence Street, less than a half mile from the clinic. Once upon a time, Lorraine had tried to explain the meaning of independence. About how easy it was to fall into the habit of *dependence*. How easy it was to surrender. Melissa had replied with a characteristic snort.

"Girl, you have to cross Flatbush Avenue. Are you fool enough to think those fool drivers give a damn about your independence?" Another snort, this one even more contemptuous. "Not to mention the animals out there. Those animals see you comin', they won't be thinkin' about your *independence*. What they're gonna think is 'easy pickin's. Knock you down, snatch your purse in a heartbeat. And it might be they'll snatch more than *that*. If you take my meaning."

Lorraine hadn't bothered to argue. Melissa Williams had as good a heart as anyone Lorraine knew, despite her assertion that, "Being as I'm a black woman in a white man's world, I can't afford to be soft."

For Melissa, not being "soft" meant leaving the Downtown Brooklyn Medical Center at five o'clock on the dot. No matter how many unmailed insurance reports lay on her desk. The medical staff—the nurses and the techs—could stick around until six or seven. They really didn't have any choice. But the clerical staff was under no such obligation. Melissa had a husband and two children waiting in a condominium on First Avenue and Thirty-eighth Street in Manhattan. Their needs came first.

Lorraine sat quietly for a few minutes, listening to the hum of her IBM Selectric. Remembering Melissa Williams' patience when faced with the prospect of training a blind typist. Lorraine Cho knew her employment may have been a spontaneous bit of charity on the part of the doctor who decided to "give her a chance," but for Melissa Williams, Lorraine's "chance" meant long months of reviewing each report Lorraine typed, of quiet corrections and explanations.

For Lorraine, on the other hand, mastering the unfamiliar jargon that poured through the earphones attached to her mini-recorder was just one more battle in a war that had begun five years earlier when she'd gotten drunk at a friend's house and plowed her car into a pillar supporting the tracks of the Roosevelt Avenue el.

The pain was the easiest part. In the beginning, the pain kept her from thinking about what her mother described as "your condition." As long as her face was covered with bandages, she could pretend the bandages were the cause of the darkness. That one day in the future, Dr. Marren would gently unwrap those bandages and her eyes would open to a painfully blue sky filled with soaring doves. Just like in the movies.

The only thing was that she didn't *have* eyes. (If it weren't for reconstructive surgery, she later realized, she wouldn't have a *face*.) But the funny part was that the fantasy persisted, even after the bandages were removed, even after they weaned her off the Demerol, even after she went home to her parents' apartment in Kew Gardens.

Organize and memorize. A place for everything and everything in its place. It took months to get it right. Until she could move from the kitchen to the bedroom without cracking her shins against the corner of an end table. Or brush her teeth without sending the toothpaste and the plastic cup on the sink crashing to the floor.

The effort to learn that tiny piece of the world represented by the six rooms of her parents' apartment was enormous. But once the effort had been made, Lorraine was content to rest, to revel in the safety after so much insecurity and physical pain.

And why shouldn't she? Her parents were invariably supportive. Supportive and protective. "We'll always be there for you," they told her again and again. "Don't worry about *anything*."

The Library for the Blind sent her books on tape—sent them free of charge along with a sighted braille tutor. If she wanted fresh air, all she had to do was step onto the balcony and take a deep breath. True, television meant nothing, but the New York radio bands, AM and FM, were crowded with stations offering every kind of music along with call-in shows, public radio stations, religious broadcasting, twenty-four-hour news . . .

Why should she leave? Ever? What was the point? Sure, if you didn't have anyone to care for you, to go out and buy the groceries, cook the food, clean the house, do the laundry . . . then you'd have to venture out into the dark and dangerous world. The world that had taken your sight in the first place. But she wasn't in that position. Her father was an electrical engineer with a doctorate from MIT. Money would never be a problem for Lorraine Cho.

What I did, she decided much later, was drift, a puffball in a gentle stream. Still expecting my sight to be restored. Still waiting for the cure.

The event that changed her life took place ten months after she left the hospital. With her father at work and her mother out shopping, she reached into the refrigerator for a can of Coke and sent a bottle of grapefruit juice crashing to the floor. Her first reaction was anger. Juice bottles were supposed to be on the left side of the top shelf, not stuck in the middle. How could they be so stupid? Didn't they know she was blind?

It took Lorraine a full minute to realize that she was standing barefoot on a floor littered with broken glass and her mother wouldn't be back for hours and she couldn't call a neighbor because she couldn't get to the telephone. She would have to deal with it herself.

The first thing she did was squat on her heels and brush shards of glass off her feet. It was the obvious place to begin and the last thing she expected, as she fought the anger and panic, was to find herself transformed. Nevertheless, as her fingertips slid across the linoleum floor, she awoke to a sensitivity beyond anything she'd ever dreamed. Her fingers were alive, searching the floor as if they had eyes. As if *she* had eyes. She could handle the sharpest piece of glass with no concern for her safety; the jagged shards might have been spilled marshmallows for all the danger they posed.

She cleared a small space around her feet, then dropped to her knees and made her way across the kitchen to the broom closet. Removing a plastic dustpan, she began to systematically clean the floor, brushing glass chips into the dustpan with the sensitivity of a lover caressing the flesh of her beloved. The force of her concentration, as she read the sensations traveling through her fingertips, drove every other consideration from her mind.

When she finished, when she'd emptied the dustpan into the small garbage pail by the stove, she became aware of a mix of emotions radiating just outside her body like the halo surrounding the head of a medieval saint. Overwhelmed, she continued to sit on the floor for a moment, then got up and made her way into the bathroom.

Still bemused, she disrobed, turned on the water, adjusted the temperature, and stepped into the shower. When the water hit her face and chest, it was as if the sensitivity in her fingers had been transferred to every cell in her body. She was aware of individual streams cascading off her flesh, of trickles running along her ribs and down her thighs, of steam rising to envelop her body. She could hear droplets strike the surface of the tub, hear them over the intense hissing of the showerhead.

It was miraculous. And impossible, too. Of course, she'd heard that blind people enjoyed heightened sensitivity as a kind of compensation. But if that was the case, where had that sensitivity been hiding all this time? And, more important, what would she do if it suddenly vanished?

But it didn't vanish. True, over time, the excitement and emotion diminished. She began to take her abilities for granted, even as they expanded. Within a month, she could identify people she knew by the sound and rhythm of their breathing. Within two months, she could enter a room and know someone else was there, even if they were completely silent. Five months later, she left her parents' Kew Gardens apartment, entered a group home for the blind, and began to train for the rest of her life.

"I'm leaving, girl. You sure you'll be all right?"

Melissa's voice jerked Lorraine back to her little cubicle. "I'll be okay, Melissa. Let me get back to work."

She listened to Melissa's retreating footsteps for a moment, then put on her earphones and pressed the foot pedal controlling the dictaphone.

Focal area of decreased echogenicity in the tip of the spleen. Differential diagnosis would include artifact vs splenic abscess vs splenic infarct vs tumor. Splenomegaly. Cholelithiasis. Phleboliths vs distal urethral calculi on both sides of the true pelvis.

She continued to work for another twenty minutes. The typing was purely mechanical, though it hadn't been that way at first. In the beginning, her coach, John Tufaro, had set her down in front of an ancient Smith-Corona and said, "If you could type when you were sighted, you can type now. Do it."

But she couldn't do it. Not at first. What bothered her was the fact that she had no way to check her work. If she made a mistake, she wouldn't (and didn't) know it. Not knowing caused her to hesitate, to make mistakes. It wasn't until after John took her into the lounge and played several cuts from his George Shearing collection that she finally took the hint. Shearing was a blind pianist, yet he never missed a note. In a way, his situation was worse than hers, because if George Shearing made a mistake, he *would* know it. And so would everybody in the audience.

What she needed, she'd realized, was confidence, and the best way to get it was to bang away at the keys with the abandon of a toddler stacking a pile of blocks. At first, she insisted that John Tufaro check her work. But after a few weeks she discovered that she could tell when she made a mistake. The same fingertips that had guided her over a floor littered with broken glass could differentiate between an *l* and a semicolon, even though they sometimes pressed the wrong key.

She didn't know exactly *how* she perceived this information, but how didn't really matter. What mattered was that her craft, her typing, was one more step on the road to independence. A road that led from a wrecked car to a hospital bed to an apartment in Queens, to a group home to a . . .

She had no concrete vision of the next step, but she was sure that each prior step was an expansion, and as long as she kept expanding, she was on the right track.

Half an hour later, Lorraine Cho flipped off her IBM. The waiting room was quiet, which meant the last patient had been taken to one of the screened cubicles that served as an examining room. She sat for a moment, enjoying the silence, then pushed her chair away from the desk, grabbed her long white cane, and stood up. Marching across the floor without hesitation, she took her wool jacket out of the staff closet and put it on. New York was in the middle of a cold spell, and it could easily take half an hour to walk the few blocks to the group home. After all, despite what she told Melissa Williams, she still had to cross Flatbush Avenue.

Lorraine moved quickly through the patients' waiting room, sweeping the floor in front of her with practiced ease. She knew the territory well, but there was always the chance that some patient had left a surprise for her, had moved a chair or dropped a magazine on the floor. (Stepping on a magazine was like stepping on a patch of ice.) But she found nothing untoward as she made her way out to the street.

A bracing wind chipped at her nose and her ears, but instead of trying to pull her head down into the collar of her coat, she flared her nostrils and sucked in the clean, cold air. She could feel the sun's heat despite the forty-five-degree temperature and gusty winds. The mix was delicious.

She made her way to the corner of Flatbush Avenue and Willoughby Street, stopping next to the mechanism that regulated the traffic light. The problem with Flatbush Avenue was that its eight lanes led directly to the Manhattan Bridge. At six on a weekday, it was inevitably packed in both directions with bumper-to-bumper traffic. Traffic that, as often as not, spilled back across the intersection when the light turned red, so that even though Lorraine could hear the light flip from green to yellow to red, she couldn't be sure the intersection was clear. Nor could she be certain that vehicles making the turn from Willoughby Street onto Flatbush Avenue would respect her right to cross the street unimpeded. In New York, pedestrians and drivers seemed to be in a constant state of war, a fact she'd joyfully exploited when she was sighted, ignoring traffic lights and pedestrian crosswalks like any good citizen.

Now she had to pay the price. And there was only one way to do it. One way that didn't involve a high probability of physical injury. Lorraine walked to the edge of the curb, then stood stock-still and waited for some good citizen to come to her rescue. A traffic agent usually worked this intersection, a man named Joe who guided her across the street whenever possible. Unfortunately, Joe wasn't on duty. Lorraine knew he wasn't around because Joe blew his whistle, stopping traffic, whenever the light changed. Lorraine could smell the stink of mixed gasoline and diesel exhausts, hear the animal roar of buses pulling away from the curb and the vicious chorus of car horns that challenged their right-of-way. But there was no whistle.

One day, she decided, she'd have to ask Joe why he wasn't on duty every weekday at this time. Lord knew it had nothing to do with the volume of traffic. Traffic volume varied in direct proportion to the number of horns blaring at any given moment. The more frustrated the drivers, the louder the symphony. Tonight, she was listening to Tchaikovsky's cannons.

"Do you need some help, miss?"

Lorraine smiled, relieved to hear a voice, especially a female voice. That was another thing Melissa was right about. The animals who roamed New York City streets looking for prey would respect neither Lorraine's blindness nor the seeing eyes of potential witnesses. She was the quintessential victim, ripe for a takeoff, and the only surprise was that it hadn't already happened. Everybody else in her group home had been attacked at least once. Vulnerability was the price of independence; there was no way around it.

"I'd surely appreciate it," Lorraine answered. She waved at the unseen vehicles. "They don't seem like they're about to stop for me. Or for anything else."

"Well, I must say that I'm new at this. If you will tell me what to do, I'll be glad to help you."

Lorraine listened closely, knowing the woman through her words. The accent was definitely southern, the voice young but serious, the phrases oddly separated. *Well, I must say . . . that Ah'm new . . . at this. If you will tell me . . . what to do . . . Ah'll be glad . . . to help . . . you.*

"Let me take your left arm. Then walk normally."

"All right." As the woman moved around her, Lorraine caught a trace of flowery perfume. Lilac predominated, but there were other scents as well. The perfume reinforced Lorraine's sense of the woman's rural origins. Lilac was definitely not New York. "Are there any potholes?" Lorraine asked.

"Well, the road *is* bumpy, but isn't that just like the roads in New York? There is a crew—I believe they are from the telephone company—workin' on the far corner, but we can pass around them. Are we ready?"

Lorraine took the woman's arm, noting the slender limb and the underlying muscle.

"I did have an auntie," the woman said as they stepped off the curb, "who was blind. But that was back in Atherton? In Mississippi? She surely did not have to worry about streets like this. And everybody did know her, so they would stop and help. I think it's just awful that you should have to go out on your own. But isn't that typical? Of New York City? It is such a *cold* place. Back home, people care about each other."

Lorraine paid little attention to her Good Samaritan's chatter, saving her concentration for the task at hand. She knew, from bitter experience, that small imperfections in the road, imperfections a sighted person wouldn't notice, could send her sprawling. Nor could she entirely rely on the judgment of her benefactor when it came to larger obstacles. On one occasion, a well-meaning stranger had run her into the tail pipe of a small truck. Between the collision and the deep burn, she'd been hobbled for the better part of a week.

"Only a few more steps, miss, and we will be on the sidewalk. We just have to go around this truck."

Lorraine stretched her left arm out to gauge the distance between herself and the truck. She didn't want to insult the woman, but she could hear the truck's motor running and she knew she was very close to it.

Her arm reached out into empty space, and it took her a moment to realize the truck's rear doors had to be open. Then a hand grabbed her wrist and yanked her forward, smashing her knees into the truck's bumper as she flew through the doors.

"Close 'em and go. Fast." A man's voice, tight and urgent, followed by slamming doors and a fist smashing into the side of her head. "Shut up, bitch. Shut the fuck up."

She didn't react; her mind was spinning too fast to fashion a response, though she was aware of everything. Aware of the odor of wood smoke and pipe tobacco clinging to the man. Of the sudden jerk as the truck pulled away. Of her benefactor's tinkling laughter. Of the man's hand thrust into her crotch. Of his finger poking at the glass orbs filling her eye sockets.

"Damn, Baby, looks like we got ourselves a keeper. A slanty-eyed slope with good tits and no eyes. A definite goddamned keeper."

TWO

By the time my savior made her appearance, ramrod straight in her starched uniform, I was near madness. The preachers claim that salvation is a vision of light buried in the invisible depths of one's darkest moments. Captain Vanessa Bouton didn't fit that image, either. Mahogany skin, short and carefully styled black hair, widely spaced brown eyes—she was anything but a willowy spirit descending out of a backlit cloud. Nevertheless, the plain truth is that Vanessa Bouton saved my sorry little ass.

"Roland Means?" she said. "Detective Roland Means?"

I was standing at a workbench in the ballistics lab at the time, peering through a microscope at pairs of .22-caliber shell casings. Comparing, believe it or not, extractor marks.

This is not a fun way to spend your working days. Especially not for a street cop, which is what I'd always been and always wanted to be. Extractor marks are nothing more than scratches. Scratches made by the slide mechanism of a semiautomatic weapon as it loads and ejects cartridges. The official line is that extractor marks are as distinctive as fingerprints. Well, I've never thought much of fingerprints, either. There's a line in a song—I forget the name of the singer; most of them are as alike as the lands and grooves on a spent slug—it goes like this: *It was the myth of fingerprints/I've seen them all and, man, they're all the same.*

I'm going too far, here. Ballistics is a science, and on those rare occasions when I got a match, the exact nature of those little scratches jumped out at me like a grouse breaking cover. No matter how many hours I spent in the forest (or peering through a microscope), I was never ready for it.

The only problem was that I spent almost all of my time on random searches.

"Run this .45 through the ringer, Detective. We think it was used in a hit."

I'd begin by taking microphotographs of rifling, ejector, and firing-pin marks. Then I'd go to the files and pull similar photographs of slugs pulled from the carcasses of murder victims. Caliber was a limiting factor, of course, but mostly it was a fishing expedition. Some detective (usually a lieutenant) takes a piece off a bad guy and figures he'll become a hero if he can get ballistics to elevate a weapons violation into a murder rap.

The saddest part is that it can all be done by computer. Fingerprints, too. The computer reads a photo of whatever you're looking for, then searches for a match. It's even possible to link your system to NCIC, the FBI's memory bank. Unfortunately, the NYPD doesn't use computers. The NYPD uses slobs like me to peer at slides for hours on end.

I shouldn't exaggerate. Most of the cops I met in ballistics were glad to be there. The hours were regular and you didn't have to worry about getting shot. Or piped or stabbed or second-guessed by some fat-ass in an office when you took steps to prevent all of the above from happening. No, for most of the cops working in one or another of the NYPD's labs or crime-scene investigation teams, the work was a treat. (At the least. At the most, it was a career path laid out with microscopic exactitude.)

For me, on the other hand, the ten months I spent in the lab were pure punishment. The NYPD was that desperate to get me off the street.

"Detective Means?" Her voice was insistent (a matter of habit, I suspected), but the eyes were quizzical. Trying to figure out exactly what I was.

I was used to that reaction, had been getting it ever since I left the town of Paris, New York, more than fifteen years before. My father was a full-blooded American Indian, a wandering

Cherokee and a straight-ahead drunk. My mother was Scotch-Irish and also a drunk. Somehow they married and conceived a child. (Or did they marry *because* they conceived a child?) My father, or so the story goes, was saved by an itinerant Pentecostal preacher a month or so after my mother gave birth. Dad hung around for six months, trying to convert dear old mom, but finally gave up and headed west to rejoin his people. That was the last time anybody in the town of Paris laid eyes on him.

The end result of that brief union (namely, myself) was not a blend of the races, but pieces of a genetic puzzle glued together to make a face. I have my father's jet-black hair, narrow black eyes, high cheekbones, and forehead. Mom contributed a pug nose, thin mouth, and firm Irish jaw. Only my skin itself, a pale ivory, hints of any true union.

No, Captain Vanessa Bouton's puzzled expression was nothing new to me. People tended to view me as some kind of hybrid Asian, but at six-two and two hundred and ten pounds, I was too tall and too broadly built to fit that stereotype, either.

"What can I do for you, Captain . . . ?"

"Bouton. Vanessa Bouton. You *are* Roland Means."

"That's me."

"Let's find some chairs."

She led me out of the lab and into Sergeant Flynn's office. Flynn was nowhere to be found, the usual case in the late afternoon when he invariably found some excuse to get out of the lab and into a bar.

"Sit down, Detective."

I sat, noting that Vanessa Bouton's back was as straight and unyielding in a chair as it had been when she stood.

"How long have you been a police officer, Detective?" Her gaze had lost its former puzzlement. Now, her eyes were hard and piercing. As befits a ranking officer addressing a piece of shit.

"A little over eighteen years." I kept my voice casual. Hoping that whatever she wanted would lead me out of the ballistic wilderness in which I'd been wandering.

"And how long have you been a detective?"

"Nine years." The gold shield had been my goal even before I took the entrance exam.

"It didn't take you long to get into trouble."

"Trouble, Captain?"

"Don't jerk me off, Means. I have neither the time nor the temperament for bullshit."

Was the profanity her way of announcing that she wasn't a tight-assed, by-the-books bureaucrat? I'd have bet my left testicle that she'd gotten off the streets at the first opportunity. That she wouldn't know how to track a dead junkie through the morgue. That she hadn't made an arrest in ten years unless she'd stolen it from another cop.

"I don't know what you mean," I insisted. "I've got three commendations and no reprimands. In 1989, I was up for Detective of the Year." I have to admit, I smiled when I said it.

Bouton continued to stare at me for a moment. Her features, taken apart from her attitude, were soft. Broad nose, full lips, round cheeks, large liquid eyes. In another lifetime, she might have been motherly. In this lifetime, she was determined to be less sympathetic than a drill sergeant with athlete's foot.

"You *killed* a man."

"A man? Don't you mean a *mutt*? As far as I know, the job doesn't punish cops for killing dogs. Especially dogs with guns in their hands."

"You killed him with a knife."

The problem was that I didn't know what she wanted me to say. The facts had been established by an automatic review board that kicks in whenever there's a civilian death. I'd confronted a pimp and he'd put a gun against my chest. Being as my arms were up in the air at the time, the only weapon available to me was a plastic knife, a dagger, that I kept in my sleeve. It was the best defensive knife I ever owned, and I was more than a little pissed when the review board kept it. I'd never seen a plastic knife before I took that one off a street junkie. It was virtually weightless, yet sharp enough to cut circles in a sheet of newspaper. A perfect little double-edged dagger that I miss to this very day.

The pimp should have killed me on the spot. (God knows he had plenty of reason; I'd been in his face for months.) But he didn't pull the trigger right away. What he did was indulge his ego, telling me that I was a piece of shit he had to scrape off his shoe. What *I* did was grab the knife with the fingers of my right hand, then sweep the gun aside with my left hand while I dragged the blade across his throat. He stood there for a moment, pumping blood all over my Evan Picone jacket, then dropped like a rock. Leaving, I'm happy to say, his Glock 9mm in my hand.

(I'm not trying to make myself out to be a hero. There was no risk at all. The asshole had made two mistakes. Not only had he gotten too close, he'd let me make the first move. He could *not* have pulled the trigger before I hit his hand. I had no doubt about it then. I have no doubt about it now. Taking him out amounted to no more than having the confidence to do it without hesitation.)

"What's the point, Captain? The killing was investigated and I was cleared."

"The point is that I have to know whether you're a run-of-the-mill hotdog or a genuine psychotic. The department took you off the streets because it couldn't make up its mind."

"You want proof? I can't give it to you. You want *evidence* on the other hand, take a look at the last ten months. I came into work, on time, every day. I peered through a microscope until my eyes refused to focus. And I never complained. *Never.* I know I'm on probation, Captain. I'm not a fool. But the question I have to ask is if there's *anything* I can do to redeem myself."

I let my eyes go hard for a moment, trying to show her a little righteous indignation. Hoping she'd fall for it. The truth, as far as I could see it, was that the NYPD would be much better served by keeping me right where I was. The truth was that I'd never been a team player and never would be. The truth was that what I wanted from the job had very little to do with a paycheck and a pension. I felt like a game warden trying to explain how an out-of-season deer got into his trunk.

"It wasn't the first time, was it?" Her expression didn't change. It *refused* to change. She wasn't going to let me wriggle off the hook until her question was answered. I've known any number of ranking officers who pretended to be hard asses because that's what they thought they were supposed to be. Vanessa Bouton, Captain, New York City Police Department, wasn't pretending.

"The first time?"

"The first time you *killed* someone. I believe you were still on patrol the first time it happened."

That one got a genuine smile. "The first time happened long before I joined the department, Captain. In a country called Vietnam. You wanna hear about it?"

"Not especially."

"Not especially? Listen, you say I'm a hotdog? You say I worked on my own time when I could have been drinking in some cozy cop bar? When I could have been rubbing against some aging cop groupie? I say it was that extra hustle that got me out of uniform. That got me knocked up to grade one. That got me those commendations you don't wanna talk about. And I'll tell you something else, Captain. I'll never be the kind of cop who does his tour and goes home. Never. I'd leave the job first."

Suddenly I was disgusted. Why was I sucking up to this fat-ass desk jockey? For Captain Vanessa Bouton, creeping down a dark hallway in some abandoned South Bronx tenement was the cop equivalent of jumping out of a helicopter without a parachute. For me, it was the ultimate superfly dope.

"What do you know about King Thong?"

That got me. I actually burst out laughing, then continued to laugh at Vanessa Bouton's unchanging expression. I don't know which one of the tabloids gave that name to New York's latest serial killer. (At the time, I'd thought it incredibly insensitive, even by New York standards. Then I'd discovered that reporters in the Seattle area had routinely identified Ted Bundy's victims as Miss March, Miss April, Miss May, and so on.) In any event, King Thong had spent most of last year killing and mutilating male prostitutes. He'd earned his nickname by wrapping his victims' penises with a narrow strip of leather, a thong, then tying the ends around the victims' waists in what amounted to a permanent erection. The tabloids and the counterculture weeklies (especially the *Soho Spirit*) had injected a certain bizarre humor into their coverage from the beginning. I suppose the fact that each victim was a homosexual *and* a prostitute entitled them (at least in *their* opinion) to a little license, but the humor had ended abruptly when the *Spirit* published a cartoon depicting the Empire State Building wrapped in a long, leather strip. The caption, "Thong Lives," had said it all. So had the two thousand protesters who spent the next month picketing the headquarters of the *Spirit*.

"Sorry." I dutifully wiped the smirk off my face. "You caught me by surprise."

"You always find murder funny, Means?"

"Not always, Captain. But, then, not every murderer gets a name like 'King Thong.'"

Vanessa Bouton finally managed a smile. A smile and a deep chuckle. "The best part," she said, "is that we'd decided to hold the leather back. Somebody in the task force leaked it."

I nodded sympathetically. Detectives regularly hold back details as a way to separate a true confession from the ravings of a maniac. They just as regularly hand information over to their favorite reporters, despite a professed hatred of the media.

"Tell you the truth, Captain, the only thing I know about your serial killer is what I read in the papers."

And the only thing I wanted to know. Homicides where killer and victim have no prior connection are a cop's worst nightmare. Where do you begin? Every detective catches his share of professional hits, and I was no exception. After a while, I dreaded them, because I knew I'd never solve one. Not *one*.

But I still had to make the rounds. Had to send out whatever evidence I recovered to the labs. Question the locals in search of a witness. File my DD 5's after every tour. NR, NR, NR. Negative Results. Every inch of the way.

When it comes to serial killers, you can take all that frustration and multiply it ten thousand times. The media pounds the public every day with the simple truth: no suspects, no clues, no nothing. Despite the creation of unimaginable six-hundred-cop task forces that, in turn, create tons of useless paperwork.

"You don't know *anyone* on the task force? Nobody?"

"I don't spend my off-duty time with other cops."

"Off-duty time? My information is that you're a cop twenty-four hours a day. Is it true that back when you were in uniform, you used to ride the subways looking for muggers to arrest?"

"I used to ride the subways looking for muggers before I became a cop." I leaned forward, smiling. "Tell ya the truth, Captain, looking for muggers is *why* I became a cop."

It was her turn to hunch forward on her chair. She kept on coming until her face was a couple of inches from mine. "Listen, you sorry-assed motherfucker, if you think you can intimidate me, you're sadly mistaken. Now, sit back in that chair and try to use your brain instead of your hormones."

"I thought that was my line."

Stalemate. But not altogether unpleasant.

"You like punch lines, Detective?" she asked, ignoring my witty remark.

"Only if I'm not the one getting punched."

"The King Thong victims were *not* selected at random. They were not serial killings as we understand them. The motivation was not sexual, not the product of a demented psychopathic personality. One of the murders had an everyday, understandable motivation. The rest were committed to cover it up."

That got my attention. The Thong murders had begun more than a year ago. One killing a month for seven long months, then nothing. The department, in its infinite wisdom, had tried to bury the first three, assigning them to Homicide as if they were routine incidents. Then some cop had leaked the facts to a CBS reporter with close ties to New York's considerable homosexual community. That considerable community had responded with an organized fury not seen since the heyday of the Vietnam protest era.

And why shouldn't they? Devastated by a disease called AIDS, subject to attack by roving packs of demented teenagers, how could they view the NYPD's response as anything but another demonstration of the city's indifference to their plight? Indifference that was a logical extension of the conventional wisdom that whatever happens to a faggot is part of God's punishment for a demonstrably evil lifestyle.

For the first few weeks, the crowds at City Hall and Gracie Mansion, the mayor's residence, were massive, with large numbers of ordinary citizens as well as a dozen gay advocacy groups in attendance. A serial killer was walking the streets, a predator seeking victims. How could the cops (and, as far as the demonstrators were concerned, the mayor and every other politician) try to cover it up? A year later, months after the killings had suddenly stopped, small groups of demonstrators holding lit candles continued to follow the mayor from one public event to the next.

The NYPD (following a series of carefully orchestrated *mea culpas*) had been forced to go public. The sixteen cops assigned to investigate the first three killings quickly grew to a hundred, then two hundred, then six hundred at the peak of the investigation. A hotline had been set up, the FBI called in, and psychologists galore invited to speculate on the killer's motivation.

All to no avail. The killings had stopped five months before Vanessa Bouton appeared in my life and the task force, with nothing new to investigate, had begun to wind down.

"What's the matter, Detective, cat got your tongue? Is the wise guy out of wisdom?" Her grin had broadened considerably.

"I admit you've got my complete attention." I shifted in my seat, trying to get my brain to pursue exactly what this piece of information meant to *me*. "Is that the official position of the NYPD?" I knew it couldn't be even as I asked the question. If the task force was buying Vanessa Bouton's theory, it'd be doing its own investigating.

"No, it's not." The grin faded as she returned to her formidable former self.

"Does the department know you're here?"

"Do you think that's a proper question for a piss-ant detective to put to a captain? You might want to do yourself a favor, Means, and not presume *anything*. Not unless you plan to stay in this lab for the rest of your career."

She obviously expected a response, but I refused to give her one. The only thing she could do (as she so kindly pointed out) was leave me where I was. I was already being punished.

"What do you know about serial killers?" she asked after a moment.

"They don't get caught unless they make a mistake."

"That's not very much."

"Look, Captain, the last serial killer we had in New York was the copycat Zodiac killer. He managed to kill one man and wound several others before he disappeared. How many homicides have we had since then? Two thousand? Three thousand? *Five* thousand? Serial killers are big problems for politicians, not cops."

It was the truth and it was obvious. The myth of the serial killer—that he's out there and waiting to get *you*—terrifies the voters, who put pressure on the pols, who put pressure on the department. But the department is not, and never has been, the individual cops who do their jobs every day. The whole, in this case, is not the sum of its parts. The whole, meaning the New York City Police Department, is a political bureaucracy out to cover its ass. Even when covering its ass means sacrificing individual parts.

"You don't think this particular serial killer was a problem for the six hundred cops relieved of their regular duties to work on the task force?"

"You take the man's pay, you do the man's job." The universal cop explanation for accepting distasteful assignments.

Suddenly, Vanessa Bouton stood up. "You came well recommended, Means. But you also came with a warning. Now that I've read the label, I think the possible side effects outweigh the possible benefits."

"Wait a second, Captain. You asked me what I knew about serial killers. You didn't ask me what I know about homicide in general." You can't have your bluff called unless you're bluffing. Which I undoubtedly was. "Tell me why you believe Thong isn't a serial killer? Please."

She stepped forward without resuming her seat. "Thong *is* a serial killer. By definition, any series of homicides with a cooling-off period between them falls into the category of serial killing. *Assassins* are serial killers. *Hit men* are serial killers. What I said to you was that the King Thong murder victims were not chosen at random. Or, at least, *one* of them wasn't chosen at random. Now, are you at all interested in how I came to that conclusion? Or do you intend to play your bullshit macho games until I walk out of here?"

THREE

The sneer on her face was truly wonderful. It dripped contempt like the fangs of a rattlesnake drip poison just before they sink into the flesh of a browsing rabbit. I studied that sneer for a moment, realizing that Vanessa Bouton, like any other ranking officer addressing a subordinate, expected me to play the part of the rabbit. To play it consciously and willingly.

Well, bad for her; good for me. Bad for her because if she wanted anything but the scalp of a serial killer (if for instance, she also wanted *my* scalp), then she was vulnerable. Good for me because I could be the snake inside the rabbit. Contenting myself with green, leafy vegetables until the opportunity for red flesh presented itself.

"Please tell me why you believe Thong wasn't choosing random victims," I said as sincerely as possible. "If you're right, it would make police history."

That got to her. She managed a broad smile and nodded her head. "So, you finally figured it out. And the best part is that we don't have to share it. The department is committed to the serial killer theory. If we bring Thong in, you and me, they'll be talking about us for a long, long time."

And visions of the "Today" show danced in her head. Did she want to be promoted to inspector? Chief? Commissioner? Her current rank, captain, was as high as civil service exams could take her. The rest of her career path (if there was to be a rest) would be paved with appointments and politics.

"I said, '*if* you're right,' Captain. I'm willing to be convinced, but I can't take it on faith."

The perfect mix of respect and skepticism? I felt like I was conducting an interrogation. Trying to coax a statement from a reluctant perpetrator.

"Rule of thumb: Sexually motivated serial killers begin tentatively. There are no schools for murderers. They learn by doing. The Thong murders were *identical*. The victims were all street prostitutes, all working at the time they were taken, yet there was no sign of sexual assault. Each was killed by a single shot to the head from the same .22-caliber automatic and the bodies mutilated after death occurred. I don't want to get into the details—you'll have plenty of chances to learn them for yourself—but the mutilations were so exact, it was as if the killer was working from an instruction manual. Look at it from your own point of view. You've conducted hundreds of interrogations. In the beginning, you must have been tentative. You knew what you wanted, but you had to learn how to get it. It's the same with serial killers. They have to learn, and our man started at the top."

"You think he read a book or something?" I maintained my half-smile, nodding idiotically.

"That's *exactly* what I think." By this time, she was out of the chair and pacing. Her hands, palms up, fingers splayed, were moving in excited half-circles. "There are thousand of books on serial killers. Everybody wants a piece of the action. Psychologists, criminologists, cops, lawyers, reporters. There's no reason why our boy couldn't have studied the subject for a few months before he made his move. What surprises me is that the FBI, with all its experience, hasn't been expecting this."

I raised my hand. "Excuse me, Captain, but aren't you overlooking something. Maybe he took his show on the road before he came here. I seem to remember hearing that serial killers tend to drift from place to place."

She stopped pacing and jammed her fists into her hips. Broad-shouldered and solid, she presented a formidable image. Even in that uniform with the two gold bars on the shoulders.

"Don't you think I thought of that? Are you making me for

stupid, Means? Black people don't care to be taken for stupid. If I was you, I'd keep that in mind as we go along."

I suppose I could have come back with the "dumb injun" bit. Moaned about how *all* minorities have suffered from the same accusation. But I didn't. I held my ground and waited for her to get to the point.

"The first thing I did, after I became suspicious, was tap into VICAP. You have any idea what VICAP is?"

"Not the faintest."

"Why am I not surprised?" She was pacing again, her hands moving as rapidly as her mouth. "VICAP is run by the FBI out of Quantico. The letters stand for Violent Criminal Apprehension Program. Theoretically, all unsolved murders are reported to the FBI and entered into VICAP's database. The programmers designed the system to track killers who move from one jurisdiction to another. If Thong was out there killing before he came to the Big Apple, he wasn't doing it anything like the way he does it now."

"No disrespect, Captain, but you used the word 'theoretically' to . . ."

"Yes, yes." She waved me off impatiently. "Reporting is voluntary and there's no shortage of cops, like *you*, who don't even know what VICAP is. But we're talking about mutilated male prostitutes tied up with strips of leather. It's not the kind of thing you can file away and forget about."

I could picture her making this same pitch to whatever chief was running the task force. I could also picture said chief looking down his nose at this upstart black woman who, in his opinion, like all women officers, could best serve the department by resigning forthwith. Vanessa Bouton couldn't have been more than thirty-five years old. She'd already passed the sergeant's, lieutenant's, and captain's exams. Half the brass at the top of the NYPD would hate her for that alone.

"Consider this," she continued, pausing for a moment to fix me with a penetrating look. "The victims were taken from various locations around Manhattan: the 'strip' on Fifty-third Street, the West Street piers, Queens Plaza under the Fifty-ninth Street Bridge, Hunts Point in the Bronx; Roosevelt Avenue in Jackson Heights. He got them off the street without anyone knowing, then murdered them, mutilated them, and cleaned up the bodies. Why would he dump them where they were sure to be found? Why would he take the risk of being discovered *as* he dumped the bodies?"

"Maybe he's stupid." It was exactly what she wanted to hear.

"Stupid? Face it, Means, he's crafty as hell. By the time he was ready to take his fourth victim, half the homosexual population in the city was looking for him. Not to mention every cop on patrol and the largest task force ever assembled by the NYPD. Yet he managed to kill four more people and leave their bodies on street corners without being caught. That doesn't sound stupid to me. It sounds like he wanted to make *sure* the bodies were discovered."

"Why couldn't he just be proud of his work? Maybe outwitting twenty-seven thousand NYPD cops is part of the kick."

"Then why not a note of explanation? Contact with the media? Something to tell the world exactly what he was doing. Another rule of thumb: Serial killers do not want to get caught. Some kill and leave their victims right where they are, but the ones who transport bodies almost always make an effort to conceal them. Believe me when I say that I've reviewed the literature carefully."

She sat down facing me, her expression earnest, almost entreating. "And there's something else that bothers me. The victims were very different types. Thong took a ten-year-old boy from Hunts Point, a pre-op transexual from Queens Plaza, a leather-and-studs biker from West Street, a twenty-two-year-old country boy from Fifty-third Street . . . "

"Wait a second. A twenty-two-year-old man from the strip? Fifty-third Street is chicken heaven. It's where the hawks go when they're hungry. Twenty-two seems ancient for Fifty-third Street."

"That's the point, isn't it? Thong was very careful. Too careful. It was as if the only thing that mattered was not getting caught. He didn't have sex with his victims. It's one of the few things we managed to keep from the media. There was no semen in (or on) any of the bodies. And no fresh anal fissures so we're pretty sure he didn't use a condom." She leaned forward, eyes blazing with conviction. "Add it up, Means. He didn't care who he picked up. He wasn't interested in sex. He left the bodies where they had to be found. He mutilated and trussed up his victims in a way that guaranteed media attention. Something's wrong here. Something doesn't smell right."

I didn't buy it at the time. Mainly because I assumed that men like John Wayne Gacy and Henry Lee Lucas (and our boy, King Thong) were crazy. How else could you explain random killings? Later, I found out different, but just then, looking into Vanessa Bouton's passionate eyes, the only thing I really saw was my ticket out of ballistics.

"Let's say I buy it. Let's say I buy that bad smell you mentioned. What does it have to do with me?"

"Simple enough, Means. The victims were all male prostitutes and you spent ten years working Vice. I spoke to Inspector McIntyre, your former commanding officer. He said you had a genius for street work. In fact, he said you were the best street cop he'd ever seen."

"Most of that was before I became a detective. It was a long time ago."

She was right, as far as it went. The Vice Squad had given me an opportunity to identify targets. Most pimps have a vicious streak and many of them are heavily involved in the cocaine business. They have to be to keep their stables happy. I think I mentioned that people don't know what to make of my physical appearance. The whores I was expected to arrest were no different. Believe me when I say they were mightily pissed off when I flashed my shield and uttered the magic words. But not so pissed off they weren't willing to trade a little information for the chance to continue lives of violence, disease, and drug addiction without the inconvenience of spending a night in jail. Or a few months, if they happened to be carrying drugs in their shiny little purses.

"Are you telling me you have no connections out there? No informants?"

I watched her eyes darken, realizing that I'd made a major mistake.

"No, I'm not saying that. But you can't expect miracles, either. I've been working in Manhattan for the last ten years. You said that some of the victims were taken from Queens Plaza and Hunts Point in the Bronx. I can't just walk into those neighborhoods and pluck snitches out of the air." I paused for a moment, as if reflecting. It was time to give her something to hang her hat on. Something she'd already considered. "Can I assume you're thinking blackmail? That one of our victims recognized a famous john and decided to supplement his earnings?"

Bingo. She smiled like a little girl contemplating her first Christmas tree.

"It's the right place to start."

How would *she* know. One thing about NYPD brass, they never lack for arrogance.

"What size task force are we looking at here? There's a lot of ground to cover."

"You and me, Means. We're the task force."

I managed a frown and a shake of the head. Despite the fact that my heart was pounding with joy.

"You can forget about thorough," I said. "Forget about quick, too. Seven victims . . . it could go on forever. Unless we get lucky."

"Maybe." Her eyes got that glow again. "But if we succeed, it's all ours."

"Look, Captain, no disrespect intended, but I know what's in it for you. You're young, you're smart, and you're ambitious. Why not? New York is more than half minority. There's no reason why you can't make inspector in a few years. Or chief, if you hang on long enough. A failure here won't make much difference to your career, especially if you keep the investigation low profile. *My* problem is that I don't know if I can take being sent back here again after going out on the street."

She snorted, pulling her head back to contemplate me along the length of her nose. "You've got a lot of nerve, Detective."

"Isn't that why you came to me?" I looked her right in the eye. The hook was set. All I needed to do was land her. "You're asking me to give my best effort to the longest of long shots. I need to know that I won't take the heat if we fail. I need to see the pot of gold at the end of the rainbow."

"Taking a serial killer off the street isn't enough for you?"

"Taking a serial killer off the street *is* enough for me. I'm not worried about the consequences of success."

"You're worried about the consequences of failure."

"You got it, Captain."

She finally let herself relax, let her shoulders drop to their normal set and took a deep breath. "You're not as dumb as you look."

I think she was expecting a response, but I had no intention of changing the subject.

"All right," she said, "here's the deal. Win, lose, or draw, I guarantee that you'll return to regular duties. Maybe it won't be homicide, where you were before the . . . the incident. But you *will* be on the street again. Is that what you want to hear?"

"That's it."

"There are some conditions, though. Or, actually, one big condition."

She paused dramatically and I leaned forward, a half-smile on my lips. Just as if I didn't know what she was going to say.

"We work together, Means. You don't do *anything* without my personal okay. Nothing. You don't breathe until you clear it with me. You don't *fart* until you clear it with me. Understand?"

I nodded wisely. "Sure, no problem, Captain."

"It's not a joke, Means. You fuck up here, you'll never see the streets again. Never."

"Damn, you'd think I was a criminal." It was my turn to pause and her turn to exhibit the great stone face. "Captain, you said we were going to work together. Does that mean on the street, too?"

"It means everything and everywhere. I don't want you out of my sight."

"Sounds like you're ready to move in with me."

"I'll be knocking on your door in the middle of the night. You can count on it."

"Bed checks? Are we in summer camp?" I tried to smile, but the truth was that I was pissed off again. If I wanted out of the lab, I was going to have to kiss her butt until she got bored and went back to her desk. Well, maybe I could wake her up a little bit. Show her how the other half—the street half—lives. Even if it wasn't exactly in my own best interest.

"No, Means," she said without blinking, "it isn't summer camp. It's parole with intense supervision. I'd put an electronic bracelet on your wrist if I could get my hands on one."

"You afraid I'll go out and knife somebody?"

She took a deep breath and shook her head. "You still don't get it?"

"Oh, I get it, all right. You want to fail. Which doesn't exactly surprise me, being as you're a typical department bureaucrat."

"You bastard . . ."

That got her. She stood up, fists clenched. For a moment, I thought she was going to take her best shot. Not that I planned to leave my face in front of her knuckles.

"If you wanted somebody to conduct a textbook investigation," I said as calmly as possible, "you could have chosen any one of a hundred detectives. You came to me because you thought I could get results in a hurry. My problem is that I don't think you're willing to do what's necessary to get those results. What you *ought* to do is back off and let me operate, but you're too scared to do that, either. All of which adds up to a guarantee of failure. Face it, Captain. You can't have it both ways. You *can't* say, 'Excuse me, Mister Pimp, I'm conducting a murder investigation and I need your cooperation.' If you want Thong, you're gonna have to take some risks. Those gold bars on your shoulder might be enough to impress other cops, but they don't mean shit on the street."

She turned and walked out of the room without another word. I listened to her footsteps for a moment, then heard a door slam. Then, nothing.

It didn't take me long to begin reminding myself that of all the assholes I'd met in the course of my life, I was far and away the biggest, the most stupid, the smelliest. It'd taken all my self-discipline to show up at the lab every day. To give it my best effort without the consolations offered by the street. I'd gone home and stayed home every night. Whenever the tension got to me, I'd contented myself with beating the hell out of a heavy bag chained to a steel beam in my loft. Instead of the criminal psychopaths I preferred.

Compared to the life I'd enjoyed on the streets of Manhattan, working in the lab and going home at night was worse than dying. It was death with your eyes open. The only thing that kept me sane was the hope that eventually I'd be freed. That an angel would appear with a magic wand and open the prison doors.

So, why had I dumped on that angel? Why did I have to be as compulsive as the criminals I liked to hunt? Everything was going perfectly. I could (and should) have gone out with Vanessa Bouton and conducted a textbook investigation. The results would have been entirely negative, but that, too, would have been to my advantage. Captain Bouton wouldn't have lasted more than a few weeks. What was that compared to the ten months I'd already spent in ballistics? Or the ten years I'd *be* spending?

My self-incriminations were interrupted by footsteps. Vanessa Bouton's footsteps as she made her way down the hall. I struggled to compose myself, to keep every trace of triumph or exaltation off my face.

"Here's what I want you to do, Means." She stood in the doorway, shoulders squared, hands at her sides. "I want you to go directly to 655 Jane Street and report to Sergeant Pucinski. He's in charge of accumulated evidence for the task force. Spend all night, if you have to. By tomorrow, I want you familiar with the evidence. Is that a problem?"

"No problem, Captain."

"I'll be at your place at ten o'clock in the morning. I want to get started as soon as possible."

I couldn't suppress a smile. "Captain, the people we have to find don't operate during the day. Ten o'clock at *night* would be a much better time to begin."

Her face softened for a moment. "Okay, Means. It really doesn't make sense for me to hire an expert, then disregard his advice. I'll come by your place around two. By that time, I'm sure you'll be ready to name the perpetrator. Just don't do anything on your own. Risks are one thing. Stepping off a cliff is something else entirely."

FOUR

Lorraine Cho gently touched the sheet of aluminum covering the room's only window. Wondering if she'd made it through another night. The metal was cool to the touch, but that only meant the sun wasn't shining. It might be morning; it might be cloudy; it might be . . .

What was the point? Why this need to mark each passing night?

Because she knew she was never getting out of there. Because the only thing she could hope for was some hunter stumbling across the cabin (even though hunting season was six months away) before Becky and her husband (she still didn't know his real name) did what Becky claimed they'd already done to twenty-three other women. Twenty-three women and seven men.

"Now, the men . . . well, Lorraine, the men simply do not count. Daddy said we had to kill those men, but we did not enjoy it one bit. No sireee. I swear on the Lord's Book, Lorraine, it gave me the creeps just being *near* those homosexuals. I surely do hope I don't get the AIDS. Course, we were careful about the blood and Daddy insisted that I wear rubber gloves. But, still, those boys were *homosexuals*."

Lorraine shuddered, pulling the blanket a little tighter. They'd taken her clothing, though she couldn't understand why.

"Daddy says we took your clothes so you would not run away from us, Lorraine. You're like the baby we couldn't have because Daddy can't have babies. Oh, I have wanted a little girl for so long and now you *are* my little girl."

"But there's no place to run to, Becky. Clothed or naked."

How many hours had she spent with an ear pressed to the window? Listening for any human sound—for voices in conversation, a distant factory whistle, the whine of tires on pavement, the lowing of cattle in a meadow, the call of a rooster at daybreak.

At another time, in another place, the forest sounds would have delighted her. The birds sang out with a hundred voices, while the sigh and hiss and howl of the wind changed from second to second. A nearby stream (her bathtub) babbled over a rocky bed, forming a base for the darting hum of bees and flies, the persistent whine of mosquitoes. Squirrels and chipmunks quarreled from first light until sunset, their tiny claws scratching over the bare earth as they competed with cooing doves and bawling jays for the cracked corn Becky thoughtfully spread on the ground.

But there were no *human* sounds. None at all. And the only human odors were the stink of the outhouse and the sharply acid smell of the bucket in the corner.

They'd driven for hours and hours before dumping her in the cabin. Fucking her, the two of them, as they traveled the interstates. Taking turns; one driving while the other played.

The man had been rough, twisting her body with powerful hands. The woman had been gentle, chattering away as if she were sitting down to a church supper.

"Don't you fret, Lorraine. If Daddy says you're a keeper, then, by the Good Lord above, you *are* a keeper and we will not hurt you. Not one darn bit."

Lorraine wondered how Becky defined "hurting." Because Lorraine had never been in more pain. Those weeks in the hospital were nothing compared to this; now she was afraid most of the time, and the terror was absolutely physical. The fear shook her with the intensity of a dog shaking the body of a dying rat.

It hurt so much there was no point in thinking about the pain. No point in thinking about a problem without a solution. Sure, she could get out of the cabin; she could pry the tin sheet off the window in a matter of minutes. But what would she do then? Trudge blindly into the forest? Pick a direction and hope for the best?

When she wasn't afraid, Lorraine was numb, her emotions deadened as if by anesthetic. She sat in the room's only chair for hours, not thinking, not feeling.

The hopelessness, she realized, only made her hopeless; despair producing despair. Still, there was nothing she could do about it. She was dealing with a world so foreign to anything she'd ever known it left her no point of entry, no grasp of its underlying principles. She knew she couldn't manipulate this world, couldn't change or mold its perfect madness.

Becky came every day, unlocking the cabin door, calling a cheerful, "Well how are we doing today, Miss Lorraine?" Bringing the food Lorraine wolfed down, taking Lorraine to the outhouse, bathing her in the stream. As if she were tending a show dog in a kennel.

Lorraine heard the first birdsong and knew morning was at hand. She wondered if the singing bird was a robin, the traditional "early bird" out for its morning worm. The song, a trill followed by a sharp staccato burst, was picked up by another bird, this one farther away. Then another and another.

Within minutes, a dozen songs, each with the distinct voice of its author, hung in the air. Lorraine listened intently, recognizing only the coarse, distant scolding of the crows. She imagined the birds engaged in some kind of impossible aesthetic. Imagined them celebrating the glory of the infinite cosmos. Moved to song by the beauty around them.

You have to do something.

The words came unbidden. Came at odd moments, echoing internally, a command without a commander. Blotting out the birds' celebration, the greater glory, the impossible aesthetic. Everything.

You have to do something.

She searched back through her life for pertinent data. Some relevant experience from which to draw a plan of action. She found nothing, of course. She had never been face-to-face with . . .

The word that came to mind was *evil*. She knew the word was useless, even though it fit Becky and her Daddy-husband perfectly. What could you do against evil? Pray to God for relief? There was no priest to perform an exorcism. To drive the evil back into the eternal fires of Hell. This was not a movie, no matter how unreal it seemed.

"I could make Becky love me."

Lorraine was so taken aback by the sound of her own voice that for a moment she failed to consider the significance of the words. But then, little by little, she came to understand that Becky was her only way out. Unless she decided to die.

She knew she could choose death. Even though she didn't have the courage to perform the physical act of suicide, she could simply wander into the forest until she was completely lost. Until she became trapped in mud or tumbled down the side of a mountain or fell into a frigid lake. It would amount to the same thing.

I don't want to die in the forest.

Another unbidden thought. Followed quickly by a surge of emotion that left her hands trembling. Outside, rain began to fall, spattering on the leaves, the roof, the bare, packed earth surrounding the cabin. Lorraine felt she had an obligation to name the emotion that'd left her shaking, but her mind wandered to the trees outside her prison cell. Each morning, she passed beneath their branches when Becky led her to the outhouse. She couldn't see them, of course, but the passage from sun to shade to sun was apparent enough. Now, she wondered if the trees were grateful for the rain that washed their leaves? If their roots shivered in anticipation? If they knew their own needs?

But what's the point of knowing your own needs if you can't do anything to satisfy them? Of being a thirsty tree when you can't move the twenty feet to a rushing stream?

"I've *got* to pull it together."

Once again, she spoke aloud; once again the sound of her own voice startled her. But this time she didn't allow herself to become distracted, resolving instead to begin by denying her helplessness. And her fear.

There *is* a way out of here, she decided, and I'm going to find it.

Her mind jumped to her kidnappers, to Becky and Becky's Daddy. Apart from his frenzied attacks on that first night, she knew nothing about Daddy. Each morning, Becky arrived alone. She seemed in no hurry, staying for several hours, chattering happily even when Lorraine failed to respond.

The implication that Daddy had complete faith in his ability to control Becky was obvious. But Lorraine had to wonder if Becky was really the automaton she appeared to be. Or if Daddy's faith sprang from a bloated ego.

Becky showed no remorse for the things she'd done, yet she claimed to be doing them only for Daddy.

"Daddy has needs, Lorraine, and, well, I am not one of those man-women who try to keep their husbands down. I was raised to serve my man. To love, honor, and *obey*. That may not be popular up here in New York, but it is dearly held in Atherton, Mississippi. If there's one thing we Johnny-rebs are not, it's quitters."

But suppose Becky fell under a second obligation. Suppose she felt the need to protect her little girl. Suppose it became clear, even to Becky, that Daddy was going to hurt (or *kill*) her little girl. Would Becky put her child into the back of the van and smuggle her to safety? Would she drive Lorraine back down the road that wasn't a road at all? That had tossed Lorraine about like she was a sack of flour?

Lorraine sighed, reached into the covered pot that held the

last of the food. She dug out a wrapped sandwich and sniffed at it. Peanut butter and jelly. The perfect choice for a young child.

"I should have paid attention. On that damned road. I should have paid attention."

This time, Lorraine wasn't startled by the sound of her own voice. She decided that speaking aloud was helpful, because it let her control the flow of her thoughts by slowing them down.

"I was terrified when we drove up to the cabin," she began. "I don't know if we drove through the forest or over some abandoned road. I seem to remember branches whipping the sides of the van. I seem to remember driving through a stream. Can a van go through a stream? Don't you need some kind of Jeep for that?"

She was thinking, not for the first time, about going down the road. Of following the track made by the van. She knew that it had to lead to another road somewhere. To houses and people and help. She felt she could endure almost anything if it led to escape. But what if the track ran directly to *their* house.

Lorraine imagined herself struggling, naked, along a narrow track, finding her way by following the faint impressions made by the van's tires. Her arms and legs are scratched and bruised, her face swollen by insect bites, her bare feet slippery with blood. Finally, after hours and hours of suffering, she hears a distant radio and stumbles forward. Only to find Daddy perched on the porch swing; Becky toiling at the kitchen stove.

They would kill her for sure.

A sudden gust of wind slammed a fusillade of raindrops against the cabin window. Lorraine shivered and pulled the blanket over her bare feet.

"What I need to do first," she said, "is get some little concession from Becky. It doesn't have to be much, as long as it's done without Daddy's permission. Another blanket, maybe. Or a T-shirt or a pair of socks. The trick is to get Becky in the habit of making her own decisions."

Lorraine, having made *her* decision, sat in the chair. Waiting was what she seemed to do best. She listened to the rain for a moment, then felt a cold hand pass over her flesh as the fear returned.

They can't let me live, she thought to herself. "They *can't*." The second single word began to echo in time to the drumbeats of rain. *Can't*, can't-can't, *can't*, can't-can't.

There's only one real question, she finally decided. And that's whether I'll go insane before they kill me.

Sometime later (she had no way to calculate any unit of time smaller than a day), she heard a vehicle drive up to the cabin. A door opened, then slammed shut; running feet slapped across the muddy yard.

As she did each day, Lorraine indulged a brief rescue fantasy. A rescue *daydream*. A tin-starred sheriff burst through the cabin door. Or a burly, foul-mouthed New York detective. Or an FBI agent, dressed to the nines. Or her own laughing-crying parents.

"Well, how are we doing on this rainy day, Miss Lorraine?" Becky called, unlocking the door. She rushed on without pausing for an answer. "I do have the most wonderful news for you, Miss Lorraine. Daddy says we are driving tonight. And *you* are coming with us."

FIVE

It was just after three o'clock in the afternoon when I left the labs at One Police Plaza. Sixteen minutes after three o'clock, to be exact. There are some moments you never forget. (Like December 16, 1971, 10:44 A.M., when that C130 lifted off a Saigon runway with my intact carcass aboard.) I imagine convicts released from their prison cages experience the same sense of escape. Escape mixed with exultation. I made it, you son-of-a-bitch. I survived and you got nothin' to say to me. Now or ever.

It was not the afternoon of the morning I entered the lab. Even Manhattan's sooty air smelled different now. It was the difference between the smell of the forest when you step into it on a short hike and the smell of the forest when you step into it with an M16 strapped to your chest. I automatically scanned the people on the street, separating the mutts and mopes and skels from the cops and common citizens.

Jane Street, my destination and the home of the King Thong Task Force, was on the west side of Manhattan, a couple of miles from where I stood. I might have taken a subway up or grabbed a cab, but I decided to hoof it, ignoring the fact that New York was on the tail end of a cool spell and the overcast skies threatened rain. I had a tan Gore-Tex jacket on my back, a pair of thoroughly broken-in, waterproofed Western boots on my feet, and a Policemen's Benevolent Association cap pulled low over my face. If worse came to worse, I could always unfurl the hood zipped into the collar of my jacket and make for the nearest subway.

(The boots, by the way, were my pride and joy. Custom made of fine-grained black lizard, the sharply squared toes encased a steel core. Behind the steel, a thick bed of molded foam provided the necessary cushion for my own toes. I've never had the time to study one or another of the disciplines lumped together under the generic term "karate," but I've absolutely mastered a snap-kick to the shin or knee. A snap-kick that's proven to be more effective than Mace or a Taser in bringing a desire for sanity to the consciousness of the terminally belligerent.)

I walked west on Chambers Street, dodging pedestrians as I made my way toward the Hudson River. One Police Plaza, in the heart of Manhattan's civic center, is surrounded by federal, state, and city courthouses as well as the enormous Municipal Building with its gilded angel on top. City Hall is there, too, its grimy facade plunked down in the middle of a small, even grimier park.

The few square blocks surrounding the civic center hum to the tune of the several hundred thousand low-level bureaucrats who feed and shop in the area. I suppose tourists must find it strange to discover a Blarney Castle cheek by jowl with the Ojavi West Indian Restaurant. Wong's Chinese Fast Food, two doors down, probably doesn't help matters. But that's New York. The day when you could walk into a Jewish or an Italian or a German neighborhood and know exactly what to expect from the local restaurateurs is long gone. Only Little Italy and Chinatown, pure ethnic pockets institutionalized in the name of the tourist dollar, remain.

I turned north onto Hudson Street, leaving the civic center behind. The developers call this neighborhood TriBeCa. It was created out of the old printing district by real estate sharks in the 1980s. The factories were carved up as the printers took their jobs to automated plants in New Jersey, carved up and converted into co-ops and condos. Now, the locals bustle from one trendy bar to the next while the homeless sleep on the unused loading docks of abandoned factories.

It was mostly old news, but it seemed fresh to me. I watched the life of the streets as if I was still a twenty-one-year-old veteran just back from Vietnam. I'd vowed never to return to Paris, New York, on the day I'd walked into the recruiter's office, but that didn't mean I'd been prepared for Manhattan. Manhattan was another world altogether, as different from the DMZ as the DMZ had been from Whiteface Mountain. I *breathed* New York back then, sucked it in as a kind of celebration of my ability to survive.

Well, I'd managed to survive again and now the littered streets seemed as exotic as ever. Above Houston Street, the warehouse district gives way to Greenwich Village, with its townhouses and meandering lanes. On impulse, I took a left at Christopher Street and walked down to what was left of the old West Side Highway, six lanes of asphalt punctuated with traffic lights and divided by concrete barriers.

Across the highway, a few rotting piers jutted out into the Hudson River. Between the piers and the roadway, more concrete barriers sectioned off a long promenade. On this particular afternoon, the piers were almost deserted, but after dark, winter or summer, rain or shine, West Street was the center of a homosexual meat market that had almost nothing to do with the large gay community in Greenwich Village.

That was the strangest part about it. The whores were young runaways from all over the country, and the customers were from New Jersey and Connecticut and Long Island. The newspapers claim that eighty percent of the male prostitutes working the piers are HIV positive. (Only slightly higher, by the way, than the percent of female prostitutes working Midtown.) Back when I'd been assigned to Vice, one of my jobs had been to pose as a prostitute and lure the johns into making a proposition. I was still young and pretty in those days and I never had much trouble making arrests. What amazed me (in the beginning, at least) was the simple fact that almost all of the johns were married. And they weren't anxious to use condoms, either. I know because, mostly out of boredom, I tested them.

"Forty bucks? Okay, but you gotta use a rubber. I don't wanna get AIDS."

"Ha, ha, ha. You kids sure learn to hustle early. Make it sixty. But no scumbags, sonny. I wanna *feel* something."

I continued on up to Jane Street, then turned east. The one-story brick structure housing the task force had originally been a garage. The faded sign above the door read "MANGANARO TKG." There was nothing to announce the presence of a police task force (the NYPD, if it had its choice, would probably make 911 an unlisted number) except the actual address. I tried the door, found it locked, rang the bell.

"Yeah?" The cop who answered was in uniform. He stared at my face for a moment, trying to guess who or what I was, then repeated, "Yeah?"

"Detective Means," I responded, deadpan.

"There's no Detective Means here."

"*I'm* Detective Means, you asshole. I'm looking for Pucinski."

He didn't like my answer, but there wasn't much he could do about it. Eating shit is an important part of the police experience. He let me inside and I spotted Pucinski sitting in front of a computer off to one side of the room.

I knew Pucinski from the ballistics lab. In some ways, he was the ultimate cop, a thirty-five-year man with no intention of retiring. The job was his family, his religion, his life. Five years ago, he'd run into the wrong alley and been rewarded with a shotgun blast that took off most of his right leg. He could have retired on the spot with a three-quarter pension, but, as he explained to me later, he'd never even considered the possibility. Instead, after the surgery, the prosthesis, and the rehab, he'd clomped into the office of Inspector George Dimenico, his rabbi, and begged to be assigned to limited duty.

Dimenico hadn't had much choice. Pucinski was a genuine hero, even if he had been stupid enough to chase an armed mutt down a dark alley. I suppose ballistics had seemed as good a place as any for a handicapped veteran; Pucinski had been down there for more than four years when I showed up. Somehow, despite being the ultimate burnout hairbag, he'd mastered every aspect of ballistics, including the computer link to NCIC and NYSIIS, the federal and state crime information systems. The computer wouldn't actually compare ballistic evidence, but it would match a name to a rap sheet.

I watched Pucinski (called Pooch, naturally) peck away at the keyboard for a moment before I went over. He hadn't changed much. Five-foot-eight (at the most), two hundred and eighty pounds (at the least), he was wrapped in a tan, wash-and-wear, gabardine suit, a frayed white shirt, and a solid brown tie that must have been rumpled when he'd pulled it off the five-dollar rack. Closing in on sixty, his jowls hid his collar while his gut covered his belt. Even his eyelids drooped.

"Hey, Pooch," I said. "How's it goin'?"

Pucinski turned slowly (he did everything slowly) and smiled up at me. "Why, if it ain't Mean Mister Means. How many you kill, today, Means? What's the body count?"

That was another of the many benefits of the job. Being endlessly ribbed by dinosaurs like Pucinski. You couldn't hit them and you couldn't insult them, either. What you had to do was take it.

"Well, I haven't made my quota today, but it's still early." I sat down next to him. "The captain speak to you?"

"Bouton?"

"That's her."

"Yeah, she spoke to me."

"About what she has in mind?"

"The whole deal," he smirked. "Say, Means, what was the first Israeli settlement?" Jokes, mostly ethnic, mostly nasty, were an important part of the Pucinski repertoire.

"I don't know, Pooch."

"The first Israeli settlement was ten cents on a dollar." He chortled happily for a minute, then sobered up.

"It's a piece of shit, Means," he said, grabbing the back of my hand. "You caught a piece of shit."

SIX

It wasn't what I wanted to hear, but I can't say I was surprised. I tried to dredge up some kind of a response, but failed. What's the expression—*a piece of shit is a piece of shit is a piece of shit?* I shrugged to show the required degree of macho indifference, then took a moment to glance around the room.

A row of mismatched six-drawer filing cabinets, at least two dozen, stood against the wall behind Pucinski's desk, their tops covered with boxes of what I mistakenly took to be supplies. A bank of silent telephones and a row of computer stations linked the far end of the building with the charts and blackboards covering the rest of the wall space. The center of the garage was carpeted with several dozen, mostly empty, chairs and desks.

"See them boxes, Means?" Pucinski asked. "What's in them boxes is what didn't fit in the filing cabinets. The hotline number was on the air two hundred and fifty times a day in the beginning. We got a hundred and eighty-five thousand calls in three months. After that, we stopped countin'. Things are winding down, now, but we used to have twenty cops on them phones, and the public still bitched about the busy signals.

"Then there were the known sex offenders. We interviewed five thousand creeps. Rapists, chickenhawks, pimps, madams, flashers, peepers. It didn't matter if they were straight or if they were gay. Hell, it didn't matter if they were fags or dykes. The brass got caught with their pants down and they were out to cover their asses before they contracted a windburn.

"Wanna hear the truth, Means? If it wasn't for the profile, we wouldn't have had any investigation at all. We'd still be organizing the paperwork."

I stopped him with a wave of my hand. "What's the profile, Pooch?"

"You don't know about the profile?" A quick grin sent his jowls into spasm. "Tell me somethin', Means. What do you call a Somali with a swollen toe?"

"C'mon, Pooch. Stop fuckin' around. This isn't a joke to me."

The smile disappeared. "It's a piece of shit, Means. Don't take it serious. Don't play Humpty-Dumpty and set yourself up for a fall. See, the psychs told us our boy would never stop killing. They said he might take it in his sick head to move on. They said he might get run over by a bus or commit suicide or get murdered by a run-of-the-mill New York psychopath. They said he might even do something really stupid and get caught. But he'd never decide to stop killing. He couldn't decide to stop killing. Face it, Means, there haven't been any murders in five months. Your ticket to glory is either gone or dead."

"Or recovering in a hospital somewhere. Getting ready to kill again."

Pooch leaned to the side, managed to lift a buttock off the chair, then farted loudly. "Ya know, Means, it's possible we got the key to our killer right in them filing cabinets. Or maybe it's in the boxes. Or on one of the computer disks. You might even find him if ya got, say, thirty or forty years to wade through all the crap."

It was my turn to fidget. I knew I had to surrender, to once and for all give up the possibility of actually closing the case. And not because I couldn't deal with the frustration. I needed every bit of the energy at my command for the game I had to play with Vanessa Bouton. For the show I was obliged to stage. The question I needed to answer had nothing to do with who killed seven male prostitutes. The only question was what Vanessa Bouton wanted from me.

"Tell me about the profile, Pooch. I need some kind of an angle here."

"Ah, yes, the profile." Still grinning, he picked a single piece of paper off his desk and began to read. "'Perpetrator is a white male, thirty to forty years of age, five-foot-ten to six-foot-one, one hundred eighty to two hundred pounds. He has no criminal record. He was not acquainted with his victims prior to the murders. He is a married or divorced bisexual with children. He may be employed in one of the professions associated with homosexuality: interior decoration, the fashion industry, the theater, etc. He is obsessively neat, quite formal in dress and usually wears a suit and a tie when in public. He is a heavy smoker. He owns, rents, or leases an American-made van. He is extremely cunning and will back away from potential victims before putting himself at risk. Because his economic background is both successful and stable, he cannot readily move to another jurisdiction in order to continue killing. Neither can he radically alter his tightly organized *modus operandi*. Therefore, he is at high risk to be apprehended or commit suicide.'"

"That's it?"

"That's all she wrote."

"Who did it? Who dreamed up this profile?"

"The Behavioral Science Unit of the National Center for the Analysis of Violent Crime of the Federal Bureau of Investigation." His short pudgy fingers caressed the side of his face as he peered at me through narrowed eyes. "Impressive, right? Especially when you consider that all they had was the victims' backgrounds, the crime scene material, and the autopsy reports."

I shook my head. "First, I don't see how it helps. It's too vague. Second, if it's wrong, you could walk right past the real killer. Third, there was no crime scene. The vics weren't killed where they were found."

He put down the paper and grabbed my wrist. "It's a piece of shit," he insisted. "A piece of shit."

I pulled my hand away and sat back to await the lecture. It wasn't long in coming.

"We're talking about a couple of hundred thousand phone tips. We're talking about thousands of interviews. You know Deputy Chief Bowman? Black guy works directly under the chief of patrol?" He waited for me to nod, then continued. "Bowman ran the task force up. I can still hear his voice. 'The operant concepts are organize and prioritize. Don't let the paperwork overwhelm you.'"

"That's easy to say," I interrupted. "But it's like asking a turtle to fly. Did he tell you *how?*"

"No, he didn't. But part of it was obvious. Like the known sex offenders. We did that in *spite* of the profile. We also interviewed the victims' friends, their pimps, if they had pimps, and every male whore we could get our hands on. But that only added to the basic problem. Everything we did generated more leads. Thousands and thousands of leads. *Tens* of thousands of leads. You think we could check 'em all out? Not in a fucking lifetime, Means. We *had* to put 'em in some kind of order and that meant we had to have some kind of a basic premise. A peg to hang the hats on. The profile became the peg."

He fished a smoke out of a crumpled pack of Chesterfields and lit it up. "We divided leads into five categories, A to E. A few of them were easy to place, like 'I was in a bar with so and so and he told me that he was the killer,' but most of them were vague. So and so takes young boys into his apartment. So and so works with leather and goes out late at night. So and so is a faggot priest who gets off on male prostitutes."

He was all excited now, jabbing at the air with his cigarette as he made his points. "After a couple of weeks, we finally got it through our heads that we had to do something. Half the task force was out on the streets harassing creeps. The other half was buried in paperwork. The whole fucking thing was getting away from us and if we didn't make a move in a hurry, we were never gonna catch up." He allowed himself to lean back, to relax a bit. "So we trained the phone men to ask hotline callers for age, weight, and height. What did he do for a living? Did he drive a van? Did he smoke? Was he married or divorced? Anyone who fit the profile automatically went on the A list. The idea was to check them out first, then move on to the Bs. Only we never got past the As." He looked at his hands and shrugged. "And now it's over."

"How many, Pooch?" I asked casually.

"How many what?"

"How many prime suspects you develop from the profile?"

"Twenty-three."

I shook my head in disgust. "You question their wives?"

"Naturally."

"Their coworkers? Their bosses?"

"Yeah."

"Their neighbors?"

His head jerked up. "Don't cross-examine me," he snarled. "What we did is called policing. It's not something a psycho, like you, could appreciate."

"Did you set up surveillance, Pooch? Twenty-four-hour sur-veillance?" I couldn't resist the opportunity to give the knife another twist. "Did you follow them from their homes to their jobs to their churches to their relatives? Did you totally destroy twenty-three lives on the basis of some bullshit, fucking *profile*?"

We sat there in silence for a couple of minutes. I don't know if Pooch was contemplating his sins or getting ready to shoot me, but I was thinking about my years in Vice. About busting HIV-positive, drug-addicted prostitutes. About finding those same, sad, vicious whores back on the street before I finished the paperwork. One sergeant told me to look at it like I was a sanita-tion worker.

"The streets get dirty," he'd explained, "so we sweep 'em clean. If they didn't get dirty again, why would anybody need us?"

He had a point, but I hadn't spent all those hours studying for the cops only to become a garbageman. Nor did I have a wife and kids and a house on Staten Island to support. I could've walked away from the paycheck, and I'd thought about it more than once.

The truth was that I'd come to New York to hunt. That was the long and the short of it. And not very surprising, because I'd spent most of my life hunting. I grew up in a house (call it a shack if you're the type who insists on a spade being a spade) on the very edge of the Adirondack Park, six million acres of deep dark forest that held more light for me than home, family, church, and school put together.

I got my first .22 when I was eight years old. One of the many "uncles" who came to occupy Mom's bed (only to leave in disgust after a few months or weeks or days or hours) gave me a battered, single-shot, breech-loading Stevens and taught me to plink wine bottles mounted on rocks behind the house. I proved to be an attentive student—good enough, after a few weeks, to be handed a couple of rounds and instructed to return with "meat for the table."

Bottles don't move; animals do. It was that simple, and after a few hours I returned with no bullets and no meat. Uncle John, by way of demonstrating the fact that ammo costs money, beat me for an hour. Slapping me; chasing me; slapping me; chasing me. Until I couldn't run anymore; until the only thing I could do was take it. Thinking about it now, the part I remember best has nothing to do with pain or fear. No, my clearest memory of that day is the sound of dear old Mom snoring on the couch.

The "whippin'" was not without its positive aspects. I don't recall ever coming back empty-handed again. But that may be due more to the fear of Uncle John's taking back his .22 than fear of a beating. I'd been beaten many times before, whereas the rifle was entirely new. As was the feeling of power that went with it.

"You still here?"

I looked up to find Pooch staring at me through hangdog eyes. He looked like a scolded puppy.

"Hey, Pooch, I'm sorry about what I said before. It was stupid and I was out of line. There wasn't anything else you could do, considering that you caught a piece of shit. If one of those men you put under surveillance had turned out to be King Thong, you'd be a hero instead of a goat."

He nodded his head eagerly. It was the failure that bothered him. The end only justifies the means when the end is realized. "You take the man's money," he muttered, "you do the man's job."

I nodded back at him. There was no sense in making an enemy of a man I was going to need. "Tell me about the politics here. What's Bouton's story?"

"The bitch wants to be commissioner," he answered, laughing. "And why not? The commissioner's black. The chief of patrol is black. Even the fucking mayor's black. It's the Decade of the Ape in New York."

I kept my expression neutral, though I couldn't help wondering if Pucinski referred to me as the "half-breed" or the "injun" when I wasn't around to hear it.

"I understand the ambition, Pooch. I can read it on her face. What I want to know about is the politics inside the task force. Why'd they let her loose with her cover-up theories? Why'd they let her come to me? Why didn't they give her twenty detectives so she could do a decent job?"

"It was a trap. They set a trap and she stepped right into it." He leaned forward, his voice dropping to a whisper. "One thing I gotta say for *El Capitan*, she's consistent. The task force was organized right after the fourth killing. That's when the fags hit the streets with the picket signs. Bouton was on it from day one and from day one all she could talk was bullshit about the murders being part of a cover-up. Means, when I tell you there wasn't a sympathetic ear in the house, you could believe I know what I'm talkin' about. We must've had twenty shrinks in here, every one of 'em a specialist, and they all said 'serial killer.' Plus, the first three murders were investigated as routine homicides. The dicks who caught the squeals were out lookin' for that ordinary motive Bouton kept screaming about and they couldn't come up with squat."

"Maybe it wasn't one of the first three," I suggested. "If you were gonna cover up a homicide by making it look like the work of a maniac, you couldn't make the hit on the one you really wanted to kill until the media . . . " I stopped abruptly.

"Spit it out, Means."

"Never mind, Pooch. I just got an idea about something else. You go on with what you were saying."

His voice dropped even further as he launched himself into it. "It got to the point where Chief Bowman ordered her to shut up unless she had something constructive to say."

"Did it do any good?"

"No. She managed to keep quiet when Bowman was around, but she kept talking her shit to anyone else who'd listen, including ranking officers who weren't part of the task force."

"What was she, Pooch, stupid?"

"Stupid? She ranked first on the captain's exam. *First.* She's also got a master's in psychology from Columbia and a bunch of credits toward a fuckin' Ph.D. *El Capitan's* problem was that she was too smart. She was too smart and she let everyone know it. Chief Bowman's a nice guy, but he ain't exactly Albert Einstein. If it wasn't for the fact that his boss and his boss's boss are as black as he is, Bowman would never have gone past deputy inspector. Think he liked being showed up by another black cop? A black *female* cop? A black female cop that went to his *boss* complaining about how she was abused because she was a woman? About how she might even have to file a complaint against the New York City Police Department?"

I smiled by way of encouragement. "I'm surprised he didn't have her shot."

"He played it smart, Means. He let her mouth off until there was no way she could back out of it. Then he offered to let her conduct her own investigation on the side. Completely independent, Means. No time limit. She can work it forever and she doesn't have to report to anyone until the day she arrests King Thong. Or decides to give up. On the day she decides to give up, she has to hand all her paperwork over to Chief Bowman."

"Real tidy. But I still don't get it. Why'd didn't she demand a serious squad to work with? Why'd she settle for me?"

Pucinski sat back, relaxing a bit. A grin split his face, like a watermelon being sliced with a hunting knife. "First, let me say that I was present when the offer was made. That's because I'm supposed to act as liaison between Bouton and the task force. My job is to guarantee she has access to all the files. Anyway, *El Capitan* didn't seem very surprised by the deal. In fact, I'd say she'd been thinking about it for a long, long time. Bowman asked her how many men she needed and she says, 'One. I only need one.'

"'Anybody particular in mind?' he asks.

"'Yeah,' she says, 'Mean Mister Means.'"

"Just like that?" I demanded. "Just like that? She said, 'Mean Mister Means'? Bullshit."

He slid forward and tapped me on the chest with the tip of a pudgy forefinger. "As God is my witness, Means. And Bowman knew just who she meant. How does it feel to be a legend?"

I didn't bother to answer and he let me stew for a minute before he tapped me again.

"Hey, Means, What do you call a Somali with a swollen toe?"

"I don't know, Pooch. I really don't."

"A golf club."

SEVEN

Mean Mister Means. It was an honor, in a way. The nickname had been given to me by some vicious street mutt with a penchant for rhyme. It'd gotten back to my brothers on the Vice Squad through their snitches and naturally become the vehicle of endless mindless jokes. Cops don't like to work with hotdogs, and I can't say that I blamed them, even at the time. But that doesn't mean I stopped, either. As I said, I came to New York to hunt, not to be one more anonymous soldier in what amounted to a twenty-seven-thousand-man army. Anyone who didn't like that could, as far as I was concerned, kiss my sweet red ass.

But they didn't kiss my ass, sweet or sour, red or its actual beige. The job has its own remedies for cops with Rambo mentalities, ballistics being one of them. Outright dismissal being another.

It was the dismissal part that bothered me as I sat in front of a desk contemplating the very large box of assorted reports that Pooch had thoughtfully prepared for me. If ranking officers as high as Deputy Chief Bowman were out to bury Captain Vanessa Bouton, they'd sacrifice Detective/First Roland Means in a hot second. Which meant Bouton's promise of protection carried all the force of a politician promising to end the budget deficit.

There's nothing more embarrassing to a hunter than blundering into his own snare. I'd jumped out of the frying pan and into the fire (actually, it was more like out of the refrigerator and into the freezer), but that didn't mean I had to stay there. If you stepped into a bear trap, would you scream "ouch, ouch, ouch" until you bled to death? Or would you find a way to pry open the jaws of the trap and deal with your wounds?

There was no going back. The first thing I had to do was please Vanessa Bouton. If I could keep her going for a few weeks, I might find a way to distance myself from the awful thud she was going to make when she fell on her face. I might, for instance, look up Deputy Chief Bowman and offer to be his eyes and ears. In return for a little consideration when it came time for the sentencing.

That doesn't sound nice, does it? But it wasn't altogether nice of Vanessa Bouton to use me for cannon fodder, either. It's one thing to risk your own ass for a worthy cause; it's quite another to lure some poor innocent out of ballistic hell to aid you in committing suicide.

In any event (even without a definite, long-term plan of action), I was considerably cheered by the fact that I already had my angle. It'd come to me while I was sparring with Pooch. Assuming Bouton was right in her assessment of the case (a position I was forced to take), neither of the first three victims could have been the primary target. The killer would have had to wait until the media put it together, until the cops were committed to the search for a serial killer, before he made his move.

But once his intended scenario was established, he would have had to act fairly quickly. He couldn't risk having to abandon the field because of a close call. That close call might take any number of forms. An intended victim could escape or another cruising whore come up with a partial license plate or an accurate description. Any close call would either subject the killer to extreme risk or force him to give up before he'd accomplished his actual objective.

What it came down to was victim number four or victim number five. Which was just as well, because Pooch had given me something over six hundred pages of documents to peruse. There was no way two cops (one of whom was almost certain to prove something less than proficient at street investigation) could even begin to penetrate that mass. Reducing the number of targets by five, on the other hand, would provide Bouton and myself with a few weeks of serious work, followed by a few months of bullshit repetition. After which, we could abandon the field secure in the knowledge that we'd given it the old college try.

I began to sift through the evidence, starting with the autopsy reports and the crime scene photos. The bodies were gruesome enough. The eyelids, eyebrows, and nipples had been carefully removed. The instrument, according to the autopsy notes, had been a thin, very sharp knife, perhaps a filleting knife of the sort commonly used by fishermen. The torsos, on the other hand, had been stabbed numerous times with a much longer, much thicker blade. Ribs had been snapped by the force of the blows, suggesting a survival or hunting knife. The genitals were untouched, except for deep grooves where the killer had wrapped the penis and testicles with a strip of leather. All of this, of course, had taken place after death. The cause of death for each victim was listed as a single shot to the back of the head from a .22-caliber pistol.

Toxicology reports showed the presence of various intoxicating substances in the victims' bodies. Most of them had had some alcohol in their systems, but not all. Four had tested positive for cocaine, two for heroin, two for barbiturates. One of the things that interested me (as it had the other six hundred cops who'd investigated the case) was how the killer controlled his victims until he was ready to kill them. He'd taken them off crowded streets and, therefore, was not likely to have dispatched them immediately, not with a gun.

Of course, he might have used a silenced automatic or soundproofed his van, but several other factors indicated that he'd controlled each victim for some time before administering the *coup de grace*. For instance, the .22 had been only three inches from the back of the skull when Thong pulled the trigger. (The carefully photographed scalps were severely charred by the resulting powder burns.) Plus, all the entry wounds would easily fit into a two-inch circle. And not one of the victims, as far as forensics could tell, had resisted his attacker. There was no tissue under the fingernails. No evidence of defensive wounds.

I found myself absorbed in the material despite my carefully professed cynicism. Getting the victim away from the pickup area would have been fairly easy. Most street whores, male or female, prefer car tricks to hotel tricks because there's enough risk of exposure in a car to keep the johns from lingering over their purchases. Anal and vaginal sex are equally difficult in a car (less so, admittedly, in a van), making quick, neat blow-jobs the order of the day. In and out; one, two, three; take the money and run.

But getting the victim away from the stroll was only the beginning for the killer. In each case, he had to find a quiet place to park, convince his victim to turn away from him, then pull the trigger before his victim could react. I don't deny that it's possible to intimidate someone into dying passively, but when you're talking about seven victims, it seems unlikely that one or two wouldn't fight back. Or at least move his head enough to change the position of the entry wound.

Drugs could have been the answer, if there had been any evidence of recent drug use. Johns commonly offer cocaine (along with money, of course) as an inducement to especially adventuresome sex. The killer might have concocted his own mixture of heroin and cocaine, worked his target into a stupor, then fired the fatal bullet. That hadn't happened. The stomachs and nostrils of each victim had been carefully examined for drug residue. The skin had been inspected for any sign of recent puncture marks. All with negative results.

If Thong hadn't controlled his victims with drugs, how had he controlled them? For some reason, the answer didn't leap, full-blown, into my consciousness. But it was another thing I could use on Bouton, another angle to pursue. Wasn't it possible, for instance, that King Thong was two little monkeys instead of one giant ape? Perhaps the trigger man snuck up behind his working (i.e., kneeling) target and pulled the trigger just at the moment of orgasm?

Or maybe each victim had been offered a cash inducement to wear a blindfold and play the passive partner in a round of anal sex. The killer had approached his naked, prone victim from the rear, but instead of slamming his penis into the proffered butt, he'd slammed a .22-caliber bullet into his playmate's skull. Blindfolds are not uncommon in the sewer of New York prostitution. Not for boys—or for girls, either. I noted that wood fibers had been found all over the bodies. The fibers had come from a sheet of unstained, unpainted plywood, and the prevailing theory was that it had been used to line the bottom of a commercial van. I had to presume the area surrounding the eyes had also been examined for fibers of material or for any chemical residue that might have been transferred from a leather mask. But there was nothing definite in the autopsy notes, and a blindfold theory could and would be offered to Vanessa Bouton as another proof of Detective Means' enthusiasm.

Aside from the wood fibers, the only other physical evidence found on the victims were the long, irregular strips of leather that'd earned Thong his name. They were not made from cowhide; the strips had originally been part of a deer. (This fact, along with a number of others, like the stab wounds and the removal of the eyebrows and eyelids, had been withheld from the public.) The deerskin strips must've seemed like a great lead to the original investigators, but the fact is that approximately six million hunters kill approximately one million deer in New York and surrounding states each November during the short hunting season. Most of these hunters have the heads mounted and the hides tanned in order to display their stupid macho prowess for their equally stupid macho friends.

As I said, I hunted all through my childhood, but for me

hunting was never a way of proving my virility. It was not an aphrodisiac. Mom had a way of spending every penny that came into the house. She liked going to greaser bars (that's where the "uncles" came from), but she'd buy gallons of cheap wine if times were tough. The state, perhaps in recognition of my childish vulnerability, included food stamps in Mom's welfare package. Food stamps Mom sold at a fifty percent discount to a local grocer named Pierre DeGaul. The point, of course, is that I hunted in order to eat. I never equated dropping the sights of a 30-30 onto a grazing deer's shoulder with personal bravery.

Still, there was nothing in the FBI's profile to indicate the killer ever hunted anything but humans. The profile imagined Thong to be a fussily dressed executive type. It was hard to picture him crawling through a muddy forest. Or bloody to the elbows, skinning and gutting the still-hot carcass of a freshly killed deer. One more item to call to Vanessa Bouton's attention.

I moved on to the rest of the material Pooch had culled from the files. Theoretically, Pooch had excluded anything connected to the serial killer theory, especially information developed through the hotline or the profile. Included were interviews with friends, coworkers, relatives, etc. Just for the hell of it, I picked up the packet on victim number four and compared it with the packet on victim number one. Number one's file was at least five times as thick as that of number four. Clearly, once the serial killer theory had been established, standard procedure had gone out the window.

I removed the files on victims number four and five, laid them out on the empty desk, then took their autopsy reports and put them down next to their respective packages.

Victim number four was named John Kennedy. Called John-John, though his middle name was Anthony and not Fitzgerald. He'd been twenty-three years old when he'd run into Thong. Twenty-three years old; five-foot-ten; a hundred and forty pounds. No scars, no birthmarks, no tattoos.

He'd emigrated to New York from the upstate hamlet of Owl Creek six months before his murder and been arrested twice for prostitution, which meant he'd probably gotten into the life shortly after his arrival. Both arrests had been made on Fifty-third Street, better known as "the strip," an area commonly used by teenage male prostitutes. His last known address was The House of Refuge, one of many nonprofit organizations providing temporary shelter for young runaways. John-John had been taken by Thong in April of last year, April 10 to be exact. His body had been found the next morning in a parking lot on Forty-seventh Street.

I picked up a crime scene photograph showing the body as it'd been discovered and examined it carefully. John-John Kennedy had been propped up against a wall at the rear of the lot. He was entirely naked except for the infamous leather strip holding his thoroughly gray penis erect.

On impulse, I plucked a second photo (this one snapped in happier times) from the file and laid it next to the crime scene photo. Despite the removal of the eyelids and eyebrows, Kennedy's almost girlish face was clearly recognizable in both photographs. The killer had ripped his chest and abdomen to pieces; chunks of bone were visible through ragged tears in the flesh. Yet the face had been, at least in terms of potential identification, virtually untouched. Of course, Kennedy, with his police record, would have been identified through his fingerprints, but the killer couldn't have known that. Just as he'd wanted the bodies to be discovered, he'd wanted them to be identified.

I skimmed through the DD5's, hoping to find the name of John-John Kennedy's pimp, assuming he had one. Coworkers put Kennedy on the stroll at the time he was taken, but nobody had seen him at the point of contact. The name of his pimp wasn't there, either. In fact, it didn't look like the investigating detectives had any interest in Kennedy's pimp. They were looking for that license plate I mentioned earlier. That physical description of the killer.

It wasn't exactly by-the-book police work. In fact, it was piss poor. I didn't believe in Bouton's theory, but I found myself offended by the reports I held in my hand. It was easy to imagine several dozen field investigators chasing after leads generated by a hotline and filtered through a profile. One gigantic, vulgar circus, with the cops occupying center ring, the reporters and politicians as ring masters, and the public for an audience.

(I was tempted to put the word "terrified" in front of the word "public," but the mood of the citizenry was closer to the early days of AIDS than to, for instance, the Son of Sam era. Faggots were being killed, not human beings. It was all very interesting, but not especially relevant. In fact, if it weren't for the bizarre nature of the murders and the furious reaction of the gay community, the homicides probably wouldn't have been newsworthy at all.)

A detective *had* visited Kennedy's two living relatives: his brother, Robert, an upstate deputy sheriff, and his father, James. The father, as it turned out, was lying comatose in a Lake George hospital, a victim of lung cancer. The doctors had described his condition as terminal. The brother, backed by his wife, had claimed to be ignorant of John-John's life in the Big Apple, though not of John-John's sexual preferences. The two brothers had been estranged for years.

I put the files down and fetched a mug of black, bitter coffee from the ever-dirty pot near Pooch's desk. He looked up and grunted as I passed, but I made no effort to begin a conversation. I wanted to get finished and out on the street.

The fifth file was even thinner than the fourth, but it did contain a surprise. Sitting right on top was an article from *American Psychology*, entitled "Sexual Murder." I glanced over at Pooch, but he was pecking away at his computer. Had he put the article there to bust my chops? Was its presence a simple accident? Had he thought it somehow relevant? I skimmed the article quickly and just as quickly discovered the same bleeding-heart bullshit I'd been hearing for years.

Physical abuse; sexual abuse; psychological abuse. They beat me, whipped me, kicked me, gouged me. They sodomized me. They made me feel *inferior.*

My first reaction was, ".Gimme me a fuckin' break." Followed quickly by, "How many times do I have to hear this crap." Lots of kids go through hell without turning into criminal psychopaths. I oughta know.

Two or three times a month, as I'm drifting off to sleep, I have what amounts to a recurring vision. I don't call it a dream because I'm not really asleep. But I'm not awake, either.

In the vision, I'm low to the ground. Perhaps I'm a child; I can't be sure. A woman, her face contorted with rage, stands ten or fifteen feet away. Her eyes bulge; her skin is scarlet; her scraggly brown hair stands away from her scalp. The hair seems alive.

The woman is saying something, but I don't know what it is. Perhaps she's merely sputtering. She begins to move toward me and it's only then I notice the determined set of her broad shoulders. I can't believe how big she is; her body grows with each, deliberate step.

What I want to do is speak out, to apologize before it's too late, but I don't. Or I can't. There's no way to know.

The woman holds a length of two-by-four in her hands and slowly raises it over her head. The fact that her hands had been empty a minute ago terrifies me.

If I'm lucky, I fall asleep before the first blow descends, but I'm rarely lucky. I never wake up, though. And there's never any pain. The woman, of course, is dear old mom.

How many days of school did I miss because I was too busted-up to walk the half mile to the bus stop? Or because my face was so bruised dear old mom was afraid even the deaf, dumb, and blind authorities of Paris, New York, would have to do something? Fifty? A hundred? Two hundred?

The most amazing part was that I did well in school right from the beginning. And I didn't blame the teachers who knew and did nothing. Quite the contrary. I was glad when their eyes turned away from me. That way, I, too, could pretend it wasn't happening.

"Means, you all right?"

"Huh?"

"You're staring off into space like some kind of a zombie."

"I'm all right, Pooch. Better than ever."

I dumped the article on top of the other useless material and went back to work. Victim number five was Rosario Rosa, a twenty-year-old Dominican national with a forged green card. A Polaroid in the files showed him on the stoop of some anonymous tenement, arms defiantly folded across a broad chest. He couldn't have been further removed from John-John Kennedy if Thong had dragged him out of central casting. Six-foot-three, two hundred and fifteen pounds, and dressed in a studded leather jacket, his black eyes glared at the camera. Rosa's skin was swarthy, his cheeks pitted, his nose broken so badly it twisted an inch to the left. Every bit the top-man, he looked five years older than Kennedy, though he was actually a year and a half younger.

I put Rosa's picture next to Kennedy's and stared at them for a minute. Bouton had been right again. Thong hadn't made his selections on the basis of physical type. More likely, he'd imagined himself to be on some sort of a crusade. Maybe he was a trick who'd come down with AIDS and blamed all male prostitutes.

Rosa's DD5's were no more revealing than Kennedy's. He'd been working on West Street when he'd been taken, but nobody had seen anything of significance. His last known address was

Rikers Island. Acquaintances described him as a mean, unpredictable bastard.

I glanced at the autopsy photos and found the same powder burns, the same entry wound. Rosa had been facing away from his killer, that much was certain, but it was impossible to imagine Rosario on his hands and knees. That wasn't how top-men operated. Besides, tricks who like to dominate would have no interest in studs like Rosario Rosa.

"Hey, Pooch," I called.

He snapped off the computer and turned to me. "What's up?" He seemed relieved to be away from his work.

"You have any idea how Thong controlled his victims? I'm looking at Rosario Rosa here and the mutt's completely butch. I can't see him turning his back long enough to get taken."

Pooch laughed happily. "Means, you want a definite answer to that one, you're gonna have to get it from the killer."

EIGHT

I made arrangements to leave the material with Pooch for a few hours, then hit the streets. That box with its little mountain of information was depressing enough for me to abandon it until the wee hours when I was usually depressed, anyway. Though I never lack for energy, I don't sleep much and never have. Before my exile to ballistics, I used to walk the streets at night, sometimes looking for trouble, but just as often to soak up the available energy. Urban renewal of the soul is what I called it.

New York, despite the popular misconception, does not cool off at night. No, while all those well-meaning, well-intentioned day people are sitting in front of their fifty-inch Mitsubishis watching the late news and wondering if they still have the energy for sex, the city actually *burns*.

Most people equate light with energy. According to conventional wisdom, the world is supposed to slow down when the sun drags its fire below the horizon. But this is bullshit, and I advise all those who believe it to spend one night in a virgin forest without benefit of tent or lantern. If there's nothing out there, why are you so afraid? You know full well those bats and possums roaming the night forest can do you no harm. That the *only* thing you inspire in their tiny brains is a desperate need to avoid you at all costs. That *you* are the great monster in *their* forest.

So, why are you afraid?

I was somewhere around six years old the first time I was exposed to that particular fear. The edge of the forest, a grove of fifteen-foot hemlocks whose branches swept the ground, came to within fifty feet of the house. I'd made a little tunnel into the hemlocks during the day (when I was usually free to explore while Mom scoured the town for booze or the money to buy booze) and somehow found it again one night when Mom went berserk. I seem to remember that her anger wasn't directed at me, but at one of my "uncles." They were fighting, but it wasn't the kind of picky argument usually associated with that word. Mom and her lover of the moment were pounding the crap out of each other.

I was already experienced enough to know that Mom was as likely to shift targets in midstream as she was to pass out on the bed. The door happened to be open, so I ran out of the house, but instead of standing in one of the elongated patches of light cast through the windows, I kept on going. I plowed into my little tunnel and came to rest in a small hollow where three hemlock trunks met the forest floor.

It was funny, in a way. I was sitting on a scratchy mix of forest earth and dead needles, delighted with my narrow escape, when the lights in the house went out. Maybe it was Mom's way of punishing me for evading her tantrum. More likely, she and her lover had decided to patch it up between the sheets and Mom had no idea where I was. Either way, I was stuck with the dark. And the noise.

I spent the night waiting for the "cannibal injun" to come and get me. The cannibal injun was Mom's invention, the boogeyman she used to control me when she was too tired or too drunk to use her hands. Seven feet tall and red as a fire engine, the cannibal injun came in the night to sink his glistening white teeth into the soft flesh of disobedient children. Like half-Indian me, of course.

At five years old, with no one around to say, "Oh, Roland, there's no such *thing* as monsters," I fully accepted the cannibal injun. As well as my own badness. The forest is never really silent. The wind moans in the trees just like a monster yearning for the flesh of a tiny child. Small animals (mice, voles, skunks, rabbits, raccoons) stir the dried branches and dead leaves, breaking into occasional panicked flight at the approach of (who else?) the cannibal injun.

Like I said, it was funny, in a way. (And from a distance.) The only thing I could do was sink *deeper* into the darkness between the hemlock branches, hold my breath lest the slightest noise lure the monster to my hiding place. I had to embrace the night and the life that came with it simply in order to survive. A life that, as I came to understand later, fed on me even as it sustained me.

Do nocturnal animals fear the sun? Fear it the way humans fear the dark? By the time dawn made its appearance, by the time I could see my uncannibalized flesh, I was no longer afraid. Even at five years old, I knew dear old mom would never follow me into those deep, dark woods. Like any other night-blind human, she could only pass the hours of darkness in a safe, well-lit den.

(What I think I did was become Mom's cannibal injun. Big joke on Mom, right? Not that I eat human flesh. Like any other wraith, I feed entirely on spirit.)

Later, after I came to New York, I discovered an unsuspected truth. The special life that emerges after sunset has nothing to do with the absence of light. Because it was there waiting for me in the Big Apple, despite the fact that New York (like every other place where humans dwell in numbers) both fears and fights the dark. High-intensity streetlights; shimmering, hissing neon; blazing restaurant windows; glowing theater marquees; the great white fucking way—none of it matters because there's nothing humans can do to restore the sun, to hold off the boogeyman.

It was still early when I left Pooch to his misery. The sun had been down for an hour or so and it was raining lightly. I flipped the hood of my jacket over my head and rammed the PBA cap into my pocket. PBA stands for Patrolmen's Benevolent Association, and the errand I had in mind called for some small measure of concealment. I say "small measure" because the drug dealers in New York would solicit a ham sandwich if it had the money to buy a quarter of a gram or a ten-dollar bag.

I made my way up Tenth Avenue, cruising through the neighborhood called Chelsea toward Midtown and Times Square, the sleaze capital of America. Chelsea is one of those "used to be" neighborhoods the real estate industry keeps trying to resurrect. They'd succeeded in one, the Upper West Side, and partially succeeded in another, Hell's Kitchen, but Chelsea had eluded their best efforts. Perhaps it had something to do with the Robert Fulton Houses, a three-square-block housing project as grim as any in Manhattan.

The dealers were out in force when I strolled by, preying on coke and dope junkies who, in turn, preyed on local citizens. I could feel their eyes scanning me as I walked past; this was not the neighborhood for a casual hike. An emissary approached me on the second block.

"You wanna party, bro?"

I stopped and turned to face a tall, slim Latino. He had sharp *Indio* eyes, somewhat like my own, though his skin was quite a bit darker. I stared at him for a moment, then flipped my shield in his face.

"I have no business with you; you have no business with me. *Comprende?*"

His eyes widened momentarily, then he laughed. "You sure don't look like no cop!"

"What do I look like?"

His laugh actually deepened. "You look like me."

I left him to pursue his trade, continuing Uptown. I was looking for a lone dealer, but I didn't expect to find one until I got to Times Square. The street dealers on the deuce usually come from distant neighborhoods. True entrepreneurs, they rarely work in packs, preferring to set up shop on the quieter side streets and pick off whatever business happens to walk by.

I found the man I was looking for on Forty-fourth Street, between Eighth and Ninth avenues. A short black kid in a soggy, hooded sweatshirt, he couldn't have been more than seventeen. I tossed him a questioning glance and he whispered the magic words.

"Coke? Coke?"

I hesitated, started to walk away, then turned to him, wiping my nose with the back of my hand like any other coke junkie.

"What I'm looking for is an eight-ball. Can you handle that?"

An eight-ball is an eighth of an ounce, three and a half grams. Not every street dealer can (or will) sell that much to a stranger.

"No pro'lem, bro. Cost you three Franklins. Up front."

I cocked my head to one side and regarded him skeptically. His head barely came up to my chin, but he looked like a runner.

"You think I'm stupid?" I asked. "You think I'm just gonna hand you three hundred dollars? Do me a favor, man, don't disrespect me."

He gave me a hard look, but I held my ground. I didn't want to threaten him, but it wouldn't hurt if I came off like I'd spent a few years in the joint.

"Wha'chu thinkin', man?" he finally demanded. "Think ah'm gon' take yo money? Shiiiit, this here is my *spot?* Ah'm steady on this block." He glared up at me, his face set. "How do I know it ain't *you* come to rip *me* off?"

I fished out my roll, peeled away three hundred dollars and held it in front of his face. "Your move, pal."

His hand started up toward the money, then hesitated before diving down into his pocket. "Ah shouldn't do this here shit," he explained, "but Ah'm gon' make an exception to the motherfuckin' rule." He came up with three small packets. "Ah'll hold the money. You hold these halves. Got the rest of my shit down them steps."

He gestured toward a brick stairwell leading to the basement entrance of a shoe store. Telling me his main stash was down in that darkness, which is exactly what I wanted to know. I dumped the money into my pocket, noting the confused, disappointed look on his face, then hauled out my shield.

His head jerked right, then left, looking for a way out. I tapped him on the shin with the toe of my boot, then drove a forearm into the side of his face. It was my way of explaining that humans can't fly.

He hit the ground fairly hard, landing smack on his butt, then gripped his right leg as if trying to contain an explosion.

"You goin' somewhere, mutt?" I asked quietly. "You got an appointment?"

He looked up at me, eyes blazing with pure hatred. Soul food is what I like to call it. I slid my .38 out of the holster clipped to my belt and showed it to him.

"Your hands go in your pockets, they're not comin' out again. You understand that?"

He hesitated and I drew my foot back.

"Yeah, I ain't stupid."

I might have debated that point, but I didn't. "Get your ass up. Get on your feet."

Once he was standing, I stepped in close and pushed the business end of the .38 against his ribs. Then I frisked him quickly, finding a small knife in his jacket pocket. The media like to pretend that every street dealer carries an Uzi, but the truth is that street dealers expect to be busted, and carrying an illegal handgun translates into a lot more time then selling a few half-grams to a narc. A lot more time and a guaranteed dose of curb-side justice from the arresting officers.

"What do I want, mutt?" I pushed him away from me, careful

to keep the weapon against my body and away from the eyes of virtuous pedestrians. "No cuffs on you, right? I didn't read you no bullshit about lawyers, did I? So what do I want?"

He knew what I was after, and he didn't like it a bit. If I took his coke *without* arresting him, he was going to have a hell of time explaining it to the dealer who'd fronted it to him in the first place. On the other hand, he *damn* sure didn't want to go to jail.

"This is what you call your basic approach-avoidance situation," I explained. "And I can see as how you're having trouble deciding on the best course of action. So allow me to make your choice a little easier. If you don't give it up willingly, I'm gonna drag you down them stairs and beat you to a fucking pulp. After which I'll find it myself. Understand?"

He got the point, and a few minutes later I sent him on his way, ten half-grams poorer for his night's work.

"Life is hard, mutt," I called to his retreating back. "One goes up, another goes down. It's called the Law of the Teeter-Totter."

I gave him a half-block, then turned and walked the other way. The hookers, including more than a few transvestites in full drag, would be out in force on Eleventh Avenue, near the Javits Center. It'd been a while, but I was sure I'd recognize one or two and just as sure those one or two would lead me to others. I wanted to listen to the street gossip, hear what the players had to say. That's what the coke was all about. The mutt had gotten the vinegar so I could go out and catch flies with honey.

NINE

Lorraine Cho decided, tried, and failed to count backward from one thousand; to concentrate all her attention on the beating raindrops; to fully explore the small cabin for the tenth time; to recite every line of high school poetry locked in her memory. She didn't do any of it. Didn't complete a single resolve.

What she thought about, with Becky gone and Daddy soon to come, was the chipper.

Becky had been at her bubbly best yesterday, chattering away about her and Daddy's various attempts to conceive a child.

"Why it nearly broke Daddy's heart, Lorraine. When the doctor said he could not make any babies? Not now or ever? And all the time he blamed me. Even after the tests. Well, it was not fair and don't I know it, but Daddy just hates to be wrong. Oh, Lord, he does hate to be wrong. You must never tell Daddy he's wrong about *anything*. Even now, when life is going along so nicely, his temper just flies out the window if he makes a mistake."

Becky had stroked Lorraine's hair. "I shouldn't tell you this, Lorraine. And you must promise not to repeat it under any circumstances. Believe me when I say if Daddy finds out, the both of us will be in a whole *heap* of trouble." Her voice dropped to a whisper. "After the doctor told Daddy he couldn't make any babies? Why Daddy wasn't able to have sex at *all*. I swear, Lorraine, it didn't matter how I tried to stimulate Daddy's appetites (and I did try my very best; it was my Christian duty), Daddy was just as limp as last night's macaroni." She had giggled again. "That's why we started driving."

"Becky?" Lorraine finally had gotten up the courage to give her plan a try.

"Yes, Lorraine?"

"It gets very cold at night, Becky. I can't seem to sleep with the shivering and all. Do you think you could get me an extra blanket?"

"Oh, Lorraine." Becky's voice had been filled with genuine sorrow. "I have already asked Daddy and he said no. But don't you worry. It's spring, now, and it's going to get a lot warmer."

Lorraine had allowed a silence to build between them. She'd waited until she could hear Becky stirring before speaking out. "Couldn't you bring me one on your own, Becky? A blanket, I mean. What I could do is hide it whenever I hear the car pull up. Daddy would never know."

"Well, you see, Lorraine, I have already thought about that. I mean considering you are my little girl and everything, it seems only right that I take proper care of you. But Daddy says that if I bring you anything without getting his permission first, he'll put me in the chipper."

Chipper? A series of associations had floated through Lorraine's consciousness: chipper, alert, cheery, energetic, bright, cute, perky.

"I don't understand," she'd finally said.

"Well, he *would*, Lorraine. No matter how bad it may sound, Daddy would do it."

"Do what, Becky?"

"Put me in the chipper."

Once again, Lorraine had failed to make any sense of the message. She'd been about to give up, to attribute the whole business to the manifest insanity of the situation, when Becky, slid her fingers beneath the blanket.

"My, you *are* cold. But I am so afraid of that chipper."

"I don't know what you're talking about." Lorraine had been close to crying.

"I'm talking about the *woodchipper*." Becky's hands had continued to stroke Lorraine's body. "Daddy told me all about this man in Connecticut who killed his wife? You must have read about him in the newspapers. He killed her, then he cut her up and froze her, then he put her body through the chipper. And you know what, Becky? They could never prove a darn thing against him. That's what Daddy said. He says if I give you *anything* without his permission, he'll put me in the chipper. Only he will not kill me first. He'll do it while I'm *alive*. Can you imagine, Lorraine? While I am alive. And they will never prove a darn thing against him."

The minute she heard the car, Lorraine knew that Becky wasn't driving. The van came fast, the engine roaring in protest as it pushed toward the cabin, then screeched to a stop. Two sets of feet crossed the wet yard.

"Hurry up with the goddamned door. I don't see why we're bringin' her in the first place." The low, gravelly voice belonged to Daddy.

"Everybody needs recreation," Becky replied. "Everybody."

The door flew open, slamming against the wall. Daddy pounded across the room, yanked the blanket away, slammed a ball of clothing into Lorraine's chest.

"Put 'em on. And do it fast."

Lorraine noted Daddy's short, quick breathing. She imagined him wide-eyed with excitement. Standing with his feet apart, his fists balled.

I want to live.

The sentence reverberated for a moment, then resolved itself into a determination to overcome the fear burning in every cell of her body. Daddy, she understood, would settle for nothing less than complete obedience. She could not obey if she was paralyzed by fear. Her hands found the bundle of clothing, fumbled with the different items.

"Now, Daddy, it is just not fair to ask Lorraine to do that all by herself. She's *blind*."

"Help her. No, wait a minute."

The hands that pushed her down on the bed were large and strong. Lorraine felt rough wool against her breasts, heard the metallic hiss of a zipper sliding open.

In an instant, she was gone. It wasn't happening to her. None of it. Not the scratching of a calloused hand against her breast. Not the indifferent animal grunts that accompanied each thrust. She did not will this reaction. It happened in the only way it could. With her body floating above her body. Listening carefully. Actually pitying the woman on the bed.

Daddy stood up as soon as he finished. Lorraine noted his indifference as she came back into herself. She was surprised to find her body wracked with sobs.

"Let me help you, Lorraine." Becky's voice had lost none of its perky cheer. "Now, I have to tell you that we are going to tie you up in the van. We simply cannot have you jumping out into traffic. I don't want to lose my little girl now that I've found her."

Ten minutes later they were on their way. Lorraine's chest and arms were lashed to cleats in the plywood lining the van's interior and a coarse rag covered her mouth.

She tried to memorize the route. Or at least get some grasp of its character. The van whined and bounced over the rough ground; branches scratched and tore at the side of the vehicle. Once, they plunged into a stream, rode through the water for a moment, then lurched onto the bank.

Did we go upstream or downstream? she asked herself. Followed by, I should have kept track of the time. The time is more important than the route.

But it was already too late, and she resolved to be alert for anything suggesting a human presence. A dog barking, cooking odors, anything.

Sometime later (half an hour, an hour—she couldn't be sure), they bounced onto a level surface and sped up. She had neither heard nor smelled anything of interest.

"My Lord, but that was a rough ride. I hope you are not *too* uncomfortable, Lorraine. Daddy is a real cowboy when it comes to the driving."

Lorraine, unable to answer, nodded her head.

"Would you like to listen to the radio? If it's all right with Daddy?"

"Great idea, Baby. Get us some music."

Lorraine heard the radio click on. Heard quick, sharp jabs of sound punctuated by static as Becky flipped the tuning knob, finally what sounded like a church choir. *Jeeeeesus loves me.* Followed by a slap and a choked cry from Becky.

"I've told you about that Jesus shit before, Baby." Daddy's voice was dead flat, as offhand as if he was commenting on the weather.

"Well, I just figured this one time we could make an exception, Daddy. For Lorraine's sake." Nevertheless, she flipped the dial again, tuned in a rock station.

Lorraine listened eagerly, though she'd never cared for rock music. She was waiting for the station to identify itself; she was waiting to get some idea of where they'd taken her. Despite knowing the information was useless.

The radio faded in and out as the van rose and descended through what had to be mountainous terrain. The signal was at its strongest when they stopped for the infrequent traffic lights; at its weakest when they dropped down into the valleys. Finally, a woman's voice announced, "This is Robin Love with the Voice of Love. WLOV-FM in beautiful, downtown Pottersville."

Lorraine began to cry, silent tears running from her eyes into the gag covering her mouth. She'd never heard of Pottersville, and the sense of having sailed over the edge of the world became nearly unbearable. Perhaps she'd been kidnapped by aliens.

Maybe she wasn't on Earth anymore; maybe she was on Planet Crazy. Maybe she was going to die tonight.

She pulled gently against the ropes that tied her to the van. Tied her like a side of beef or a crate of machinery that couldn't be allowed to slide. Her bonds were not terribly tight. She might even escape.

But, no, that wasn't right. She might get free, but she couldn't escape. She was blind.

She wondered what Daddy would do if he found her with her hands free. Then imagined Daddy putting her frozen body in the chipper. Imagined what would spew out the other end.

"Daddy, I have to pee real bad."

"Damn."

"Well, I do. I can't help it. When we go driving, I get so nervous I just have to go."

"Yeah." Daddy voice was resigned, the voice of a parent with a predictably annoying child. "What about that chink bitch in the back there?"

"Don't call her that, Daddy."

In an instant, they were fighting. Slapping, screaming, cursing at the top of their lungs. Lorraine felt the van weave back and forth across the road; she felt the insanity, the chaos, as well. When she finally began to sob, they stopped abruptly.

"Do you see what you have done?" Becky's voice whistled between her teeth. "You and your filthy mouth?"

They drove for hours; Lorraine slept and woke and slept again. Rock music pounded continually, Becky dutifully working the dial as individual stations faded out. Occasionally, they stopped for burgers and Cokes, or to use the bathrooms. Lorraine's needs were taken care of a few yards off the side of the road, but she appreciated the opportunity to stretch her cramped body. To breathe something besides the stink of Daddy's cigars.

They did not remove the gag, however. Not when she left the van. The gag was only removed when she ate.

She wasn't afraid anymore (though she was sure she would be again); she knew she had somehow settled in for the long haul. Questions popped up from time to time, questions about what Daddy and Becky were doing out on the highway. At first, she'd been sure they were going to kill her and dump her body in the woods. But that couldn't be right; they would have done that immediately. Of course, they might be perfectionists, might be looking for the absolutely perfect spot the way a photographer looks for the perfect sunset.

Once, they pulled into a parking lot and Daddy whispered something to Becky, then came into the back of the van to squat by the side door. Becky got out and Lorraine listened to her firm step for a moment, then turned her attention to Daddy. She could smell his sweat, as well as his excitement. He was waiting for something, and suddenly she knew exactly what it was. He was waiting for prey.

Becky returned a few minutes later and they left the parking lot without speaking. Lorraine listened to the rising pitch of the tires as the van accelerated onto a highway, a highway somewhere, in some place, in some time.

Sooner or later, she decided, they'll have to give up. They can't drive forever.

Within fifteen minutes, the van left the highway, bumped along a dirt road and came to a stop. Becky and Daddy climbed into the back, ignoring her altogether. They laid down on the floor of the van and went to sleep.

Lorraine listened to them snore for a while, then suddenly saw them as seasoned veterans. They knew exactly what to expect. Exactly how to pace themselves. They were like soldiers who learn how to sleep in muddy foxholes, to ignore incoming fire not directed at their positions.

A harsh June sun slowly heated the closed van and Lorraine,

knowing she was in for a very long day, began to sweat. She was tired, too, but she couldn't sleep. Instead she drifted into a memory that was closer to vision than to dream.

Her parents had taken her to a beach in Far Rockaway. She couldn't have been more than five years old and may, in fact, have been a good deal younger. It was very hot, actually sweltering, and they were without the protection of a beach umbrella. After a couple of hours, the ocean was no longer enough to keep them cool, and her father suggested they go for ice cream cones. Her mother was asleep on a blanket.

The line at the concession stand was fifteen people deep, but her father, stuck with his promise, took a place at the back. After a few minutes, Lorraine, in the manner of bored children everywhere, wandered off to see what she could see. The other bathers interested her briefly, but then she heard a voice coming from the back of the concession stand and tiptoed around the corner to investigate.

She found a child standing with his face a few feet from the wall, a young boy. He was talking excitedly, but there was no one to listen. His hands jabbed away as he made his case. *I didn't; I didn't; I didn't.* Over and over and over. As if those were the only words he knew.

Lorraine was fascinated; she felt no fear whatsoever. This was something new, something clearly alien to the calm world of her parents. She felt a need to name it, to understand what her eyes were seeing. The universe was much bigger than her parents' apartment. She was old enough to know that. And to want to bring that larger world inside. To master it.

The boy turned slightly and saw her. His expression jumped from surprise to anger; the change was almost comical. Then he sneered and jerked his bathing suit down to show off his small white penis.

Lorraine stared at it, nearly dumbfounded. She knew something was wrong, but she wasn't sure what she should do about it. Maybe she ought to run. Or to cry out for her father. But she'd never seen a penis before.

Suddenly there were people everywhere. Lorraine was snatched up by her father, his hands rising to shield her eyes. The last thing she saw, before she was hustled away, was a grown-up, a fat woman in a very tight blue swimsuit, slap the boy right in the mouth. She heard the boy proclaim his innocence, both before and after the blow: *I didn't; I didn't; I didn't.*

There's no relevance, Lorraine finally decided. This is all desperation. The mind throwing out anything to pass the time, to push away the fear. I can't surrender to this; I can't become insane. I can't become like them.

I want to live.

A few minutes later, Lorraine fell into a dreamless sleep. When she woke up, the van was already moving. She tried to stretch, but of course she was still tied. Her cramped arms ached and she groaned through the filthy gag covering her mouth.

"Are you okay, Lorraine?" Becky asked sweetly. "We'll be stopping soon. For food? Daddy says we can get take-out and eat it in the woods. It will be so much fun, Lorraine. Just like an old-fashioned country picnic. The kind we used to have back in Atherton when I was a little girl. Oh, I do remember those church picnics. . . . "

"Becky." Daddy's voice was sharp, almost choked. The van slowed markedly. "See there? I think someone's in that car."

"Why I believe you are right, Daddy. And there's a white cloth tied to the antenna. Do you suppose it is a damsel in distress?"

"Unless it's some kind of leftover, long-haired hippie. You go up there first, Baby. I'll get the tools and be right behind you."

The van slowed further, then stopped. Doors opened and slammed shut. The van's side door was yanked back and Lorraine smelled the cigar smoke on Daddy's breath. She heard something heavy scrape along the floor, then Becky's voice from a distance.

"Hi, you seem to be in a whole heap of trouble. May we help you?"

"It died. Just like that. Brand new and it just died." A woman's voice. Young and nervous. "I think I killed the battery trying to get it started."

"Sound like that darn computer." Daddy's voice.

"Computer?" the woman asked.

"Yeah, they got computers in all these new cars. They don't give no warning when they go. And there's nothing you can do but replace 'em. Guess these tools won't do us any good."

"I know what you *can* do," Becky said. "If you don't want to wait for some trooper to come along? Lordy, you *could* be waitin' till sunrise for one of them boys. But we have a telephone in the van. The new portable kind? You could call your husband. . . ."

"I'm not married."

"Well, your boyfriend or your parents. Someone to come pick you up. I mean I just *hate* to see a woman stranded. In these lawless times? You don't know who is going to come driving by."

"Don't think I haven't thought of that."

"Why, I just bet you have. I know it would be the first thing to cross *my* mind. Do you live far away?"

"About twenty minutes."

"In that case, we'll wait right here until someone comes for you."

"That's not necessary. . . ."

"I wouldn't even *think* of leaving you all by your lonesome. It would be so un-Christian. Wouldn't it be un-Christian, Daddy?"

"Definitely."

"All right. And thank you. I'll get someone here as fast as I can."

Lorraine heard relief in the woman's voice. Relief and gratitude, then steps approaching the van. She knew what was going to happen, wanted to scream a warning: RUN! She tried to spit out the gag, but it was already too late. The footsteps reached the door and she heard a solid thud, then something heavy pushed into the van.

"Drive," Daddy said. "Take Route 9 out to the reservoir. You know where. I'm gonna see if I can wake this bitch."

The screams began long before the van stopped. They went on and on and on and on. Until time ceased to have any meaning. Until they become nearly abstract. Like a police siren heard at a great distance in a large, violent city.

Lorraine was far away. Drifting, dreaming. She smelled the coppery smell of blood even as she walked through a fragrant spring garden; smelled the ammonia stink of Daddy's sweat as she sat alongside a bed of red and yellow tulips. Cherry blossoms dropped onto her shoulders; the delicate white petals carpeted the grass. Lorraine heard the screaming, of course. She heard the begging, but she knew it wasn't her. It wasn't her, because it couldn't happen to her. Now that she was safe in her garden.

TEN

I woke up at ten the next morning, hit the bathroom, inhaled a glass of orange juice, and began to work out. I didn't bother turning on the lights. I was living in a converted manufacturing loft on Fifth Street in Long Island City, and the floor-to-ceiling windows lining the western wall threw plenty of daylight.

My "gym" was down at the northern end of the two-thousand-square-foot space. The four-story building (my loft covered half the top floor) had once been the headquarters of Parenti Machinists and was built to hold heavy equipment. Steel beams ran from east to west in a mockery of the exposed ceiling beams common to upscale suburban homes. I'd attached heavy bags to these beams—thirty, forty, and seventy pounds of stuffed canvas—setting each of them at a different height.

The bags dangled invitingly, but they were not the place to begin. A Precor treadmill sat in a corner; it beckoned to me like a drooling sadist contemplating a bound virgin. I hated that treadmill, hated slapping one mindless foot in front of the other. But it was the fastest way to start a workout, and I needed to get done with the running the way a constipated child needs to gulp a dose of castor oil. With all due speed.

I stretched my calves for a few minutes, then stepped onto the platform, started the machine, and began to run. Slowly at first, then faster and at the steepest incline the machine had to offer. Half an hour later, dripping sweat, I flipped the switch and slid off. It would have taken me two hours to get the same workout on the streets.

I moved on to the seventy-pound bag and began to drive my right forearm into its rough surface. Over and over. I have my own method of street fighting. Forearm, elbow, palm-heel, ridge-hand, forehead—those are my weapons. I never use my fists; broken knuckles take months to heal, and sometimes (as more than one promising boxer has discovered) they *never* heal.

For some strange reason, the idea of going out on the street with a damaged hand terrifies me. I want every advantage I can get. Being in shape is part of it. As is packing a weapon; wearing a badge; striking hard, fast, and first. But my biggest edge is a willingness to accept pain without turning away. If I'm still conscious, I'm still coming. You can smell it on me.

That's undoubtedly part of Mom's legacy. If you're beaten often enough and hard enough, the only thing you really fear is losing a fight. But Mom did leave me something besides a hard head and a scarred body. Mom had enough good luck to win the New York State lottery and enough good taste to get drunk on a foggy night six months later and step in front of an eighteen wheeler. There was no will, of course, but as I was an only child and my father turned out to be dead, all other claims were dismissed in probate.

The payoff, $48,000 a year for twenty years, accumulated interest for the better part of three years before the courts decided to pass it over. In a way, the endless meandering of the system worked in my favor. When they finally handed me a check for $102,486 (the remainder having been eaten up by fees), the New York real estate market was in a state of near panic. My loft would have gone for close to three hundred thousand in 1987. In 1990, I picked it up for a little more than half that figure.

I switched positions, adopting a relaxed, natural posture, then drove the heel of my right hand into the center of the bag, right where the solar plexus would be on a live human being. I followed this with a shot to the nose, then returned to my original position and started the process all over again.

From any objective point of view, the sequence was every bit as mindless as running on a treadmill, but it never struck me that way. Probably because I was able to put a human being on the receiving end of the blows. A human being without a body, a face, or even gender, but a human being nonetheless.

I'd done quite a bit of fighting as a kid (even by the rather broad standards of Paris, New York, I was considered a strange child), but despite learning to win, I was never accepted by my peers. Which was fine by me. I wasn't looking for love; respect was more than enough to get me through.

It was only noon and I was still working out when the doorbell rang. My first reaction was annoyance—Marie Koocek come for a morning romp despite her knowing my schedule. Marie was a sculptor, one of a small colony of artists who lived and worked in Long Island City. I was never able to figure out whether she liked me or not. She'd come to my apartment, usually late at night, and rake me over the coals. In the morning, she'd go back to work without ever mentioning anything as stupid as love. I admit to having had some curiosity about her motives, but not enough to actually ask her and ruin a good thing.

One glance at the monitor above the door, however, revealed that my visitor was not Marie come to drag my sweaty ass into bed; it was Vanessa Bouton come for a bed check. Electronics was a hobby for me, and I'd long ago installed a tiny surveillance camera in the door's peephole. The camera's lens framed a determined, imperial Vanessa Bouton standing with her legs apart and her hands clasped behind her back. Her features were stolid and expressionless, but at least she wasn't wearing a uniform. Thank God for small favors.

I opened the door and she stepped inside without saying a word, then stopped dead at the sight of my apartment. I let her take a good look, let her think about what she was seeing. She'd come to all the wrong conclusions, of course, but that was okay, too.

The area around my little gym was unfinished, and I'd walled off a small bedroom, but the rest of the space was wide open. I'd sanded down the oak floors, bleached them until they were almost white, then covered the boards with a coat of polyurethane. A white leather couch, a matching love seat, and a glass coffee table rested close to the eastern wall, the wall without the windows. The kitchen was white, as well—white cabinets, white sink and stove, white Formica table, white leather chairs on polished chrome frames.

Over the last few years, I'd invested (with Marie Koocek's assistance) in half a dozen abstract glass sculptures. Set on black lacquered platforms and lit from beneath, their sharp, primary hues provided the only genuine color in the room.

With two exceptions, the walls themselves were empty. The first, my gun collection, hung just behind the couch. I won't bore you with a piece-by-piece recitation, but the collection was fairly extensive and mostly modern with as many handguns as long guns. At its center was a .45-caliber Thompson Model 27 A-1 fitted with every accurizing option available and finished off with an LS55 Lasersight. Fully automatic or not, I'd long ago voted it the weapon I'd most like to carry into a fortified crack house.

The second exception came about accidentally. A few years ago, I became interested in locks and how to open them. It didn't take more than a week to master the basic theories, but the application was something else again. Picking locks or taking impressions requires endless practice; it's a great deal more difficult than, for instance, learning to shoot accurately.

What I'd done was nail together strips of one-by-four, then attached various locks and mounted the completed frame low on the wall nearest the gym. On one level, the construction was undoubtedly an insomniac's response to the empty hours; still, I'd given it enough time and effort to be very good on the easier locks (the Yales, Arrows, etc.) even by professional standards. My ambition was to master the electronic stuff, but I hadn't gotten there yet.

"Captain?" I said when her few minutes were up. "You wanna take another step so I can shut the door?"

She turned to look at me. "Nice apartment."

It was more a question than a statement. Her eyes were calling me a crook, assuming the loft and everything in it had been purchased with dirty money. My answer was a conspiratorial smile. I was willing to let her believe I was on the take; if the headhunters ever decided to come after me, I *wanted* them to start with the money. I wanted them to think I was *motivated* by money.

"Thanks. I've spent a lot of time on it."

"It's very clean. Not exactly what I expected from a bachelor cop."

My apartment was clean for two reasons. First, and most important, was an obsession with *not* being the typical unmarried cop who blows his pay in cop bars, then comes home to collapse between filthy sheets. The second reason was Olga Pizarro, who did the actual work.

"Living up to movie cop standards is not one of my ambitions," I replied as neutrally as I could.

She seemed to notice me for the first time, notice the sweat drying on my body, the soaked gym shorts.

"I was working out," I explained. "Being as you weren't expected for another two hours, I figured I had plenty of time."

Her mouth widened into a totally unexpected grin. "We have a problem, Means. You work all night and sleep during the day. I work during the day and I hate soap operas. Noon was the best compromise I could manage without going crazy." She held out a paper bag. "I brought some bagels. I'll toast them while you're in the shower."

Great. We were starting out on the big adventure and she couldn't wait to get going. It was all a game to her. Which I found strange, being as her career was on the line.

Still, I took her advice and headed for the shower. I wanted a little time to compose the presentation she was certain to demand. My sojourn among the sisters (and brothers) of New York City's night had been discouraging to say the least. King

Thong *was* a hot topic of conversation among the ladies on the stroll. As were his victims. The names John-John Kennedy and Rosario Rosa were instantly recognized, but nobody, male or female, believed the killer was anything more than an especially deranged trick. Each time I suggested another motive, I was met with a blank stare.

John-John, they told me, was a baby, an innocent. And far too new to the life to pull off a crime as tricky as blackmail. Rosario, on the other hand, though born guilty, was too unstable to handle anything more long-term than a mugging.

My cocaine, however, did buy me an intriguing rumor. John-John Kennedy, they insisted, was being harassed by a pimp at the time of his death. The only thing was that nobody would admit knowing the pimp's name.

The rumor put me in an interesting position. On the one hand, it was an obvious place to begin. On the other hand, I wasn't supposed to operate on my own. I was tempted to throw my night's adventure into Vanessa Bouton's face. To see how she'd react, if for no other reason, but a little voice kept whispering, "It's a piece of shit, Means. A piece of shit."

I turned off the shower and grabbed a towel. Thinking, the hell with it; don't tell her a goddamned thing. Just give her a few theories and let her try to run with it.

"Means, you drown in there?" The voice of authority. Booming through doors and walls.

I dressed quickly: black, double-breasted Karl Lagerfeld jacket; gray, slightly wrinkled linen trousers from Basco; lemon yellow Armani silk shirt. I buttoned the shirt all the way up, then slipped on my gold shield. Most detectives carry their shields in a leather billfold as old and worn as the suits they wear. Mine, mounted on a thin sheet of onyx, dangled at the end of a gold chain. Reversed, with the shield against my back and covered by my jacket, the chain slid under my narrow collar, effectively replacing a tie.

The end result was as far from Columbo as I could get. A fact Vanessa Bouton was quick to appreciate when I stepped out of the bedroom.

"Damn," she said, then repeated herself. "Damn." Another pause. "I feel like Cinderella. *Before* the ball." She was wearing a dark blue pants suit and a white silk blouse topped with a gold pin, a sunburst.

"Don't worry about it," I said. "It's just me. I want people to know I'm coming. And to remember me after I'm gone."

"Why, Means? Tell me why?"

I looked at her closely. Wondering if she'd grown up on the mean streets, if she was trying to forget.

"Because crime goes on forever. Because law enforcement is a play without a final act. Because it's just no fun if it isn't personal."

She turned to the stove and began to arrange hot bagels on a plate. "You know something, Means? Your ass is screwed on so tight I'm surprised you don't shit through your nose."

I thought about it for a minute, then decided it was *my* line.

"That's *my* line," I said.

It sounded lame, even to me, but Captain Bouton had the grace to ignore the comment. "Why don't we get down to business," she said, spreading a thick layer of cream cheese and chives on a bagel.

I ignored my own bagel and sipped at a cup of coffee. "I went through the material last night, and while I can't really say the evidence supports your theory, the investigation did center on this idiot profile the FBI developed."

I laid it out slowly, mentioning the physical types, the problem with control of the victims, the lack of a drug pattern, and my blindfold theory. Then I hit her with my conclusion that Thong's intended target must have been victim number four or victim number five.

"Besides," I finished, "we have no practical way to investigate seven homicides. Not the two of us. We *have* to zero in."

She chewed her bagel thoughtfully. Her teeth were small, even, and very white. I watched her for a minute, then restated my theory.

"Homicide treated the first three murders as unrelated. They did a textbook investigation; they found nothing. The profile only came into it later, after the media put Thong on the front page. If the perp wanted to use the serial killer bit to deflect the investigation, he'd *have* to wait until somebody was talking about a serial killer. Don't forget, before it hit the papers, the perp had no idea how or where the investigation was going. But once we were committed, the perp would have had to act quickly. He couldn't take a chance on being made before he got the job done."

She nodded thoughtfully. "You're talking about Kennedy and Rosa, then."

"Right. See, my idea is to start with those two, and if we come up empty, work backwards and forwards. Victim number three and victim number six, victims two and seven. Like that. We have to narrow the scope, or we'll be overwhelmed with information."

"Just like the task force."

I smiled. "There's only the two of us, Captain. The task force doesn't have an excuse. By the way, can I assume you're thinking blackmail?"

"It doesn't have to be, but it's the logical place to start."

I picked up a bagel, looked at it for a moment, then set it down. What I wanted to do was get started.

"The problem is I don't believe anything in the files," I said. "The interviews were half-assed; the cops were just going through the motions. Which means we're gonna have to begin at the beginning, run down all the friends and enemies, shake out the bullshit and see if there's anything left. Kennedy spent time at The House of Refuge, and it happens the director, Barry Millstein, is a friend of mine. I think we should start there."

The House of Refuge was a shelter for young runaways, male and female, many of them former (and soon to be again) prostitutes. Street whores usually come with pimps who consider their ladies to be property. More than one girl had been beaten or slashed when she left the shelter on an errand. The pimps used to congregate in an alley across the street, waiting like cats for the mice to come out of their holes.

Barry had complained about it one day when I'd come to his office on an unrelated matter. Asking me why the police (meaning me) didn't do something about it.

"Beats me," I'd said. "You have any names?"

I think it's called symbiosis. We fed off each other right up until the start of my exile. In fact, the pimp I'd killed had been one of his.

"The director," Bouton said, "Millstein, he's the one who's homosexual, right?"

"I don't see what that has to do with it. The guy gets checked out every time Cardinal O'Connor preaches a sermon on the evils of the homosexual lifestyle. He's clean."

Millstein, like every other sane homosexual in New York, was terrified of AIDS. Both he and his longtime lover (an ex–football player who would, incidentally, have broken Barry into a hundred pieces if he'd caught him screwing around) had tested negative for the virus. The last thing Barry needed to do was sleep with street kids, male or female.

Bouton shook her head, smiling softly. "You're obsessed, Means. And like most obsessed people, you think you're charging into something when you're really running away. What you need to do is loosen up."

"And what do you need, Captain?"

"What I need is to get you obsessed with King Thong. And I'll thank you not to interrupt me when I'm pontificating."

I didn't bother to respond. Eating shit, as I've already said, is an important part of the police experience.

ELEVEN

I left Vanessa Bouton sitting at the table and went back into the bedroom. My .38 was lying on the night table where I'd left it. The department requires its officers to carry a .38, and not wanting to offend the powers that be, I stuck mine where it belonged, in an ankle holster. The weapon I intended to use for defense went down inside my belt. An ultra-compact Detonics .45 ACP, it'd been customized by a master gunsmith named Jim Stroh. There wasn't much besides the match trigger and slightly extended Eagle magazine to be seen from the outside. On the inside, however, most of the working parts had been replaced with custom hardware designed to accomplish three objectives: reduce recoil and muzzle flip, increase accuracy, and prevent jamming.

Loaded with 185-grain Remington Plus P's, the Detonics was the kind of weapon cops need to carry in a world of Uzis and Tech 9's. I loved it the way I'd loved my first gun, the ancient breech-loading Stevens .22 given to me by an "uncle." Technically, I suppose, the Detonics was just a backup piece, but the truth was that, except to qualify, I hadn't fired my .38 in years. Even though I went to the range at least twice a month.

I buttoned my jacket and left the bedroom. Bouton was standing in front of my lock collection; she turned to me when I closed the bedroom door.

"Christ, Means," she said, "I'm afraid to ask what you do with these."

"It's just a hobby, Captain." I was lying, of course. There are times in a cop's working life when he has to get in and out of a locked room without leaving a trace. When he doesn't have a search warrant and can't get one. Somehow I didn't think

Bouton was ready for the facts of life. Despite her newfound camaraderie.

That buddy-buddy thing was bothering me. And it didn't matter which Vanessa Bouton, the tight-assed bureaucrat or the teasing partner, was the genuine Vanessa Bouton. What mattered was that she liked to play games.

"Can you open them?"

"Eventually."

"Care to demonstrate?" She smiled when she asked me, her voice high and teasing.

"I'd rather not."

That stopped her. The smile disappeared, replaced by the disapproving frown I'd come to know and love.

"Try to figure it out, Means. We're in this together. If we don't trust each other . . . "

"Trust? Yesterday you put me on a leash. Today you talk about trust." I wanted to go on, but I didn't. Instead, I shrugged and looked down at my watch. "We have to see a man about a pimp. It's time to jump in."

We drove most of the way to The House of Refuge in silence. That is, I drove. A captain cannot drive a mere detective to that detective's own funeral. The protocol is so deeply ingrained in the minds of ranking officers like Vanessa Bouton that she got into the passenger's seat without raising the question.

From outside, The House of Refuge, a twenty-unit brick apartment building on West Fifty-fifth Street near Eleventh Avenue, looked as sooty and decrepit as any of its neighbors. Inside, it was a different story. Barry insisted that his charges become involved with their environment, that they love and protect it. The place was immaculate.

We were stopped just inside the entrance by two kids doing security duty. Bouton flashed her badge, and they passed us through. Millstein's office was on the fourth floor. I'd been there enough times not to hope for an elevator, but noted the look of disappointment on Bouton's face when I started up the stairs.

There were knots of kids, boys and girls, hanging out on the landings and in the hallways. They allowed us to pass, shifting aside without ever acknowledging our presence. Conversation ceased at our approach and all eyes remained on the floor until we were out of sight.

Streetwise is what it's called. A kind of wisdom unrelated to age. And why not? Runaways, throwaways, punchaways, fuck-aways . . . their lives have conspired to eliminate any normal avenue of escape. They don't trust, because trust has never gotten them anything but the back of someone's hand. Or the thrust of an adult penis into their midnight dreams. They gravitate to the street because the street is the only place that accepts them.

Me, I caught one break they didn't get; I had the forest, instead of the street, for my place of refuge.

I learned the forest surrounding Mom's house inch by inch, year by year. Following game trails, memorizing landmarks. Animals, especially deer, follow set patterns from food to water to food. Trails intersect, and a downed oak lying across a small pond or a moss-covered granite boulder or a rushing stream can mark individual trails the way exit signs mark an interstate. It's all very disorienting if you're thrust into it as an adult, but when you've got your whole childhood to figure it out (and the alternative to learning is dear old mom), you become very good at finding your way around.

After a few years (I was six when I began to explore), I started to make and mark trails with an old pocketknife, notching trees as I went. The Adirondack Park is crisscrossed with hiking trails, and eventually my own pathfinding efforts intersected these trails, again increasing my range. I don't claim to have memorized all two million plus acres of the Adirondack Park, but within his own territory, the only things moving faster than Roland Means were the animals that caught his scent.

We sat in an anteroom for a few minutes before the door to Millstein's office opened. A young girl, maybe fifteen, came out, her eyes on the carpet, shoulders slumped. She passed us without a word.

"Roland?" Barry's face appeared in the doorway, his crewcut as spiky as ever. That crewcut suited his perky features perfectly, and I couldn't imagine him wearing his hair any other way. Everything about him was quick and nervous, from the constantly jumping eyebrows to the sharp, staccato sentences delivered with a clipped, Chicago accent.

"Great to see you," he continued. "Long time. Missed you. Damn, but you're as stylish as ever." He was wearing jeans, a cheap blue shirt, and a plaid sleeveless sweater.

"Too bad I can't say the same for you. This is Captain Bouton. We're working together."

He ignored the jibe and reached for Bouton's hand. "A captain, eh? Impressed. Really. Good to see Roland coming up in the world. Too bad about Linda." He made the transition without a pause.

"Linda?" Bouton managed a tiny smile.

Millstein gestured toward the outer door. "Linda. Messed up once too often. Cocaine. Bad enough on the street, but she was bringing it into the house. Offering it to the other kids. Had to cut her loose." He motioned us into his office. "You can't reach 'em all. Too bad."

Bouton and I took seats near Millstein's desk while he bounced into his own chair and lit a cigarette. "So what's up, Roland?"

"We're working on the murders."

"Thong?" His features darkened. "Hard to believe the cops are interested in what the gay community has to offer. Been gathering information for nearly a year. Offered it to that inspector. What's his name?"

"Bowman," Bouton said. Her smile had widened considerably.

"Wouldn't even meet with me. Said unless I had an eyewitness, I shouldn't bother him. Tried to tell him Thong wasn't a serial killer. Patterns weren't right."

Bouton was grinning now. "Mr Millstein, those are my exact sentiments. And that's why we're here. We're looking for the true motive."

Millstein glanced from Bouton to me. He was probably wondering who was in charge. And if it turned out to be Vanessa Bouton, whether he could (or should) trust her.

"I understand the Kennedy kid lived here for a time." I handled his second unspoken question by ignoring it. Mainly because I didn't know the answer myself.

Millstein popped out of his seat and crossed to a set of matching file cabinets. He rummaged inside for a moment, then pulled out a file. "Anyone else?"

"Rosario Rosa," I said without hesitating.

He grabbed another file, then returned to his chair. "Why these two, Roland? You got something on them?"

"Not really." I briefly explained my operating premise, noting his widening grin as I went along. Barry loved police intrigue. If he weren't gay and sure to be rejected, I think he would have been a cop buff. "Anyway," I finished, "there's just the two of us, and we have to start somewhere."

His head bobbed agreement and he pressed the intercom on top of his desk. A second later, a young blond girl opened the door. She was stunningly beautiful and heartbreakingly young.

"Yes, Barry?"

"Would you copy these two files for me, Ginny? I need them right away."

"Sure."

He waited until she was gone, then turned back to us. "Ginny's all of fifteen. Comes from Iowa. Been on the streets since she was twelve. Lost her virginity to her father when she was nine. The girl's stronger than I am. Psychologically, I mean. Don't really see how she does it."

I glanced over at Vanessa Bouton. I knew she had a degree in psychology, and I could almost hear the wheels turning. Too bad she didn't have enough cop in her to stick to the task at hand.

"Tell me about John Kennedy, Barry. How well did you know him?"

"Oh, John-John. A bright kid. Sweet, but not serious. All a game to John-John. AIDS, the streets, the tricks, the cops. A big adventure. He tried to seduce me once. Not that he was the first or the last, male or female, to attempt it. Street kids think sex is all they've got to offer. A pity."

"What about Rosa?"

"Didn't know Rosa. Story going around is that he liked to hurt his tricks. A gay gay-basher. Highly unstable. Came up through the juvenile system. Foster care, Spofford, Rikers. Typical, really."

Bouton, unable to contain herself any longer, cut me off as I started to speak. "Mr. Millstein, we're thinking blackmail. Could either one of these kids bring it off?"

Millstein swiveled back and forth in his chair while he thought it over. "Don't believe it," he finally said. "John-John was bright enough. Wasn't his style, though. Blackmail's not a game, and John-John thought everything was a game. Rosa had the mentality. But could he follow through?" Millstein picked up a pencil and began to tap the eraser against the top of his desk. "Question is where they'd find a victim. (Every perp needs a victim. Right, Roland?) Talking about street prostitutes here. Get in the car, do your thing, back on the stroll. Also a problem with time. Four months between Thong's first victim and John-John. How'd the victim keep John-John quiet. Did he pay off? John-John died broke. Rosa, too. Where'd the money go?"

Standard interview procedure calls for one cop to ask the questions and one cop to evaluate the responses. I wasn't sure

Bouton understood that, but I hesitated long enough to let her ask the next question. When she didn't, I stepped in.

"Did Kennedy have a pimp?"

"One of the big reasons he came into the House. Old friend of ours, Roland. Razor Stewart."

"I thought he was in jail." At Millstein's suggestion, I'd harassed Stewart until he'd made the mistake of taking a punch at me while in possession of a quarter ounce of cocaine.

Millstein shook his head. "Cut him loose in a prisoner dump. Overcrowding. Early parole. You know the game."

"You have an address?"

"Probably get one. Just take a minute."

He popped out of the room, gone in his customary flash, leaving me alone with Bouton.

"Why are you so concerned about this pimp?" she asked. "Wouldn't Kennedy's friends know more about his personal life?"

"A pimp could set it up, Captain. If it's blackmail. A pimp would have the experience to find a target and the muscle to keep the money for himself. It'd explain why Kennedy died broke. It'd also make Kennedy's innocence an asset. Besides, I like pimps. I like the way they hate."

"You think this is a game, Means?"

"Tell you the truth, Captain, I was gonna put the same question to you."

Millstein bounced into the room before she could reply. Dragging a young girl behind him. I wasn't surprised to see her. Stewart, I knew, pimped girls as well as boys. Bouton, on the other hand, sat up in surprise, eyes widening as she took it in.

"This is Taisha," Millstein said. "She knows Razor Stewart."

"How ya doin', Taisha?" I asked.

"Okay." Her eyes bounced from me to Bouton. Trying to put it together.

"Taisha, do you know where Razor Stewart lives?"

"You gonna bust him?"

"I don't think so. Most likely, I'm gonna kick his fuckin' ass, then ask him a few questions before I cut him loose."

She grinned at that. "Razor lives with some of his girls on West 147th Street. Number 865, apartment 2B."

"How many rooms, Taisha?"

"Three bedrooms, but Razor sleeps out front. That's so the girls don't be sneakin' out on him."

"He bring tricks up there?"

"Naw, he don't mess with no house tricks. Alls he got are street girls."

I nodded. "You want me to give him a message? You got something you wanna tell him?"

"Yeah." Her face screwed up in anger. "You tell him Taisha's doin' fine. Tell him I passed my GED, and I'm trainin' to be a nurse's aide. Razor always told me I was nothin'. Said I couldn't do shit without him. But Taisha's doin' just fine."

Taisha left and we chatted with Barry Millstein until it became clear he had nothing to tell us that wasn't in the files he and his associates had painstakingly compiled. I stood up to leave, but Millstein held me back.

"Captain Bouton, would you mind if I talked to Roland alone for a minute?"

Captain Bouton minded like hell, but there wasn't much she could do. She could treat me like an old sock in front of other cops, but civilian witnesses were a different matter. When she was gone, Barry turned to me.

"What's the story, Roland? Thong going down? You really on the case?"

"Why, Barry? You wanna be there when I put the cuffs on? How 'bout when I put one through his forehead?"

His eyes glittered, but he knew when he was being kidded. "Need a straight answer, Roland. Friends'll wanna know."

"A straight answer, huh? Well, the straight answer is that I'm gonna give it my best, but it's a piece of shit from beginning to end. It should put me back on the street, though, which is all I'm asking. Do me a favor, Barry, put the word out that people should cooperate with us. It might help a little bit. I don't know if Thong had another motive besides insanity, but if he did, we're not gonna find it unless someone points the way."

"No problem, Roland. Fact, I could round up some of the people in those files if you want. Make it faster for you."

"I don't think so, Barry. I wanna string it out for a little while, but I don't wanna have to muscle any of the kids. Just put the word out."

I left him with a nod. Bouton was waiting in the hallway, a little frown on her face.

"What'd he want?" she asked.

"He wanted to know if we were serious."

"What'd you tell him?"

"I told him I had an appointment with a pimp. For me, that's as serious as it gets."

TWELVE

We were close enough to jump on the West Side Highway and be Uptown in ten minutes, but I decided to take Amsterdam Avenue instead. I needed to find out how far Bouton wanted to go, and I wasn't sure I could do it in ten minutes. Razor Stewart was a pimp, and pimps live by violence. Not the occasional violence of the armed robber or the street mugger. Pimps live by the minute-to-minute threat of imminent painful reprisal for any transgression, real or imagined. Prostitutes are beaten, stabbed, burned, and killed every day by New York City pimps who justify their behavior with the claim that sadistic violence is the only way to maintain social order.

The pimps may be right. It's hard to imagine women hopping into cars with eight or ten or twelve strangers each and every night unless something hangs over their heads. I've met prostitutes who claim to love the life, but I've never met one who loved turning her money over to a sadistic psychopath. The only thing worse than living with a pimp, they told me, was living without one and being the legitimate prey of every maniac on the street.

"Means?"

"Yeah, Captain." I was glad she broke the ice, and I kept my voice friendly. She was sailing into uncharted waters; if she was afraid, I wanted to know it.

"You've dealt with this guy? Stewart?"

"I busted him. About a year ago. He threatened to kill one of the girls living in The House of Refuge, and Barry asked me to take him off the street."

"You always take orders from Barry Millstein?"

"I was on my own time, Captain."

"I was kidding, Means. Lighten up."

"Sorry, Captain. Guess I'm just sensitive. Ten months in ballistics will do that to you."

"Tell me about Stewart. What are we in for?"

"Stewart's a pimp, and from what I can see, all pimps are the same. They're wife beaters in a polygamous culture. The only good thing about them is that they don't run in gangs. You take off a pimp, you don't have to worry about seven other pimps coming after you. Unless he decides to put out a contract." I let the idea dangle for a minute, then laughed. "Just kidding, Captain. The bad guys don't put out contracts on the good guys. Killing doesn't happen unless you corner them like rats. Which is exactly what we're gonna do to Razor Stewart. You gotta close your eyes and imagine it: There's Razor, nodding out on his bed, thinking he's the baddest badass in New Jack City. Then, here *we* come. Busting into his life. Pushing him around. Asking questions and expecting answers. We're not gonna ask politely, Captain; we're not gonna make any *requests*. If he refuses to answer (or if he asks for a lawyer), we're gonna kick his brains out and he knows it. He . . . "

"You're crazy, Means."

"You can still call it off, Captain. Maybe we can get a judge to issue a subpoena. Question Stewart with an attorney present."

"Uh-uh, Means." She was staring straight into the side of my head. "I have no intention of calling anything off. But you're *still* crazy."

"I see it as a vocation."

No doubt about it, my adrenals were starting to pump. We'd just crossed 110th Street, and the Cathedral of Saint John the Divine, bathed in afternoon sun, loomed on our right. The saints carved into its facade seemed to beckon. Some pointed to scrolls cradled in their arms, others to heaven. I ignored their accusing eyes, ignored the ambulances off-loading wheelchair patients in front of Saint Luke's Hospital, ignored the fresh young Columbia students heading to and from their classes. None of it had anything to do with me. The waters of my life flowed from another source altogether.

We crested the peak of Morningside Heights and drifted down into Harlem proper, crossing 125th Street, projects lining both sides of the avenue. Harlem is not the deep, dark hell it's cracked up to be. (No pun intended.) The neighborhood has always been spotty, with middle-class enclaves tucked away between the projects and the rotting tenements. Middle-class enclaves housing middle-class families forced to raise their middle-class children behind locked doors and barred windows.

"Means, you all right? You're awful quiet."

Some people fear silence; they need words the way alkies need fortified wine. Bouton, apparently, was one of them.

"I'm girding my loins for battle. In a manner of speaking."

She hesitated so long, I thought she was going to leave me alone with my thoughts. No such luck.

"Means, you think we should get some backup?"

"You've been watching too many TV shows. The last thing we need is more witnesses. Besides, it's a good day to die, right?"

There wasn't much traffic, but every fifth or sixth block, a red light brought us up short. I could feel Bouton's impatience, but the delays didn't bother me. I'd come to the point where I liked to draw it out. In some ways, there's more pleasure in the anticipation than in the act itself. I was busy imagining the look on Razor Stewart's face when I came through the door. Bouton was imagining what he'd do right after he recognized me.

We stopped for a light at 138th Street, just across the street from CCNY's north campus. Like Columbia, it hummed with the comings and goings of young, fresh-faced students. Only here the faces were black or Latino instead of white or Asian.

"I went to this school," Bouton said. "A long, long time ago."

"You from around here?"

"Not anymore. I grew up in the Riverton Houses, fought for

everything I have. Now I live in Forest Hills." She managed a wistful smile. "With the white people."

"You have a family?"

"The job's my family."

"Gee, where have I heard that one before?"

"I'm divorced, Means. My daughter's away at Princeton. In her first year. I'm not looking to remarry; I'm looking to get ahead."

"Seems like you put all your ambition eggs in one basket."

She didn't answer and I let it drop. What was the point? My focus had narrowed past the point of idle conversation.

I turned left on 147th Street, heading for the Hudson River and the domicile of Razor Stewart, as nervous as a nymphomaniac in a men's prison. Some people race motorcycles for kicks; others jump out of airplanes. Me, I disrespect New York criminals who structure their entire lives around being respected. Junkies brag about the "rush" of mainlined heroin or inhaled crack cocaine; I'll put the rush of danger up against any drug. I wasn't kidding when I told Bouton it was a good day to die. *Any* day is a good day to die. As long as you go down fighting.

The 800 block of West 147th Street looked like it belonged on a movie set. The tenements lining both sides of the street, the few left standing, had been ravaged by the twin terrors of impoverished New York neighborhoods: abandonment and fire. Battered apartments, the windows broken out by firemen and never replaced, marked every building. Black stains, shaped like the flames that made them, crawled over the window frames and up toward the roofs.

Yet the apartments weren't empty. Odd pieces of fabric, from gay prints to stained, yellowed sheets, hung over many of the gaping holes that passed for windows. They announced the fact of possession. Shouting, here I am and this is my home. Maybe the floors are busted open and the ceilings burned out; maybe the stink of the fire still scorches my lungs and there's no heat and the junkies stole the plumbing; maybe I stole the plumbing out from under myself, but here I am and this is my home.

It was a beautiful afternoon, and the locals were out in force. We were driving a four-door Plymouth sedan with blackwall tires, one of tens of thousands owned by the city. As we slowly cruised the block looking for number 865, the citizens, making us for the cops we were, began to drift away. By the time we found Stewart's building, the street was deserted except for the very young and the truly insane.

One of the former, a little girl who looked all of ten years old, sat on the stoop of 865 West 147th Street. She was wearing pink pants and a blue Mickey Mouse T-shirt. Someone had taken the time to braid her hair into neat cornrows. That same someone had allowed her to go out onto the mean streets by herself.

Poverty creates its own contradictions, and like any good cop, I'd learned to ignore them. As far as I was concerned, that kid was just another part of the landscape. There was no reason to acknowledge her existence. Bouton didn't see it that way.

"Hello, baby," she said, touching the girl's cheek. "What's your name?"

The child looked up at Bouton and grinned a grin as wide as the mouse on her T-shirt. "Lena," she said.

"What're you doing out here by yourself? Where's your mama?"

"She upstairs with a trick." Her voice was matter-of-fact. As if she were reciting her breakfast menu.

"Welcome to hell," I muttered.

The girl looked at me, then back at Vanessa Bouton. "Bombo geekin'," she said solemnly.

"Pardon me," Bouton answered. "I don't understand."

Lena pointed to a man on his hands and knees in the rubble-strewn lot next to the building. "Bombo geekin'," she repeated.

"What's 'geeking,' baby?" Bouton asked.

The kid's eyes opened in surprise. She cocked her head to one side and explained, "Bombo lookin' for rocks."

"Rocks? I don't get it."

"For Christ's sake, Captain," I said, "this just isn't the time for social work." All I got was a blank stare in return for my words of wisdom, so I compounded the felony by continuing. "It's like this, Captain. Every night the crack junkies go into that lot and every other lot on this block to smoke rock cocaine. Being as the rocks are mostly sold in little vials and the people handling them are stoned out of their minds and all the street-lights have been shot out, rocks get spilled and lost. Bombo is searching for those lost rocks. Now, can we get going?"

"Bombo geekin'," the girl repeated, her smile gone now.

"Lena," Bouton squatted in front of the girl, "do you know Razor Stewart?"

"Yes."

"Is he upstairs?"

"I don't know."

"Have you seen him today?"

"No. He mostly don't come out before dark. If he need some-thin', he send one of his bitches for it."

That did it. I turned my back and started into the building. If Bouton wanted to hang out, that was her problem. The last thing we needed to be feeling, at that point, was compassion or pity.

I heard her coming after me, but I kept going until I reached the second-floor landing. Then I turned the gold chain around to let my shield dangle against my chest. Bouton's eyes widened when she saw the way I had it displayed. They grew into saucers when I slipped the Detonics out of my belt.

"I think you wanna go in with your piece in your hand, Captain. We're not planning to knock."

I walked over to apartment 2B and examined the lock, a small

Medeco installed just above the doorknob on a wooden frame. That was another advantage to going after pimps instead of drug dealers. Pimps just aren't security conscious; they don't have that much to protect.

I took a deep breath, then stepped forward, kicked the lock out and walked into the apartment. It was a perfect moment, as good as they get for me. Stewart was sitting on the bed. A tall, heavy woman (a girl, really, all of seventeen or eighteen) bent over him, her naked breasts hanging right in front of his face. A second woman, an emaciated junkie with dark tracks crawling over both arms, stood in front of the stove, cooking something that smelled like breakfast.

Nobody moved for a long time. I suppose I could have shifted things into gear, but I wasn't in a hurry. I wanted to preserve the scene, to give it the sharp reality of a photograph. The kind you put in a scrapbook.

Stewart finally broke the spell by dropping his head into his hands. "Oh, shit," he muttered. "I thought you was dead."

The woman standing next to Stewart reached for a robe on the back of a chair and I instinctively swung the Detonics around to cover her.

"Don't touch anything," I said. "Not a fucking thing."

She froze in place, squeezing her eyes shut. "Please don't kill me." It came out a whisper. The whisper of a very small child confronted by a raging parent.

"Captain, would you secure the women?"

Bouton knew the drill. Like any good bureaucrat. She put both women on the floor, slapped on the cuffs, then stood them up and carefully frisked them.

"Sit them against the wall," I ordered, knowing I'd hear about it later. "I want them to watch."

"Why you doin' this, Means, why . . . "

"*Means?*" I shouted, taking a step toward him. "You know what to call me, Stewart. I taught you last time we met."

"*Mister* Means. I forgot, man." He put his hands in front of his face.

"Stand up, Stewart. Stand up and strip."

"Damn, why you doin' this. I ain't been near that shelter. All I'm after is mindin' my own bidness."

"Do what he says, you piece of shit."

I glanced over at Bouton to find her face contorted with rage. At first I thought she was pissed off at *me*, but her narrowed eyes were focused on Razor Stewart. I made a mental note to ask her about it when we were alone.

Stewart's own eyes were fixed on the two women as he stood up and stripped off his shirt and trousers. He was being disrespected and they were watching, perhaps even enjoying, his discomfort. The glance he shot them was more than a warning not to laugh or smile. He was announcing the fact that they were going to get their butts kicked as soon as we were gone. Not only was it a matter of principle, it also made good business sense.

"Damn," I said, "now I can understand why you girls stay with old Razor. That's not a dick, that's a goddamned bazooka. You take transfusions to keep it supplied, Razor?"

"Oh, man. I mean Mister Means. Please, tell me what you want from me."

I slipped the Detonics into my belt and folded my arms across my chest. "It's simple, Razor. You killed John-John Kennedy and I want you to confess."

His eyes shot up and his jaw dropped down. He couldn't have been more shocked if I'd just announced his candidacy for Citizen of the Year.

"Who? John-John Kennedy? Wasn't he the president?" The attempted lie, given the expression on his face, was actually pitiful.

"Ahhh, you're bullshitting me. I was hoping for that." I smiled and let my hands drop to my sides. "Kennedy went to The

House of Refuge to get away from *you*. A dozen kids at the shelter told me so."

There's something about nudity that takes the fight out of people. Or maybe Stewart was remembering that he and I had gone hand-to-hand before. He'd taken a bad beating that night. A bad beating in an even-up contest.

"Look," he said, "I don't want no trouble. There ain't no cause to get in my face. You ain't got to dog me here, Mister Means. Ah'm ready to cooperate."

The fun was over. He'd said the magic word and it was time to go to work. The first thing I did was toss the apartment, looking for any indication that blackmail was part of Stewart's financial strategy. I found a cheap .32 and a small amount of cocaine, but nothing else. No photos, no videos, no hastily scribbled notes.

I put him up against the wall, searched his clothing, had him dress, then marched him into one of the bedrooms. By that time, Bouton had released the two women. There was no point in confining them, because they no longer had an obligation to defend their man. He was cooperating.

"All right," I said, once the door was safely closed behind us, "let's hear the confession."

Stewart's jaw dropped again. As did Vanessa Bouton's. She was standing right next to me and clearly having a problem understanding my strategy. Which didn't surprise me, because what I was doing was having fun. Fun was not Vanessa Bouton's strong point.

"You said you were going to cooperate," I continued.

"I never killed *nobody*," he hissed. "Least of all some damn sissy wasn't worth shit anyway."

"I know that, Razor. But I really *need* this confession."

"You crazy, Means. You out your fucking mind." He turned to Bouton. "The man is a damn *psycho*." His voice had risen two full octaves; he was actually pleading. "Ah didn' do nothin' to that boy. Word, Officer, the boy was sellin' his butt 'fore I ever knowed he was alive. Ah was doin' him a solid-gold favor. Kid like him don't know shit about the street. How he gonna survive out there by hisself? Little skinny thing lookin' like a damn *girl?* How he gonna make it 'thout somebody watchin' his back? Alls I did was tell him where it's at."

"And then?"

"Then he go hide in that damn shelter you so worried about."

"The one I told you to stay away from?"

"I *did* stay clear. I ain't come within a mile of that shelter."

"Before or after you slapped Kennedy around?"

"I never . . ."

I smashed the heel of my palm into his chest and he went over on the bed. He was lucky, in a way. I could have jammed his solar plexus, but I didn't want him unconscious. Just scared.

"Don't lie to me, Razor. I'm not gonna take it."

Anger replaced his initial surprise. Enough anger for him to consider doing something about it. I could see it in his eyes.

"Make up your mind, Razor," I said, calm in spite of the blood pounding in my temples. "Shit or get off the pot."

He heaved a sigh and shook his head, resigned now. Ready to give me what I wanted. "Okay, Ah *did* get in his face, but it wasn't nothin' serious. The boy was fly, Mister Means. He was beautiful. Why he wanna sell that good shit on the street when he could be makin' serious bank? See, Ah gots me an arrangement with a sissy lives on East Sixty-fifth Street. Knows *everybody,* specially the kinda faggots that's too scared to buy they ass on the street. Understand what ah'm sayin'? Married faggots. *Politician* faggots. *Rich* faggots. The boy coulda got two, three hundred for his butt. Instead, he givin' twenty-dollar blow-jobs. Didn' make no sense."

"Keep going, Razor. And don't leave anything out."

"Ah tried to talk some sense to the boy, but he don't take nothin' serious. He ain't a bidnessman. Thinks everything's a damn joke. Ah 'splained to him about what could happen to a boy on the street by hisself, but it didn't do no good. Way ah sees it, the boy done had his faggotness cooped up so long, he steady believin' he havin' hisself the great adventure. Ah got so mad, ah jus' hada smack him. Word, Mister Means, ah wasn't after gettin' him into mah stable. Ah was jus' mad, 'cause ah hates stupid. If y'all don' believe what ah'm sayin', y'all could ask Dolly Dope. She right outside and she knowed the boy good. Dolly the one firs' call the boy to my attention."

I turned to Bouton. "You wanna get Dolly Dope?"

I was ordering her around again, but I think she was too involved to notice. As soon as she was gone, I returned to Razor Stewart.

"Face the wall, Razor. Sit on the bed facing the wall. I don't want you passing her any signals. I want her to speak for herself."

I took a chair off to one side and waited for Bouton to come back. The idea was to let the female officer interview the female witness. Even the most bigoted male cops were willing to concede females an edge in this one area.

Dolly Dope turned out to be the skinny whore with the needle tracks. Big surprise. I looked at her a little closer, noting that she had those sad, sad eyes common to terminal drug addicts. Eyes that'd seen everything. At that moment, I'd have bet my soul (assuming I had one) that she was HIV positive and knew it.

Bouton glanced at me uncertainly and I signaled her to go ahead. The first rule of cop interviews is to assume that everybody lies. Even if they don't. My job was to catch the lies.

"Dolly," Bouton began, "did you know John Kennedy?"

"John-John? Yes, I knew him." Her voice was smooth and educated; it betrayed no surprise whatsoever. She glanced at Stewart for a minute, then back at Vanessa Bouton.

"He was a friend of yours?"

"Yes."

"A *good* friend."

"He was kind to me."

"What can you tell me about him?"

"He's dead."

"I know that, Dolly. What else?"

"He was happy."

Bouton took a deep breath. "What can you tell me about his tricks?"

"John-John was doing car tricks."

"Did he have any regulars."

"Not that he talked about. He used to move around a lot."

"Did you try to get him together with Stewart?"

Dolly shifted uncomfortably. She was claiming Kennedy as a friend. Bringing him into Stewart's orbit could only be understood as betrayal.

"Yes," she finally said. "I thought he could make a lot more money and I told him so. John-John was fresh, unspoiled. The streets would have ruined him."

"But he didn't want to work for Stewart."

"That's right. He told me that his father had money and was dying of cancer. John-John expected to inherit enough to get off the streets. That's what made it a game. The streets, I mean. He thought it wouldn't be permanent."

"Kennedy had a brother, didn't he?"

"Yes."

"Did he ever talk about his brother?"

"John-John told me that his brother couldn't deal with his being gay. He did write to his brother from time to time. I don't think he ever got an answer."

Bouton looked at me for some sort of guidance, but all she got was a shrug. There was no way Stewart could have anticipated our arrival and, therefore, no reason for him to make sure his and Dolly's stories matched. Which they did.

"Is there anything you want to add?" Bouton asked. "Anything more you can tell me?"

Dolly Dope thought about it for moment. She looked down at her ruined arms, raising them slightly, then shook her head from side to side.

"He was happy," she whispered, "and now he's dead. That's all there is to it."

THIRTEEN

There was good news and bad news.

The best news was that it was seven o'clock in the morning and the worst news was over. Vanessa Bouton had gone home to her bed about an hour before, leaving me in front of a twelve-inch Goldstar, Heineken in hand, watching *Moulin Rouge* on Cinemax.

The bad news had begun somewhere between Razor Stewart's apartment and our first stop on West Street when Bouton fixated on saving Dolly Dope by getting her into a long-term rehab program. Even if I'd been interested, which I wasn't, it was the wrong time and place. We were in the middle of an investigation, and her mind belonged on the business at hand. It was that simple.

I tried to explain it to her. Along with the obvious fact that Dolly Dope was beyond redemption, that her eyes reached all the way to an inevitably painful death in a city-supplied hospital bed. Naturally, Vanessa wasn't buying. She was far too busy with Dolly's resurrection to listen to a poor schmuck like me.

Once Bouton got started, there was no stopping her, and about thirty minutes into her verbal daydream, I realized that she had two problems. The first was that she'd grown up in the projects, so she knew what the streets were like. She had to know. The second was that she'd spent most of her adult life running away from her childhood. She could have chosen to come up in the job by way of the streets. Lots of cops have done it. But she'd gone a different way, burying herself in personnel and earning her brownie points one ranking officer at a time.

I'm not saying the insight elevated me to the level of Sigmund Freud, but it did show me just how complex keeping

Bouton happy was going to be. I'd been charged (*ordered* might be a better word) with finding a suitable drug rehab program, after which Bouton would apprise Dolly Dope of her glorious future. Manufacturing a real investigation out of a piece of shit was challenge enough as far as I was concerned. Saving Dolly Dope was beyond my abilities.

I did catch one break, however. Between the cocaine I'd spread around the night before and Barry Millstein's putting out the good word, the whores, male and female, as well as a handful of pimps, were eager to talk with us. Bouton, I could see, was impressed. I'd come advertised as a super street cop and I was producing. Unfortunately, *what* I was producing confirmed Razor's and Dolly's assessment of John-John Kennedy as a nutty little hick with a deeply entrenched Pollyanna complex.

We didn't do any better with Rosario Rosa. Rosario had had plenty of enemies; in fact, we couldn't find a single person, not even the pimps, who had anything good to say about him. Over the years, he'd cheated, assaulted, or hustled just about everybody he knew. Rosa, so the story went, had a fondness for angel dust, a drug widely associated with mindless violence. When he was high, he was completely unpredictable. Nobody cared, as long as he limited his attacks to common citizens, but whenever Rosario beat on one of the girls, her pimp was forced to seek revenge. Protection is the only tangible thing pimps have to offer.

Even two cops committed to finding a motive for murder couldn't make Rosario into a blackmailer. Blackmail is too complex. The carnal encounter has to be carefully set up and recorded. The victim has to be approached and convinced that paying off is the only option. It takes time, patience, and diplomacy to do it right, none of which Rosa possessed.

At one point, Bouton dropped her Dolly Dope fantasy long enough to suggest that I'd targeted the wrong victims. Yes, she admitted, my theory had *sounded* good, but it wasn't working out. Kennedy and Rosa were too ordinary to inspire a killer like Thong. Maybe we should move on to someone else.

I countered with the assertion that we'd already found a motive. Namely that Kennedy's father had money and was close to death. Suppose Kennedy's brother wanted the inheritance for himself? Suppose he'd concocted a diabolical scheme to divert the investigation?

"Face it, Captain," I finished, "if Kennedy had been found in his room with a knife in his back, the suits would've been driving upstate the next day."

And that was the problem. Upstate. The task force had interviewed Kennedy's brother, and while they hadn't been terribly interested, they'd pegged him as a rural type without any direct connection to the Big Apple. Thong, on the other hand, had a detailed knowledge of male prostitution in New York. He'd pulled his victims off five different strolls; he'd posed as a horny john; he'd killed, carried, and disposed of his victims on city streets.

Any port in a storm, right? The idea was to stretch out the investigation for as long as possible, right? Don't blame me, I'm only the messenger. Right?

The messenger of doom.

Zsa Zsa Gabor was whirling around Jose Ferrer's deathbed when I hopped off my own bed, trotted over to the phone, and dialed the task force's number.

"Yeah?"

"Sergeant Pucinski, please."

"Speakin'."

"Pooch, it's Russell Means."

"Whatta ya say, Means? You bring in the perp yet?"

"Not now, not ever. Pooch, you were right. It's a piece of shit."

"Great insight, Means. So, what can I do for ya?"

"I want to get to Chief Bowman. Without Bouton finding out about it."

His laughter quickly degenerated into a choking, phlegmy cough. "And what're you gonna tell him?" he finally asked.

"I thought he might want to be apprised of our progress."

"Why couldn't he just ask Bouton?"

"Maybe he'd like an *independent* opinion." I hesitated long enough for him to think about it. "Look, Pooch, my ass is on the line here. Bouton's out of her mind. I don't wanna go down with her."

"I could understand that. I could *definitely* understand that. Tell ya what, Means. Why don't you keep *me* apprised and I'll pass the information to Bowman. He likes having a white cripple for a mascot."

"I can't go to him direct?" Somehow, the idea of trusting Pucinski wasn't all that appealing.

"You could do anything you want if you don't mind it gettin' back to *El Capitan*. Face it, Means, there's no reason for you to be going into Bowman's office, and he ain't the kind of officer meets with schmucks like you on dark streets in the middle of the night. You and me, on the other hand, are supposed to work together. I'm your liaison with the task force."

"And you have access to Bowman?"

"Absolutely."

"You're asking me to trust you here, Pooch."

"Please, Means, you're hurtin' my feelings."

"I'm gonna hurt a lot more than your feelings if you fuck me. I'm gonna take that wooden leg and beat you to death with it. You think I'm bluffing, just try me."

"That ain't right. What've I ever done to you that you should threaten me?"

"Nothing. And that's the way I want to keep it."

I quickly outlined what Bouton and I had done over the last twenty-four hours, then hung up, went to the refrigerator and made myself a ham sandwich. The sandwich went on the table along with a jar of pickles, a jar of hot peppers, and another cold

Heineken. I left it all sitting there while I went off in search of the pile of material supplied by Pooch.

The box was lying next to the bed where I'd left it the night before. The idea was to compare the names supplied by Pooch with those Barry Millstein had supplied, then compare both with the people we'd interviewed on the street. The end result would be a list of those we'd missed. Searching them out (or so I hoped) would take a couple of days. After which we could drive upstate to interview Kennedy's brother. Three days ahead was as far as I could think.

I made a mental note to pick a warm, dry day for the drive, then dug into the sandwich and the work. Half an hour later, I'd come up with a very short list of people who'd already indicated they had nothing to offer. Now it was time to read myself to sleep.

As usual, I picked the most boring material I could find. Namely the *American Psychology* article entitled "Sexual Murder." It was a fairly long piece, almost thirty pages, and more objective than I'd expected. The author, a psychologist named Miriam Brock, had managed to locate and interview more than twenty serial killers who'd exhausted their appeals and therefore had no reason to hold anything back. In the opening paragraphs, Brock emphasized how eager her subjects were to be interviewed.

> I wasn't the first to visit these men. A dozen journalists had been here before me, but they had gotten their stories and left, usually within a day. I made it clear that I expected much more, and the response was enthusiastic.

I'll bet. Brock's killers had accumulated a grand total of seventy-five life sentences and three thousand years between them. They were going to die in jail and they knew it.

Who wouldn't be willing to talk under those conditions? Every single one of Brock's murderers was being held in protective custody because they, themselves, were subject to being murdered by cons looking to make a reputation. Protective custody is no more than solitary confinement with a few amenities (like televisions and books) tossed in to make it look good. Time is the enemy, and interviews help to pass the time.

Brock began the study proper with an analysis of the relationship between child abuse and fantasy. Abused children—whether the nature of that abuse was physical, sexual, or psychological—all feel helpless; they must achieve some kind of psychological equilibrium in order to survive. Fantasy becomes their only avenue to empowerment.

> *Typically, these men recounted fantasies in which they, as children, became the abuser, the most powerful figure their inexperienced minds could imagine. The object of this fantasy-abuse varied considerably. Sometimes it took the form of the abusing adult and can be understood as a fantasy of revenge. Just as often, however, the object of abuse was another child or an animal.*

She went on for some time, recounting individual fantasies, then noted that, with few exceptions, her subjects had asserted the absence of *any* nurturing adult in their early experience. They were completely unprotected and thus completely vulnerable. Their fantasies, over time, became fixed and obsessive. And, over time, they began to act out their fantasies. The most common form of this acting out was cruelty to animals.

I laid the article on the floor and dropped my head onto the pillow. Wondering if it's cruel to kill animals if you eat them after you kill them? If you're hungry? If someone puts a weapon in your hands and *tells* you to kill them? If coming out of the forest with the body of a squirrel or a rabbit in your six-year-old hand means a pat on the head and a muttered, "The kid's good. He's real good."

Try as I might, I could not remember the details of my first successful hunt, but the effort put me in touch with another hunt, one that took place when I was eleven years old. My first deer.

My carefully chosen killing ground is a long-abandoned homestead several miles from Mom's shack and buried in the forest. There's almost nothing left of it—a gaping rectangle of piled foundation stones, a busted brick chimney, a few rotten planks buried in weeds and earth. The walls and floors are long gone. As is the road leading up it, if there ever was a road.

The waters of a shallow beaver pond stretch to within fifteen feet of the house. I've seen the beavers a few times, their dark triangular heads at the narrow end of a long wake. They swim in straight lines, with fierce determination, diving and emerging on an exact course.

The beavers would be easy to kill, but there'd be no sense to it because they'd only sink to the bottom. Food for the snapping turtles, but not for me. No, if I want to kill them, I have to catch them on land, and they only operate after dark when I am blind and they can see and smell and hear.

In the moonlight, their wakes are twin silver bars dissolving into flashing lace.

But it's not the wreck of the house or the muddy beaver pond (which was probably a stream or a small clean creek when the house was built) that brings me here on a weekday morning in early October. I'm here because the apples are ripe and dropping to the ground.

Because deer love apples.

As orchards (even long-abandoned orchards) go, it's not much. Maybe a dozen gnarled trees ringed by skeletal birch and crowded by densely packed young hemlocks. Eventually the hemlocks will overspread the apple trees and the birch, closing out the sun and killing them. But that means nothing to me. At eleven years old, the idea of plant wars has never crossed my mind. All I know is the orchard continues to produce shrunken wormy apples and the deer will come for the fruit.

I'm in place an hour before sunrise. Sitting behind the brush atop a granite outcropping forty feet above and seventy yards away from the orchard. I need the height for two reasons. First, because the hemlocks will hide the browsing deer from any line of fire at their own level, and second, because deer (like humans, incidentally) rarely look up.

I've been watching ever since I discovered the orchard, watching long enough to know that the deer bed down in a marshy area at the headwaters of the pond, that they'll come out before sunrise to feed, circling the pond and the homestead to get to the half-rotted fruit.

The air is cold and wet. A mist hangs over the pond, moving in thin clouds, driven by a breeze so light it barely exists. The pink light of dawn tints the mist a pale, pale rose. A blush thrown over aging features.

But, again, I know nothing of this. These are details to be observed in reflection. I'm an eleven-year-old boy with enough sense to remain still, but with too little experience to be patient. I have a new rifle (or, at least a different rifle, a borrowed, lever-action 30-30) and I can't wait to put it to the test.

Suddenly the air is filled with noise. At first, I'm at a loss, and I almost stand up to see what it is. Then I recognize the honking of geese. I know the geese are migrating, that most of the birds are fleeing the onrush of winter, and I wonder where they're coming from. If their summer home is a lake in some remote Canadian province, a lake completely unknown to humans. A lake where I could be entirely alone.

As the geese approach, I strain to see them, turning my head to pinpoint the sound. They're coming in just above the tree-tops, but the mist hides them for a moment. Then they appear, white breasts flashing up, webbed feet extended, slicing through the mist as they skid onto the surface of the pond. For a time they continue to call to each other, the dominant males, necks extended, menacing the weaker members of the flock. But they are too tired and hungry to pursue old quarrels for long and soon begin to feed.

I turn away from the geese to find a deer in the orchard, a small doe. Seconds later, another doe follows, trailed by a half-grown fawn. Then a third doe, this one older and wiser. She halts every few feet, sensing me, but unable to pin me down.

Finally, the buck trots into view. His head is up, his nostrils flared. He stops beneath an apple tree and begins to duel with the lower branches, pawing the ground as he slashes an imaginary opponent. The buck has an impressive rack, the kind city men lie about as they stoke the fires in their cabins. As they sip at their whiskey, their six-packs of beer.

The buck's antlers mean nothing to me. I want a tender young doe, and for a moment I consider taking the half-grown fawn. She's not more than forty pounds, and I can pack her out in one trip. But, no, she's so small she disappears beneath the hemlocks. If I fire and miss, I'll never see these deer again.

I bring up the rifle slowly. Very slowly. I'm not excited, but my concentration is narrowly focused. I see only the sights of my 30-30 and the smallest doe's shoulder. My finger squeezes the trigger gently, caressing it until it explodes. The doe drops immediately, slammed to the ground by the force of the bullet. The buck, without a backward glance for his consort, leaps twenty feet and disappears into the forest.

FOURTEEN

Lorraine Cho knew that night had fallen. She was lying on the small bed, enclosed from her feet to the top of her head in the woolen cocoon of her blanket, trying to fight the cold.

She listened to the scrabble of tiny claws on the bare wooden floor and imagined an army of rats massing for an attack, a continuous undulating gray wave about to charge across the cabin. She imagined this army baring yellowed teeth as it contemplated the taste of her flesh.

Or rats' feet over broken glass.

The single line of poetry repeated in her mind, but try as she might she could not recall more of the poem. Couldn't even remember the name of the author.

Or rats' feet over broken glass.

She told herself not to be so dramatic. That she had plenty to fear without worrying about a few mice come to pick at the crumbs. If they bothered her all that much, she need only tell Becky and Becky would take care of it.

But that wouldn't do, either. Becky would set traps to kill the mice, and Lorraine knew she couldn't bear another death.

Suddenly, without warning, a long-forgotten memory surfaced. She was down in the basement of her parents' apartment building, heading for the tenants' storage area to retrieve her bicycle. Her best friend, Linda Fried, was already outside and Lorraine was in a hurry. Still, when she saw her buddy, Joe, the super, kneeling by the furnace, her curiosity got the best of her, and she skipped over to see what he was up to.

"Hi, Joe," she said, trying to peek over his shoulder, "wha'cha doin'?"

He turned, grinning his customary broken-toothed grin at the sound of her voice. "Looky what we got here, Miss Lorraine. Look at how we got this critter."

Lorraine saw the narrow pointed face and the long naked tail and knew it must be a rat. Her parents were always complaining about rats in the basement. One bar of the trap was lying directly across the animal's back, as if the rat, sensing danger, had turned away at the last second.

To Lorraine, all of nine or ten years old, the rat seemed to be two animals. The lower half, the legs and tail, lay motionless, while the upper half writhed furiously. The rat bit at the trap, at itself; its front legs tore at the dirty concrete next to the furnace. Blood trickled from its nose and ears.

"That's one rat won't be botherin' nobody," Joe observed.

Lorraine watched as the animal's frantic efforts slowly diminished, as the volume of blood increased, as the rat emitted a final piercing squeal. She watched Joe lift the bars of the trap, hoist the animal by its tail and carry it to the compactor.

> Or rats' feet over broken glass
> In our dry cellar.

The next line of the poem came to her. Along with a decision not to let *anyone* kill her mouse. *Her* mouse.

She wondered if the mouse (it was a mouse, now, she noted, not a rat or even mice) would take food from her hand. Or if she had the courage to put her hand out there. To await her mouse's attentions without being able to anticipate them.

She fell asleep without deciding to, and when she awakened, her mouse was gone. Or at least quiet; she had no way to know. But she was sure that it was finally morning because she was sweating beneath the blanket. And also because she was hungry.

"Your throne awaits," she said out loud.

Her "throne" was a bucket in the corner, and she used it as quickly as possible. Now she would have to live with the smell until Becky arrived.

What, she asked herself, will I do if one day Becky *doesn't* arrive. If nobody comes.

Whatever she *would* do, in that event, was what she *must* do now. Because it was only a matter of time until Daddy killed her. Or until he took her riding again. In which case she would go mad.

She was half-mad already, and she knew it; she held the madness off by dreaming of a mouse taking food from her hand. There was a limit to how long that would work. How long before the screaming returned.

The question she asked herself again and again was if there was anything she could have done to stop him. She wanted to be able to say, "I didn't know what was going to happen and if I didn't know, how could I have been obligated to prevent it?"

But she couldn't say the words. Because she had known. Because she *will* know if Daddy takes her riding again. Because remembering the screams crush her words like a trap crushing a hungry rat.

She crossed the room and ran her fingers along the edge of the sheet metal covering the window. Counting the four nails that held the metal in place. Daddy had built a prison fit only for the blind. He must have thought she was too crippled to escape. As if she were a paraplegic confined to a wheelchair. But, then, why did he bother to cover the window at all? Why bother to lock the door?

The whine of a car's transmission pushing up a steep incline sounded in the cabin. Becky on the way. It seemed a little early, but Lorraine was too hungry to worry about tiny inconsistencies. She wanted to eat, to get out in the sun, even to bathe in the cold stream.

The car skidded to a stop, and a moment later hands fumbled at the lock on the door. Lorraine listened for Becky's "Well how are *we* today?" What she got in return was a silence that brought her near to panic. Wondering exactly what she was going to do if it was Daddy instead of Becky.

"Becky? Is that you?" Lorraine labeled herself a coward for asking the question.

"Yes, Lorraine, it's me." The voice was oddly muffled, as though the speaker had a swollen tongue or a toothache. "Here is your dinner. I am afraid it's cold, because I did not cook this morning."

Lorraine accepted the basket, then, without thinking, reached out to run her fingertips over Becky's face. She felt the spongy swelling around the eye and beneath the checkbones, the deep split running across both lips.

"What happened, Becky? What happened to you?" Lorraine's mind began to move even as she asked the question. Because she knew what had happened to Becky. Daddy had happened to Becky, and there had to be a way for her to use that.

"Oh, Lorraine, I just can't understand Daddy. I know I am not perfect, but I do try so hard to please him."

"How badly were you beaten?" No response, and Lorraine's fingers continued to explore until Becky pulled away.

"My ribs are sure a'hurtin'." Becky managed a short laugh. "Whew, I guess you will have to carry your own bucket today, Lorraine. I don't believe I could manage it. The drive nearly shook me to pieces. But I did bring something for you, and if you will give me a minute, I'll go fetch it right now."

Lorraine listened to Becky's retreating footsteps. She didn't really care *what* Becky had brought her. The important thing is that Becky had brought *something*. That she had managed one small act of defiance.

Lorraine was not surprised when Becky wrapped a blanket around her shoulders. "Thank you, Becky. I know how much courage it took for you to bring it."

"Well, Daddy is just so darn wrong about this. I mean if you got sick, what would we do? I said I would not let anything happen to you, Lorraine, and I did mean it. I swear I did."

Lorraine put her arms around Becky and, very gently, drew her close. She tried to feel some sympathy for Becky's predicament, for her life, but the effort threatened to summon up rage instead. Better, she decided, to do it cold.

"Daddy's going to kill me, Becky. He's going to kill us both." She tugged Becky's head down onto her shoulder. "He's going to kill me because he kills all the women he kidnaps. He's going to kill you because you know what he does."

Lorraine released Becky and stood up, fetched the bucket, and walked outside without asking permission. Noting that her feet were already accustomed to the rough, broken earth. Listening to Becky's shallow breathing as she followed behind.

"Are you coughing blood?" Lorraine asked, kneeling to empty the bucket into a narrow trench.

"No, I guess it is not all that bad."

"How did it happen?"

"Well, see, that is just what bothers me so much. I was frying up some veal chops when Daddy came walking by the stove to get himself a beer. You know how men are in the kitchen, Lorraine. They don't see a doggone thing, especially when they are a bit tipsy. Anyway, I did try to get my body out of Daddy's way, but he bumped into the frying pan and the fat spit up onto his arm.

"'Quick, Daddy,' I said, 'run your arm under the cold water.'

"You know what he did, Lorraine? He grabbed me by the hair and put *me* under the cold water. He kept me there until I was nearly *drowned*. And he was hitting me while he did it. Hitting me and hitting me. Why, I just thank the Lord above that I passed out. Otherwise it would have been terrible."

"Did you fight back?"

"Lord, no," Becky said, "I would never do that. That would be the worst thing I could *ever* do."

"Why, Becky?"

"Because if I fight back, Daddy will put me in the chipper for sure."

"I guess you can't resist. You're right about that."

"Yes indeed I am, Lorraine."

"But you could escape. We could escape together."

"I can't believe you are saying this, being as how you know me so well. How many times have I told you that I was raised to prize loyalty? I am not from this new breed of female that runs from man to man without giving it a second thought. No sireee. I believe the Lord put us on this earth to serve our men the way we serve Him. And that I intend to do."

Lorraine heard the coldness in Becky's voice and sensed the danger in going on. But she ignored her instincts. Telling herself there must be some way to reach out, to touch this strange woman.

"We could be gone before Daddy knows it, Becky. We could just get in the car and drive away before he kills us both. I don't want to die. . . ."

Lorraine heard a sharp crack and froze. She thought she knew what it was, a branch being snapped off a tree, but the first blow cut into her naked flesh before she could react. A second, then a third blow followed before she fell forward and began to crawl.

Small rocks jammed into the soft spaces between the bones of her knees. The knobs of protruding roots bruised the palms of her hands. In a moment, she became totally disoriented; she wanted to flee to the cabin, but crawled, instead, into the frigid waters of the stream. The blows continued to descend, ripping into her flesh. Above it all—above the sharp whiz of the branch as it fell, the crack of the whip on her back and legs, the indifferent bird song, the rush of fast water—she heard Becky screaming . . . Becky's pain-muffled diatribe echoed in Lorraine's mind.

"Bitch, dirty fucking bitch. Cunt. You're no good; you're pathetic. You don't deserve to live. Bitch, dirty fucking bitch. Cunt. You're no good; you are pathetic."

FIFTEEN

Bouton wasted no time in putting me on the receiving end of a not-unexpected chewing out when she finally showed up at two o'clock the following afternoon. Maybe I should call it a critique, because she went about it fairly gently. She started by asking to see my "automatic," and since I had no choice in the matter I handed it over, pointing out that detectives are permitted to carry backup guns. She nodded solemnly, and I went on to list the Detonics' various attributes.

"It's accurate enough to shoot competitively," I told her, "and it has less kick than a 9mm. Maybe even less kick than your .38." I went on to explain the mechanics of slide tighteners, compensators, and barrel bushings. "Everybody knows," I concluded, "that a .45 is a proven man stopper. It makes a big hole going in and a crater coming out. The only problem is that it's hard to shoot. Off-the-shelf .45's (the cheaper ones, anyway; the kind most cops can afford) are just not accurate. Not without careful training and constant practice. The weapon you're holding goes for a thousand dollars new. Add in the customizing and you're looking at two and a half, large."

"It weighs a ton." She handed it back to me. "Do they price them by the ounce?"

"I'm willing to admit that it might not be the ideal weapon for a woman." I gave her my brightest smile, but she wasn't about to let it drop.

"How is it a backup gun if you pull it before you pull your .38? If your .38 is on your ankle and that thing is in your belt?"

"Actually, there's no set rule about when you pull what."

"No set rule?"

"Not that I know of."

"And you think a technicality will get you off the hook if you actually *use* it?"

"I have used it, Captain. On a scumbag who was about to kill one of my brother officers. I sent him off to a closed-coffin funeral and they handed me a commendation." I gave her a second to think about it. "Look at it this way, Captain. Your butt has to be on the line before the job'll let you pull that trigger. Now, when it's really *your* butt on the *real* line, you have to know you can fire one shot, center of mass, and conclude the discussion. I've been around guns all my life; I've seen a deer run two miles with half a lung and a big chunk of his heart missing. You can't rely on your .38, especially with the cheap loads most cops use."

Somehow, I got the mistaken impression that I was reaching her. Maybe it was that absorbed look on her face. At the time, I thought it showed some interest in what I was actually *saying*. I should have known better.

"See this, Captain." I got up, walked over to my gun collection, pulled down the Thompson and flicked on the laser sight. "Forty-five caliber. Thirty-shot magazine. Fully accurized. It fires as fast as you can pull the trigger, and the bullet goes wherever you put the little red dot. You don't have to jam the stock up against your shoulder, and that's a big advantage. It's hard to keep track of what's going on around you when you're sighting a long gun."

"Most officers manage to negotiate their careers without ever using their weapons."

Her voice was soft, but the expression on her face had passed from "absorbed" to "what the hell am I looking at." It's a look I've been getting all my life.

"I'm not 'most officers,' Captain." I kept my voice as low and neutral as hers. "That's why you came to me."

"Is that why you wear your shield on a gold chain?"

"I want people to remember me."

"What people?"

"The ones who sport those gold medallions. You know, the automatics, the maps of Africa, the anchors, the pitiful street names. I want them to know who I am. That I'm not afraid of them. That my juice is greater than theirs, my power more powerful."

She sighed and crossed her legs. "Do me a favor, Means. Put your shield where it belongs. But carry the . . . what do you call it?"

"It's a Detonics. That's a manufacturer's name. New Detonics."

"Carry the Detonics, Means. If you flip out, I want you to be able to back yourself up. Me, I'm heading for the hills."

She burst out laughing, and I found myself grinning in return.

"It's nice to know you're committed, Captain."

"I *should* be committed," she said through the tears running down her face. "For taking up with *you*."

"Ready for lunch?" It was the slickest rejoinder in my repertoire.

"What have you got, Means?"

"Salami and provolone on Italian semolina with hot and sweet peppers, shredded lettuce, and Chinese mustard. I can rustle up a couple of Heinekens if you're drinking this afternoon. Otherwise it's Snapple lemonade."

"I'll take the Snapple."

It wasn't too bad, once we got down to business. Bouton had spent the morning contacting VICAP, looking for any sign that Thong had begun to kill again. She did this once a week, and not because she expected to find anything useful. She did it, she explained, to check on herself. To keep her ego under control.

We went from VICAP to a review of the interviews we'd conducted the previous night. Neither of us had taken notes on the spot, but Bouton pulled several sheets of paper from her purse and laid them on the table. They contained the names of those we'd interviewed and a short synopsis of what had been said. Our immediate task was to review the notes, then transfer them to the supplementary report forms known as DD5's.

"By the book, Means," Bouton explained. "The paperwork has to be perfect."

"Not if we find Thong."

She dropped her sandwich onto the plate and sipped at her lemonade. "Theoretically," she explained, "we're operating independently. In fact, Chief Bowman could ask for the paperwork at any time. Big Brother *is* watching, Means. And Big Brother has a big stake in our failure."

I nodded wisely. Just as if I wasn't part of that review.

"Did you locate a rehab program for Dolly?" she asked after a moment.

"Not yet, Captain. Tell you the truth, aside from asking Barry Millstein for advice, I don't have any idea how to go about it."

"Well, you can forget it. I found a place myself. Not that it was easy. The waiting list for drug rehab is six months and growing."

I probably should have kept my mouth shut, but I didn't. I couldn't. "Tell me something, Captain. Aren't you putting the cart before the horse? How do you know Dolly Dope *wants* to go into a program?"

She gave me a pained look, her eyes narrowing as she shook her head. "Don't call her that, Means. She's a human being."

"That's the problem, isn't it? She's human and we're cops. Not social workers."

"Spoken like a true warrior." She wiped her mouth with a napkin (paper, not linen) before continuing. "Means, on the day I walked into the academy, I swore that I'd never be a twenty-four-hour-a-day cop. I'm black, in case you didn't notice, and there isn't a black man or woman in this city who doesn't have mixed feelings about the po-leese. What I wanted from the NYPD was a secure job with decent pay and good retirement benefits. It's called civil service, Means, and it's the only industry that's really open to blacks. Despite affirmative action and all the rest of the bullshit. You pass the exams and you move up the ladder. That doesn't happen at IBM."

By this time, she was leaning forward, palms down on the table. "What was it you said yesterday? 'Law enforcement is a play without a final act?' If that's the case, it's important to have something else in your life besides the job. Something to hold you down. I've been working in the community for years. Working with kids who want to move up when everything around them conspires to beat them down. I see that struggle as noble, Means. Noble."

And it doesn't look bad on your resume, either.

I thought it, but I didn't quite have the courage to say it. No, what I said was, "Who's going to break the bad news to Razor Stewart? Who's going to tell him that a chunk of his income is about to be rehabilitated?"

"I'd have thought you'd be looking forward to it."

She was right, I was looking forward to it, but when I finally confronted Stewart a few hours later, it turned out that he couldn't have cared less.

"Take the bitch," he said. "She costin' more than she's worth. Word, Mister Means, they ain't enough cock in New York to keep that bitch high. Not when she can't do no more than give fi'-dollar blow-jobs." He motioned me closer, his voice dropping to a whisper. "She think she so smart. Went to *Vassar*. Treat me like shit in the beginnin'. Me, ah took it. Kep' feedin' the bitch steady dope. Tellin' her how much ah love her. How she the only bitch for me. How all these other bitches don' mean nothin'. They jus' workin' under my protection. Tellin' her it's all bidness. Except for her, mah onliest true love."

It was a familiar story. Take one inexperienced girl with a fondness for the fast lane. Romance her until she's hopelessly strung out. Put her ass out on the street. Beat her into submission when she balks. Dump her when she's finally used up. The only added ingredient in the recipe was Razor's hatred of Dolly's education. That and his obvious pleasure in her downfall.

"Has she got the virus, Razor? She been tested yet?"

His eyes jerked up, trying to figure out where I was coming from. If I was pissed off, he'd try to deflect my anger, even if he didn't know exactly why I was mad.

"Ah can't say as how I rightly know. She ain't never been tested; not so she told me about. But she been shootin' up so long I figure she gotta have it. She gotta have it and she gotta be steady givin' it out to her tricks. Ah say it serve the motherfuckers right. Tricks ain't nothin' but massa comin' to the slave quarters. Only difference, he wavin' a few bills, 'stead of passin' out hair ribbons. Ah hopes they give it to all they wives."

"If the tricks are 'massa,'" I said, "then who are you? You the slave who administers the whippings?"

When he finally responded, his voice showed careful respect, though his eyes remained defiant. "I hear you some kinda Indian, Mister Means. If you a Indian, tell me what the white man ever done for yo people, 'cept kill 'em. Shit, you jus' a damn nigga like me. Takin' massa's pay to keep the rest of the niggas quiet. But that ain' nothin', but nothin'. Even niggas gotta get paid."

I suppose I should have been angry, but I wasn't. Razor Stewart had as much chance of understanding me as a mouse of understanding a lion. Meanwhile, he wasn't making a fuss about losing one of his whores, which was all I cared about. At the moment. Later, once I was back in business, I'd look up old Razor and teach him something about lions.

But that was for later. For now, my job was to keep Vanessa Bouton happy. She was in the other room, pitching Dolly Dope on the joys of detox. Apparently, Dolly wasn't an easy sell, because they were in there for the better part of an hour before Bouton opened the door.

"We're ready," she announced without bothering to look at Razor Stewart.

I walked into the living room to find Dolly Dope standing with a battered gym bag in her hand. Her eyes were glued to the ragged carpet, her shoulders slumped, her back bent. I won't deny that she was pitiful, but there are thousands of pitiful souls in New York. What was the point?

The point, I reminded myself for the fiftieth time, was to please Vanessa Bouton, and that's exactly what I did. I played the part of the silent chauffeur on the drive from 147th Street to the Brooklyn rehab center Bouton had chosen. Bouton sat in the back, literally holding Dolly's hand. It was a performance worthy of Mother Teresa.

Or, it would have been if Mother Teresa had been running the rehab center. The real director, a practical, no-nonsense woman named Lottie Douglas, didn't spend more than ten minutes with Dolly before announcing that she'd have to detox before she could be admitted.

"We're not equipped," she insisted, "to deal with an addiction this severe. The law does not allow us to dispense drugs, and this woman is in no condition to go through cold turkey withdrawal. When she's ready, I promise to make room for her. In the meantime, I suggest we get on the telephone and locate a proper setting."

It sounded simple enough, but it ended up taking more than eight hours (even with Lottie Douglas pulling the strings) to find a clinic with a free bed that also accepted Medicaid. There's an old Billie Holiday tune that sums it up nicely: *Them that's got shall get. Them that's not shall lose.*

The clinic Douglas finally located was out in Bayshore on Long Island, and we made the drive in rush hour traffic. On the way, Mother Bouton managed to extract Dolly Dope's life story. Me, I didn't bother listening. And not only because Dolly's history (her real name, by the way, was Lydia Singleton) had already been recounted by Razor Stewart. Somewhere along the way, I'd come up with an idea that could add weeks to our little investigation, and I was too busy mapping it out to worry about Dolly Dope's childhood.

Thong's last victim was a thirty-year-old transvestite named Reese Montgomery. It was his age that'd caught my attention. The original investigators hadn't spent any more time on Montgomery's personal history than on Rosario Rosa's, but there was a hint in their reports that Montgomery, who'd been pulled off the streets of Long Island City, had once run with a much better crowd.

I was hoping that Montgomery had made that personal descent into hell common to many prostitutes, male or female. They begin by selling their youth, and they usually get enough compensation to live fairly well. To pretend, for instance, that it's not really happening even *while* it's happening. But little by little, the life wears them down. Drugs, time, disease, jail—the bloom is off the rose within a few years, and their pimps move them along (or outright sell them) to other pimps with less discriminating clientele.

The final stop is a stroll on the Queens side of the Fifty-ninth Street Bridge. Or on Delancey Street where, at six o'clock in the evening, whores service the Hasidim on their way back to Williamsburg. Or in the Hunts Point section of the Bronx where, at six o'clock in the morning, whores make mechanical love to exhausted long-distance truckers.

The point was that if Reese Montgomery had made that same journey, he'd undoubtedly left a trail of clients, some of them influential (or at least rich), behind him. Supposing Montgomery, finding himself at the end of the line, had decided that the patrons he'd known in his youth (who'd *stolen* his youth) owed him something besides an indifferent good-bye. Isn't there at least the possibility that he, like a drowning man grasping at a straw, had decided to extort what was rightfully his in the first place? Had decided to extort it from the wrong john?

It sounded good to me, and I intended to bring it up to Bouton as soon as we were alone. Unfortunately, she began to speak even before I started the car.

"You think I'm stupid, don't you?" she accused. "You think I'm an idiot."

"Stupid? Idiot? I don't get it." And I didn't. As far as I could see, I'd been a good little worker, chauffeuring her about, handling Razor Stewart, not complaining.

"You think we wasted the whole day. You think Lydia Singleton isn't worth the effort. You think I don't know how to conduct an investigation."

"Look, Captain, what I think is you just set the world's record for saying the word 'think.' As for the rest of it, you're a captain and I'm a detective. It's not my job to make judgments."

I glanced over to find Bouton with a clenched jaw and a narrowed mouth. She was angry, all right, but there was something else going on as well. Her eyes had drifted away. They were remote black shadows in her dark face. I remember wondering exactly what they were looking at and deciding it must be some childhood memory. Some long-dead relative, maybe even a sister or brother, who'd succumbed to the lure of the street.

Not that it mattered to me, one way or the other. My first objective, as I defined it at the time, was to avoid having to hear the sad story.

"I've been through your records, Means. You like to play the tough guy, but I know you've got a degree from John Jay College. In sociology."

"I don't think I've ever denied it."

"You've *avoided* it." She leaned back in the seat, relaxing a little.

"Look, Captain, I'm not trying to piss you off, but the degree doesn't amount to a hill of beans. Sure, I went to college. So do thousands of other cops. Everybody, from the youngest recruit to the thirty-year veteran, knows that school is a way up. I was young and ambitious. Plus, I was always good at schooling."

"But why sociology, Means? It has to mean something, whether you want to admit it or not."

"Sorry to disappoint you, Captain. What happened was that I bounced from one department to another—from police science to criminology to psychology to history—looking for some discipline that wasn't entirely bullshit. By the time I realized I'd never find it, I was a senior and I had to choose a major. I picked sociology because it was easier than the others. At least for me."

"You're telling me that you spent six years getting a degree and you learned nothing?"

"Nothing I didn't know before I took my first class."

"I feel sorry for you, Means. In fact, if I was you, I'd make a serious effort to find professional help."

"Wouldn't do any good, Captain. You been in shit as long as I have, there's no getting rid of the stink."

SIXTEEN

I managed, after a long, respectful silence, to bring up Reese Montgomery and his theoretical life history. Bouton listened, I'll give her that much, but she didn't jump at the bait. She remained at a distance throughout the long drive. At first, I assumed that she was angry because I was unable to share her enthusiasm for social work. After all, nobody likes having their hobby rejected, especially ranking officers who expect subservience from the hired help. But after a while it became obvious, even to me, that something was really bothering her. Her expression, eyes narrowed, mouth pursed, jaw rigid, became more and more fixed as she continued to stare through the windshield.

If we were in a movie, I remember thinking, this would be the poignant breakthrough scene. The one where the callous detective reaches out to pluck the traumatic memory from the psyche of the sad, sensitive captain. Where the two of them finally achieve a mutual understanding that transcends rank. Our hands would touch, our eyes meet; I'd lean forward, and her trembling mouth would rise to engulf my own.

Nude scene to follow. Nude scene with a twist. Sex by the side of a highway. The lovers' moans punctuated by the coarse squawking of a police radio.

But, of course, we weren't in a movie, and lacking a director, I remained my usual indifferent self, leaving her to stew in her own juices. I assumed that she'd come out of it, but even after we'd crossed the Triborough Bridge and hit the streets in search of Kennedy's friends, she continued to sulk.

For my part, I simply refused to acknowledge her mood, almost dragging her from place to place. Maintaining what must have been an extremely irritating enthusiasm. I couldn't forget the simple fact that as long as she held my career in her hands, friendship, or anything like it, was impossible. Not that I pined for contact.

Two hours later, Bouton surrendered to whatever was bothering her and called it a night. I can't say I wasn't happy to be rid of her, though I admit to feeling some contempt for her professional attitude. In any event, it was much too early for a dedicated insomniac to consider sleep, so I threw myself into a heavy workout. For months, I'd been trying to add a new move to my ragtag system of self-defense. (Or offense, depending on your point of view.) The move, an uppercut, required me to rotate my left shoulder into my opponent, drop my right, then run the heel of my hand up his chest and into his jaw.

The effect, assuming I could deliver the blow properly, would be devastating (mostly because it would take place out of the recipient's line of sight), and I admit to entertaining visions of severed tongues and fractured jaws as I worked. The problem was that the combination took forever to complete, while dropping my right hand meant that I was exposing my own jaw to a left.

After an hour of practice, I made a decision never to begin a fight with the uppercut. There might be a place for it later on, especially if it came down to a wrestling match, but not early when my opponent was likely to be on his guard. Still, I continued to practice for another hour. First, I assumed a defensive posture, then visualized the move as a single motion, a long graceful curve, down and up, so fast it was never really visible. Then I did it, over and over and over. Smashing the heel of my hand into a short piece of padded plywood until my right arm was dead. Until I couldn't raise my shoulder.

Then I switched to my left arm.

I didn't allow myself to think about anything except what I was doing until I was finished and in the shower. I'd always seen my workouts as a kind of meditation. Inside them, I was purely focused; nothing I did was halfhearted. There was no equivocation, no "should I or shouldn't I," no questions of any kind.

I'd taken enough psychology courses to know that shrinks dismiss the validity of such behavior with a simple label: obsessive.

"Look, ma, he's doin' it *again*."

My favorite shrink, Ms. Brock of *American Psychology* fame, used the word "obsessive" in every third sentence. What I wondered, as I dried off, was whether she was obsessive enough to really put herself in the place of a beaten child. To actually feel what it's like to be trapped in a world of unpredictable violence. A world that can (and does) flip from tranquil to deadly in an eyeblink. I doubted it. Knowing that if she had felt that insanity, she would not have used a word like "obsessive" to describe her reaction to it.

The truth, I decided, standing in front of the mirror, is that once the cards are dealt, you have to play your hand because it's the only hand you have. If you're strong, you eventually make peace with yourself. You react positively to those turning points which eventually define you.

Big Mike was my particular turning point. He was one of dear old mom's lovers, a perpetually unemployed lumberjack who needed a place to stay. He was nice to me, in the beginning, but I was used to that. The uncles were always nice while they were trying to curry favor with Mom. Later, after it became clear that Mom, far from being protective, liked to use me for a punching bag, they usually turned mean. Big Mike didn't take that route. Instead, he began by playing the part of big brother, teaching me how to use an axe and a chain saw efficiently, how to climb to the tops of the tallest trees.

I can't say I responded enthusiastically; I was far too wary by then. But I did want to master the skills Big Mike was willing to teach, so I spent a lot of time with him. At first, things didn't go badly; I didn't find it strange when Big Mike ran his hand along my thigh as he boosted me into the lower branches of a tree. Or even when he suggested we skinny-dip in the creek.

But when he began to go further, to soap me up, to let his hand drift from my thigh to my butt, to press my crotch into his when he hugged me, his intentions became painfully obvious.

So, what to do? Should I "take arms against a sea of troubles" or let the scumbag fuck me in the ass? I don't think I ever made a real decision, but there came a time when character took command. Big Mike and dear old mom went on a monumental bender; they began drinking in the early afternoon, finishing off two quarts of vodka by sunrise on the following morning. Mom passed out on the floor, her favorite spot, but Mike somehow managed to stagger into the yard and call my name.

"Roland, Roland. Where are you, Roland?"

Mike was staggering for two reasons. First, he was blind drunk, but second, and more important from my point of view, his trousers and underpants were down around his ankles.

I was too familiar with drunks to fear him at that moment. (At thirteen years old, I wasn't about to be trapped by a staggering alcoholic.) Instead, I became more and more angry. I was tired of being kicked around, tired of being subject to a new father every month. The sight of Mike's cock dangling in the breeze may have been the final straw, but it wasn't the only straw. An individual piece of straw may not weigh very much, but when you're at the bottom of the haystack, you either fight your way clear or you get crushed. There are no other possibilities.

Big Mike's mating dance didn't last very long. He stumbled over to the shed, managed to collapse into a sitting position with his back against the wall, and passed out. I watched him for a few minutes, until he was snoring away, then went to my room and got my .22.

Like I said, I didn't have a plan of action as I crossed the yard; it wasn't until I was a few feet away that I knew what I was going to do. And even then it wasn't a real decision. I knew what was going to happen the way a psychic knows the future.

"Wake up, motherfucker."

I smashed the rifle butt into the bridge of his nose without waiting for a response.

He woke up screaming. Blood was pouring from his nose. It ran over and into his mouth, momentarily choking him. I took advantage of his confusion by crushing his right ear. That got him to his feet, got him up and running. Unfortunately, he'd forgotten about his dropped trousers and he fell, head first, onto the grass.

"What're you doing? What're you doing?" His hands were in front of his face. As if they could stop a bullet.

"I'm tired," I muttered, my voice ten years older than my body. "I'm tired. I'm tired. I'm tired. I'm tired."

It wasn't that I couldn't remember what I was tired of. There were so many things, I didn't know which to mention first.

"Don't shoot me, Roland. I'll do whatever you want. I'll leave right now."

I hated him even more, then. I hated him for not fighting back, for taking it, for accepting the idea that might makes right. I had a gun and therefore I was stronger. And therefore he would submit as he'd expected me to submit.

My finger tightened on the trigger. I was a veteran hunter by that time and knew, to the millimeter, exactly how far that trigger would have to move before Mike's luck ran out. And he knew it, too. He could see it through the alcohol, through the pain, through the blood.

He began to crawl away, and this time I didn't follow. I watched him drag his body through the dirt, watched drops of blood fall from his chin to mix with the dust. When he was thirty feet away, I released the trigger.

"Why don't you pull your pants up, Mike?" I said, my voice as calm as if nothing had happened. Nothing at all. "You look stupid."

• • •

After my shower, I soaped my face and began to shave. Bouton and I had agreed to interview Kennedy's brother and, if possible, his father, the next day. The drive upstate would take at least four hours, and Bouton had insisted we get an early start, which meant I'd be lucky to snatch a few hours' sleep. It also meant I'd be in no shape (or mood) to shower and shave in the morning.

It didn't take me long to shave; I don't have much of a beard, an inheritance, most likely, from my Indian father. Still, I was careful about it, soaping and dragging the razor across every inch of my face. When I was finished, I walked into the bedroom, stripped, laid out the day's wardrobe, and got into bed with my favorite sleeping pill, Miriam Brock's treatise on the sexually motivated murderer.

I skimmed through what I'd read, fairly disgusted by the dry, academic tone which I took to be a disguise for her psychologist's bleeding heart. I kept waiting for her to mention the simple fact that tens of thousands of children had gone through similar experiences without becoming murderers. To somewhere discuss the role of choice.

It never happened, of course. She spoke about these men as if they were machines, as if, the ingredients having been mixed, the recipe followed, their fates were sealed. As for me, I'd rather be thought of as a vicious killer than a programmed robot. Killers, at least, are human.

Ms. Brock wrote:

Social isolation was the final and, in some ways, the most important factor in the progression from abused, terrified child to adult murderer. As children, children sustained by obsessive, often sadistic fantasy, these men might have been saved (and, we theorize, many children were saved) by the give-and-take of peer association. Our murderers, virtually to a man (see Table 4), report little or no meaningful contact with other children. They remained isolated, not only through their childhoods and ado-

lescences, but virtually throughout their lives. This not only intensified their retreat into fantasy, it also reinforced the value of fantasy to their fragile psyches.

Their *fragile psyches?* It's hard to imagine a grown man who stalks and kills strangers for the fun of it, who relives his triumphs again and again, gloating in the fear of his victims, as fragile.

As for me, I passed my childhood in a shack five miles from my closest neighbor. By the time I started school, I was already pretty odd, having spent more time in the forest than most of the other kids had spent out of their parents' sight. My yellow skin and narrow, slanty eyes compounded that oddity, and somewhere along the line, my peers, male and female, began to call me Hiawatha. I put an end to their teasing in a hurry, but, as I've already said, my ability to kick their mean little butts all over the schoolyard didn't make them like me.

Looking back on it, I didn't remember shedding any tears over my unpopularity. The forest had been my refuge (and my friend) before I ever started school, and it continued to be my refuge right up until the day I took off for boot camp. The only curious part was the fact that I'd never gone back to it. That I hadn't, up to that point, left New York City in ten years.

I dumped Miriam Brock on the floor by the side of the bed and turned off the light. Imagining her in a prison interview room, face-to-face with her homicidal subjects. Wondering if she'd ever examined her own motivations. If there hadn't been a slight sexual motivation underlying her interest in serial killers. Perhaps some itty-bitty, teeny-weeny twinge when she asked them for the gory details.

"Did you have sex with your victims before or after you killed them, Mr. Smith? Was the intercourse vaginal? Or did you bury it in their sweet, round butts? And, of course, I'll have to know many times you ejaculated."

SEVENTEEN

I'm standing on a railroad track in the middle of a remote, dense forest. A train approaches. I can't hear it, but I can see it; I can see the train's headlight as it alternately fixes me in its glare, then disappears behind the trees. Or, I *assume* it disappears behind the trees. I can't see the trees, and all I know for sure is that I am sometimes bathed in a merciless glare and sometimes left in absolute darkness. Should I be afraid? Should I face the onrushing locomotive? Should I leap off the tracks and take cover? Is there any cover to take?

I don't know how long it went on, but at some point I realized that I was dreaming and began to wake up. The only problem was the dream persisted, even after I opened my eyes.

POP!

The constellation of dancing lights was beautiful. Baffling, but beautiful.

POP!

"What the hell?"

"Perfect, Means. I've finally got it."

"Marie?"

POP!

"Jesus Christ."

I put the pillow over my face, trying to buy enough dark to restore my sight. The author of my nightmare was Marie Koocek, monumental sculptor, uninhibited lover, dedicated lunatic. Marie had been trying to capture my "essence" with a cheap Instamatic for the better part of a year. For the life of me, I couldn't see what she'd do with it, since most of her work consisted of welded I-beams decorated with rubbish she picked up ("rescued" was the word she preferred to use) off the streets. Marie, when she wasn't lonely enough (or horny enough) to seek my company, spent her nights roaming the boroughs in a dilapidated pickup truck.

I flipped the pillow in her general direction, grabbed for the camera, and caught a piece of her wrist.

POP!

As wrestling-foreplay goes, it was a fairly even match. Marie had never been demure, and years of pounding chisels into chunks of stone (when she wasn't welding five-ton I-beams) had turned her arms to steel. Nevertheless, I managed to strip away the camera and her clothing (mostly because she was too busy stripping away mine to resist) and get down to business.

Marie and I had a perfect relationship. Each of us knew what we wanted and, more importantly, what we didn't want. It was a union without the need for possession or jealousy. Which is not to say it was based entirely on sex. I can't remember a time when I wasn't glad to see her, and I took her efforts to capture my true, final, irreducible self for the compliment it was. There was nothing Marie hated more than mediocrity.

She took me inside her, wrapped her legs around the backs of my thighs, and locked me down. I settled into a long, slow grind (exactly what she wanted) and ran my tongue over the broad bones that framed her face. She responded with her lips and with hands sensitive enough to transform a lump of clay into a rainbow.

We were both soaked with sweat by the time we finished. I started to pull away, but she held me close, demanding that I remain inside her until I softened completely.

It didn't take all that long, and within a few minutes I was headed for the john to dispose of the condom we were both smart enough to insist on. When I came out, I put my hands over my face, expecting another Instamatic onslaught, but Marie's camera lay forgotten on the carpet. She was sitting on the edge of the bed, absorbed in Miriam Brock's *American Psychology* article.

"What's this all about, Means? You going back to school?"

"I'm trying to figure out why I'm not a serial killer," I said, surprising myself with the bitterness evident in my voice. "Being as I've had the required education."

She looked up, fixing me with pale gray eyes. "Maybe it's because you don't sprinkle your victims with Cheerios. Before you eat them."

"You think it's funny?" I ignored her protest and dug the autopsy photos out of Pooch's evidence box. "Because this is what all the bullshit in that article really looks like."

I laid them on the bed in nice, neat rows, then stepped back to give her a close look. She didn't pull away, but then I didn't expect her to; she picked the photos up, one at a time, carefully examining each of them.

"This is Thong's work, right?"

"*Work?*" I paused, but she was too smart to reply. Instead, she stared up at me, her mouth curved into a bemused smile. "You know what bothers me about people like Miriam Brock?" I continued. "They really *believe* they're describing something. They think they're fucking scientists. And that's not the worst of it. The worst part is that someone *pays* them to pursue their bullshit delusions. They're government funded. Or they get time off from their teaching duties. Or they milk private foundations for grant money. I'm telling you, Marie, morons like Miriam Brock will *never* know why people like Thong do what they do. Or why millions of kids experience everything the men in that study experienced and don't become killers."

She stared at me for a moment before she finally spoke. "Jesus, Means," she said, "I really love the way your cock bounces against your leg when you pace. And I wonder what it feels like. That's the whole game, of course. Knowing what you can't possibly know."

"Thanks for the insight. Think I should write it down?"

She gathered her clothes and began to dress. We had a game we liked to play in the shower, play with our hands and a greasy bar of soap. I'd been looking forward to it, but . . . ring up another victory for Ms. Brock.

I sat down next to Marie and said the wrong thing. As usual. "What's the matter, Koocek? You got a hot date with a dumpster?"

She stopped, turned, and fixed me with one of her piercing stares. Marie was small-breasted, and I remember thinking that her pale nipples, set in that broad muscular chest, looked like an extra pair of eyes.

"It's not a curse," she said, her voice almost a whisper. "Going inside, going back? It's not a curse; it's an obligation. If it hurts? If it changes you? If it lifts you out of your comfortable chair and propels you into another life . . . well, that's what obligation's all about."

"Yeah? And what's your obligation? To get out of here as fast as you can?"

Her eyes widened slightly. In shock, I think. We weren't in the habit of controlling each other's time. But I didn't want to be alone, and I wasn't strong enough to conceal it.

"You up for a blow-job, Means?" Marie didn't smile much, but when she did, her face opened to reveal deep, childish dimples.

"Up? Not yet, but soon."

Soon turned into an hour of very slow, mostly oral sex. I wouldn't call it love, but there was a great deal of tenderness in the way Marie stroked me. She'd once told me that in the early days, when she was still working in clay, she insisted on touching her models because she wanted to see with her fingers instead of her eyes. Now, as those same fingers traced the lines of flesh and bone, from my face to my feet, I knew she was reaching beneath the surface. Looking for something she could hold up for my inspection. Like an obstetrician displaying a wet, red-faced baby.

She didn't find it. Or, maybe I didn't want to look. But, either way, I was grateful for the effort, though not grateful enough to tell her so.

It was a little after eight when Marie finally left. I didn't waste any time getting on the telephone. Bouton was due in an hour, and I wanted to finish my calls before she arrived. I began with Pooch, identifying myself and outlining the previous day's events.

"Rehab?" he asked, the minute I paused for breath. "A fucking junkie whore? I bet she was a nigger, too. Am I right? Was she a nigger?"

"Look, Pooch, I'm just telling you what happened. So you can pass it on to Bowman. I don't have time for your bullshit."

"C'mon, Means, you must'a laughed. Don't tell me you didn't laugh." He was clearly offended.

I was at a loss for an answer. On the one hand, I didn't want to defend Vanessa Bouton's flight of fancy. On the other, I didn't want to come down to Pooch's level, either. The fact that I wasn't *painfully* conscious of my own race didn't mean I looked into the bathroom mirror and saw a white man.

"Have you spoken to Chief Bowman yet?"

"As a matter of fact, I have."

"What'd he say?"

"You wanna know exactly?"

"Just tell me, Pooch. I'm startin' to lose my temper."

"As near I can remember, what he said was, 'That goddamned Cherokee's no dumb injun.'"

I could still hear him laughing after I hung up, still hear him as I dialed Barry Millstein's number at The House of Refuge. Millstein picked up on the fourth ring.

"Barry? It's Roland Means."

"Roland, how are you?"

"Pressed for time, Barry. I want to talk to you about Reese

Montgomery, Thong's last victim." I quickly outlined my thoughts, emphasizing both the lack of a detailed history in the NYPD's investigation and my theory that Montgomery had once run with a more affluent crowd.

"I need to put his life together, and it'll take me forever if I have to do it a piece at a time," I concluded. "I was hoping you could give me a boost."

"I don't think I want to do that, Roland." His voice was matter-of-fact, as if he'd thought it over before I'd called. "See, the community's been taking it on the chin ever since Thong hit the papers. Everybody—the cops, the politicians, the media, the entire homophobic swamp—they just assumed the killer was gay. I don't want to get into the details, but hundreds of our people were hounded. . . ."

"That was the profile."

"The profile?"

"The FBI has some kind of a team that invents profiles of murderers. They give this profile to the local cops and it becomes the basis of the investigation. According to the profile team, heterosexual serial killers kill women and homosexual serial killers kill men. What the cops do is target individuals based on the profile."

"Does it actually work? This profile?"

"What do you think, Barry? You think it comes with a name and address? Is Thong in jail? Hell, we'd get better results consulting a psychic."

He laughed appreciatively. "I guess there's no substitute for shoe leather."

"That's the point, isn't it? That's exactly what I'm trying to do, and that's why I need your help. I'm trying to take it one step at a time. I'm . . . ."

"Don't scam me, Roland. Don't play me for an asshole."

"I'm not. . . ."

"It's a piece of shit, remember? That's what you told me

when I asked you if you had any hope of actually finding Thong. Now, if I were to give you a list of Reese Montgomery's clients and lovers, you'd visit each of them, right? You'd *interview* them, ask them to provide alibis, demand their life histories. And every time you found somebody with a potential motive, he'd become a target. No, Roland, I don't think I want to put the community through that for a piece of shit. We've already paid too high a price for King Thong."

I tried to come up with some counter to his argument, but failed miserably. Millstein was absolutely right. I didn't believe in Bouton's theory, but I was perfectly willing to bounce a few lives around to get myself out of the hole.

"It's gonna happen anyway, Barry. It'd happen even if I walked away altogether. Bouton's the driving force here, not me. And you can put this in the bank—as time goes by, she's gonna be under more and more pressure to pin this on somebody. She's ambitious and her career is on the line."

I could almost see him fidgeting behind his desk. Bouncing in his chair, scratching at his crewcut, shuffling papers. "That doesn't change anything. Look, I'm not operating under any delusions. The question is whether or not I should help you, not whether I should try to stop you. We're talking about complicity, Roland."

"That doesn't mean we can't make a deal."

"Keep talking."

"Look, I happen to agree with you. There's no reason to burn innocent people for bullshit. Now, I'm not saying I'm in charge of the investigation, but what I *can* do is keep it light. Bouton doesn't know a damn thing about police work. She relies on me. If I tell her so-and-so isn't a realistic suspect, she'll go along with it. I'm not kidding. . . ."

"Forget it, Roland. I know you well enough to be a hundred percent convinced you'll do whatever's necessary to protect yourself. I don't blame you, but I won't help you."

I hung up, silently cursing my big mouth. I should have conned him from the beginning. Instead, I'd quoted Pooch, the ultimate authority, when I'd used the phrase "piece of shit." Now, the chickens were coming home.

I walked into the bedroom and consoled myself with my wardrobe. Bouton and I were spending the day in the country, and I'd already decided to dress appropriately—brown Harris Tweed jacket with suede elbow patches; ribbed white turtleneck; medium-weight pleated wool trousers; cordovan loafers (Bally, of course); brown and red argyle socks. The socks, I decided, standing in front of the mirror, were definitely country.

EIGHTEEN

When Vanessa Bouton finally showed up, nearly an hour late at ten o'clock, she wasted no time in making her bad mood abundantly clear.

"The goddamned car broke down," she announced, plopping herself onto the sofa. "And we can't get another one before noon. I swear to Christ this miserable city's falling apart. We'll have to put the trip off. Phone those idiots at Bird Creek, or whatever the hell it's called, and cancel the interview." She was wearing a black suit over a white silk blouse. A vivid tribal scarf draped her right shoulder, dropping across her chest and back, while a soft, wide-brimmed hat, banded in the same tribal pattern, sat squarely on her head. The effect was stunning.

"It's *Owl* Creek, Captain, and there's no reason we can't take *my* car. It's parked in a garage about a block from here."

"You have a car, Means?"

"It's not a crime. Even in New York." You'd never know it, though. Not with the price of gas, the eighteen percent parking tax, the tow program, the registration surcharge, and the three-dollar toll on the tunnels and bridges.

"What kind of car?"

"It's a Buick."

"In decent condition?"

"In *perfect* condition."

What I didn't say was that it was a 1968 Electra 225 with a high-performance cam, two Carter 4-barrels and a Hurst 5-speed shifter. Four thousand, five hundred pounds of rolling thunder bearing the nickname Big Pollute. The car was more than perfect. Rollie Burdette, who'd sold it to me in the first place, spent more time caring for the Buick than he did caring for his six kids. It was Rollie who'd applied ten coats of pearl gray lacquer to the aging body; Rollie who'd rubbed down each coat by hand before applying the next. In fact, the only thing Rollie loved more than Big Pollute was his 1949 Ford. Which he called Little Pollute.

Bouton, as expected, nearly fell down when I yanked the dustcover off the car. The look she gave me, pure poison, lifted my spirits considerably, and I began to anticipate a pleasant afternoon. Which is the way it *finally* worked out.

We bounced over New York's gaping potholes (the Buick was tightly sprung; it had to be to keep it on the ground) through Queens and the Bronx. The city's annual road-repair frenzy was in full swing, and crews of workers blocked lanes everywhere, slowing us, then stopping us, again and again. Bouton announced her royal displeasure by cursing under her breath at each new obstacle. I tried to make things easier by flipping on the radio, but one look at her expression had me turning it off in a hurry. Maybe, I thought, she doesn't like Black Sabbath.

"I don't see why we're doing this," she finally said.

We were on the Major Deegan Expressway, approaching the exit for the George Washington Bridge, a stretch of highway notorious for traffic jams. I was in the far left lane, hoping to skirt the exiting eighteen wheelers, but we were barely crawling. Even the Buick seemed impatient.

"You're right," I answered. "I should have ducked into Manhattan and skipped the Bronx altogether."

"I'm not talking about the traffic, Means. And you damned well know it."

"What I damned well know is that we *have* to interview Kennedy's brother, even if he is a cop. We can't leave a big hole in the middle of the investigation. That's not the way it's done."

"Don't tell me how it's done, Detective."

"Somebody has to."

"What did you say?"

"What I said was that somebody has to tell you how it's done, because you don't have the slightest clue." I gave her a second to think it over, then continued. "What do you want from me, anyway? I've been busting my ass from day one. Why don't you try to imagine where you'd be if I *wasn't* here."

"It's your fucking attitude, not your work, that bothers me."

Lacking a sane choice (and having *already* gone too far), I gave her the last word. The traffic broke up a few minutes later, as it always does north of the bridge, and I eased the Buick up to seventy. Cops don't worry about tickets.

Gradually, a mile at a time, the city gave way, first to the shopping centers and used car lots of the suburbs, then to the hills and woods of Rockland County. Bouton's sullen mood seemed to give way, too. It was a beautiful morning, nearly seventy-five degrees with a bright sun framing small, swiftly moving clouds. Wildflowers blossomed all along the side of the road—yarrow, buttercups, sweet clover, and trefoil so perfectly golden yellow it seemed an arrogant exaggeration, the conceit of some photographer shooting nature through a filter. Oxeye daisies carpeted the open pasture like clouds come to earth; dogwood trees, nearly lost in the forest, spread floating tiers of pink or white petals. Surrounded by towering maple, oak, beech, and hickory, the dogwood had always seemed brave to me, hurriedly thrusting its blossoms at the sun before the larger hardwoods could produce more than a few buds.

"Pull over a minute, would you, Means?"

Bouton opened the car door before I came to a full stop. At first, I thought she was car sick, but when I got out to help her, she was leaning against the fender, a bemused smile lighting her face.

"Would you look at that," she said.

I followed her eyes to a fenced meadow. A mare cropped the spring grass, while a chestnut foal, a colt, gamboled alongside her. He'd approach on wobbly legs, bump her belly as if he was about to nurse, than jump back with a shake of his head, nearly falling down in the process. We watched for about ten minutes before the mare, followed by her leaping, snorting foal, trudged off.

"Lord, it's so beautiful," Bouton said once we were moving again. "I never get out of the city, and I should. I really should. You could live up here and pretend it's all perfect. The crime, the poverty, the dirt . . . just gone, vanished. Something to read about in a magazine. Watch it on PBS."

"Yeah, Captain, it's real picturesque. Idyllic. That old shack set up on concrete blocks? The one with the crooked chimney and the rusting refrigerator in the front yard? The wind doesn't crash through it in the winter. The kids aren't living a curtain away from their parents' bedroom. And nobody gets hungry, either, when the mill shuts down and papa drinks up the unemployment check. In fact, the tourists don't even have to see it. They can just keep their eyes on the mountains, the lakes, the rushing rivers. They can just slide on by."

It was the wrong thing to say, but I couldn't help it. Bouton reacted like any good social worker; she probed for the details.

"That where you grew up?" she asked, turning toward me.

"I grew up about fifty miles north of where we're going." I kept my eyes on the road.

"That's not what I meant." Her voice was soft and gentle. Filled with enough pity to make me puke.

"You peek through bedroom windows, too?"

"I don't get it."

"Why am I not surprised?" I noted the puzzled look on her face. "It's not your business, Captain. It's not *our* business."

She gave me her best penetrating stare for a moment, then turned away. What I couldn't say was that it was too late for kindness. For understanding. There may have been a time when some adult could have stepped in and made a difference, but it hadn't happened. No, the good citizens of Paris, New York, turned their collective backs and kept them turned.

They all knew what was happening. In a small town, everybody knows everything. And when I think about it, there's no way I could have been the only one. Maybe they justified their indifference by embracing good old family values. Maybe they went home to their kids and passed out extra hugs. Maybe they remembered me in their hypocritical prayers. Maybe they figured I was a bad seed and deserved everything I got.

I remember one morning when I caught a terrific beating, bad enough to justify staying home. Unfortunately, it was too cold for me to seek refuge in the woods (later, I'd learn to deal with the coldest days, but I was nine years old at the time) and too dangerous to hang around with dear old mom. So I pulled a watchcap over my swollen right ear and got on the school bus.

Everything went okay until I walked into the classroom and refused to take my hat off. Mrs. DuPont, my fourth-grade teacher and a stickler for discipline, demanded that I conform to the rules, but I stubbornly refused, even when she threatened to take me to the principal's office. Our principal, Mr. Knott, liked to use a barber's strap on "obnoxious" students, male or female. He liked to fold them over his desk until their pants or skirts were drawn up tight against their sweet young buttocks and flail away.

Which is not to say that I was afraid of him. Mr. Knott might hurt me, but, unlike dear old mom, he wouldn't kill me.

"Take off the hat," he commanded, "or I'll take it off for you."

When I didn't comply, when I just stood there staring, he stepped around his desk and fulfilled the prophecy. I knew my ear was swollen and my hair was stiff with dried blood, but I wasn't prepared for the look of horror on his face. Nor for the sharp cry from Mrs. DuPont. The two of them literally recoiled, and for some reason their reaction filled my boyish heart with joy.

After a minute or two, they managed to close their mouths and go into a huddle. Thinking back on it, I realize that I couldn't have been allowed to return to the classroom, either with or without my hat. But what to do? Should they "take arms against a sea of troubles" or let dear old mom beat me to a pulp?

What they did, after due consideration, was exactly nothing. Mr. Knott dismissed Mrs. DuPont, then sat me in a chair and left me there until the bus came to pick me up at three o'clock. I wasn't offered food; I wasn't allowed to go to the playground. I was simply ignored, a vanished, invisible child.

I was mad by the time that day ended. And mad by the time Bouton and I pulled into the parking lot of Guardian Angel Hospital in Lake George an hour later. There was no point to what I was doing. To revisiting a locked and frozen past. Nobody fishes in a septic tank. Not if they want to eat what they catch.

Aloysius Kennedy was, indeed, comatose, a be-tubed skeleton with just enough brain activity to justify the two or three grand a day it cost Medicare to keep him alive. The nursing supervisor who took us to him, a tall, thin, black woman named Shanara Townsend, was much livelier. She couldn't stop talking about the tribal scarf Bouton wore. Did Bouton know the pattern, the tribe? Was it made in Africa? Bouton answered each question as if she'd just been reunited with a missing relative. I took it as long as I could, waiting for my captain to get to the point. The *cop* point.

"Ms. Townsend," I said when I'd had enough, "may I speak to Captain Bouton privately for a moment?"

"Should I leave?"

"No, please, we have a few more questions. It'll only be a minute."

I drew Bouton a few feet away and whispered my instructions. "I'm going to go find Kennedy's doctor. I want you to pump this woman. Find out what Kennedy's like. If he's really got money. Who visits him. See if she knows the two sons. Were they ever in the room together? Give her your goddamn scarf if you have to." I walked off before she could respond.

Dr. Ehrlich's office was on the fourth floor, and, miracle of miracles, he was actually in it. Kennedy, he told me, had been unconscious for the better part of six months, and he wasn't going to wake up. The administration wanted to transfer him to a nursing home, but the family insisted he be treated in the hospital. What Ehrlich didn't say was that Medicare would pay for the hospital bed. Nursing homes weren't covered beyond thirty days.

"Is the matter in the courts?" I asked.

He lifted his chin and looked down his nose at me. Telling me it was none of my business. I wondered, briefly, why he'd brought it up in the first place, then asked him who spoke for the Kennedy family.

"Robert, the son," he replied.

"Are there any other relatives?"

He clammed up at that point, insisting that I go to Robert Kennedy for any further information. I didn't know if it was a question of confidentiality or if Doc Ehrlich was simply the baron dismissing his peasant. Whichever, he was immune to any pressure I could apply, and if he didn't feel like cooperating, there was nothing I could do about it. I thanked him for his time and left.

Bouton, still wearing the scarf (and still smiling), was waiting in the lobby.

"You were right, of course," she announced before I could beg forgiveness. "Townsend was friendly, and I should have seen that as an opportunity. *Mea culpa.*"

"Nice speech," I responded. "Did you get anything worthwhile?"

"Couple of things." She pulled a little notebook from her purse and checked it as she spoke. "Robert, the eldest of the brothers, never comes to visit. John was here a few times before he was murdered, but the old man refused to see him. Called him 'Girly' whenever he showed up. It seems that Aloysius was a straight-out racist and referred to Shanara as 'that colored bitch.' Claimed to be a lifelong member of the Klan, a dedicated cross burner. Bragged about driving the niggers out of Herkimer County."

"What about the money? Did he have any money?"

"Hold your water, Means. I'm getting to it." We were in the car by then, pulling out of the lot. "Shanara didn't know anything about the Kennedy finances. Why should she? The important thing is that the old man has a regular visitor, a drinking buddy named Seaver Shannon, who's asked to be notified when Kennedy dies. I've got his phone number. By the way, I keep calling Kennedy an old man, but he's only fifty-two."

"What about a wife? There must be a wife somewhere."

"His admitting form lists him as widowed."

"Occupation?"

"Businessman."

"What kind of business?"

"Shanara said she thought he once owned a liquor store. Maybe still does. She wasn't sure. He isn't the kind of patient who takes you into his confidence."

"So what we have is exactly nothing?"

"I wouldn't say that, Means." She slouched in the seat, pushing her shoes up against the fire wall. "We've got this beautiful day and this beautiful car and we're not working the streets of New York. Thank God for small favors."

NINETEEN

We took Route 14 northwest out of Lake George and immediately began to climb into the heart of the Adirondack Mountains. The landscape presented to us was a long way from the friendly, rolling Catskills. Two Indian tribes had hunted the Adirondacks, the Iroquois and the Algonquins, but neither chose to live there. They called the region *Couchsachraga*, the Habitation of Winter. The average temperature in the Adirondack Park is twenty degrees colder than, for instance, Kingston, less than two hundred miles to the south.

Which is not to say the Adirondacks aren't beautiful. The high peaks, deep valleys, and granite outcroppings, the evergreen forests so dense they appear black, present a landscape as majestic as anything east of the Rockies. The entire region is dotted with lakes, some more than a mile across. At this time of year, streams and rivers, swollen with snow melting off the high peaks, flow through the valleys, while the ponds and bogs, home to beaver, otter, and every kind of fighting fish, are choked with lily pads.

I watched Bouton watch six mallards, their perfectly round heads flashing an intense, iridescent emerald, glide across the roadway and come to a splashing halt in a small lake. They continued to quack away for a moment as each member of the flock reported, then settled down to feed.

A little farther away, a flock of ring-necked ducks, their black and white bills making them instantly recognizable, dove under the water in search of any creature slow enough to catch and small enough to eat. They disappeared without a ripple, only to pop to the surface fifteen yards away, drops of water glistening on oily feathers.

"This is amazing," Bouton said. "Just amazing. It's summer in New York. The roses are blooming. Up here, it's barely spring."

We passed a dairy farm and the bucolic images—barns, fields, a dozen Guernseys around a bale of hay—seemed to intrigue her.

"So, humans actually live here," she observed. "I was beginning to wonder."

"A hundred and twenty thousand humans, Captain. On six million acres. Home sweet home."

"A hundred and twenty thousand? We had that many in the project where I grew up." She laughed happily, then shook her head. "But in some ways, I was as isolated as if I lived in the middle of all this. I was a homegirl in the old sense. Back when 'homegirl' was an insult. My mama didn't let me play in the streets. Wouldn't even let me go to the store by myself."

"Probably checked your homework, too."

"Every night. You?"

"Me?"

"Did your mama check your homework?"

"She didn't have to. I always did well in school." It was the truth, though there was no good reason for it. I missed so many days that if I hadn't aced my ninth-grade exams, I wouldn't have been allowed to go to high school. By that time, dear old mom (chastened, perhaps, by the bandages covering Big Mike's broken face) was past raising her hands to me. Still, I continued to spend most of my time in a forest that, for all its frigid temperatures, its swarms of biting flies and ravenous mosquitoes, was at least ordered and predictable.

We were just east of Indian Lake, still plowing along on Route 14, when the north country put a damper on Bouton's wistful mood. A town cop in a white cruiser passed going the other way, made a quick U-turn, then powered up to us, lights flashing. Bouton frowned, shaking her head, and muttered, "Snake in paradise."

"Correction, Captain, *redneck* in paradise."

I pulled the car off the road, buoyed by the prospect of venting my ugly mood on someone besides my superior officer. The town cop, a small, skinny asshole in an ill-fitting uniform, got out of his car and sauntered over, a shit-eating grin spread across his pimply face. The name tag on his chest read "Beauchamp."

"Well, well, well. Would you look at this? Lemme see some ID." His glance took in my narrow eyes, Bouton's chocolate skin, the vintage Buick.

"Sure." I pushed my gold shield into his face. *Right* into his face. He jumped back, his eyes focusing on my badge as his hand dropped to his .357.

"What?" he managed to say.

"Detective Means. Roland Means, NYPD. This is *Captain* Vanessa Bouton."

"You don't have to say it like that." Deprived of the possibility of using his weapon, he looked merely confused.

"I'll say it any fucking way I like."

"What?"

"Listen, you redneck prick, you got business with me, tell me what it is. Otherwise, you can crawl back to that cruiser like the piece of shit you are."

"Means!" Bouton's voice was halfway between amused and amazed.

"Now, now, now, now," Beauchamp stuttered, "listen here, you don't have no jurisdiction. This is damn far outside your territory."

"Really? How 'bout I come out there and pound my fucking jurisdiction into your face?" I refused to give him any slack, any chance to save face. Leaving him with a very simple choice: total humiliation or a serious battle. Most street-hard city cops would have taken the second option, no matter what the consequences. Beauchamp, on the other hand, with no excuse to use his .357 (and no buddies around to spread the tale), accepted his defeat like a good bully. He got back into his cruiser and drove away.

"You're crazy, Means."

"Well, you know how it is, Captain. Some days you wake up and you just *can't* eat shit." I tossed it off, but if Beauchamp had called me out, I would have busted him up without a second thought. It didn't make sense and I knew it. But who says it's supposed to make sense? The first thing you have to do is live with yourself, and that's what I was doing. In my own silly way.

We pulled into the headquarters of the Algonquin County Sheriff's Office an hour later. Kennedy wasn't there, but the deputy handling the telephones told us that Sheriff Pousson was expecting us. His office was in the back, last door on the left. As we walked down the narrow hallway, I reminded Bouton that protocol required that she do the talking for both of us.

"See if he knows where Seaver Shannon lives," I added. "It'll save us some time."

"Why don't we try to look him up in the phone book?"

"Because the address will probably be a post office box. Or something like Star Route 4. Except for Main Street, the roads around here don't have names. I'd like to talk to this guy without calling him first."

Sheriff Pousson managed to greet us without doing a double-take. He was a tall, serious-looking man, with high cheekbones, a narrow face, and a sharp, hooked nose. As predicted, he spoke directly to Vanessa Bouton.

"Deputy Kennedy was up all night handling a bus accident on Route 11. I'll give you directions to his house. Hope it's not inconvenient."

"Not at all, Sheriff." Bouton's voice was relaxed. She sat down uninvited, smiling away. "As long as the directions are easy. I'm not used to streets that don't have names."

Pousson nodded, his thin white lips splitting into what I took to be a smile. "Know how you feel, Captain. I was in Manhattan last year. For a conference. Got lost five times and the hotel was only six blocks from the convention center. Never felt so out of place in my life."

He drew a simple map for us, ticking off the various landmarks—a creek, a lake, a battered barn—as he went along. Finished, he handed the map over to Bouton and cleared his throat.

"Uh, Captain, when I spoke to you on the phone, you said you were still investigating the death of Bob Kennedy's brother, John. I know it's none of my business, but are you getting any closer to an arrest?"

Bouton, much to my delight, threw him an appropriate line of bullshit. No, we weren't getting anywhere, but the NYPD, with its proverbial tit caught in the proverbial wringer, couldn't let it drop. With no recent killings, the powers that be had decided to review every facet of the case, to do it all over again. It was a waste of time, but what could a mere captain do? Orders being orders.

"By the way, Sheriff," she concluded, "we'd like to speak to a man named Seaver Shannon, a friend of the father. Do you have his address? And some directions?"

"Seaver? Sure, I know Seaver." He took off his wire-rimmed glasses and wiped them carefully. "Is Seaver somehow connected to John's murder?"

"Not at all." Bouton laughed softly. "We know that John occasionally visited his father in the hospital and that Seaver Shannon was a constant visitor. It's just barely possible the two of them were there at the same time and that John said something about his life in New York. You see, Sheriff, we don't know how this killer targeted his victims. The forensic evidence indicates that he had their complete confidence. Maybe there was contact prior to the actual murders. If we don't ask, we'll never put this chapter behind us. And that's exactly what we're trying to do. To close these doors once and for all."

Five minutes later, still on Route 14, two sets of directions in hand, looking for a Texaco gas station and the dirt road a hundred yards beyond it. On the way, we passed a wide, swiftly flowing stream. Several fishermen, their hip boots held up by wide suspenders, were casting brightly colored lures into the water. Their graphite rods and expensive reels pegged them as tourists.

"Did you fish, Means?" Bouton asked out of nowhere. "When you were young?"

"Not like that."

"Not like that?" She turned in the seat to look at me. "And how did *you* fish."

"The first thing I did was take thirty feet of line and attach hooks every two feet or so. Then I went out in the woods and shot a squirrel. Then I took the squirrel and the line to a lake or a pond, baited the hooks with squirrel guts and threw the line into the water. Then I roasted the rest of the squirrel over an open fire and ate it. Then I retrieved the line, pulled off whatever fish I'd caught, rebaited the empty hooks, and tossed the line back in. When I was out of squirrel guts it was time to go home."

"Doesn't sound very sporting."

"It wasn't about sport, Captain. It was about dinner."

Seaver Shannon's house was a notch or two above ramshackle. Small, no more than four or five rooms, its roof was intact and all the windows were glazed. The small front porch, on the other hand, sagged badly, and the step leading up to it was no more than a one-by-six supported by a pair of cinder blocks.

I knocked on the door, knocked again. No response. I pounded it with my fist and heard a faint, "Hold your horses. I'm a'comin'," followed by the sound of shuffling feet.

Seaver Shannon was very small and very old. Wizened is the word that comes to mind. Shrunken. Thick tufts of gray hair sprouted from his ears and nostrils. His eyebrows poked out and up, twin fans over horn-rimmed glasses held together with black electrician's tape. He peered at us through those glasses, scrutinized us with the frank, puzzled look of a toddler. Or of an old man past disguising his feelings.

"Yessir?" he said to me, ignoring Bouton.

I showed him my ID and my badge, actually passed the billfold over and let him take a good look. "And this is Captain Bouton," I added. "Also, NYPD."

Shannon closed the billfold and passed it back. "You folks are a long way from home."

"Not so far," I said. "I grew up in Paris. It's only about forty miles from here."

"Paris?" He broke into a wide, toothless grin. "Used to hunt up there when I was younger. Around Black Brook. You hunt, Officer?"

"Started with squirrels and rabbits. Soon as I was strong enough to hold my .22. I'll never forget that old gun; she was a breech-loading Stevens went for sixteen dollars. New, that is, not when I got it. That gun sure didn't look like much. Stock was all chipped away as I remember. But it shot straight."

"Well, come on in. I'll go find my teeth and put some coffee up."

I waited until the coffee was ready before turning the conversation away from the glories of bloodletting. By that time, Shannon seemed perfectly comfortable, though he still refused to look at Bouton.

"I guess you're wondering why we're here," I said.

"Did cross my mind," he admitted. "Don't wanna rush you none."

"We're investigating the murder of John Kennedy."

"Still?"

I couldn't restrain a smile. The little bastard knew how to

twist the knife. "Yeah, still. You're a good friend of John's father, Aloysius, right?"

"Near 'bout his *only* friend, truth be told. Fact, some ways I ain't *even* a friend. He just sorta tolerates me."

"Are you saying the father wasn't such a nice guy?"

"Son, you can take that to the bank. And it ain't only that Aloysius, man and boy, was mean as a snake. Hell, this ain't no country for sissies; nobody'd hold that against him. No, the reason why people mostly didn't take to Aloysius was that he'd squeeze a dime till it was bleedin' silver 'fore he'd pay for a candy bar. Did okay for himself in life; owned himself a liquor store in Lake Placid, smack dab in the middle of all those resorts. Had the ski people in the winter, the summer people in the summer, the fishermen and hunters in between. Think he'd spring for a drink down the tavern? Hell, Aloysius bought a new Ford pickup in '72 and he's *still* got it. Fenders all rusted out. Windshield wipers don't work. No heat in the winter. Damn thing is a horror."

The meeting ended up being "everything you ever wanted to know about Aloysius Kennedy and more of the same." Kennedy's roof leaked, his plumbing backed up, he heated with wood, mowed his lawn with a push mower, shoveled his own snow, ate macaroni and hash three times a week.

I let it go on as long as I could, then gently shoved the old man in a new direction. "Well, I guess he doesn't do any of those things now," I said. "He's too sick."

Shannon looked down at his feet. "Won't do 'em again, neither," he whispered. "Doctors say he's a goner." He shook his head. "Don't know what he was savin' his money for. Can't take it with him, can he?"

"Probably all go to the son, Robert. Unless he's got a will somewhere."

"Nope," the old man shook his head, "no will. Aloysius once told me couldn't stand the idea of his boys endin' up with his money, but he couldn't stand the idea of leavin' it to nobody else, neither. Man, that Aloysius was some kinda cheap."

"Tell me, Seaver, did you know John Kennedy?"

Shannon wrinkled up his nose and spat on the floor. "That *he-she?* Oh, yeah, I knowed him. Wasn't a bad kid growin' up. Always smilin'. Always tryin' to please everybody. Thought maybe he'd turn out okay. 'Spite of Robert beatin' on him." Shannon took a deep breath. "See, Robert was just like his daddy in that way. The damned school terror. Aloysius was always goin' to that school, try to get Robert out of some kinda trouble. Take the boy home and beat him till he was blue in the face. Tell the boy, 'Why can't you be like your brother?' Didn't do no good."

"The father liked John? Favored him, maybe?"

"Much as he favored anybody. Fact, he mostly treated the boy good. Right up to the day he caught John . . . " Shannon looked over at Bouton for the first time, then back at me. "Up to the day he caught John performin' an oral perversion on his brother. After that, he didn't have no use for none of 'em."

"Did John visit his father?"

"Come one or twice, but Aloysius wouldn't see him. Would you?"

I left the question unanswered; I wasn't there to debate an old man. "How about Robert? Did he visit?"

"No sir. Robert ain't seen his old man in five years. Maybe more."

"They have a fight?"

"Sure did. A humdinger. Robert knocked out his father's teeth. Over money, too. The boy wanted to borrow money to buy himself a house. This is when he was just startin' out with the sheriff. Aloysius had the money, but he wouldn't part with it. *Couldn't* part with it. No more than a snake can fly."

"Shannon, I take it you don't know anything about John's life in New York?"

He snorted, breaking into a wheezy laugh. "That's another snake can't fly. What I *heard* was that John did what come natural to him. Got paid for it, too."

"But you don't know anything about his friends? His associates?"

"Nothin'."

"What about the mother? Aloysius' wife."

"Dead. Robert kilt her."

"What?"

"They called it somethin' like 'accidental discharge.' Boy was around nine years old at the time. John was still a baby. Robert claimed he was cleanin' his daddy's 30-30 and it went off. Weren't no witnesses, but lotsa people 'round here had suspicions. Bullet went right through Virginia's head. Hell of a thing, really. Hell of a thing." He shook his head grimly, then managed a thin shrug. "Hard life up here. Hard country; hard life. No place for sissies. Guess you know the four seasons?"

"Sure," I said, "I know them. Black flies; Fourth of July; Labor Day; winter."

TWENTY

As we drove away from Shannon's, Bouton's mouth went into overdrive. As far as she was concerned, Robert Kennedy was already tried and convicted. He fit the pattern, she informed me. Fit it a hundred percent. He was cruel to other children (his brother), abused by his father (and his mother, for all we knew), killed his own mother, attacked his father. Throw in money as a motive and all the psychological pieces came together.

I suppose I should have warned her about tunnel vision. About forcing big round pegs into small round holes. About locking onto a suspect and ignoring any evidence pointing in another direction. The rule is motive, means, *and* opportunity. It wouldn't have surprised me to learn that Bob Kennedy didn't want to share his inheritance. And I suppose he could have lured his brother and the others into that van everybody assumed Thong was driving when he committed the murders—all it would take was a few twenty-dollar bills. But for the life of me, I couldn't see an upstate, hillbilly cop targeting Thong's victims. They were too varied, worked too many different strolls. Where would he find the time?

"What we ought to do," Bouton concluded as if reading my mind, "is subpoena Kennedy's work records. See if he was off-duty when the murders were committed."

I didn't bother to answer. I kept seeing a nine-year-old boy with a rifle aimed at his mother's head. Wondering if I'd ever done that, if I'd ever thought about it. Had I seen my mother's face superimposed on the bodies of squirrels and rabbits? I could remember every detail of my confrontation with Big Mike, but I couldn't recall ever standing up to my mother.

No, what I'd done, when the opportunity presented itself,

was flee. That was the literal truth, and I suppose I must have experienced fear. What I wanted to know, as we drove through the forest, Bouton chattering away, was if there was anger as well. Did I hate her? Did I wish she was dead? Did I ever play out the deed in my childish daydreams? And if I hadn't, if the idea of putting an end to the torture had never occurred to me, why not?

But wanting, as far as I could see, had nothing to do with receiving. (Just ask the millions of souls who pray for the miracle cure, the unexpected check in the mail, the one true love of their miserable lives to ring the doorbell.) And the more I thought about it, the more convinced I was that far from wishing her dead, I'd somehow expected her to change. To press my face between her breasts and draw out the pain the way you'd suck poison from a rattlesnake bite.

Without warning, I found myself drawn back into an almost-forgotten memory.

Mom is in the early stages of a serious binge. She's sitting on the floor, her back to the wall, clutching a bottle. The bottle is filled with cheap bourbon, so she must have had a good day. If she hadn't, she'd be drinking wine. Tears pour down her face. She mutters something about her husband, my father, long gone, then reaches out to me. I fly into her arms, grateful even for this false comfort. Accepting the sour smell of her unwashed body, the touch of her greasy, matted hair. Accepting anything I can get.

"Why don't you pull in here." Bouton's voice drifted up to me. "Let's get some lunch before we see Kennedy."

"Where?"

"This place just up ahead."

The sign said "Pete's Eats," which I suppose Bouton found encouraging. The pickups and motorcycles scattered over the gravel parking lot told a different story. We'd be anything but welcome.

I started to explain the facts of life to her but held my tongue at the last moment. A little hostility, I figured, would put things back into perspective. Would turn me away from a road I didn't want to travel.

I found all the hostility I needed the minute we walked through the door. Conversations stopped; heads swiveled; slow, knowing grins swept across white, north-country faces. The only sound, as we stood in the doorway, was the hard whine of a country guitar issuing from a battered jukebox.

"I think we better get take-out, Means." Bouton was faintly amused. "Considering that we've just wandered into a story my grandmother told me about life in Mississippi."

The low, persistent laughter began as we walked over to the cash register. One rogue, making no effort to keep his words of wisdom between himself and his buddies, said, "I know we need the tourists, but *daaaamn*." Someone at the same table, eager to elevate the discussion to more abstract principles, said, "I know what *she* is, but what the fuck is he?"

"Which one gets to hold the leash?"

"Are we talkin' about some disgustin' babies, or what?"

The counterman grilled our hamburgers without comment. It wasn't that he didn't want our business—up there, you take a dollar where you find it—but we'd be gone in fifteen minutes and he'd need another dollar tomorrow.

At one point, Bouton put her hand on my arm, telling me to stay calm. She needn't have bothered. As a matter of law, mere speech, no matter how nasty, cannot justify an assault. I'd need much more, and when I heard chairs scraping behind us, followed by a squeaky door opening and closing, I knew I was going to get it.

"Don't back out, motherfucker." I thought I'd said it to myself, but apparently I'd spoken aloud.

"What, Means?"

"The burgers look good, Captain. Can't wait to get my teeth into them."

The counterman took our money and made change without a word.

"Why don't you take this?" I handed the package to Bouton and much to my surprise, she accepted it without protest. Cradling it in her left hand while she opened her purse with her right.

"There gonna be a problem here?" she asked.

"I hope so."

"Then do what you have to do." She was grinning broadly. "I'll be in the car."

There were three of them waiting outside. Two were leaning against an ancient pickup while the third, the biggest (naturally) stood in front of my car. Maybe forty years old, round-faced and bearded, he wore an Oakland Raiders cap, a red wool shirt-jacket, and a shit-eating grin.

"Hiawatha, I presume," he said. "And little black Sambette."

I walked straight at him. He looked surprised for a moment, then determined. His shoulders hunched and his hands came up.

"Come on, bitch," he muttered. "Come and get it."

I maintained control until he threw the first punch, a slow, powerful left that I allowed to graze the top of my head. That gave me the legal right to respond, which was all I needed to justify losing control. I don't remember seeing him or hearing him; can't remember the feel of his flesh against the heel of my hand or the outside of my forearm. According to Bouton, I went through him like a hurricane through a cornfield. She insisted that except for that first punch, he'd put up no resistance, as if he'd suddenly come to understand (and accept) his fate.

Whatever way it happened, when I came back into myself, he was lying on the gravel, hands over his face, whimpering like a beaten child. Bouton was standing five feet away, displaying her .38 and her badge. The two buddies were still leaning against their pickups, but now their mouths hung open. Behind us, a small crowd had gathered near the entrance to Pete's Eats.

"Arrest him," Bouton said, her voice firm and committed.

"Why you wanna do that?" One of the buddies found his voice. "*He's* the one got the beating."

"He assaulted a police officer," she returned, stretching the truth more than a little bit. I'd neither displayed a badge nor announced my profession.

I yanked the man's head up, noting that the left side of his face was bright red and badly swollen. "You're not going to resist, are you?" I asked.

Before he could make his intentions known, I heard the wail of sirens in the distance. I let his head drop and turned to face an onrushing cruiser as it roared into the parking lot.

Sheriff Pousson got out first (thank God, I was afraid it was Beauchamp, the town cop), followed by two deputies. He stared at us for a moment, then nodded at someone standing in the doorway.

"Pete?" he said. "You called about a riot? I don't see any riot."

The counterman who'd taken and prepared our food separated himself from the crowd by the door and walked across the lot. He and Pousson huddled for several minutes while the rest of us stood around, then Pousson strolled over to where I was standing. His stern, closed face showed nothing of his intentions, and I wasn't sure of how he was going to handle the situation until he stepped on my adversary's hand, then twisted his heel like he was grinding out a cigarette butt.

"Why are you always in the middle of my problems, Burdette?" he asked. "Why is it always you?"

"I need a doctor," Burdette said, without bothering to deny the central allegation. Apparently, I'd picked the right target. Or, credit where credit is due, the right target had picked me.

"Captain," Pousson said, raising his eyes to meet Bouton's, "allow me to apologize on behalf of the people of Algonquin

County. If you'd like to press charges, I'd be glad to accommo-
date you."

Bouton folded her hands across her chest and took a step
back. "Well," she said, "now that I look at the situation a little
more closely, I'd have to say that Mr. Burdette has been duly
punished for his big mouth. If you don't mind, Sheriff, we'll be
on our way."

Pousson smiled, then turned to me. "You do this all by yourself?" He waited for me to nod before continuing. "What's your
name, again?"

"Roland Means. Detective Roland Means."

"You ever decide you had enough of the big city, Means, you
come and see me."

"I'll take that as a compliment."

"Which is what it is. I'm only sorry you didn't kill the bastard."

Robert Kennedy's home was about as far off the main road as
he could get without using a helicopter. A well-built, well-main-
tained frame house with an attached garage and several storage
sheds scattered over the property, it sat at the end of a dirt road
that wound through dense forest. It was the only house on that
road, and as we drove up I tried to imagine how he kept it free of
snow in the winter, concluding that he probably didn't. That,
most likely, he used a snowmobile to get back and forth when
the snow was deep. Even the four-wheel-drive van parked in
front would be useless once the snow piled up. The brown
Toyota parked next to it wouldn't get two feet.

I stopped the car near the house, but didn't open the door
because two very large German shepherds were biting at the
tires. In lieu of my leg.

"How do you want to handle this?" Bouton asked, ignoring
the dogs.

"If they scratch the paint, let's shoot 'em."

I have to admit, I was feeling a lot better. My encounter with Mr. Burdette outside Pete's Eats had done me a world of good.

"Get serious, Means. How should we handle Kennedy?"

I shrugged. "It's a reasonable question, but I don't have any idea how we *should* handle Kennedy. All I can see are negatives. We shouldn't say anything to make him think he's a suspect. Mainly because he isn't; not at this point. That means we can't ask him to provide an alibi for any of the murders. Or about his potential inheritance. Or about his personal relationship with his brother. Or about anything Seaver Shannon told us."

Bouton nodded as I went along, patiently waiting for me to finish. When I did, she said, "Let's just get him on the record about not having contact with his brother. After that . . . "

"All right, all right. King. Wolf. Enough, enough." A tall, thickly set man emerged from the house and gathered up the dogs. He took each by the collar and half-dragged them to the side of the garage before chaining them.

"He knew we were coming," Bouton said. "He could have chained the dogs before we got here."

"Captain, when you're right, you're right."

As we got out of the car, the man approached us, a smile spread across his long, horsey face. The smile seemed genuine, but when he got close enough for me to look into his light blue eyes, I couldn't find a trace of warmth. I saw calculation, but nothing beyond that, not even surprise at the odd couple that'd come to interview him.

"Mr. Kennedy?" Bouton asked, extending her hand.

"Robert," he responded, accepting a quick handshake.

"I'm Captain Bouton." She smiled (rather graciously, I thought). "And this is Detective Roland Means."

The introductions finished, Kennedy led us into the house and had his wife, Rebecca, pour out the inevitable coffee. She was a small, pretty woman, sturdily built and a good deal younger than her husband, with a heavy Southern accent. Her blond hair was braided and wound tightly around her head. The effect was not especially flattering, nor was her shapeless, faded housedress, nor the bruises on the side of her face.

"Well, you boys have certainly come a long way," she said. "I hope you find what you're looking for."

Her husband tossed her a nasty look, but made no move to exclude her. Which, even at the time, I found strange.

"Well, how can we help you, Captain?" he asked.

Bouton gave Robert Kennedy the same line she'd given Sheriff Pousson about the possibility that Thong had had contact with his victims prior to the actual killings, then asked him if he knew anything at all about his brother's life in the big city.

"Not a damn thing, Captain." He responded without hesitation. "You know, when I was much younger, I spent a year with the Albany Police Department, the Vice Squad, and I saw things you wouldn't believe." He managed a short laugh, but his eyes remained empty. "Oh, well, I guess you would believe them. Bein' as you're from New York City and everything. But it sure enough disgusted *me*. Men dressin' up like women. Practicin' their perversions in city parks. Children havin' to step over condoms on their way to school. And that was the least of it. There were murders *every* night. I mean I suppose I sound like an old country boy, but I got sick of it in a big hurry. We may have our troubles up here in Owl Creek, but we're not given to perversion and murder. So, to answer your question, I didn't have any contact with my brother after he left. No letters, no phone calls, no visits."

"And you never saw him in New York?"

Kennedy's wife answered before he could speak. "New York?" she drawled, laughing softly. "Lord above, I have been after my husband to take me to New York or Boston for ages and ages. But he is the most stay-at-home man I have ever known. I was born in Mississippi—I suppose that must seem obvious—and I have been to a few places in my life. But Robert never wants to go anywhere. If it wasn't for church suppers and the like, I do believe we wouldn't go out at all."

There being no point in hanging around, we left a few minutes later. Bouton, naturally, didn't waste any time getting started; she began to run off at the mouth before we reached the end of Kennedy's private road.

"The wife alibied him," she declared, arms folded across her chest. "Why'd she do that? Nobody asked her."

"Maybe she was just making conversation. Unless you want to make her part of it. Unless you want to make her a serial killer, too."

"It wouldn't be the first time a wife lied to protect her husband. I assume you saw the van?"

"I saw it. What does it prove?"

"And you saw his eyes."

"His eyes?"

"Don't bullshit me. You know exactly what I'm talking about. Those eyes were dead empty." She gave me a minute to answer, but I drove on without commenting. "I thought you were supposed to be the street cop. Where are your instincts? Robert Kennedy is dirty as hell."

"A man's wife makes a chance comment, most likely the kind of complaint she's been making to her friends for years. 'My husband doesn't take me anywhere.' So what? A man has cold eyes. Just like the eyes of a dozen cops I've known. Again, so what? Look, Captain, I'll go as far you want with it. But let's not convict the man of seven murders without a tad more evidence."

My sarcasm slowed her down, but I couldn't slow the thoughts and images rolling through my own mind. The house at the end of that long, long road; the bruised, mousy wife in her old housedress jumping into the interview as if she'd been told just what to say; the dogs circling the car when Kennedy should have tied them up before we arrived; Kennedy's eyes as they weighed and measured every syllable.

"Tell me something, Means. Didn't you find Kennedy's little speech about perversion in the big city a bit forced? Considering that he blew his mother's head off and had sex with his brother?"

TWENTY-ONE

Lorraine Cho woke to pain. And not only in her bruised body. She felt herself to be on fire, saw images of burning cities in a mind that wandered like the wind outside her cabin.

She told herself, "Get a grip, girl." Decided she liked the sound of that. All those *g*'s.

"Get a grip, girl." She said it out loud. Then giggled. Then began to cry.

But there were no tears, and when she touched her face she remembered why. Becky hadn't come since . . . She couldn't remember. Two days? Three days?

She asked herself what difference it made. Knowing that the real question was, Do I want to live? Or, even more real, Do I want to die *this* way? To die of thirst with the sound of running water echoing in my ears?

She could hear the birds singing outside the cabin and knew that it was early morning. The birds quieted when the sun was high; they got down to the business of eating, building nests, feeding young.

Becky would come later, if she came at all.

"I'll wait," Lorraine said. "I'll just wait and if she doesn't come, I'll do something."

The smell of her bucket-latrine was so powerful she imagined herself a rat living in a sewer. A trapped rat.

Wondering how her body could make urine if she hadn't taken any fluids. Garbage in, garbage out, yes. But nothing in, something out? It didn't make sense.

She picked up the water jug and tilted it to her mouth. Looking for that single, overlooked drop. But, of course, the jug was empty; her efforts no more than ritual. Like saying grace over meals.

Thanks for the grub, bub.

"I'll just wait. I'll just wait for Becky to come and bring water. She'll take me outside to bathe in the stream, to lie in the sun."

She recalled hearing a description of the Muslim paradise somewhere. A land of running waters, cool winds, and lush valleys where servant girls served chilled sherbet. A land far, far removed from the deserts of Arabia.

But Lorraine was not in the desert. She didn't know exactly *where* she was, but she knew she wasn't in a desert. Knew it by the sound of the wind running between uncountable leaves, the sound of water bubbling over rocks. And by the smell of the forest which assaulted her whenever Becky took her outside. The overwhelming, invasive odor of green things growing. Of the frantic rush of spring.

She walked back to her bed and sat down. Knowing that if she waited too long, she might not have the strength to get out. Even this small effort had tired her. Perhaps if she slept . . .

Her eyes closed and her mind filled with water. Bottomless black lakes, pounding surf, tumbling, crashing rivers. She imagined herself a twig in a river. Dancing in the whitewater, slithering over the rocks, curling upstream in the eddies. Tumbling over the edge of a waterfall, suddenly free and floating in the air.

It's not right, she decided. It's not right, and it should be. Human beings could make it right, but they make it a horror instead. They hurt each other all the time, in millions of small ways, for no good reason.

I can't die this way.

The thought had the force of revelation because it removed the element of choice. There was nothing to decide. Nothing.

. . .

When Lorraine awakened, the air was still and quiet. No birds, no wind. No Becky.

Time to go.

She fetched the metal water jug, then crossed to the window. Forcing the lip of the jug under the sheet metal until it backed up against one of the nails, she levered the jug back and forth. The first nail, much to her surprise, loosened within a few seconds. She had no way of knowing that the window frame hadn't been painted in a decade, that the frame was thoroughly dry and weathered. She knew only that she would soon be free. That she would soon have water.

Five minutes later, the sheet metal came off in her hands. She was working feverishly now, driven by the fire in her throat. The window stuck momentarily, and she pounded on the frame with the heel of her hand until it suddenly came free, sliding outward on ancient screeching hinges.

Warm, clean air rushed in, cutting the fetid atmosphere of the little room. Lorraine squeezed into the small opening, thrusting one leg forward. The frame dug into her naked flesh, and her bruised body cried out in protest. She hesitated, then pushed forward, letting herself drop feet first to the ground outside the cabin.

The babbling of the stream seemed as loud as the roar of an interstate, as compelling as the cry of an infant. She stumbled forward, tripped on an exposed root, fell heavily, rose, stumbled again. Nothing mattered except water, and when she finally reached the stream, when she dropped to her knees and lowered her lips to the water, the overwhelming sense of relief and fulfillment was as real to her as the liquid running down her throat.

She drank as much as she could (drank until her swollen belly threatened to push the water back up where it came from), then plunged her head beneath the surface of the stream. The water flowed through her hair, cooling her face and scalp. She remembered the first time she had bathed in the stream, how her body had resisted the cold. How she'd had to lower herself an inch at a time while Becky encouraged her with soft, motherly chuckles.

"Now, Lorraine, it won't hurt a bit once you get used to it. You don't want to be all yucky, do you?"

Now Lorraine sat up on the bank. She was first aware of the water running from her hair over her shoulders and chest. Then of the fact that she was naked and alone. And blind.

I'll go back the way I came, she thought. I'll just go back inside and cover up the window. All I have to do is line up the nails with the holes and pound them in with a rock. It won't be that hard.

Then she added the obvious: If I stay out here, I'll starve to death even if Becky and Daddy don't find me. If I stay out here, I'll die.

But she was likely to die either way and she knew it.

The June sun warmed her body, evaporating the moisture as it slowly dripped from her hair. The sensation was delicious, a pure physical delight. She cupped her hands and scooped water from the stream, holding it for a moment before letting it run onto her breasts and belly and thighs.

This is what it means, she thought, to give up life. To surrender the moment to the promise of eternity. There is no present in forever, no here and now. No pain, no release.

She heard the strident call of a crow in the distance, heard an answer, then another. Wishing herself to be as free as them. Free of . . .

Her mind hesitated for a moment, then filled with a single idea: the knowledge of good and evil. So much better not to know. Such a curse, to know and not be able to change. She recalled another line from her childhood Bible classes, this one from the Gospels. "For ye know not the day, nor the hour."

Maybe not, she decided, but you do know there will *be* a day and an hour. And that makes a difference. That makes *all* the difference.

She lowered her mouth to the stream and drank again, this time more slowly. The sun was very strong, strong enough to negate the cool breeze on her wet body. An airplane passed overhead, a small plane from the sound of it, flying very low. She stood and began to wave her arms frantically.

"Help me! Help me!"

The plane droned on, the roar of its engine gradually fading. Lorraine stumbled away from the stream, following the sound of the plane until it disappeared altogether.

She had never felt more alone.

"I have to make a decision," she said out loud. "I have to do something."

She remembered losing her mother on a crowded beach. Asked herself, How old was I? Old enough to talk. Old enough to get lost. She recalled looking out at the ocean, then back at the hundreds of faces. Faces on big beach blankets. Stuffing food into their mouths. How could they do that when she'd just lost her mommy?

She'd concluded (she can remember this clearly) that they didn't care. They were all devils, and they laughed to show that her condition pleased them. The condition of being lost.

But when she began to cry, they had come to her. Talked to her, led her to a lifeguard who took her to the hotdog stand and fed her ice cream and soda until her mother finally showed up.

Lorraine sat on the grass, plucked blades of grass and put them into her mouth. Maybe, she thought, I can eat grass. Like a cow or a sheep. If I could eat, I could escape. I could somehow find my way out.

But when she thought about food, she found Becky's face in her mind. Becky, the source of nourishment. The nurturing maniac.

Lorraine managed a laugh. The irony was too powerful to resist. And there were so many ironies here. Every possibility negated by a drunken moment on a Queens street. And then the worst of it, the most cutting irony of all—if she weren't blind, she'd already be dead. They'd allowed her to live *because* she was blind. And helpless. And hopeless. And so forth, and so forth, and so forth.

She lay back on the grass. Remembering screams inside a van. Remembering bloody, violent, painful death. Her death, eventually. If Becky returned. If Daddy returned. If she didn't starve.

"I'm not going to go like that," she said. "Without fighting back. Why should I, when I know what's coming?"

Her mind began to form a plan. She didn't rush it, didn't try to shape it. What was the point? It wasn't as if she had anywhere to go.

Sooner or later, she finally decided, Becky or Daddy or both would come to her. They hadn't abandoned her to starvation and thirst. No, far from it. If Daddy wanted her to die, he'd do it himself. He'd do it and enjoy it. In fact, sooner or later, he *would* come. He'd come to kill her.

If Becky came, she'd bring food. If Daddy came, he'd bring death. Either way, they'd arrive with the conviction that she, Lorraine, was helpless. That she couldn't fight back.

"And that's where they're wrong. The fatal flaw in their fatal argument."

The plan was simple: Find a weapon, a rock or a sharpened stick, then go back into the cabin. Replace the window and wait for one of them to show up. Wait until they open the door, until they're standing in sunlight, peering into the darkened room. Wait until *they* are blind, then strike. Again and again and again.

If I can walk into a room and know someone else is there, she concluded, I can find the body of my enemy. If I can find the keys on a typewriter, I can find the body of my enemy. If I can cross Flatbush Avenue, I can find the body of my enemy. If I can clear a floor of broken glass, I can find the body of my enemy.

It was, she realized, a litany. One she vowed to repeat until it became impossible to forget. Until the assertion became rock-hard reality.

Whoever came, she told herself, would come in a car. She might find a telephone in the car. Or a CB radio. Or a canteen. Or a backpack. Or a gun that she could fire off as a signal to rescuers.

Whoever came would bring a day's supply of food. She could ration that out for a week. A week of travel toward civilization.

Whoever came would come clothed. That would mean shoes; she knew she would not get far if she couldn't protect her feet. It would mean a jacket and pants to shield her body from tree branches, shrubs, and brambles. It would mean extra warmth at night.

Lorraine picked herself up and began to look for a stick large and sharp enough to be a spear. Ten minutes later, she settled for a dead branch snapped off a dead tree. It seemed sharp, but she had no way to know if it would actually penetrate flesh, and she decided not to rely on it.

No, she would use rocks instead, lots of small rocks. All she needed to do was find one with a sharp edge, then gather the rest. She knelt on the bank of the stream and let her fingers drift over the stones at the bottom, finding a piece of slate after the briefest of searches. Even in water, she could feel its oily surface and polished edges. Then, quickly, she located the rest—half a dozen palm-sized, rounded rocks—and began to carry her ammunition back to the cabin.

Twenty minutes later, she was back inside, the window recovered, the water jug full, the bucket-latrine empty. She felt almost serene. Something was going to happen, and she would be the agent of that something. She was no longer helpless, no longer hopeless.

"Let the chips fall where they may," she muttered, "as long as I get to throw the dice."

She sat at the edge of the bed, took up one of her blankets, and carefully hacked a large square, then a narrow strip. She folded the larger piece into a pouch, then began to add rocks, stopping occasionally to test the weight. It had to be light enough for her to swing quickly, yet heavy enough to incapacitate, at least temporarily.

When she was satisfied, she made a series of slits just above the rocks, wove the narrow strip through the openings, then knotted the strip. The stones were now tightly packed, the outer part of the wool square extending two feet. It would make an effective handle.

She crossed to the door, taking a position alongside it. The door opened outward, and she imagined Becky stepping through. Becky chattering as she came.

Should she strike at the head? Or go for the body, the larger target, and count on a second opportunity? And what would happen if Daddy showed up? Or if they came together? Or if they showed up while she was sleeping? Or if they didn't come at all?

"If I can walk into a room and know someone else is there, I can find the body of my enemy. If I can find the keys on a typewriter, I can find the body of my enemy. If I can cross Flatbush Avenue, I can find the body of my enemy. If I can clear a floor of broken glass, I can find the body of my enemy."

TWENTY-TWO

When I finally got home, twelve hours after my day had begun, I found that my trip to the country had put me in a decent mood. Maybe it was just the stress-blower outside Pete's Eats—I won't deny smacking that redneck had done me a world of good. But there was also the fact that I'd gone back to the north country (if not quite as far north as Paris) for the first time since the day I'd left it to enter the army. The day's journey had had its share of bad memories, but they hadn't crushed me. In fact, you could make a decent case for the proposition that my bad memories had crushed someone else. Which, I suppose, was par for the course.

In any event, when I picked up Ms. Brock's article (and there was no doubt that I was *going* to pick it up), I thought I was ready to deal with any new revelations. They weren't long in coming.

> *Rocky W. killed and mutilated five women in a period of six months in 1963 when he was nineteen years old. He didn't deny his guilt at time of trial, though the judge hearing the case refused to accept a guilty plea because of the distinct possibility of a death sentence. The killings, it should be noted, were clumsily executed, the product of a typically disorganized serial killer. Rocky did not stalk his victims; he chose them impulsively and in so doing left behind enough forensic evidence to guarantee his eventual conviction.*
>
> *Rocky W. came from the abusive background typical of our sexually motivated murderers. His father, George W., an alcoholic, drifted in and out of Rocky's life. His mother, Simone, was obsessed with religion and dragged Rocky to various church functions, sometimes as often as four or five times a week. Rocky, an only child, had virtually no contact with other children before beginning school and reports engaging in sadistic fantasy "as far back as I can remember."*
>
> *It should not surprise us to learn that Rocky did not share these fantasies with his parents, but we should also understand that he would have been unlikely to relate them even to trained personnel. Rocky's fantasies sustained him; they belonged to him alone. He saw them as his property.*

The goal, of course, from society's point of view (and from the point of view of the individual therapist), must be early identification. If the progression from abused child to sexual murderer is to be halted, intervention must begin early on. If society cannot identify children at risk, such intervention is unlikely, if not impossible.

We must, therefore, discover observable behavioral indicators of eventual sexually based aggression. Two of the most common of these indicators are cruelty to animals and/or cruelty to other children. More than 70 percent of the men in our cohort reported one or the other or both.

Rocky W. is typical of those children who actualized their fantasy lives by exhibiting long-term cruelty to animals. He began by killing the family's parakeet, though it is not clear that killing was his aim. Rocky, over a period of two weeks while his mother was at work, sprayed the bird with an insecticide, then settled back to watch as the animal convulsed on the floor of its cage. He did not do this every day, because, as he reports, "If Tweety died, I wouldn't be able to spray him any more." Rocky, according to his mother, was five years old when the bird finally expired.

Rocky admits to being "turned on" by the experience, but as his mother did not buy another family pet, he was unable to continue what he called "my experiment" on a regular basis until he reached adolescence. By that time, still friendless, he was spending most of his free time on a series of long-abandoned piers and wharfs extending into a major river near his home. The piers were populated by large rats, animals that both fascinated and repelled young Rocky. At first, he was satisfied to throw stones at them, but his efforts quickly accelerated. He reports, for instance, sprinkling the piers with rat poison, only to be disappointed when the rats ate the poison without noticeable effect.

Finally, Rocky discovered a method of entrapment that afforded him maximum satisfaction. He took a bird cage (Tweety's old cage, ironically enough) from a back closet, baited it with food stolen from the refrigerator and devised a way to close the door of the cage once a rat was inside. He would then take cage and rat onto a pier and lower the cage into the water. With practice, he was, he reports, able to gauge exactly how long the animals could remain below the surface and still survive. He would pull the cage up, give the trapped rat a chance to recover, then lower the cage, repeating this sequence until . . .

The sound of a key turning in the lock on my front door interrupted Ms. Brock's somewhat passionate recital of Rocky's childhood obsessions. A moment later, the door opened and Marie Koocek appeared.

"Wha'cha doing, Means?" she called as she crossed the apartment. "You alone?"

"Actually, I'm cuddling in bed with Miriam Brock."

"Well, save some for me."

By that time, she was close enough to see that I was alone. I won't say she was disappointed, but I don't believe she would have been embarrassed if I'd actually had company. Marie tended to take events in stride. The only thing she couldn't handle (that I knew about, at least) was her work going badly. At such times, she would pace my apartment, swearing at the top of her lungs while she announced her determination to put the art business behind her once and for all.

"So, who's Miriam Brock?"

I handed her the article without comment. "Oh, that," she said, then began to scan the pages I'd just finished reading.

"Did you torture animals, Means?" she asked when she was done.

"Well, I *killed* enough of them. Does it count as torture if you eat them after you kill them?"

She thought about it for a moment, then said, "Only if you don't cook them first."

"In that case, I declare my innocence. You know . . . "

"What're you thinking about, Means?" Koocek had a way of doing that to me. Of asking the wrong question at the right time.

"I'm thinking about a little birdy." I didn't expect it to get me off the hook, but it was the first thing that popped into my head.

"And?" Her eyes were filled with intense curiosity.

"Well, I guess I was eleven or twelve when this happened. By that time, I was just about living in the forest, hunting for meat, cooking it right there. As I was pretty experienced, I rarely had trouble finding prey, but unless it was high summer when there were berries available, or autumn when the hickory nuts and acorns dropped, meat was all I could get my hands on, so I used to filch a few pieces of bread or a couple of muffins before I went off on my expeditions.

"It's a funny thing, Marie, about animals. You fire a rifle, you *kill* something, and for a few minutes the forest is completely silent. But then it's as if nothing ever happened. The birds come back first, moving through the branches, claiming territory, scrabbling in the underbrush. Then I'd begin to see a rabbit or two, maybe squirrels in the trees. It was like they knew it was all over. That I'd done what I had to do and the danger was gone.

"Anyway, I'd cook up whatever I'd killed and have my dinner. I guess I wasn't all that neat about it, because after I finished, the birds would come for the crumbs I left behind. Chickadees, juncos, sparrows, doves. Eventually, they got to be pretty bold, especially the chickadees. The chickadees dove like black and gray bullets. *Swoooosh.* Hit the ground, snatch a crumb, and back into the trees.

"What I decided to do, for no reason better than idle curiosity, was get one of the birds to eat from my hand, so I started going to the same place every day, a small pond loaded with catfish. I'd catch, cook, and eat, then scatter crumbs around my legs and freeze in place.

"I should say something here about sitting still and how good I was at it. There's a popular myth that has the mighty hunter moving silently through the forest in search of prey. Well, anybody who's ever gone into a forest knows that moving silently is just about impossible. The animals hear better than you, smell better than you, and, for the most part, see better than you. Your only advantage is your brain, and if you've got one, you find a place where the animals go, sit your ass down, and wait for them to show up.

"But still-hunting has its own problems, biting insects being the worst of them. But there's also cold, rain, and cramps. You've got learn to sit through anything, to ignore the bugs and the weather. You've got to put your body to sleep while your mind stays focused. It's not as easy as it sounds, especially the last part. Your mind tends to wander and many's the time, especially in the early days, when I woke up to find a squirrel or a rabbit staring at me from fifteen feet away. It would have been pretty embarrassing if there'd been anyone else to see it.

"What finally happened, after years of practice, was that I'd go into a kind of trance. I'd lose my body altogether, like it wasn't even there. My mind would empty as well. I mean *really* empty. No fear, no anger, no Mom, no nothing. But at the same time, I never lost focus. I saw anything moving in my field of vision. *Anything.* And if what I saw moving was food, I killed it.

"Birds live by sight, not by hearing or smell. From up in those branches, they can see anything close enough to hunt them. They could see me, too; me and the crumbs I scattered within inches of my hands. I know they didn't like the situation, because they kept screaming at me, especially the chickadees. *Dee-dee-dee. Chicka-dee-dee-dee.* The essential message being 'get your ass outta there so I can have my lunch.'

"But I wasn't about to leave, and after a while I guess they figured it out, because, one by one, they fluttered to the ground and began a very slow approach, hopping toward me, then hopping away, then hopping forward again. Finally, after two days, the first chickadee snatched the first crumb.

"I sat motionless through it all, sat there until the chickadees approached without hesitation. The rest of the small birds, the sparrows and juncos, never worked up the courage to leave the safety of the trees. Smart sparrows, dumb chickadees.

"What I did, when I was sure they'd come, was hold the crumbs in my outstretched palm. That got them nervous again, but they were still intensely curious, perching in the lower branches of a maple, turning their heads from side to side while they checked me out with tiny black eyes. Finally, one of them, the boldest, took the plunge, fluttering down to land on my palm.

"I didn't know what I was going to do; incredible as it seems, I hadn't thought it through. But what I *actually* did—did without deciding to do it—was close my hand, trapping the animal."

Dead silence. I shut up and waited for Marie to ask the inevitable question. When it came, I was ready.

"Well, Means, you gonna tell me what happened? Or do I have to beg?"

"What happened, Marie, was the little bastard drilled his beak into the heel of my hand, then flew away. The wound bled for an hour."

Another silence. Then a "hoo, hoo, hoo" from Marie, her version of laughter. I heaved my ass off the bed and began to light the small halogen bulbs around my abstract glass sculptures, the ones Marie had selected. When I was finished, I shut off the rest of the lights in the apartment and yanked down the window shades. The effect was like dismantling a rainbow, separating the colors, then re-forming and compressing them.

But I wasn't after an effect, no matter how dramatic. What I wanted was time. Marie had accepted me at my word, but if she'd gotten a good look at my face, she'd have known better. The chickadee hadn't punctured my hand. Or maybe it *had*. The truth was that I didn't know. And I hadn't known that I didn't know until I'd gotten right to the end. Someone or something had closed down the movie, snipped off the final frames. I could literally feel the bird in my hand, feel its wings fluttering against my fingers, its heart beating wildly. But I couldn't remember what I'd done. I didn't have a glimmer, and it scared me the way an imagined boogeyman in a deep, dark closet frightens a small, helpless child.

TWENTY-THREE

By the time Vanessa Bouton showed up, some twelve hours later, my good mood had been gone for so long it seemed more abstract than one of Koocek's I-beam sculptures. Everybody knows the one about the magician who shows the hero two doors, saying, "Behind one of these doors is a dragon. Behind the other, a treasure. You *must* choose one of the doors, because the way back is guarded by a thousand rabid psychoanalysts, all of whom are programmed to save you from yourself. A fate, my friend, worse than life itself."

Now suppose the magician is a practical jokester (or, better yet, a rabid psychoanalyst), and the treasure is not a treasure at all but a lifetime partnership with Vanessa Bouton, while the dragon is King Thong wrapped in a pink ribbon. Suppose the dragon is the reward and the treasure is the punishment. What do you do then?

What you do, if you're part of the NYPD, is say, "Good morning, Captain," and let your superior officer inside. Despite the sad fact that her broad, toothy smile proclaims the even sadder fact that she's happier than a pig in shit.

"Morning, Means. How'd you sleep?"

"Sleep? I don't believe I'm familiar with that term."

"Bad as that, eh?"

"And getting worse."

But the truth was that I wasn't tired. Not physically.

"What's on today's agenda, Captain? We arresting Robert Kennedy?"

"Not exactly, Means. We've got an appointment with a psychologist named Miriam Brock."

It's funny how you learn things about yourself. For instance, I knew I wasn't a paranoid schizophrenic as soon as Bouton spoke those words. If I were, I would have killed her, myself, or the both of us. On the spot.

"Would you repeat that, Captain?"

She looked at me looking at her for a moment, her smile slowly falling away. "Miriam Brock. Teaches at Columbia. She's been studying sexually motivated killers for more than a decade. I want to run Kennedy's profile by her. See what she thinks before we take it any further. That a problem?"

I retrieved the article in *American Psychology* and passed it over to her. "This was included in the package of evidence Pucinski assembled for me. Did you know that?" Maybe I was a *little* paranoid, after all.

She looked it over for a minute, then giggled. "Actually, I didn't. But it's just as well. She's the best there is on the subject. I studied with her when I took my master's." She raised her nose and sniffed the air. "Is that coffee I smell? We've got a couple of hours to kill. Let's generate some paperwork on what we did yesterday."

I led her over to the kitchen area, poured her a mug of freshly ground French Roast, then poured one for myself.

"By the way," she said, pulling out a stack of DD5's, "I got a letter from Lydia Singleton."

"Who?" I wasn't being sarcastic. The name didn't ring a bell, and I suspected that Lydia Singleton was another psychologist.

Bouton frowned and shook her head. "She still Dolly Dope to you?"

It took me a minute to put it together. Lydia Singleton was Dolly Dope's real name.

"What does she want now?" I asked, rather stupidly.

Bang! Bouton smacked the mug onto the tabletop. "What's the matter with you? I'm starting to think there's nothing under there. You hear what I'm saying? You're like an onion, Means—all layers, no core."

Very clever, I thought, you should have been a poet. Or a psychologist. Anything but a cop.

"What can I say, Captain?" I said. "You caught me off guard."

"Can I read you part of her letter?"

I was tempted to remind her that "may I" was the correct way to phrase it if she was asking permission, but what I actually said was, "Sure, Captain. Read away."

I let the doctors do an AIDS test the other day, and it came out positive. No surprise, right? But the funny part is the results didn't get me down. Maybe I won't have a long life—I know the odds are against it—but at least I'll have a life. The way it was before I got here wasn't life at all. I have hope, now, which is sort of funny. I mean, hope in what? It's kind of confusing, so I'm playing it one day at a time. And what I want to do is thank you and Detective Means for seeing something human in a creature that couldn't see it in herself.

Bouton dropped the letter and looked up at me. "There's more," she said, "but I just wanted you to hear that part of it."

A pregnant pause followed, right on cue. I was expected to make some sort of a comment, that was obvious enough, but I didn't know what to say. On the one hand, I couldn't bring myself to fake an enthusiasm I didn't feel. On the other, I knew that a cynical remark would only prolong the agony.

"Well, you know, Captain," I finally said, "it's all well and good, but I can't say I had very much to do with it."

"You convinced Razor Stewart to let her go. Doesn't that count for anything?"

"Actually, he was glad to be rid of her. She was costing him more in dope than she was earning on the street." I shrugged my shoulders, hoping she'd change the subject and let me off the hook. No such luck, according to her expression, so I said, "Tell me something, Captain, how long have you been in the rehab business?"

Before she could answer I had a sudden flash of rather repulsive insight. *I* was one of Vanessa Bouton's projects. One of those sad, sad souls to be lifted from the muck and mire. To be pitied.

"Excuse me a minute," I said. "I have to get something."

Bouton looked surprised, but not as surprised as she would have been if I'd surrendered to my first impulse and slammed my fist into her mouth. She started to speak, then thought better of it. Maybe she read the look on my face. Or maybe she simply couldn't think of anything to say. Whichever it was, I managed to get out of the room without another word being spoken.

Safe inside the bedroom, the only enclosed space in my loft, I picked up the phone with the intention of calling Sergeant Pucinski. I hadn't reported in in a couple of days, and this seemed like as good a time as any. But I couldn't bring myself to punch out the number. There didn't seem to be any point to it. I'd spent my whole life trying to make order out of chaos. Chaos isn't much in the way of raw material, but if that's all you have . . .

I walked into the bathroom and splashed my face with cold water. The problem—*my* problem—was that I wasn't all that sure of what I wanted. At that moment, staring at my reflection in the mirror while I toweled off, my professional career seemed remote, something that had happened to me rather than something I'd actually done. For the life of me, I couldn't see the difference between torturing small birds and torturing vicious pimps. If you enjoy delivering pain, you're a sadist. It doesn't matter if the individual on the receiving end deserves the pain.

Much calmer, I went back into the bedroom, punched out Pooch's number and waited for him to pick up.

"Yeah?"

"Pooch? It's Roland Means."

"Means, whatta ya say?"

"Not much, Pooch. Look . . . "

"Say, Means, what's the difference between karate and judo?"

"I don't have time for this."

"Don't be mean, Mister Means." He chortled happily. "What's the difference between karate and judo."

"I give up, Pooch."

"Karate is a martial art. Judo is what you make bagels from."

"Nice, Pooch. You ready to listen, now?"

"I'm all ears."

I ran down our visit to the north country, including our conversation with Seaver Shannon and Kennedy's wife, Rebecca, providing him with an unrequested alibi. Pooch took a minute before responding.

"Not bad, Means," he finally said. "You actually got yourself a suspect. It's more than I expected."

"Guess I'm just an overachiever, Pooch. You have yourself a nice day."

I hung up and rejoined a solemn Vanessa Bouton. She was leaning back in her chair, holding her coffee mug in both hands.

"That feels better," I said as cheerfully as I could manage. "Too much coffee this morning. Too much coffee and not enough sleep. Shall we get to work?"

Two hours later, we were sitting in Miriam Brock's Columbia University office, waiting for her to come back from a class. The place was a mess. Books and manuscripts were piled on every flat surface. The ashtrays and wastebaskets were overflowing. Her wooden desk (what I could see of it) was dusty and scarred.

"What's the image here, Captain?" I asked innocently. "Eccentric genius? Or fuzzy academic?"

Bouton grinned amiably. "I think some of this crap was here when I was a student. I don't know how she lives with it. But don't jump to any conclusions. Miriam Brock spent ten years working for the FBI. She still consults on virtually every major case involving multiple homicides. Whatever you may think of civilian experts, at least be open enough to accept the fact that she's the best there is."

The "best there is" made her entrance a couple of minutes

later. At least thirty pounds overweight, she sported an enormous bosom, several jiggling chins, and a pair of shrewd black eyes. Her smile was so warm as to be positively motherly.

"Vanessa," she said, "it's been too long."

The next several minutes were filled with hugs and coos and murmured clichés. Then Ms. Brock turned to me.

"You must be Roland Means." Her voice was honey smooth, but her eyes tore into me like a pair of sharpened forceps.

"There's a rumor, but I'm not admitting anything." My smile was easy enough, the way for it having been prepared by Captain Bouton's solicitude.

"Veee haf vays," Brock said in a mock-German accent, "uff making you talk."

"Promises, promises—that's all I ever get."

The amenities observed, Brock took her place in a swivel chair behind her desk and folded her pudgy hands. "Now, I believe the subject is King Thong."

"Right," Bouton said eagerly, "Kennedy . . . "

Brock silenced her with a casual wave. "Before you start, Vanessa, I want to remind you that whatever I say off the top of my head should be taken for exactly what it is—casual conversation. *Not* analysis."

Bouton looked crestfallen. "You *have* studied the Thong killings, Miriam. It's not like you're unfamiliar with the case."

"That's true, Vanessa, and I came to the conclusion, as did you, that the killings were not sexually motivated. Now, sexually motivated homicide is my *only* area of expertise. The rest is pure speculation."

"Ms. Brock, " I said, "are you telling me you haven't thought about this case? That you don't have any theories?"

She turned to me with a happy grin. "I won't say that I'm not opinionated. That I don't have theories about *everything*, up to and including dam construction in the Pacific Northwest. But that doesn't make what I say valid."

"Would it make you feel better," I asked, "if we promise not to use your theories to get an arrest warrant for Kennedy?"

"That's just the attitude I was hoping for," she responded, leaning back in her chair. "Now, Vanessa, hit me with the goodies."

Bouton related our trip to Owl Creek in detail, referring to her notes as she went along. When she finished, she put her notebook into her purse and looked up at Miriam Brock. "Robert Kennedy's being a deputy sheriff puts me in a ticklish position, Miriam. I mean, how in hell can I conduct a nice, quiet preliminary investigation? How can I ask for his duty records, records that might provide him with an alibi, without his finding out about it? I'm not saying that I won't do it, but I'd like to have a little more input. *Before* I turn up the heat."

Curious, how she kept saying "I" instead of "we." Curious, but not altogether surprising.

Miriam Brock swiveled sideways in her chair, looking at us over her shoulder. "Very interesting," she began, "*very* interesting." She swiveled back, leaned forward, and placed her refolded hands on the desk. "When did we last speak about this case?"

"Three months ago? Four? Five? I'd have to consult my notes to be sure."

"Forget the notes." Brock's smile was that of an indulgent parent. "It doesn't matter. What does matter is that I've been thinking about this case ever since, trying to make some sense of it. I never bought the FBI's assessment of the murders. There were too many details at odds with my own personal research. The disparate types, the identical patterns of mutilation.... We've been through this in detail. The simple fact is that those homicides literally haunted me. Something (perhaps the ghost of Dr. Freud, if I may be permitted to stretch the metaphor) kept telling me that *my* conclusions simply didn't fit the pattern any more than the FBI's.

"I'd been theorizing an individual who'd never killed before, an individual, motivated by greed or jealousy, who'd suddenly stepped out of his safe skin to commit seven grisly homicides. This individual (the one in my neat little theory) could not have been a 'hit man' or a professional criminal of any kind. A professional would have devised a much simpler plan. Nor could this individual have been acting on impulse, because the crime scenes clearly indicated an organized type who'd taken great care to plan and execute his crimes."

She took a deep breath and lit a cigarette. "See this," she said, waving the cigarette before taking a deep drag. "Cigarettes kill thousands of times more often than serial killers, but nobody quakes in fear at the image of a pack of Marlboros running amok. According to the FBI there are fewer than a hundred serial killers at large at any given time, yet serial killers are the subject of book after book after book. Misplaced paranoia is what it's all about.

"Anyway, back to King Thong. I've come to the conclusion that the perpetrator of the King Thong homicides is a heterosexual who killed *women* before the King Thong homicides began, and who continues to kill women now that they're over. That would account for a number of the anomalies in this case—no indication of sexual assault, no pattern of escalating violence, the victims left where they were sure to be found. Thong, if my present theory holds up, gained little satisfaction from murdering those seven men. His motive was not sexual, but his evident skill was developed during the commission of prior, sexually motivated homicides. Robert Kennedy, as you've presented him to me, is a man driven by greed and, perhaps, anger. His background, as outlined by Mr. Shannon, seems consistent with that of the typical serial killer, but what you've presented to me is only an outline. A *vague* outline. Plus, you must also remember that many, many individuals endure horrific childhood abuse without ever committing a crime. If I were you, I wouldn't draw any conclusions about Mr. Kennedy, but I would certainly take the next step. Whatever that may be."

The silence following Brock's lecture was so profound, I felt an urge to break it by applauding, an urge I resisted mightily.

"It fits." Bouton finally broke the spell. "Not Kennedy. I'm not thinking about Kennedy. I'm thinking about Thong. The FBI profiling team was sure that Thong was a serial killer, and they were right. I was sure that Thong was not sexually motivated, and I was right, too. What a clever bastard he was. *Is.* Let me not forget that. Let me *never* forget that. Clever and vicious."

"May I ask a question?" I said, interrupting the accolades.

"Sure." Brock turned to look at me.

"The victims were all shot in the head. In almost exactly the same spot."

"Yes, I know that. I've reviewed the autopsies."

"How'd he do it? How'd he get all seven into the right position and keep them there? Why didn't one or two of them fight back? Or at least turn around?"

"That's a cop question," Bouton interrupted.

"Not so, Vanessa." Brock silenced her student with a wave. "It's a question that caught my attention as well. A very intriguing question. Initially, I understood it as an indicator of just how premeditated these crimes were. How cold-blooded. *Your* question only occurred to me later, but in the absence of any forensic evidence, hair samples, tissue samples, fibers, et cetera, I'm not willing to draw any definite conclusions. I assume you've come up with theories of your own, Detective."

"Not one that I'm happy with."

"Have you considered the possibility that King Thong might be two people? There are many examples of serial killers acting in consort."

"I have. But I can't see the victims getting into a vehicle with two men. Not once the killings became public."

"Why does it have to be two *men?* Maybe it was a man and a woman."

"Say that again?"

"Do you know the history of Gerald and Charlene Gallego?" She smiled and shook her head. "No, obviously not. Well, Gerald Gallego was a lifelong criminal, always in and out of trouble, who'd survived an incredibly brutal childhood, while Charlene Williams was a rather prim would-be violinist from a 'good' family. They met, fell in love, and married.

"Things went reasonably well (though Gerald continued his criminal activities and abused Charlene from time to time) until one day Gerald came home to find Charlene in bed with another woman. This undercut his own virility, making it impossible for him to perform. Charlene, driven, presumably, by guilt, suggested they spice up their love lives by kidnapping sex slaves. Gerald thought that a great idea, as long as they killed the sex slaves when they were finished with them. And that's just the way it went for the next seven years. Charlene lured the women into their van, whereupon Gerald controlled them with words or violence while Charlene drove to a remote spot. The women were sexually assaulted for hours, then beaten to death and left to rot.

"The initial investigation was hampered, as many of these investigations are, by two factors: The bodies, when found, were badly decomposed, and the killings took place in multiple jurisdictions. Gerald and Charlene weren't caught until one of their victims escaped. Not surprisingly, Charlene testified against Gerald in return for a life sentence with the possibility of parole after nineteen years. She claimed that Gerald forced her to help capture the victims, that she did not participate in the sexual assaults or in the actual killing. Forensic evidence, however, indicates otherwise. Gerald Gallego, I should add, was sentenced to death."

TWENTY-FOUR

You can run, but you can't hide.

Maybe the old cliché ought to read, "You can hide, but sooner or later the mosquitoes will drive you into the open." It had taken a long, long time; I'd managed to stretch it for all it was worth. But there were no forests in Miriam Brock's office. No dark groves. Something inside me downshifted, popped the clutch, and put the pedal to the metal. The sensation wouldn't have been all that terrible, if I'd known whose hands were on the steering wheel.

"Congratulations, Captain," I said, turning to Bouton, "looks like you've got yourself a suspect. One that actually fits."

She looked surprised, then pleased. "Did I miss something? You seemed pretty skeptical a few minutes ago."

"Ignorance is what it was. A man and a woman operating together? Chalk it up to an overdeveloped macho attitude if you want, but the idea never occurred to me."

"Actually," Bouton nodded happily, "it never occurred to me, either. I'm still not sure I believe it, Charlene Gallego notwithstanding. There may be other factors. . . ."

"Other factors don't mean squat to cops," I interrupted. "Look, when I was on the streets I had maybe a dozen male prostitutes snitching for me. Not all at one time, but over a period of years. I got to know a few of them pretty well. Understand, these were mostly kids, small-town boys from broken homes, and I played the father figure for all it was worth. 'Tell me everything, son. Listening's what I'm here for.' Now, understand something else, most of these kids were scared shitless. Not only were they on unfamiliar turf, but the johns kept doing horrible things to them, not to mention the pimps and the rest of the

208

street sharks. So what's the chances that with all the publicity surrounding the murders, these kids would get in a car with *two* men? Like I told you before, the question of how the victims were controlled jumped out at me the first time I looked at the autopsy photos. I've run it through my head with every variation I could dream up and the only thing that works is two perpetrators, one to distract and one to kill. But two perps, two males, anyway, would have made the victims even more skittish. Somewhere along the line, somebody would have fought back. A man and a woman, on the other hand . . ."

"Detective?" Brock's voice was almost amused. "Does that happen?"

"Does what happen?" As far as I was concerned, Brock was yesterday's news.

"A couple hiring a male prostitute?"

"Professor, in New York everything happens. In New York, men in chauffeur-driven limos pay to give head to disease-ridden, middle-aged, South Bronx prostitutes. Get yourself a copy of the *Village Voice* and look in the personals. If there isn't an ad there from a 'bi white male' or a 'bi black male' or a 'bi couple' looking to party with a married couple, I'll buy you dinner."

"Does it happen on the street, Means?" Bouton asked. "Bisexual encounters?"

I took a deep breath. Having smelled blood in the water, I was having a very difficult time sitting in that office. "Not often, Captain, and not to everybody, but when it did happen, the kids talked about it for weeks afterwards. I mean, as far as I could make out, most of those kids believed they were straight. They were out there trying to survive, and peddling their butts was the only way they could see to do it. What they'd tell me was, 'I don't do nothin'. I let 'em go down on me, but I don't do nothin' back.' I knew it was mostly bullshit—and there were exceptions, like John-John Kennedy—but it was just the kind of bullshit that'd get a streetwise whore to jump into a van with a man and a woman. And here's something else to consider—according to forensics, Thong probably used low-velocity, .22-caliber hollow points to kill his victims. A big gun, a .45 or a 9mm, would have been a lot more efficient, especially if there'd been a struggle somewhere along the way. Now, the conclusion that I (and everybody else) reached was that our killer used a small gun simply because small guns are quieter, but there's a second possibility. Maybe he needed to make sure the bullet he fired into the back of his victim's head didn't go right through his victim's head and kill his wife. Who just happened to be lying under his victim. Captain, tell me something. The M.E. couldn't come up with any evidence of sexual assault from a male. No semen samples, no anal penetration, no male pubic hairs. But did anyone check for vaginal secretions, female pubic hairs?"

"If they did, it's not in the report."

"Why am I not surprised?" I stood up. "I think it's time we got moving, Captain. Time to go to work. Professor, it's been instructive. To say the least."

Brock took my hand, then turned to Vanessa Bouton. "My God, Vanessa, he's exactly as you described him."

Bouton tossed me a guilty look, but I didn't react. Between the three of us, we'd found a scenario that fit all the known facts and a suspect who fit the scenario. That didn't mean Kennedy was guilty. Nor did it mean that my inflamed cop radar was anything more than wishful thinking. But it was enough to prevent my responding to Bouton's games.

The way I saw it, there were three problems in my immediate future. First, we, Bouton and I, had to find a way to pursue the investigation without alerting the task force. Chief Bowman might have been willing to let Bouton chase the proverbial wild goose, but if that goose ever came into sight, Bowman and his task force would take over in a hot second.

The second problem was how to check on Robert Kennedy without alerting *him*. Sheriff Pousson, if pressed, might be persuaded to let us have a look at Kennedy's work sheets without a court order. But Kennedy would almost certainly find out about it. He'd find out and, like any good serial killer, destroy whatever trophies he'd accumulated over the years.

My final problem was Vanessa Bouton, *Captain* Vanessa Bouton. If she opted for the rules and regs, problems one and two wouldn't be problems at all. Both the task force and Robert Kennedy *would* know. The task force would take over the investigation and Kennedy *would* have a chance to work on that van before we could impound it.

I watched Bouton and her professor go through the ritual of vowing to keep in touch, to call more often, to do lunch, while I considered a fourth problem. I'd been playing the part of the snitch (not without good reason) all along. If I now decided to withhold information, I'd probably spend the rest of my career in a little booth outside a foreign embassy. Especially if Kennedy turned out to be Thong. The brass would have to promote Bouton; she'd make deputy inspector, at the least. But Detective Means? Somebody would have to pay the price for making Chief Bowman look like a jerk, and the only someone I could think of was me.

We made our way out of the building and onto Amsterdam without saying much of anything, but that was as long as we could contain ourselves.

"Captain, I—"

"Means, I—"

We stopped, then grinned, then began to laugh.

"I think we should get some lunch, Means."

"Lunch, yes."

"And formulate a plan of action."

"Action, yes. By all means. That's a pun."

"A bad one. You know any restaurants on Amsterdam? I haven't been here for years, and I don't feel like walking across the campus to Broadway. These kids make me feel like a relic from another age."

"Not my neck of the woods, Captain. A little farther Uptown and I might be able to help you out."

It was just after noon, and the streets were filled with Columbia students. I stopped one, a boy, and requested the name of a decent restaurant.

"What's decent?" he asked, looking from Bouton to me to Bouton.

"Anything between consenting adults that doesn't involve an exchange of money."

"Pardon me?"

"How about anything within six blocks with a liquor license."

He gave me the name of an Italian place, *Stella Mare*, near 111th Street, and ten minutes later we were uncomfortably seated on wobbly chairs in what could only be called a neighborhood joint. (A joint which, I was pleased to note, hadn't added goat cheese pizza with broccoli to the menu.) I ordered a beer and the shrimp *fra diavolo*. Bouton settled for linguine with white clam sauce, extra garlic, and a diet Coke.

"What do you think, Means?" Bouton didn't waste any time. She was literally rubbing her hands together.

"I think we have a genuine suspect. In fact, I think we've got two genuine suspects. And I want you to remember who steered you onto Kennedy. In case we get lucky and these suspects turn out to be perpetrators."

"Don't worry, Means. Even if Kennedy comes up clean, I'll still remember who steered me onto him."

"You play fair, Captain. But you don't play nice."

And neither did I. I wanted her happy when I hit her with the facts of life, and judging from her broad smile, I wasn't going to get a better chance. I waited for her to say, "It's a good thing I've got you for a role model," then jumped into it with both feet.

"You've got some decisions to make here, Captain. I mean *right* here and *right* now. You make the wrong decision or no decision at all, you're gonna lose control."

Her grin dropped away, but it wasn't replaced by annoyance or anger. More like curiosity.

"Spell it out, Means."

"Tell me something—how do we go about accessing VICAP? Can you do it from any computer?"

That brought a quick frown. "Why do we want to contact VICAP?"

"Because, Captain, if, as *Brock* suspects, Thong is out there killing women and if, as *I* suspect, Thong turns out to be Kennedy and his old lady, we should be able to find some evidence of it in VICAP's little computer."

"Actually, it's not so little. It's tied into one of the biggest mainframes in the country." She was nodding as she spoke, thinking it over. "What would you want to look for? And where would you want to look?"

"If Kennedy works a rotating schedule at the sheriff's department, he'd do five days, five swings, and five nights, then get six days off. That gives him a lot of driving time. I'd say, Maine, Vermont, New Hampshire, Massachusetts, Connecticut, and New York."

"You forgot Rhode Island."

"*Everybody* forgets Rhode Island. It's a culture thing. Now, as to what we're looking for, that would depend on how the computer works. Which is not my department. Ideally, we'd like to ask the computer for unsolved homicides with evidence of a woman perpetrator. If that doesn't work, we can broaden out. Ask it for any evidence of a serial killer working in Kennedy's territory."

Bouton sipped at her Coke, then leaned back as the waiter approached with our food.

"Clams for the lady," he said, setting a plate in front of Bouton. "And shrimps for the gentleman."

I watched his back for a moment, then popped a shrimp into my mouth. "Bland," I said, "as usual."

"Not enough garlic," Bouton responded. "As usual."

"So how do we get in touch with VICAP?"

The question caught her chewing a mouthful of linguine. Which wasn't all that bad, because it gave her a minute to consider what I was really after.

"I take it," she said, "that you don't want to go through the task force."

"That's right."

"Why?"

I laid down my fork. "You know about stealing collars?" I paused, got no response, then continued. "Stealing collars is one of the job's oldest and least publicized traditions. Sergeants steal collars from patrolmen; lieutenants steal collars from sergeants; captains . . . "

"I get the point." Now Bouton wasn't eating either. She was sitting straight up, holding her fork like a baton.

"We're working on the biggest case in New York since Son of Sam," I said, rubbing the point in as hard as I could. "Do you really think Chief Bowman (who, by the way, is at least as ambitious as you are) is gonna sit by and let you bring in King Thong? Do you *really* believe that?"

"Never." She spat the word out.

"How many times did he make you eat shit, Captain? How many times did he make you eat shit with other cops in the room? How many times did he make you eat shit because you're a woman?" I paused, but she chose not to respond, though her eyes were blazing. "Like I said, you've got a decision to make and you have to make it now. As for me, I'm not sure I care. I'm not saying the idea of hunting down a multimurderer doesn't appeal to me, because it does. I'm a hunter; it's as simple as that. But on the other hand, I've done exactly what you asked me to do when you dragged me out of the ballistics lab. If Bowman takes over and you're out of it, then it's time for you to make good on your promise to have me returned to Vice."

Bouton smiled, then took a sip of her Coke. "You're very persuasive, Means. You should have been a lawyer. But you're forgetting one thing. The paperwork. Filing a false report is a serious violation of NYPD procedure. Not to mention a criminal act."

Her statement caught me by surprise. According to Pucinski, she didn't have to file the paperwork until after the investigation was completed. Not that I could bring that up.

"Look, Captain, today's Friday. Nobody will say anything if you don't file any reports before, say, next Wednesday. In the meantime, I'll go visit Sergeant Pucinski. I'll tell him you've got this fixation on an upstate cop named Kennedy just because Kennedy's father has money. You wanna hear how it goes?"

"Yes, I do."

"'She's crazy, Pooch. She thinks some redneck, hillbilly cop murdered and mutilated seven men so he wouldn't have to share his inheritance. And me, I have to sit there and nod my head like I was dealing with a real cop instead of an ambitious desk jockey. I'm tellin' ya, Pooch, I take much more of this bullshit, I'm gonna kill some people on my own. And I'm gonna start with that worthless bitch.'"

She flinched at the B-word, then leaned forward again. "That's very convincing. You practice? Or does it come naturally?"

"You want the five days or not, Captain?"

"Oh, I'll take them, Means. Being as there's no price to pay. But what happens then? Where do we go for the subpoenas? The search warrants? The personnel to set up surveillance?"

I didn't answer right away. And not because I didn't have an answer. I had answers, all right, but not answers she was ready to deal with. Not yet.

"You've got a point, Captain. A good point. And right now, I can't see a way around the task force. Not if the shit really hits the fan. But if we take good notes and find the right ghostwriter, we just might be the first ones out with a book. *Thong Lives*. By Commissioner Vanessa Bouton and Chief of Detectives Roland Means."

TWENTY-FIVE

VICAP. Somehow, despite all my professed cynicism, I'd envisioned Vanessa Bouton tapping away at a computer keyboard. Envisioned her reaching directly into VICAP's bowels for the information we needed to connect Kennedy and spouse to the King Thong homicides. I should have known better.

VICAP's files could only be accessed by FBI personnel. For the rest of us piss-ant, law-enforcement types, using VICAP meant submitting a fourteen-page, fill-in-the-blanks report, followed by a three-week wait. And even that wouldn't do us any good. We were looking for any unsolved series of homicides in the Northeast involving a woman. The official VICAP form assumed knowledge of a specific crime. Fishing expeditions, apparently, were out of the question.

But, in law enforcement as in everything else, it's not what you know that counts. It's who you know. And Bouton, as it turned out, had been working closely with a special agent named Timothy Donovan, VICAP's official liaison with the King Thong Task Force. Their phone conversations, Bouton explained as we drove toward my Long Island City apartment, had been especially lively.

"See, Donovan's no jerk," she explained. "He knows the murders don't fit established theories, but he doesn't buy my explanations. He thinks he's onto something entirely new, an intellectual who's spent time in the library. Someone smart enough to pull off a series of homicides, then move on to establish an entirely different M.O. in a new jurisdiction. Donovan thinks Thong masturbated into a condom to throw us off the track."

"That's all well and good, Captain, but how does it help us?"

"It helps because Donovan will run our request through the

computer without asking too many questions. All we need is a fax machine to receive the case files."

The fax machine wasn't a problem. Nearly every small printer in town has a fax machine. For a price, they send and receive information. The printer we found on Vernon Boulevard, four blocks from my apartment, was more than willing to call us if anything came in. The ten-dollar bill I pressed into the clerk's palm virtually guaranteed that he wouldn't forget.

Once inside the loft, Bouton wasted no time. She was dialing the phone before I finished locking the door. Her manner was quick and imperious as she dealt with the switchboard down in Quantico, but once she got to Agent Tim Donovan, her tone changed abruptly. Low and rich, punctuated by deep chuckles, it cajoled and flattered its way through the pitch, shifting only at the end, when she had to ask Donovan to keep the request under his hat. At that point, she became apologetic, slightly embarrassed, like a little girl caught peeping into the boys' bathroom.

"Well done, Captain," I said as she laid the phone down. "Really impressive. If I could do that, I'd be mayor."

She frowned at the backhanded compliment, then shrugged. "It's a butt kisser's world," she admitted. "But what are you gonna do?"

"Get ahead by getting behind?"

I thought the pun was rather witty, but it appeared to sail over her head.

"We've got some time to kill. Three or four hours, at the least. Why don't we kill it with paperwork?"

"Actually, I have another idea. While we're waiting for the FBI, I'm gonna get in touch with the Albany cops. You remember how Kennedy bemoaned the horrors of urban life? Like we're supposed to believe that he left the APD because he was too sensitive to be a big city cop? With a little luck and a lot of begging, I just might be able to find out why he *really* left."

The begging began almost as soon as I got started. First I

begged Albany information for the phone number of APD personnel. Then I listened to the phone ring thirty or forty times before a civilian clerk informed me that all requests for information on "Members of the Force" had to be submitted in writing. It wasn't until I got Sergeant DiMateo, a supervisor and a cop, that the phrase "multiple homicides" produced results.

"We're talking about seven homicides, Sergeant. And we're sure the killer's still active. We don't have two or three weeks to screw around with this."

The last bit of begging got me the promise of a return call. It also bought me a little time. I hung up, then leaned back in the chair and stretched out. "You know, Captain, there's something we should talk about. Being as we've got nothing better to do."

"Step two in the corruption of Vanessa Bouton? Is that the hot topic?"

I was tempted to make a joke of it, but something in her eyes warned me off. She wasn't angry; more like sad and puzzled. This wasn't the way it was supposed to go. I almost felt sorry for her. Almost.

"I'm only here to give you the facts of life," I said. "That's why you asked for me in the first place. For me, specifically. I won't be insulted if you don't take my advice. In fact, if you tell me you don't wanna hear it, I'll keep my big mouth shut altogether."

She waved me off impatiently. "You already gave the propaganda speech, Means. Don't repeat yourself. The question, I believe, is what comes next. Assuming VICAP pays off."

"Tell me something, Captain," I said, trying to lead her away from her quite justifiable anxiety. "Do serial killers really keep trophies? Trophies that can be used as evidence against them?"

"Many do. Not all of them, but enough. Part of the fun comes from reliving the murders. It goes back to the obsession with fantasy. The trophies make the fantasies more . . . rewarding."

"If I remember, pieces of Thong's victims were missing, the eyelids and nipples, along with the clothing and personal effects.

What's the chance that he kept some of that? Maybe has little pieces of his triumphs mounted on a mirror over his bed?"

"Get to the point, Means."

Bouton's expression had passed from annoyed to pissed off. Her lips were pressed together, her nostrils slightly flared.

"You remember that van? The one parked near the house?" I waited until she favored me with a cautious nod. "It'd be real nice to let the lab boys have a go at it. See if Kennedy over-looked something when he cleaned it up."

"Means, if you don't tell me something I don't already know, I'm gonna tape your mouth closed."

"A couple of hours ago you told me this was fun, now you're get-ting upset. I need to know which Captain Bouton I'm talking to."

"How is it fun if you can't trust your partner?" She gave me a minute to think about it, then continued. "You want to go in there, don't you? You want to break into Kennedy's house."

"It wouldn't be a problem, Captain." It was my turn to be annoyed. Annoyed at my own predictability.

"No? You're ready to *guarantee* that you can break into a house sitting at the end of a half-mile-long private drive with no possibility that you'll be caught? Because if you do get caught, you'll blow the case forever."

"What do you think I'm gonna do, drive the Buick up to the front door? Leave my police parking permit in the window?"

I couldn't keep the sarcasm out of my voice, and I expected a sharp response. Instead, I got a hard stare and a muttered, "Keep going, Means?"

"You know what topographical maps are?"

"No."

"Topo maps, which you can buy at any decent sporting goods store, show elevation as well as geography. Now, we've all been raised to believe that the shortest distance between two points is a straight line, but if the straight line happens to run over a mountain, you're gonna be awful late getting to the party. So, if you're operating in a forest, you've got to know the terrain, and that's part of what topo maps show you. They also show things like old logging roads, hiking trails, streams, lakes, swamps, rivers, abandoned railroad grades. This in addition to ordinary paved roads and highways.

"The point, Captain, is that the Adirondacks are honeycombed with hiking trails. I can use one or another of those trails to get within a mile or two of Kennedy's house, then bushwhack to a point where I can put the house under surveillance without any possibility of being spotted. Once the place is empty, the rest is easy. When I'm finished, I'll go back the way I came."

Bouton leaned back in her chair, opened her purse and took out a roll of Tums. She stuffed one into her mouth, then returned the roll to her purse.

"What about the dogs?" she asked. "Are you going to Mace the dogs?"

"Mace doesn't work well on dogs, Captain, because they don't have tear glands. There's a spray called Punch II, made from hot chili peppers, that'll stop the best-trained attack dog. It wears off in forty-five minutes with no permanent effects."

"And if the house is locked?"

"Locked with the Yale lock on Kennedy's front door? No problem, Captain. It won't even slow me down."

Bouton stood up and turned her back; she strolled over to a window and stared at the street for a moment, then spun around to face me.

"What you've been doing all along," she announced, "is trying to stay one step ahead of me. As if I was some nasty aunt who had to be tricked into giving you a cookie. What I think you do is blame it on authority. Never trust a ranking officer, right? But the truth is that you don't trust *anybody* and you never have. Well, you're going to have to make an exception here, because if you don't fill me in on steps three, four, and five, I'm not going to let you out of my sight. You can start by telling me what you plan to do if you find evidence in that house."

"If we find evidence," I said, stalling while I formulated a plan I hadn't had a moment before, "we'll *know* Kennedy and his wife are guilty. The way it is now, we could spend weeks getting search warrants and subpoenas. . . ."

"Don't bullshit me. What do you plan to do?"

I stared into her round, dark eyes for a moment, then it came to me. "One thing I might do, Captain," I said, letting my eyes drop, "assuming I find those trophies, is take one or two and hide them somewhere in the house. Like in a suitcase at the back of a closet. That way they'll still be there on the day we arrive with the paperwork."

"You're not going to remove anything?"

"Anything I remove can't be used at trial. There's no point to it. The next step, assuming I find that incriminating evidence, is to contact Sheriff Pousson in his own home and get his cooperation. Kennedy's duty sheets might give him an airtight alibi; if they don't, they'll give *us* enough circumstantial evidence to get the warrants we'll need to search the house and impound the van."

Bouton walked back to the desk, frowned, and shook her head. "I can't say as I trust you, Means. How do you trust a man who's been a lone wolf all his life? But I'll be damned if I'll go into that forest with you. The deep, dark forest scares the crap out of me." She sat down heavily and closed her eyes for a moment. When she reopened them, they were sharp and committed. "We're jumping the gun here. There's no reason to make a decision now."

"That's true, Captain. We haven't heard from VICAP, yet. Or the Albany cops. Why don't we let nature take its course and make our final decisions when we have to?"

As luck would have it, both VICAP and the Albany Police Department gave us tantalizing glimpses, but nothing conclusive. DiMateo came through first, calling back, as promised, just after four-thirty. Kennedy, DiMateo reported, had resigned from the APD, just as he'd claimed. He'd never been charged with any violation of the rules and regs, but his service record did show that several women had accused him of what DiMateo labeled "coerced sexual activity." Unfortunately, as all of the women were active prostitutes with extensive rap sheets, and no desire to sign a complaint, the charges had remained allegations, and Kennedy had never suffered anything more severe than an unofficial reprimand from his commanding officer.

Both DiMateo and I, even as we discussed the matter, knew full well that many a vice cop has traded a free pass on a bust for a sexual favor. It wasn't that either department, the APD or the NYPD, condoned the activity, but it was too common to make Kennedy a serial killer.

"If you wanna take this further, Detective," DiMateo said toward the end of our conversation, "I'd suggest you go to Kennedy's former commanding officer, Captain Forey. He's retired now, but his phone number's on record. You can have it, as long as you don't tell him who gave it to you."

Promise delivered, I hung up and dialed Captain Forey's number. He picked up on the second ring, listened suspiciously for a moment, then perked up on hearing the phrase "multiple homicides."

"Robert Kennedy," he said, the whiskey evident in his slurred vowels, "was a miserable son-of-a-bitch. One of those cops who handles every problem by punching it in the mouth. I knew he'd get himself in deep shit, sooner or later."

"I don't want to disappoint you, Captain," I said, "but we're only in the initial stages of our investigation. Right now, I'd say it's more like we're trying to eliminate Kennedy, not convict him."

That got him going. He took a deep breath and practically screamed, "Eliminate! Try, *exterminate!* Make the goddamned world a better place for the rest of us."

"That bad?"

"Worse. The boys used to call him Boffing Bob Kennedy. He was quicker on the draw than them liberals from Massachusetts he's named after."

"You know, Captain, it sounds like he was having a ball with the APD. What made him decide to leave?"

"What happened was old Boffing Bob went a little too far one night and beat one of his concubines into the hospital. She was all set to press charges, but he managed to wriggle out of that, too."

"How?"

"He married the bitch. Married her and took off for the boonies. That's how."

"You remember her name, Captain? The one he took off with? I'd like to know if he's still married to her."

"Sure do, Detective. I spent hours tryin' to persuade the miserable whore to sign a goddamned complaint. Had to kiss her repulsive butt every five minutes. I couldn't forget her if I tried. Bitch's name was Rebecca Knott."

"Did she have a record?"

"Not a criminal record. Except for prostitution. Mostly she'd been in and out of the crazy house. Made her first visit when she was eight years old."

VICAP came on board, as promised, at five o'clock, when Agent Donovan called to announce that he'd found something interesting and was faxing it even as he spoke. Bouton had me on the way to the printer before she'd hung up the phone. There, along with a hefty bill, I found twelve pages of material and a note suggesting we analyze the top three pages first. I was tempted to read the case files on the spot, but I couldn't see any point to it beyond self-indulgence, so I took them back to the loft, dropping them in front of Bouton like a puppy dog delivering the newspaper. Bouton accepted the report solemnly, passing individual pages to me as she finished reading them.

The two homicides outlined on the first three pages were of women whose bodies had been found a hundred miles apart in deep forest. Each had died as a result of a severe beating; there were fractured bones all over their bodies. What made them relevant to Bouton's inquiry were a series of bite marks found on each body, bites on the abdomen, buttocks, and thighs. FBI forensic specialists in Quantico, after careful analysis, had concluded that the bites had been made by a woman, not a very small man.

The rest of Donovan's report involved twelve associated homicides. All the victims were women between twenty and thirty years of age. All had been found in deep forest within seventy-five miles of Owl Creek and all showed extensive bone fractures. The bodies were too badly decomposed for any soft-tissue analysis, and while the various coroners and medical examiners had declared the beatings severe enough to be the cause of death, stabbing, shooting, or even poisoning couldn't be ruled out.

Nine of the victims had been identified; of these, only one had a criminal record, and her brush with the law (a minor pot bust that'd resulted in a year's probation) had occurred six years before she'd met her death. Of these nine, an astonishing six (including both bite-mark victims) had had their disabled cars found, apparently abandoned, shortly after they'd been reported missing.

One individual, the husband of victim number eight, had been charged with murder, brought to trial, and convicted. This in New York State. An appellate court had reversed the conviction on a technicality (an expert witness for the defense hadn't been allowed to testify), and the prosecution had declined a retrial because the body had been discovered in the interim and linked with the other homicides.

"Try to imagine it, Captain," I said as soon as we'd digested the case files, "you're a woman in . . . "

"I don't have to imagine that I'm a woman, Means. No matter how difficult it is for you to admit a woman can wear captain's bars."

She was in a good mood and I was glad of it. Decision time was coming. I could feel my heart flutter as I thought about it.

"Okay, don't imagine that you're a woman. Imagine that you're yourself and your car has broken down on a small county road in the middle of nowhere. The first thing you hope is that a cop'll come by, but that doesn't happen. Then you think about walking to a pay phone, but you know they roll up the sidewalks at ten o'clock in most of the towns, and you're not at all sure you'll find anything open. Finally, a van passes, brakes, rolls to a stop. A thousand terrible thoughts flash through your mind, and for the first time, you realize just how alone you are. But then, joy of joys, the passenger door opens and a *woman* gets out. A sweet, butter-wouldn't-melt-in-her-mouth, deep-drawling, Southern lady. The last thing you think is that she's checking you out—making sure you're alone, that you're young enough to be acceptable, that you're not armed. No, that idea never crosses your mind until it's way too late. Until you're subdued and the van is speeding you to your death."

"I take it you still want to go into his house?" Bouton's voice was neutral.

"More than ever."

"Then convince me. Prove that you can pull it off without getting caught. We'll start with those topological maps you mentioned earlier. Where did you say we could buy them?"

"They're called topographical maps, Captain. We can probably get them at Eastern Outfitters on Third Avenue and Seventy-seventh Street."

"*Probably?* It wasn't *probably* a couple of hours ago."

"Don't get your back up. We can definitely buy them from Rand-McNally. As far as I know, selling maps is all they do. Only it's after seven o'clock and Rand-McNally's sure to be closed. On the other hand, it's Friday and Eastern Outfitters might be open till nine. Selling tents and sleeping bags to last-minute campers. If you want the topo maps tonight, that's our only hope."

Fortunately enough, our only hope came through, producing a bound collection of survey maps for the princely sum of thirty-seven dollars. We paid the salesman, then carried the book to an unused counter near the gun racks and began to work with it. The store manager came over, apparently to protest, but changed his mind when Bouton flashed her tin.

"Problem, sir?" Bouton asked.

"No, no. I was just wondering . . ." He slowly drifted away.

"Get on with it, Means," she said, turning back to me. "I think this guy wants to close."

The first thing I did was look up Owl Creek in the index, then turn to "Map Number 45."

"This is Owl Creek here," I said, circling it several times. "And here's the road that runs past Kennedy's private driveway." I circled that, too. "See this dotted red line? That's an unimproved road, probably an overgrown logging road. We passed it about fifty yards from Kennedy's driveway. That road's gonna be my landmark." Once again I circled vigorously. "And this little blue dot here is the actual building. Let's call it Point Zero." Another circle. "All right, now we need a hiking trail that comes within striking distance. This one here ought to do the trick. It runs up to the summit of Black Mountain. From this point on the trail, I can intersect the logging road and use that to pinpoint Kennedy's house."

"It sounds too easy."

"Captain, for you it would be impossible. But I grew up in those forests. Here, take a look at this. You see these irregular concentric ovals? Look close, they're faint."

She bent over the map for a moment, checking me out all the way. She needn't have bothered. This was one area where I didn't have to bullshit.

"Okay, I see them."

"They show changes in altitude. The fainter lines mean twenty feet of elevation from the larger to the smaller. The darker lines represent a hundred feet. Now, when you see dark ovals real close together, that means the way is very, very steep. You want to avoid that whenever you can."

"The trail goes right through those lines."

"That's because the view from the summit is spectacular and there's no way to get there without going up. But me, I don't plan to make it that far. I'm only going about half a mile on the trail, then I'm gonna cut down into the valley and follow this stream to the logging road. They intersect right over here."

"All right, enough." Bouton closed the book. "I'm convinced that you *can* do it."

"Thank you, Captain." I bowed my head. "I appreciate your confidence."

"But that doesn't mean you *should*."

I looked at her for a moment, trying to read her mind. Trying to guess what I should say next. When I couldn't think of anything really clever, I settled for the merely practical.

"I'm going to need a good deal of equipment, Captain— sleeping bag, backpack, compass, canteen. I mean, as long as we're in a sporting goods store. . . ."

She heaved a deep sigh, then shook her head. "Can you do the job in one day?"

"C'mon, Captain, how would I know when the house'll be empty? Plus, it'll take me four or five hours just to get there.

She continued to stare at me, continued to shake her head. "I may be crazy enough to do this, but not so crazy that I'll let you go by yourself. No, I'm going with you. Not into those mountains. I'm going to drive you to that hiking trail, find a decent motel, then come back every afternoon at six o'clock to pick you up. I don't want you making any side trips, no matter what you find. Is that a problem?"

"Not with me." I kept my voice calm, despite the fact that my adrenals were shooting pure electricity into my veins.

"And while you're in the woods, I'm going to have a long talk with Sheriff Pousson about Deputy Kennedy. That means you'll only have one shot at the house. Is that a problem?"

I answered by displaying my one credit card.

"The only serious problem, as far as I can see, is what we're gonna do if I don't have enough room on my Visa to pay for everything I'm gonna need."

TWENTY-SIX

I arrived back at my loft an hour and a half later. Loaded down with packages (my credit card having, in fact, held up), it was all I could do to slide the key into the lock and push the door open. I failed to notice Marie Koocek sitting in the dark until I'd closed the door and switched on the light.

"What are you doing, Means?"

"What are *you* doing, Koocek?"

"I asked you first." She was holding a piece of charcoal in her left hand, waving it like a baton. A sketch pad lying on her knees fell to the floor, landing on the heap of discarded pages scattered about her feet.

"True," I said, "but it's my loft. And right at the moment, you're the intruder."

"Intruder's not the right word. Being as you gave me a key. You might want to try 'unwelcome guest.' Or, 'material witness.'"

"Okay. Tell me what the hell you're doing, Unwelcome Material Witness."

"I'm sketching out an idea for a new piece."

"In the dark?"

Her black, Slavic eyes narrowed under heavy brows. "The ideas come from the darkness of the void, and I use the darkness to trap them in matter."

"Bullshit."

She grinned happily and stretched out, arching her back like a lazy cat. I noted her small breasts punching into the fabric of her blue T-shirt and wanted to jump her bones on the spot. There's nothing like the prospect of a good hunt to get the testosterone flowing.

"Okay, it's bullshit," she said. "What I'm doing now is very preliminary, and the streetlamp gives enough light for what I

228

want to accomplish at this stage. Besides, I like to work in the dark. It's peaceful."

I couldn't argue with that, because I also liked to work in the dark. Although I preferred a .45 to a piece of charcoal.

"What's the piece called, Koocek? *Moonbeams 'n I-beams?*"

"I'm going to call it *Crushed Bird.*"

"Oh, Jesus!" I shivered, the sensation flashing up my spine hard enough to jerk my shoulders. Marie Koocek had a way of surprising me (which might have had something to do with the fact that she was much smarter than I was), but on that particular night, she couldn't get more out of me than a single, involuntary shudder. I had better things to do. Much better.

"You all right, Means?"

"Who are you supposed to be, Sigmund Freud?"

"*Anna* Freud. If you don't mind."

There was no point in arguing with her. And no point in convicting myself of bird murder when I couldn't remember what had actually happened. If *anything* had happened. I was beginning to think the whole incident was a dream. How else could it be so vivid and not have an ending?

I crossed to the dining-room table and began to lay out my gear—heavy-duty frame backpack; wide, rectangular down sleeping bag; emergency first-aid kit; hard-soled Timberland hiking boots; waterproof, strike-anywhere matches; jellied charcoal starter (for those moments when life's choices boil down to *make a fire in the rain or die*); two plastic water bottles and a package of water purification tablets; very light, very expensive compass; camouflage T-shirt with matching wool sweater; canister of pepper spray; ten freeze-dried meals (just add boiling water and puke); hooded poncho suitable for a ground cloth; small hatchet and smaller canvas daypack; extra-large bottle of Cutter's bug juice.

"You going hunting, Means?"

"That's exactly right, Marie. I'm going hunting."

How she knew I was going hunting, since I hadn't unpacked anything resembling a weapon, didn't occur to me until she added, "Who's the lucky prey?"

That stopped me. I turned to her and said, "Do you think you could limit yourself to defaming my childhood and lay off the mind-reading act? I really want to get this right."

When I was reasonably sure she wouldn't interrupt me again, I took one of my rifles off the wall, a bolt action Anschutz 1700D. I'd given a lot of thought to just what sort of weapon I wanted to pack. My Thompson had enough power to cut down trees, but it weighed more than eleven pounds (not counting the ammo) and wasn't accurate enough for me to trust it beyond fifty yards or so. The Anschutz, on the other hand, would shoot the eyes off a mosquito at a hundred yards, but the bolt action was relatively slow and it only held five .22LR cartridges in its small clip. What I'd decided, as I'd listened to Bouton chatter on about when she was going to pick me up and what car we should use, was to carry the Detonics (on a holster and not tucked behind my belt) for close-up work and rely on the accuracy of the Anschutz to compensate for its slow rate of fire and small-caliber ammo.

I carried the rifle over to the table, then retrieved a mounted ANPVS-2 starlight scope from a cabinet built into the wall behind the couch and brought that to the table as well. Using the screwdriver blade on my Swiss army knife (which was all I'd have when I reassembled it), I removed the Anschutz's barrel and rolled up stock, barrel, scope, sling, and Detonics in the sleeping bag, then strapped the bag to the top of the backpack. The rest of the junk, except for the compass, went inside the backpack, along with several changes of underwear and three pairs of socks.

"Here's the choice, Koocek," I said, sliding a pair of very lightweight binoculars, the compass, and a Buck folding knife, each in a nylon holder, onto a heavy leather belt. "You're investigating two individuals, husband and wife, suspected of killing at least twenty-one people, mostly for the fun of it. You break into their home and find absolute proof of their guilt, but, unfortunately, you can't use this proof, because you've obtained it illegally. Now, do you replace this proof, then back out and wait a month or two until you've accumulated enough evidence to make an arrest and maybe obtain a conviction? Or, do you 'take arms against a sea of troubles' and eliminate them from the face of the fucking earth before they go out and kill again?"

She didn't answer right away. Instead, she walked across the room and laid a hand on my arm.

"You forgot the most important part," she said.

"What's that?"

"'Eliminate them from the face of the fucking earth' while loving every minute of it."

I turned to look into her eyes. We were getting to the point where there were no more secrets left. Koocek had been an institutional child, moving from foster homes to group foster homes to out-and-out orphanages.

"Whether you love it or hate it, you still have to choose, Marie. Even if the point of choice is entirely your own creation, you still have to choose. Even if you originally thought the whole deal was a piece of shit, you still have to choose."

I took the bottom of her T-shirt, pulled it over her head and halfway down, pinning her arms. She kept her eyes on mine, a quizzical half-smile playing with her lips. I rubbed the calloused heel of my right hand over her nipples, back and forth across her chest while my left hand yanked open the belt of her jeans and slid the zipper down. She began to breathe heavily, her eyes fluttering for a moment before they closed. I dropped to my knees and tugged her jeans and panties down.

"Open your legs."

She obeyed, moving them as far apart as the jeans around her ankles would allow. When I ran my finger down between the lips of her cunt, her knees buckled. She was sopping wet, her clit as hard as any male erection. I circled it with the tip of my finger, so gently the contact was almost imaginary. Her T-shirt fluttered to the floor and she pressed her hands against the back of my head.

"Lie on the couch and pull your legs up into your chest."

She was into it now, kicking her jeans away as she crossed the room. I watched her buttocks rise and fall as I followed. Already tasting them. She lay on the couch, shivering slightly at the cool touch of the leather, hesitated just a moment, then lifted her legs. I left her in that position while I slowly undressed. Until my own state of arousal was more than obvious.

"Don't move; don't make a sound."

I began with the tip of her spine, with her coccyx, working my tongue in a slow half-crescent to her navel, then made the return trip, hesitating briefly as I crossed her clit, taking her to the brink of orgasm, only to let her fall away. She lay completely still, though the muscles on her belly hardened into thin flexible ridges and her breath hissed between clenched teeth.

When I couldn't stand it anymore, when my own heat threatened to set my hair on fire, I lifted her into a sitting position with her ass on the very edge of couch, then knelt in front of her and pushed inside. That was the end of the self-control, the end of the game. Somehow, I found myself on the floor with Marie pounding into my crotch, determined to get what she wanted. Her breasts danced above my blurry eyes as she leaned into it; they bobbed madly. I watched drops of sweat roll from her throat down across her breasts and nipples to fall on my face. At the very end, as I slid into oblivion, I heard a scream that I thought was hers, then knew to be my own.

We slept and fucked and slept and fucked, until it was six o'clock and time for me to get into the shower. Marie crawled in after me, bleary-eyed. We took turns soaping each other, but neither of us had the heart for any more sex. Or for any superfluous talk. After we'd toweled off, I went back to the living room, double-checking every item in the backpack, then taping my heels and toes to avoid the otherwise inevitable new-shoe blisters.

At seven-thirty, the buzzer from the lobby sounded. It was Bouton come to pick me up. I told her I'd be down in a minute, then turned back to Marie.

"Did you make a choice?" I asked. "Did you choose for me?"

"What difference does it make? You've already made up your mind."

"Not true, Marie. All this?" I raised the backpack. "Well, as the Boy Scouts say, it ain't smart to go into the forest unprepared. But as for what I'm actually going to do? I haven't gotten to the point where I have to choose. Until I get in the house and actually find something, it's all hypothetical."

She gripped my arm as I opened the door, her fingers digging into my bicep. "You be careful, Means. I don't need you dead. Or in jail."

I turned to go, but she pulled me back again. "You have to take arms against a sea of troubles, Means," she hissed. "You *have* to. There's no glory in submission."

TWENTY-SEVEN

You see how it is, **Lorraine Cho** thought, just when nature seems to be forcing you to make a decision, nature forces you to stay right where you are. In purgatory.

The pain of purgatory was alive in her belly. She had already given it a name; she called it Betty. After Betty Compton, who made her first-grade reputation by punching her fellow first graders in the stomach. Betty did this so often and to so many children that after a while she became a kind of force of nature. An earthquake or a volcano, to be avoided whenever possible, to be endured when there was no other choice.

Lorraine saw her hunger as a force of nature. Relentless, it acted on blind instinct, pounding at her viscera until she bent over, clutching her belly, trying to push it back inside. Which didn't make a whole lot of sense, because it was killing her right where it was. Better to let Betty out. Better to let Betty punch someone *else* in the stomach.

Lorraine heard the rain pound on the cabin roof and smiled bitterly. An image popped into her mind, a pompous politico in a top hat. Pronouncing the nostrum: *Something Must Be Done About Betty*. But there was only one something to be done and that was to find a way out of this wilderness. So why, after a week of bright sunshine and warm temperatures, was it raining like hell?

She remembered a beer commercial that asked the same question over and over again: "Why ask why?"

Because Betty was eating her alive. Because, for the ten thousandth time since this nightmare began, she was telling herself that she had to do something. Because she didn't believe she could survive in that rain. Because Becky wasn't coming, today or tomorrow or tomorrow or tomorrow.

She heard a set of claws scrabble across the floorboards. Her friend. Not a rat, of course. Not even a teeny-weeny mouse. Lorraine pictured a furry brown chipmunk. All ready to sing its falsetto song. And why not? Are the blind to be allowed no advantages? Not one?

"Sorry, Alvin," she said, "no dinner, yet. Maybe no dinner, ever."

Once again, the rattle of tiny claws. Then silence. Lorraine took up the pitcher and drank. The warm water hit her stomach, found the accommodations unsuitable, came right back up.

The force of the retching drove Lorraine to her knees. Her stomach heaved again and again. Heaved until bitter acid burned into her sinuses and down through her nose.

She stayed on her knees for a while, then sipped at the water, rinsed her mouth, sipped again. Finally, she got up the courage to swallow.

This time it stayed down, and amazingly enough, she felt better. The pain disappeared, and with it her preoccupation with hunger and food. She listened to the rain outside, thought she heard a car's motor in the distance, shook her head in disbelief. Then she was sure.

Panic. Her whole body shook before she could pull herself together. Before she told herself that it was time to act. That there were no more decisions to make. She stumbled across the room, retrieved the bag of rocks, hurried over to the door.

"Please, Lord," she said, her prayer as fervent as that of a cloistered nun, "let it be Becky. Becky alone. Please don't let it be Daddy. Please, Lord, please."

She twisted away from the door, twisted at the waist, allowing the greatest possible arc to her swing. Telling herself to strike as soon as the door opened, before Becky's eyes adjusted to the interior shadows.

The sound of the engine grew louder, roared into the clearing around the cabin, suddenly shut down. A door creaked on its hinges, then slammed shut. Footsteps slapped into the mud; hands rattled the padlock on the cabin door.

"Oh, Lord above, Lorraine. Things have just been so awful. Daddy and I have been driving for days and days, but we have had no damn luck at all. I swear I thought Daddy was going to kill me, but I said, 'Daddy, we should go back and get our little girl. Remember how much good luck she brought when we took her driving? We should just go back and take her with us. Then our luck will change.'"

The lock snapped open and dropped to the ground. Becky grunted, the sound rising as she straightened up.

Lorraine took a deep breath, prayed that she was not frozen in place, heard the door open, knew her life was on the line. That this was her first, last, and only chance.

"I have got a wonderful lamb stew for . . ."

Lorraine swung with all her might. Willing the rocks toward the sound of Becky's voice. The impact of rock on bone ran through her arms, rattled into her shoulders. Packages crashed to the floor, followed by the solid thud of a body.

Silence for a moment, then a long, drawn-out groan.

I've got to kill her, Lorraine thought, stepping through the doorway. I can't let her get up.

But she didn't strike until Becky began to move. Until fear propelled her into action. This time the force of the blow snapped her improvised sling, scattering rocks across the yard. She dropped to her knees, feeling about until one hand found a large stone while the other found Becky's unconscious body.

"Do it," she said aloud. "Don't think about it. Do it. Do it. Do it."

But the sound was too much for her. The sound of a stone crashing into the skull of a helpless human being. That first *crunch* and the trickle of blood that would surely follow. She could not bring herself to strike again.

Lorraine sat back on her heels. Realizing that the tears running down her cheeks echoed the cold rain falling on her hair and shoulders. She was suddenly hungry, suddenly ravenous; she cast about for the dropped package, found a plastic bag and felt the warm food and broken dish inside.

Her fingers tore at the bag even as she backed into the shelter of the cabin. The effort to separate the bits of meat and vegetable from the broken dish left her shaking. She knew, dimly, that she had to prepare to flee, that she could not wait for Daddy. Knew, too, that she'd better not eat everything. Knew it even as she pushed the last scrap into her mouth, as she tore at the apple, the slice of pie. Even as she turned the plastic bag inside out to get at the spilled gravy.

She finally rose, crossed to the water jug. The pain in her belly was gone; now she must face the rain and the forest. Unlikely as it seemed, even to her, she was suddenly calm and purposeful. Feeling as if she'd accomplished something for the first time in her life. Feeling like a four-year-old who's just recited the alphabet to her doting parents.

The water slid down her throat, sat comfortably in her stomach. She felt her strength returning and wondered if she was strong enough to take the next step. The cold rain made that step unavoidable, though not necessarily easier.

"What cannot be cured," she muttered.

Lorraine walked to the doorway, squatted, grabbed Becky's feet, dragged her inside the cabin. She reached for the zipper of Becky's jacket, but her hands strayed to Becky's throat, finding a pulse. Lorraine was relieved and frightened at the same time. Knowing that if Becky revived before she, Lorraine, could escape . . .

Knowing, too, that she could not kill.

"What cannot be cured," she repeated.

The job turned out to be harder than she'd envisioned. Becky's jacket and sweatshirt were soaked with rain, and with blood. The body was curiously fluid, seeming to flow away from Lorraine's grasp as she rolled it over, tugged the jacket off, yanked the sweatshirt over the bloody head.

"Ignore the gore," Lorraine muttered, then broke into a laugh. Thinking, I *can't* be doing this.

But the weight of the soggy sweatshirt on her own flesh was too real to be part of any dream. The weight and the shiver that followed reminded her that she had no time to waste in idle speculation.

Becky's worn sneakers came off easily, but the jeans were another problem altogether, and Lorraine pulled Becky halfway across the cabin before they slid off in her hands. She stepped into them, yanked the zipper up, snapped the top closed. The jeans were tight, very tight, but in a way, that was good. At least she wouldn't have to hold them up. The sneakers were more important, anyway, and the sneakers fit.

Fully dressed, Lorraine wrapped a blanket around her shoulders and picked up the stick she once intended to use as a spear. Of course, she could still use it for that purpose. She could drive it into Becky's unprotected chest, into her belly.

Becky moaned once, then fell silent. The sound echoed in the little cabin, echoed in the rain outside. Lorraine, purposeful again, found her way through the door, remembered to replace the padlock, groped her way to the van. The keys were in the ignition, and she pocketed them before beginning a systematic search of the vehicle.

She found tools and, of all things, an utterly useless flashlight and a stack of equally useless maps wrapped in a rubber band. But no food, no knife or gun.

Sitting in the back of the van, she remembered her last ride, the screams, the hollow thump when Daddy shoved the body out onto the ground.

Time to go. To step out into the unknown, the unknowable. A solitary figure driven through a shadowy forest. Branches clutched at her face; animals stalked her in . . .

Don't give in to it, she reminded herself. Don't surrender to self-pity and fear. If you wanted to surrender, you could have stayed where you were. No, think about what Daddy will do if he gets his hands around your throat. Think of dying slowly. Think of that woman in the van and decide not to share her fate. Better to stumble over the edge of a cliff.

Nevertheless, as she stepped out into the rain, she recalled a painting seen long ago in a museum. A bent, wizened monk struggled to cross an endless, empty plain. There was no water, no trees, just a few blades of dry grass and a sky filled with angry clouds. The painting was entitled *The Inexorable Winds of Karma*, which seemed to have no connection to her situation, because her only break was the lack of wind. The rain was falling straight down.

But it's not, she knew, the literal scene that brought this painting to mind. That small figure, that monk with his wispy beard and hunched back, had seemed so alone, so lost, so help-less, that his silhouette had burned its way into her memory, whereas the rest of the exhibit had been long forgotten.

She felt that loneliness now. Or, rather, that aloneness. She could not expect any help, couldn't call on the community of human beings. The forest awaited her, ancient and implacable; she had to cross it, driven by the inexorable wind of her captors' insanity.

"Stop feeling sorry for yourself," she said again. "Pay attention."

And, a few minutes later, she had to admit that it was not as bad as she expected. At least not yet. She found the track with-out much difficulty, two ruts with a hump in the middle. If she followed it faithfully, she'd come out at the other end. Come out into that community of human beings she'd denied a few min-utes before. It was that simple.

Cold at first, she began by shivering. Only to find that as the rain penetrated the two blankets, the jacket, the shirt, her body warmed the moisture next to her skin until the chills dimin-ished, then disappeared altogether.

Only the uncertainty remained to cloud her concentration as she slipped, fell, struggled to her feet, continued forward. She had no real sense of how far she'd come or how far she had to go. In New York, she could measure the blocks, the intersections, but nobody had cut this wilderness into neat rectangles. The best she could say was that the track ran downhill, though even that wasn't accurate, because it switched back and forth to avoid the steeper slopes. A fact she learned by nearly stepping off the edge of a cliff.

She stopped right there, stopped to rest and remind herself to be careful. If it hadn't been for her improvised white cane, she'd have become the proverbial rolling stone. Gathering no moss until she reached bottom, where she'd gather moss until she rotted away to nothing. To bones and a few wisps of hair.

In the distance she heard a pair of crows calling back and forth, a jay screaming from the safety of a tree, a songbird still closer. But nothing remotely human.

She thought of her parents in ultra-civilized Forest Hills, with its carefully maintained apartments and private homes. Wondering if they'd given up hope, if they were in mourning. Of course, they'd already been to the police, but how could the police help? If someone had seen her kidnapping, if they'd gotten a license plate number, the police would have rescued her long before this. No, what they'd done was search the abandoned tenements, the vacant lots, put up posters: MISSING, LORRAINE CHO, 5'4" TALL, 109 LBS., BLIND, REWARD FOR INFORMATION LEADING TO. . . .

"I hope," she said to the rain, "they at least used a cute photograph."

Time passed. How much time she couldn't say, because she couldn't mark the sun's progress by the feel of its warmth on her flesh. But in a way, she thought, that was an advantage. She could travel equally well by day or night, her only limitation being the strength in her limbs and her ability to concentrate. In fact, if she could tell light from dark, she'd lay up in the daytime and travel exclusively by night.

Because sooner or later Daddy was going to come roaring up the road in search of his darling wife. That was the rub, of course, the fly in the ointment. After Daddy found Becky, Daddy would come looking for Lorraine. At which point Lorraine would be forced to abandon the road, to hide until . . .

Until when? Until all danger had passed? How would she know when all danger had passed? Because *all* Daddy would need to do is sit at the end of the road and wait until Lorraine stumbled by.

"What cannot be cured," she said aloud. Then she heard the growl of an engine.

She stood stock still, confused by the forest-muffled sound, but then she knew it was coming from in front of her. That it was Daddy roaring up to rescue his loving wife. Or to beat her to death for screwing things up.

Despite all her mental preparation, Lorraine panicked; she staggered away from the path, tripping over an exposed root, tumbling down a steep hillside, smashing against rocks and trees, hitting absolute dead zero bottom.

TWENTY-EIGHT

The best defense being a good offense, I'd prepared a diversionary tactic for Captain Bouton. She was standing beside me in the rain when I dumped the backpack into the trunk, looking grumpy and doubtful, which is exactly what I'd expected. With a little more street experience, she'd have *known* that she couldn't trust me out of her sight. As it was, she'd spent a long night with her suspicions and needed some soothing.

"I want you to take a look at this and make a decision, Captain," I said, handing her a large shopping bag. "While we're driving."

I didn't bother to wait for her reaction, because I was pretty sure what that reaction would be. I pulled the car away from the curb and began to make my way along Vernon Boulevard toward Astoria and the Triborough Bridge as fast as the early morning traffic would allow.

"Is this what I think it is?" She held up a piece of electronic equipment the size of a playing card.

"It's a transmitter, Captain. And the box contains a receiver and a tape recorder. The tape recorder is voice activated and can hold eight full hours of conversation. The box, by the way, is weatherproof. It could sit in those woods for ten years without any damage to what's inside."

"And what do you want to do with it?" Her voice was as cold as the rain pounding on the windshield.

"Look, Captain, don't take it the wrong way. I'm only offering a possibility. And what I said last night still holds true. I'm not going to make any moves on my own." I paused to let the message penetrate. "I can plant this where nobody will find it and come back to pick it up a week or a month later. I can bug the phone, too. I mean we're not dealing with the KGB here. Kennedy will never suspect, and even if he does, his kind of search won't find anything. Not unless he's a lot more sophisticated than he looks."

My only purpose was to throw her off the track. (I didn't, for instance, want her to exorcise the fear-demons by checking my gear.) She was supposed to dismiss the proposal out of hand. But that wasn't the way it went down, which was all to the good as far as I was concerned. We got into a long conversation about how I'd conceal the bugs (in the ceiling, behind the wallboard, in the base of a lamp) and how I'd retrieve them (I wouldn't) and what we'd do with what we got.

"The way I see it," Bouton said as we picked our way through the Bronx, "you're going in there for two reasons, to save us a little time by making sure Kennedy's actually involved, and to avoid the attention of the task force. I don't see the point of gathering evidence."

"Suppose I don't find anything."

"Look, Means, while you're in the woods, I'm going to be talking with the sheriff. If . . . "

"Get him to come to you."

"What?"

"Don't walk into the sheriff's office. Two visits within a week and Kennedy's gonna know he's a suspect. Get Pousson to come to you. If you can."

"I think we've been over this already." She fished a tissue out of her purse and blew her nose loudly. "Can we get back to the subject at hand?"

"Sure."

"Bugging the house gets us exactly nothing. Nothing we can use in a courtroom, anyway. You . . . Jesus Christ!"

As she was talking, an ancient Cadillac flew by us on the left, hit a puddle of water, then hydroplaned across four lanes of traffic to smash into the guard rail. An enormous eighteen-wheeler turned sharply to avoid the Caddy, began to jackknife, then came back under control. In the rearview mirror, I saw the guy in the Cadillac, a middle-aged, nearly bald man, jump out of his car and begin to kick the tires.

"Is he hurt?" Bouton asked, twisting around to get a better look.

"I hope so."

We made it through Yonkers without any further conversation. Bouton stared straight ahead, fascinated, apparently, with the windshield wipers. The rain was falling steadily, a genuine spring soaker that held the promise of real persistence.

"You sure you're going to be able to handle this, Means? In this fog? Isn't it bound to be worse in the mountains?"

"The wetter, the better. Bad weather means fewer people on that trail. I don't want anybody around when I take to the woods."

"What if you miss the stream?"

"If I miss that stream, you can figure on meeting me in Canada."

"I'm serious."

"The stream is at the bottom of the valley, Captain. It's surrounded by steep slopes. As long as I don't do something really stupid, like climb *over* the mountain, I have to hit it."

Thus reassured, she didn't say anything else until after we'd crossed the Tappen Zee Bridge. Then she let loose with a peremptory snort.

"Forget the bugs, Means. The idea's stupid. First of all, nothing those tapes pick up can be used as evidence. Second, even if you leave the hardware in the house, you have to go back to retrieve the tapes. Third, if Kennedy goes out to kill again, I don't want to hear it on tape after he's finished. Fourth, should Kennedy find those bugs, they'll compromise any case we make against him." She shook her head vigorously. "I don't see any up side at all. Not a glimmer."

I shrugged my shoulders and let it go at that. Bouton seemed preoccupied, anyway, which was just fine with me. I'd been describing my cross-country trek, from the hiking trail to the old logging road, as a stroll through Central Park. The truth was that I was going to bushwhack, in the rain, through five miles of dense forest with approximately forty pounds of gear on my back. I never doubted myself (didn't, for instance, spend a minute thinking about what would happen to me if I slipped and broke a leg); I knew I could do it. But I also understood the effort required. I'd be lucky to make it in under six hours.

Even with our leaving New York early and me pressing seventy-five miles an hour (the Dodge had a pronounced left-hand pull, adding a tension of its own to the journey), I wouldn't get started on the main event before two o'clock. Add six hours to that and it'd be near sundown by the time I got to Kennedy's house, which would have been all right on a fine sunny day. In the rain, however . . .

We had breakfast on the Thruway, slimy eggs and cold, soggy bacon. The Thruway being far more cosmopolitan than Owl Creek, our fellow diners confined their reactions to quick disapproving glances. Bouton was oblivious anyway, forking her breakfast into her mouth with robotic precision.

Fork, chew, swallow; fork, chew, swallow; fork, chew, swallow.

Finally, I couldn't stand it anymore. "Captain," I said, cursing myself for a fool, "is something wrong? You don't seem to be your bright, cheery self this morning."

She looked up at me, taking a deep breath.

"Lydia's gone," she said.

"Who? What?"

Her eyes blazed. "Lydia Singleton," she repeated, very, very slowly.

"Oh, you mean . . . " I almost said, "Dolly Dope," catching myself at the last second.

"Yeah, *that's* who I mean."

"So, what happened?" The question was strictly for the record.

"She walked out of the rehab center last night. Nobody knows where she is, and now there's nobody to go look for her. I was up all night deciding whether or not to cancel this trip."

"You were gonna do that for a fucking dope addict?" Now, my eyes were blazing, too. As a cop, you deal with the insanity of the streets every day. You get used to that insanity, adjust your tactics in deference to it. But you don't expect it from your partner, even if she *has* spent her career with her lips pressed to her superiors' buttocks.

Bouton passed the next couple of minutes trying to hard-look me into submission. When that didn't work, she got up, turned her back and marched off toward the door. Leaving me no choice but to follow.

The rest of the trip was conducted in silence. Bouton fumed, and I kept my big mouth shut even though my anger had dissipated almost as quickly as it had come. In truth, I'd been feeling a little guilty about deceiving Bouton (as I said, it'd come to the point where I actually liked her), but her attitude absolved me of all responsibility. I could not have told her the truth, could not have confided in her. Kennedy and spouse were prime suspects in nearly two dozen homicides. That should have been enough to make her forget the very existence of Dolly Dope. Add the possibility that the two of us, acting against the collective wisdom of the largest task force ever assembled (not to mention the FBI), had a decent chance to solve the crime all by our little selves, and Bouton's concern for a junkie prostitute bordered on the obsessive. I felt like ratting her out to Miriam Brock.

We arrived at the trailhead just before one o'clock. I shut down the engine and stared at the little sign with its red arrow: "Black Mountain Lookout, 7.3 miles."

"Well, we're here," Bouton said.

"Clever observation, Captain." The rain had slackened, but the mist was denser than ever, an iron-gray curtain that transformed the closer trees into stately ghosts. The ones farther away were invisible altogether.

Bouton ignored the dig. "I can't believe you're going into that. It looks like the end of the world."

"You should see it in winter."

I got out, walked around back, and opened the trunk. Despite my impatience, I went through the drill carefully. Knowing that if I made a mistake, the forest would not forgive me. The leather belt with its various attachments—knife, compass, pepper spray, hatchet, binoculars—came out first. I cinched it around my waist, noting its heft. Then I removed the poncho, slipped my arms into the backpack's shoulder strap, and heaved it up onto my shoulders.

It was heavy; I can't deny it. I hadn't carried this much weight since Vietnam. But after I'd tightened the hip straps and taken some of the load off my shoulders, it became supportable. I slid the poncho over my head, then struggled to pull it down over the backpack.

"Give me a hand, Captain. I'm getting forgetful in my old age. You're supposed to put it on from back to front."

She yanked the poncho down over the backpack, then came around to face me. "You be careful, Means." Her tone said she meant it, but it wasn't the time for reconciliations or farewells. The forest was singing to me. I believe the song was "Embraceable You." But it could just as easily have been "Helter Skelter."

"If I'm not back in three days, Captain, send in the troops."

That was it. No hugs, no tears. I could feel the mist closing around me as I marched off. Caressing me as gently as a mother caressing a fragile child. I told myself to be purposeful. Told myself that I had a job to do. But I couldn't shake off the feeling that I'd come home. And that I was welcome.

Somewhere in the distance, a cardinal sang his mating song, a complex series of sharp metallic whistles that trailed off hopefully. I looked for him in the trees and he appeared right on cue, swooping down to light on a branch overhanging the trail. He cocked his head to get a good look at me, then sang again, listened to a second cardinal's challenge, and flew away.

I marched off, stepping over the muddier patches, using exposed roots and rocks to gain purchase. The forest rose up on both sides, a mixture of beech and maples, tamarack and spruce, with here and there a thick stand of northern hemlock. The hardwoods were still in the process of spring renewal, their half-formed leaves yellow-green and nearly transparent. The evergreens looked like they'd been there forever.

Twenty minutes later, after a steep climb, I made the jumping-off point, an enormous boulder that projected over the edge of the mountain. It was supposed to serve as a lookout, inspiring hikers to continue on up to the summit. But for me, standing at the edge, looking over the crowns of the tallest trees, my inspiration came from that seemingly impenetrable gray curtain. I wanted to disappear inside it, to embrace my invisibility.

How many times had I fled, terrified, into the forest? How many times had the forest taken me under its wing, hiding me, feeding me, protecting me? I sat on the rock and leaned up against the backpack, letting the rain wash over me. There was work to be done, and time was pressing, but I intended to enjoy my welcome, even if it meant spending an extra day in the woods. Human time had no meaning here anyway. I was the prodigal idiot, wondering why I'd stayed away all those years when the only thing awaiting me was a feast. How could I have been so stupid?

I don't know how long I sat there, but when I finally heaved myself up, my jeans were soaked. Not that I'd had any hope of keeping them dry. But their weight seemed to root me in the job I had to do. I backed off the overlook, found a spot where the slope was tenable, and stepped off.

The trip to Kennedy's was going to be simple enough, even though my progress would be slow and painstaking. With landmarks like the stream and the abandoned logging road, there was no way I could miss the mark. Getting back, on the other hand, would present me with a serious problem. I had to make sure I left the stream exactly where I'd come onto it. If I missed the hiking trail, Bouton *would* be picking me up in Canada.

That's what the hatchet was for. I didn't need it to chop down trees for firewood. There was more than enough deadfall to cook my food (assuming I could bring myself to eat that freeze-dried doggie chow) and keep me toasty warm. The hatchet was there to blaze a trail from the jumping-off point to the stream, a trail I could follow back.

It wasn't a very complicated procedure. An arrow chopped into the side of a tree pointing to an arrow chopped into the side of tree pointing to another . . . But encased by a poncho, with forty pounds of gear on my back and another five strapped to my waist, it definitely came under the heading of hard work, and I was pouring sweat before I got two hundred yards down the slope.

Not that I minded. I needed to ground myself in the present, and there's nothing like smacking a hatchet into the side of a tree while standing on a steep, muddy slope to focus your attention on the task at hand. Then, too, the way was anything but straight. Fallen trees and sheer cliffs forced me to change direction again and again, to at times work back up the slope. A map of my progress would have resembled a kid's connect-the-dots puzzle.

It took me an hour and a half to reach the pounding, foaming torrent that'd looked so innocent on the map. The stream was only thirty feet wide, and probably no more than a couple of feet deep for most of its course, but swollen with rain and snowmelt, it roared over the boulders with mind-boggling intensity, reaching out to flood the dense brush and thick stands of birch and aspen lining its banks.

Too bad. In summer it'd be little more than a trickle, and I'd be able to make the streambed into my own little highway. Now, I'd have to trudge through the forest, relying on my ears to stay in contact while I worked my way around obstacles. But that's not what bothered me. There was every possibility that, at some point, the stream brushed up against a wall of solid rock. A cliff that couldn't be climbed or circled. Should that happen, I'd have to enter the water, and if the stream should drop off into a gorge at the same time . . .

My worst-case scenario never happened. I did have to cross the stream twice, working my way from rock to rock while the stream yanked at my legs like a demented crocodile. I lost my balance several times, hugging boulders, my face covered with foam, until I got my feet back underneath me. I should have been afraid, but I wasn't; I just couldn't bring myself to believe the forest would turn against me. As far as I was concerned, that wilderness was as alive as it had been to my Indian ancestors. I'd spent years placating the spirits that called it home. Paying them homage until I won their respect. And their trust.

I made the logging road in just under six hours. From there, it was another fifteen minutes to Kennedy's house. I didn't approach the house directly, because I didn't want the dogs to sound an alarm. Instead, I skirted the house on the downhill side, then climbed a slope to the east, finally coming to an enormous rock outcropping. What I was hoping for, and what I found, was a cut along the bottom where rain and wind had washed the soil away. In a billion years or so, the weather would eat away so much soil that the rock would tumble down onto Kennedy's roof, but at this point there was just enough room for me to get myself and my gear out of the rain and still keep an eye on the prize.

The first thing I did was drop that backpack and groan like an adolescent who'd just discovered the joy of orgasm. I'd carried heavy loads over a distance of ground before. (And not only in Vietnam; I'd packed fifty pounds of deer meat from the depths of the Adirondack Park on many occasions.) But that had been a long time ago, and despite all my efforts to stay in shape, the last mile had been strictly grit-your-teeth-and-bear-it.

I took a few minutes to enjoy my relatively weightless state, then got to work. It was nearly dark, and though the rain had slackened to a drizzle, the sky was blanketed with low, black clouds. More by feel than by sight, I attached barrel, scope, and sling to the Anschutz, slapped in a clip and left it, along with the .45, where I could reach it in a hurry. Then I went off into the woods, found a stand of white pine, and cut enough branches to make a mattress.

By the time I was satisfied with my accommodations, it was cold and rapidly getting colder. That was all to the good, in a way; the morning would see clearing skies and bright sunshine. But right then, with the wind picking up, my legs and feet were about to become inanimate objects. I'd already pulled on the wool sweater, but I hadn't packed an extra pair of jeans. And, of course, I couldn't make a fire. Not within sight of Kennedy's den.

I stripped off my boots, socks, and jeans, then wriggled into the goose-down sleeping bag. I'd chosen a down bag because it was much lighter than a more appropriate, flannel-lined summer bag, but now I was glad for its warmth, two wrongs, in this case, having made a right. And I was glad, too, that I'd finished the business end of my journey and could now get on with the pleasure. Kennedy's cruiser was parked in front of the house, and I imagined him sitting down to a quick dinner, then heading out to finish his shift. When he didn't, when two hours passed with no sign of him, I knew that something was wrong. Animals, predators included, don't alter their patterns, unless something drives them to it. What frightened me, as I chewed a mouthful of seeds, nuts, and raisins, was the near conviction that Bouton had made a premature move and that Kennedy, having gotten wind of it, was busy destroying evidence.

But there was nothing outside of a full-scale, frontal assault that I could do about it. And maybe it didn't matter anyway. At some point, Kennedy and I were going to have a long, pointed conversation, after which I'd know everything I needed to know.

TWENTY-NINE

It was still dark when I woke up, but a nearly full moon cast a pale light through high lacy clouds that flew across the night sky, obscuring, then revealing, a jet-black dome filled with thousands of sharply etched stars. I sat up and listened to the wind dance through the forest, whistling, whining, roaring, as it ebbed and flowed. I could feel it in my own body, feel it dance through my flesh as if the muscles that powered my bones had no more resistance than the leaves on the trees. It was a purely physical sensation, yet so overwhelming as to brush aside all resistance. I surrendered completely, feeling my breath as the wind, the wind as my breath. It didn't last very long, but for those few minutes, the past disappeared, and I was left without time or place. I was left in peace.

Then a bobcat screamed from across the valley, announcing his existence and the territory he was prepared to defend. A second cat answered from somewhere up on the mountain behind me. No life without opposition, he said. Your enemies define you.

I lay back on the sleeping bag and closed my eyes. I'd been dreaming just before I awakened, and while I couldn't remember the dream, I remembered the event that had inspired it. I was twelve years old, old enough to have grown careless, and stupid enough to disrespect Mother Nature. To be deep in the forest in mid-September without taking the precautions necessary to survive an early autumn snowstorm. When the large, wet flakes began to fall, I immediately turned for home, but when the wind picked up, when it began to howl, I knew I wasn't going to get there. I also knew that my life depended on making a fire, a clear impossibility.

The only good thing I can say about my own stupidity was that I didn't lay down and die. I stumbled through the snow, looking for something, though I couldn't have said what it was. Eventually, through sheer persistence, I came upon a pile of enormous boulders perched on the edge of a steep slope. Roughly square in shape, they sat on top of each other as if they'd originally been of one piece, then cracked like an ice cube in a glass of hot water. Down at the bottom, where several boulders met and the whole mass rested on solid bedrock, I found a deep depression. High and rounded at the top, it looked like a niche cut for a plaster saint.

Though I didn't (even in my own mind) qualify for sainthood, I was smart enough to recognize salvation when I saw it. And inspired enough to gather firewood, make that first fire, and keep it going throughout the night. To, in other words, survive.

Years later, I read Jack London's short story "To Build a Fire" and remembered my own brush with the brutal indifference of the natural world. I'd been no better prepared then London's character, and had no more right to walk away from the consequences of my arrogance. But not only had I walked away, I'd been thrilled by the proximity of death. I didn't stay home and count my blessings (dear old mom made sure of that); I continued to push the limits, knowing that a serious mistake—a broken leg, for instance, or a bad concussion—could easily result in my death.

I sat up and cleared the sleep from my eyes. Kennedy's house, surrounded by a thin mist and haloed by moonlight, seemed peaceful enough, but when I surveyed the yard through the nightscope, I discovered that his dogs had been tied to extremely long leads at the back of the house. There was no sign of any shelter for them, and no way they could have survived if they'd been exposed to the elements on a regular basis. So what were they doing out there in the middle of the night? And why were they in the *back* of the house?

The cruiser was gone, but there was a second car parked next to the van, Kennedy's ancient brown Toyota. I glanced down at my watch. It was five o'clock, time enough to find a safe place to make a fire and boil up some breakfast. Or it would have been if I'd remembered to bring a pot.

So much for Pathfinder. I settled for a meal of trail mix and water, but I didn't get to eat my breakfast in peace. A red squirrel, his tufted ears pointing straight up, chattered and squeaked at me from the branch of a tree. On impulse, I tossed a handful of seeds and nuts onto the ground. Sure enough, the little bastard flew out of the tree, grabbed an almond, then darted back into the branches before consuming his prize.

After watching the squirrel make several trips, I used all my knowledge of the natural world to reach the obvious conclusion that the beast had been fed by humans before. Squirrels don't have large territories, and there was no other house nearby. Therefore . . .

I think I would have done nearly anything to postpone climbing out of my nice warm sleeping bag and into that cold, wet denim. Anything except refuse to answer nature's call. When I got back, the sun was coming up behind me, and somebody had turned on a light in the Kennedy house. I looked down at my watch again. Six o'clock, awful early for someone who'd worked until after midnight.

Of course, it might have been the wife, Rebecca, getting ready to go to work, but I'd been under the impression that she was a housewife. She'd certainly acted the part when Bouton and I had paid our visit. I fished the binoculars out of their nylon pouch and focused on the window, expecting to find a half-naked woman putting on her makeup. What I saw was Robert Kennedy standing with his back to the window, gesticulating wildly. His arms waved like the wings of a wet chicken trying to escape a rabid weasel.

I started to collect my gear, thinking I'd move in for a closer look, when the dogs began to bark furiously. That, in itself, didn't strike me as peculiar (any small animal, not to mention bear and deer, could have set them off), but when Kennedy, shotgun in hand, came racing into the backyard, I began to get the picture.

The dogs had been tied outside in order to give an early warning. Kennedy was clearly expecting some kind of a threat, and he was convinced it would come from within the forest and not from the road, which virtually eliminated any chance that he was anticipating the arrival of the police.

I watched him march across the yard and into the woods. A few minutes later, he reappeared, kicked both dogs, then went back into the house.

Sitting there, well-concealed behind a stand of paper birch, I began to collect the things I'd need. First the belt with all its dangling tools, including the Detonics. I cinched it around my waist, then took the small daypack and shoved a bottle of water, the first-aid kit, a box of matches, the bug juice, and the trail mix inside. The rifle came next. I checked the clip, removed the bolt, sighted along the barrel, checked the batteries on the nightscope, put it back together.

I did it all as fast as I could, because just as Kennedy's back door closed behind him, I'd come to a sudden realization, a realization that stuck with me even while my brain screamed that it was only a possibility. And a remote possibility at that.

Suppose a victim had escaped and run blindly into the woods? Or suppose a victim had simply escaped. If the woman (and I had to assume it was a woman) had run out into the road, Kennedy's goose would be cooked. He could only hope that she, for whatever reason, had taken to the woods. But if that was the case, what made him think she'd come back the way she'd gone? And why, now that the sun was up, wasn't he out looking for her?

That question was answered a few minutes later when Kennedy and wife came out of the house (Kennedy still carrying the shotgun), jumped into the van, and tore around to the backyard where they disappeared into a seemingly impenetrable stand of red spruce.

I got up, slipped the binoculars into their pouch and the Anschutz over my shoulder, then abandoned my position. I could almost hear Bouton demanding that I stick to the formula. That I go into the house, search it, then get out. Following Kennedy would entail a serious risk of discovery. For all I knew, he might be camped a hundred yards away. And I had no doubt that if I was right and he was searching for a victim, he wouldn't hesitate to kill me. Kill me and bury my body somewhere out in that wilderness.

So why wasn't I afraid? Why was I so excited that my hands were literally trembling, my lips pulled apart in an almost gleeful smile? Why did I need all my self-control just to keep from breaking into a run?

I circled the yard, rousing the dogs to a frenzy. They growled, snarled, and whined at the end of their chains, desperate to sink their teeth into my flesh. I was tempted to give them a shot of pepper spray, but there was no point to it. They couldn't get at me, and what I wanted had nothing to do with them.

My objective was the pine grove at the back of the yard. It had seemed impenetrable from my lookout several hundred yards away, but I discovered just enough room between the trees to hide a well-used dirt track. I was tempted to stay with it, to take advantage of its relatively smooth surface, but the chance of an ambush was too great. I knew I had to skirt it, to remain out of sight, yet still close enough to hear that van if it came back down the mountain.

The track basically followed the ridge line, cutting back and forth because the slope was too steep for a head-on assault. Ideally, I would have kept to the uphill side. Staying above the track would give me a good view of anyone coming down, but the switchbacks made that impossible.

Still, I remained as close to the road as possible, moving from trees to brush to rock—anything to provide cover. My adrenals were pumping steadily, demanding that I speed up, an urge I resisted mightily. I'd learned the haste-makes-waste lesson in Vietnam. Also the one about fools rushing in. I maintained a slow, steady pace, pausing to sweep the higher ridges from time to time.

Half an hour later, I came upon a rushing stream, the same one I'd followed the day before. The van was nowhere in sight, but the track led right to the edge of the water, then continued on the other side. Even with four-wheel drive, I couldn't understand how Kennedy had made it through until I got close enough to examine the streambed. It was covered with small, closely packed rocks, and very shallow. Fifty yards upstream, a beaver dam held back enough water to make the stream passable. I remembered skirting the dam and the pond, but I hadn't noticed the shallow stretch of water coming out of it.

I stopped for a minute to admire Kennedy's skill and determination. The track hadn't shown up on my topo maps (it would have made my life a good deal easier if it had), which meant that Kennedy had mapped and cut it himself. There was no way he could have cleared any stretch of heavy forest, not without a bulldozer, so he'd taken advantage of the terrain at every turn. Fording the stream just below the beaver dam was one example. In other places, he'd cut individual trees, then used the trunks to fill the low, swampy sections. And he'd run his road over flat rock whenever possible.

The track turned left just past the streambed, hooking away from a steep slope that terminated abruptly at the edge of a huge patch, maybe half an acre, of cattails marking one corner of the beaver pond. I tried to stay down below the edge of the track, to keep my silhouette concealed, but the pitch was too sharp, and I soon found myself lunging from one handhold to the next.

With no real choice, I came back up to the road, expecting to cross it and work the other side, when I noticed what appeared to be a bundle of rags at the edge of the reeds. Unbelievably, my first reaction was to shake my head in disapproval. New York City is pig paradise. You expect the garbage; after a while you don't even see it. But not here, not in the heart of the Adirondack Park.

Then the bundle of rags moved, and I knew what I was looking at. I also knew that my head and shoulders were above the edge of the road, which meant that I was visible from the higher elevations. I had to get out of there, but I didn't. Instead, I froze for a moment, waiting for my heart to slow down. I'd been at the scene of a hundred homicides over the years and never felt anything more than mild disgust. Now, faced with a living victim, I had to force myself to take action.

I made plenty of noise going down, skidding from tree to tree, kicking up loose gravel and rocks. As I got close, that bundle of rags pushed itself to its knees and slowly turned to face me. I froze, my hands literally trembling, knowing on some level what I was going to see. Still, I wasn't prepared for the red, swollen face, the blood-soaked hair, the narrow, unseeing eyes, and what I saw was myself as if I'd been suddenly transported back to those first years. Those years before I learned how to escape, when I could do no more than wait for the end of my beating, then lie in bed with the pain for company. When I could neither understand nor accept.

I don't know how long I would have stayed like that. Thoughts whipped back and forth through my mind, too short, too quickly gone to form any coherent message. My hands rose up, as if in touching my face I could pull myself back into the present.

"Who? Who?" The figure stumbled toward me, one arm outstretched. "Please."

Still, I held my position as if rooted to the rock and earth. Held it until I heard the deep boom of a shotgun and felt the buckshot punch into my back. The shock propelled me forward, forcing what I could not bring myself to do.

THIRTY

I'd been exposed to any number of ambushes in Vietnam, sudden explosions of terrifying gunfire that always seemed to come when I was least prepared. What I'd learned, as had most of us who made it through alive, was a simple reflex: Take cover immediately. Do not hesitate. Do not analyze.

I shot forward, snatching up the woman who reached for me, and plunged into the reeds. The shotgun roared again and again, but what I remember, even more than the deep reports, was the *snick, snick, snick* of individual pellets cutting through long, dry reeds. I remember reeds falling all around me as I searched for some place to make a stand.

A mallard hen flew past my face, followed closely by her panicked mate, both squawking at the top of their lungs. If they were nesting in the reeds, they'd be doing it on solid ground, ground that wouldn't flood in a thunderstorm. If I could find their hummock, we'd have a chance.

As we got in deeper, I dropped low, trying not to offer my back as a target, though I knew Kennedy would have no trouble following our progress through the swaying reeds. What I wanted to do was crawl, but I couldn't think of a way to do it without dragging the woman's face through the mud. Kennedy was taking his time now, zeroing in despite my attempts to zigzag. I was ready to stop and take my chances in the muck, when I stumbled onto my patch of solid earth.

It wasn't much, maybe the size of a dining-room table and covered with some kind of dense woody shrub, but it would have to do. I worked my way behind it, then lay the woman's head and shoulders on the ground, letting the rest of her body trail off into the reeds and mud.

"Don't scream," I whispered, lying down next to her. "Please. We've got to be quiet."

The woman nodded her understanding, staring at me with unseeing eyes. I knew she was blind, had known it the minute she turned to me. I also knew I had to protect her, to die first, if that was the way it was going to be. As if her death was my own.

But I had no intention of dying. I took the Anschutz off my shoulder, laid it on the ground in front of me, then drew the .45 and set it beside the rifle. I was hoping that Kennedy, once he stopped wasting ammo, would be stupid enough to come after me. Or better yet, decide to climb up the mountain for a better view. From a distance, his shotgun would be no match for my little .22. I put my hands on my back, working my fingers in a slow spiral until I found the two small holes in my left side, just beneath the ribs. The holes weren't bleeding much on the outside, which I suppose was good news, though I knew I might be pouring blood into my abdomen. Even better, when I worked my hand around to my belly, I couldn't find an exit wound, just a small lump beneath the skin about three inches to the left of my navel. Even the pain was limited to a dull ache that I could handle without slowing down.

Kennedy maintained a calm, methodical assault, turning his shotgun into an overpowered weed whacker. I felt calmer, knowing that I had time until he decided what to do next. Time, for instance, to slip out of the daypack and retrieve the first-aid kit. There wasn't much I could do for my back (whatever was happening was happening on the inside), but I could do something for the woman's swollen face.

When my fingers touched the welts on her skin, she jerked back for a moment, then surrendered to my probing. At first, I thought the swelling was due to a blow of some kind because of the dried blood in her hair, but a closer inspection revealed dozens of insect bites. Black flies, ants, fleas . . . it didn't matter, because I had nothing specific for any of them.

"Were you unconscious?" I whispered.

"I think so. I don't know."

"You're all bitten up. I'm going to put a salve on your face. It's mostly used for sunburn, but maybe it'll help."

"No." She pushed my hand away. "I don't need anything. Kill them."

Just like that? Maybe she thought I was a character from a "Dungeons and Dragons" adventure. Means the Magician.

Her fingers reached for my face, tracing my features, hesitating around my eyes.

"What is your name?" she asked.

"Roland Means."

"I'm Lorraine Cho." She hesitated for a moment. "I heard him shooting." Another hesitation. "Are we safe?"

I explained it to her as best I could, whispering directly into her ear. Kennedy had stopped firing, and while I guessed that he wouldn't make any rash decisions, there was at least the chance of a full, frontal assault. The last thing I needed, if Kennedy came crashing through those reeds, was a blind, panicked woman on my hands.

"So, what it is," I finished, "is that we're in a stand-off. We can't get out; he can't get in."

"What if he just waits?"

I began to work the salve into her bitten face, and this time she made no protest. "If he doesn't get us out of here before dark, he's dead. That's the good news. The bad news is that it's only eight o'clock and he's got eleven hours to think about it."

She grabbed my wrist, clinging fiercely. "Kill them *both*."

"Both?"

"Becky is psychotic. You can't predict what she'll do. You have to kill her."

There wasn't much more to be said. There was certainly no sense in arguing the point. You can't expect a victim to keep things in perspective. No more than you can expect someone trapped in a hurricane to remember that somewhere the sun is shining, the birds are singing, the cows are grazing peacefully. Besides, I could understand what she'd been through, because I'd been through it as well, and though I'd had no one to champion my cause, I'd dreamed of a rescuer, a savior.

I handed her the water bottle and she pressed it to her lips, drinking deeply. Too deeply.

"Take it easy, Lorraine. That's all we've got. Unless you plan to drink the muck in this pond."

"What if he makes a fire?" She handed the bottle back to me. "What if he tries to burn us out? Because he'll do it. Daddy will do it and Becky will help him."

It took me a second to realize that she meant Kennedy. I wondered how long she'd been with him. And what role his sweet-as-sugar wife had played in the fun. VICAP had reported female bite marks on the bodies of female victims. I could visualize the words as they'd appeared on the screen. There was no emphasis, just the bare fact, as if VICAP were reporting the weather for Tucson, Arizona. And we'd been happy to read it, Bouton and I. The only emotion we'd felt was joy. Yay! Bite marks! The link to King Thong. Let's go out and have a drink. Let's celebrate.

Kennedy suddenly opened up, firing random shots into the reeds. He emptied the .12-gauge, reloaded, emptied it again, then gave up. He was obviously frustrated, obviously pissed off. As a cop and a killer, he was used to getting his own way. Now he had a problem and no good way to deal with it. He had to know that I was wounded, maybe incapacitated or even dead. And there was always the chance that some game warden had overheard the firing and would come to investigate. But he wasn't stupid enough (or frustrated enough) to come charging into those reeds. Even if he'd missed the .45 strapped to my hip, he had to have seen the rifle. If I was still in one piece, if I was lying in wait, he'd be . . .

"What if he makes a fire?"

"Huh?" Without thinking, I looked into her eyes, suddenly

realizing they were made of glass. I saw my own reflection in those dark pupils. Myself looking at myself looking at myself.

"Listen to me, you dope," she hissed. "What are we going to do if he makes a fire?"

Dope?

"If he starts a fire, we may get out of here sooner than we expected. The wind's blowing in from behind us; it'll push the smoke back at him. Plus it rained hard all day yesterday, so everything's wet except for the tips of last year's growth. Besides, it's spring, and there's a lot of new growth that's too green to burn. Here, feel this." I took her hand and placed it on the nightscope. "This is a nightscope. It amplifies available light, let's you see in the dark. It's why we have to wait."

She took a minute to think about it, then nodded at some inner decision. "Who are you? What are you doing here?"

I told her that I was a cop from New York, that Kennedy was the target of an investigation that had nothing to do with her, that I just happened to come along, that someone else knew where I was, but it'd be at least two days before she came looking for me. I also told her that I'd been wounded, knowing it would frighten her. But she didn't react with any show of fear. Instead she ran her fingers over my back, then over my abdomen.

"Do you have anything for this? Antiseptic? Bandages?"

I handed her a tube of antibiotic ointment, a package of sterile gauze bandage, and a roll of hospital tape. Thinking that none of this was necessary. If I was going to die of my wounds, it wouldn't be because of anything coming from the outside. But we had a lot of time to kill and nothing much to do with it, so I rolled onto my side and let her go to work.

There was a confidence to the way she cleaned and dressed my wounds that was unlike anything I'd ever experienced. Koocek's hands were sure and swift, as if her fingers knew things her brain could never describe, but Koocek was clumsy compared to this woman.

"Are you in pain?" she asked, finally.

"Not much. It aches a little."

"Does that mean you're okay."

"You really wanna know?"

"I *have* to know." She put her hand on top of mine. "I don't want to die here. I don't want to be killed by *them*."

I didn't see how my describing the possibilities would help to prevent that, but I went ahead with it anyway.

"Kennedy hit me with two pellets from a .12-gauge shotgun. If he'd been using a rifle, I'd be dead, but buckshot doesn't have a lot of velocity behind it. That's why the pellets didn't come out the other side." I stopped for a moment, and she squeezed my hand in protest. "All right, Lorraine. The only thing I can say for sure is the pellets didn't sever an artery or a large vein. If they had, I'd be unconscious by now. Unconscious or dead. But that still leaves the kidneys, lungs, liver, colon, spleen, and whatever else is in there. I really don't know what happens if a chunk of buckshot the size of a .38 punctures your liver. Short-term or long-term. What I do know is that right now I feel all right."

I turned my attention back to Kennedy. Imagining him crawling through the reeds, trying to get close enough to use that shotgun. The breeze was pushing the cattails back and forth, only dying down occasionally. That movement would provide him with excellent cover, assuming he had the balls to try it. Which I doubted.

Lorraine settled down beside me, but she didn't fall asleep or drift off into daydreams. Instead, she went through the daypack, went through it without asking permission until she found the trail mix. Then she began to eat.

"You're lucky I didn't have a mousetrap in there."

She didn't bother to answer. Her mouth was drawn into a tight line, her nostrils slightly flared. I suppose her features reflected the intensity of her concentration, but at the time I read it as determination. She'd come through a long journey, losing nearly everything in the process, but she would not lie down and die. She would not surrender.

Which was just as well, because somewhere around noon I began to sweat, despite the cool temperature and the fact that most of my body was lying in wet mud. Within half an hour my hands were trembling, my teeth chattering. I tried to crush whatever was going on inside my body, tried to push it down. I might as well have tried to hold back the ocean.

"You have a fever." Lorraine's hands were all over my face.

"Very perceptive." The wind had died down, and I had to remind myself to whisper.

"Show me how to use the gun."

"Use it for what? I'm not dead, Lorraine. Not yet." My first thought was that she wanted to kill herself before Kennedy got the chance to do it for her.

"Daddy's not going to come, Roland. He's going to send Becky. If you're unable to deal with her, I have to. We're not going to die here."

I took the "we're" as a sign of progress. A couple of hours ago it would have been "I'm."

"That doesn't answer the question."

"Look," she was angry again, "I wasn't born blind, and I've shot a gun before, a revolver, not an automatic. When Becky comes, she won't charge through these bushes. If I can find her with my finger, I can find her with the barrel of a gun. Just show me where the safety is and leave the gun on the ground where I can find it."

A shudder ran through my body, from my toes straight up to my scalp, and for the first time, I began to think that I wouldn't make it. Not through the hours until dark, not through the darkness itself. What I wanted to do—what I was driven to do—was close my eyes and rest.

"Give me your hand," I said. She complied without a question, and I put her fingertips on the barrel of the .45. "This gun is heavy, Lorraine, but it's been customized so it won't kick back very hard when you pull the trigger. The problem is that it's got a grip safety. Do you know what that is?"

"No. Is it hard to use?"

I guided the tip of her index finger down the lever on the back of the handle.

"You feel that?"

"Yes."

"Push it in." I waited for her to compress the safety. "You have to hold down that lever with the heel of your hand when you pull the trigger. If you don't, the gun won't fire. Remember, if you carry it anywhere, don't grip the butt and the trigger at the same time. If you do, you're liable to lose a leg."

That was the last piece of advice I had for her. Within minutes, my mind was drifting back and forth between that island of reeds and . . . I'm tempted to describe what I saw as dreamlike, but my visions didn't even have the coherence of a dream. Bits and pieces swirled into my vision, refusing to stay long enough to be weighed and counted. Big Mike was there, and dear old mom, of course. But there were teachers, too, and schoolmates, and a whorehouse in Saigon inhabited by sad, tiny women.

I don't know how long it went on. You might as well ask Dorothy how many hours she spent in the cyclone before she got to Oz. I do know that after a time, I passed into actual sleep, but I only know it because Lorraine shook me out of it.

"She's coming."

I tried to reach for the .45, but I could barely move. Not that it mattered, because Lorraine already had it in her hands. "Lorraine? Baby? It's me, Becky. Please don't shoot me. I just want to talk to you."

The wind had died away, and I could hear the steady crunch of Rebecca Kennedy's feet as she fought her way through the reeds. Once again, I tried to reach for the .45, but Lorraine sensed the movement and pushed my outstretched hand away.

For the first time, her face seemed composed, almost serene. A smile played on her lips, but the strangest part was that her face was turned toward me, her blind glass eyes fixed on my own while the gun pointed toward the oncoming sound.

"Lorraine? Please tell me where you are. These weeds are just cutting me all to pieces. I swear I don't know how you got in here. You must be a mess."

Kennedy's voice was actually cheerful. She might have been playing hide-and-seek with a naughty child. If she had any sense of her potential reception, she didn't show it. Even gripped by fever, I knew that Lorraine had been right. Rebecca Kennedy was insane.

Perhaps motivated by that sudden bit of knowledge, I felt strong enough to reach out for the rifle. I managed to pull it into my chest, but I couldn't get my fingers to stop shaking long enough to work the safety. Nor could I raise it to my shoulder.

"Now, Lorraine, Daddy is so mad at me. He says it is all my fault, and if you don't come back to live with us he will do just what he said he would do and put me in the chipper. And it will be all your fault. Will you be able to live with that on your conscience? Believe me, Lorraine, I have done some terrible things in my life and they are mighty hard to live with. I don't want you to have to go through that."

Kennedy's voice was directly in front of us now. She'd stopped moving (or, at least, I couldn't hear her steps; she might have been crawling). A thought crossed my mind, a thought I had to communicate. Once I had it fixed, I couldn't believe it hadn't occurred to me before this. I touched Lorraine's shoulder and she leaned down to me.

"Don't shoot unless you absolutely have to. Kennedy could be right behind her." I took a deep breath. Lorraine's ear seemed to be twisting and turning, as if she was a dog trying to locate a sound. I watched it grow into a teacup, then turned away. At that moment, I believed I was going to die.

Rebecca Kennedy began to move again, her footsteps some-times crunching on the new growth, sometimes splashing into the mud. She was coming at a slight angle that would take her fifteen feet past our position. I could see her body now, a vague shape, almost ghostly except for the bright red scarf tied over her hair.

My eyes were drawn to the scarf. At times it seemed disem-bodied, floating amid the brown stalks like a Disney animation imposed on a sepia-toned kinescope. The scarf told me every-thing I needed to know about Kennedy's intentions. Rebecca had been sent to locate us, not to kill us, and Robert Kennedy was following the progress of that red scarf from somewhere up on the mountain. I needed to tell Lorraine. Tell her to pull that trigger while Rebecca Kennedy was still far away, but I didn't do it.

I didn't do anything more than lay there and watch as the red scarf, ephemeral as a butterfly, changed course and came straight for us. I watched the body solidify, then the pinched fea-tures, the swollen eyes and lips, the stringy, blond hair. Lorraine kept the barrel of the gun pinned to the sound of Rebecca's progress; she had to know how close Rebecca was.

"Don't shoot." It was my voice, though I couldn't recall deciding to say anything.

"Lorraine, Baby, is that you?"

"Please don't shoot."

"Oh, I am so happy to see you, honey. I just have to cele-brate." Her eyes were riveted to the gun in Lorraine's hands as she slowly undid the knot at her throat, as she raised the red scarf high and waved it back and forth. "Yaaaaaay. Yaaaaaay."

THIRTY-ONE

Robert Kennedy's first shot tore through the back of his wife's skull. Exiting, it opened a jagged circle from the outside corner of her right eye, down across the bottom of her mouth, then up along the outside of her nose to her eyebrow. I saw it in slow-motion—or, at least, I *remember* it in slow-motion—red and white chunks of a three-dimensional kaleidoscope mushrooming outward, plastering themselves to the brown cattails and tan stalks, dripping red rubies onto the black mud.

I found it beautiful. As beautiful as napalm exploding on a distant hillside. I'd seen that many, many times. My platoon substituted napalm for television, gathering after dark, bottles of rum in most hands (joints and even dope in many others) to wait for the fighter jockeys to get to work. I knew there were human beings under that jellied gasoline, but they were enemy human beings, and I was obliged to hate them, not to pity them. Being a man of principle, I didn't shirk my obligations.

Robert Kennedy wasn't using his shotgun. Somewhere along the line he'd traded it for an AK47. I recognized its deep bark through all the fever, would have had to be dead not to know it. He was pulling the trigger as fast he could, trying to drown the area surrounding his wife in supersonic lead.

Lorraine put down the .45 and pressed up against me. There was nothing we could do, but wait and listen. Listen to the distant reports and the smack of bullets impacting wet mud. Wait for Kennedy to empty a fifty-round clip, change it, then empty another.

I lost my grip on the present long before it was over, was transported all the way back to the Mekong Delta of southern Vietnam. My platoon had been raked by a single sniper. Somebody (a close friend, perhaps, or a hated second lieutenant, or a trusted sergeant) was down and dead. It wasn't the first time the platoon had been through it, and what we did—did without any command being given—was dive into the reeking muck of a rice paddy fertilized with human excrement and sprinkled with booby traps.

Further retreat being a physical impossibility, we then responded in the approved fashion—with overwhelming fire-power. Two M60 machine guns and twenty M16's were the first on line, coming in as quickly as twenty-two desperate, shit-scared soldiers could swing them into action. Then the M79's opened up, launching grenade after grenade at the tree line.

Thwoop-BOOM! Thwoop-BOOM! Thwoop-BOOM! Thwoop-BOOM!

The sound was unimaginable, individual rounds expended so fast they became a continuous, unrelenting wall of sound. Locked within it, I couldn't hear the commands of the lieutenant or the sergeants, couldn't hear return fire, either. I jammed the trigger down, emptied a clip, reloaded, emptied another—all into a distant tree where I hoped the sniper was hiding.

What I wanted to do was keep firing, to hide behind that wall of sound forever, but after a time (long or short was a concept to be measured later, over a joint and a cold beer) the wall began to crumble. Just small gaps at first, then huge tears in the fabric as more and more soldiers let go of their triggers. Now, I could hear the shouts of our frustrated platoon commander and his buddies: "Cease fire. Cease fire," and knew I'd have to face the worst part of it.

Because somebody, once we were locked into the silence the way we'd been locked into the firefight, somebody would have to be first to raise his head, to clamber to his knees, to rise to his feet. And for all the ten thousand rounds we'd fired off, nobody was guaranteeing the sniper was dead. Maybe he'd sat it out behind the trunk of a tree. Or maybe we'd simply fired in the wrong direction. Or too high, or too low.

One thing for sure, we'd been firing in so many different directions there was no way to know if any of us had pinned the sniper's location. He might be waiting for us to show ourselves before blowing off a clip or two. He might be about to fire right now—fire, then retreat to safety again. He might be planning to do this all afternoon because Charlie would slaughter his whole family if he didn't.

Slowly, very slowly, we began to rise. I was propped up on my elbows, when I saw movement in the trees, the flash of sunlight on metal as the sniper swung his AK47 into position. I threw myself on the ground, yanked the M16 up to my shoulder, flipped the lever to semiautomatic and yelled, "Down, down, down, down."

"Quiet, Roland. Don't speak. It's almost time, now."

I opened my eyes to find Lorraine's fingers stroking my face. She was sitting with her back to the brush, holding my head in her lap. It was near dark, the sun little more than a violet haze draping the western mountains.

"Get down," I whispered, obeying her despite my fear. "For God's sake. The sniper's still active."

She smiled, offering me the water bottle. "Drink, Roland. You have to be strong. It's almost time."

I drained the bottle, stared at it for a few seconds, held it up guiltily.

"I drank it all, but you can fill it in the stream."

Then I looked around, remembering Kennedy, the beaver pond, the cattails. The air was dead calm, the water of the pond a flat sheet of smoked glass. Fifteen feet away, the dark shadow of Rebecca Kennedy's body lay on a bed of flattened reeds. I could barely see her, but I could hear the steady drone of the flies as they went about their business.

Lorraine was right; it was almost time.

"Sit up, Roland."

She guided me into a sitting position, held me there while I fought the dizziness. After a few minutes, I felt stronger; I wasn't sweating anymore and I wasn't disoriented, but I was weak and tired.

"You're infected inside," Lorraine whispered. "The bullets may have hit your bowel."

"Thank you for sharing that with me." I'd made a joke, which, feeble as it may have been, cheered me considerably. "Besides," I added, "they weren't bullets. If they were bullets, I'd be dead."

She smiled, digging the bag of trail mix out of the daypack. "You already told me that. Do you want to eat? Before you go after him?"

The sun was completely down, now, and the moon wouldn't rise for another hour. The sky was clear, the rain and wind having driven out every bit of haze. I knew I wouldn't get a better chance, that whatever was happening inside my body wasn't about to heal itself. My choices, as I saw them at the time, were very simple—go now or die.

And if I died, Lorraine would die as well. That was also very simple and very clear.

The Anschutz's clip held five rounds, and I had two spare clips. I was using Remington High Velocity ammo, but that didn't make my .22 a match for Kennedy's assault rifle. No, a shoot-out at twenty paces would only result in chunks of my flesh turning up in Nebraska. My advantage was that I could see in the dark. And that I'd spent my life seeking prey that could fight back. I hadn't scoured the countryside in search of defense-less women. I hadn't used my wife to lure men onto their knees while I fired into the backs of their heads.

"I'm not exactly hungry, Lorraine. I suppose I could look on it as a last meal. That might get my appetite up."

Another joke; the future was looking positively rosy.

"There's something you have to do for me, Lorraine," I continued. "See, the thing about it is that I don't know where Kennedy's hiding, and I'm not strong enough to spend the next three hours trying to find him. I want you to give me enough time to get back up to the road, then fire several shots into the mud. Hopefully, he'll return fire and I'll be able to spot him by the muzzle flash."

"What's that? Muzzle flash?"

"That's the flame that comes out of the barrel of the gun. You can't see it in the daytime, but at night it's like sending up a flare."

She thought about it for a minute, nodding her head as she ticked off the possibilities.

"What happens after I do it? After I fire the gun?"

"After you fire the gun, you duck."

"I thought you said you could see in the dark with your . . . your night-thing."

"Look, Lorraine, Kennedy could be anywhere, even behind us. Imagine a point maybe three hundred yards away, then draw a circle with us in the middle. That's an awful lot of area to scan, even with a nightscope. Me, I feel a lot better than I did half an hour ago, but that doesn't mean I'm anything like back to normal. In fact, I think what I'm doing is living on borrowed time and that I've got to find Kennedy right away. I've got to find him and kill him while I'm still strong enough to walk out of here. What I'm after is one clean shot when he's least expecting it. When he's standing up, shooting at you."

I was lying, of course; I had no intention of letting Kennedy off that easy. I wanted to look behind his eyes. To see if I was hiding there. I wasn't afraid of dying; didn't give it a second thought. (Though I *did* give it a first thought.) Maybe it was the fever doing the thinking. Or maybe it was just my own Brockian obsessions finally taking control. Either way, it amounted to the same thing.

"How much time to do you need, Roland? And how will I count it off?"

"I need enough time to get up to that little road. I should have a clear view from there. It'll take maybe twenty minutes."

"There's no way . . . "

"I know that, Lorraine. Once I get in position, I'll take a rock and toss it into the water. Maybe we'll get lucky and Kennedy'll open up then and there. I doubt it, because he grew up in these woods, and he'll know it could be an animal, maybe a beaver slapping its tail against the water. If Kennedy doesn't respond, you have to go to work. Remember, shoot the gun down into the mud. If you shoot up into the air, he'll see *your* muzzle flash."

"What if he doesn't respond at all?"

"You could always stand up and wave." I smiled, but, of course, she couldn't see the smile. Or the joke, either. "If he doesn't respond, I'm gonna have to go and look for him. I don't know how long it will take or what direction to go in. You can wait for me or walk out and take your chances. If you go straight ahead and up the slope, you'll hit the road. From there it's about half a mile, mostly downhill, to Kennedy's house. Then it's another quarter of a mile along his driveway to the main road. He's got two dogs tied in his backyard. When they smell you, they'll come to the end of their leads, and they'll be making plenty of noise. Imagine it as a half-circle and go around them. There's probably a phone in the house if you want to try that route."

There wasn't much more to be said. I was thirsty again, but there was nothing to drink, not unless I cut back to the stream. But that didn't make much sense. The stream flowed into the pond which, in turn, flowed into the stream again. If I could drink from the stream, I could drink directly from the pond. Unfortunately, the idea never crossed my mind. The stream was clear and moving, the pond was dark and murky, and that was the end of that. I didn't remember the water purification tablets in the daypack either, which would have rendered the whole thing academic.

"I've got to go," I said. "My head's starting to spin."

She reached out and put her fingers on my face. "I think you're going to take chances." She waited for me to respond, but there wasn't much to say. It was up to me to handle Kennedy;

how I did it was none of her business. "Don't let yourself die, Roland Means. I need to see you again. I'll never be finished with this if you die."

Her face was composed, her small mouth free of tension. I'd just finished telling her that she might have to make her way up a very steep hillside, then follow an obscure track half a mile through a stream to a house with two vicious dogs in the backyard. All without being able to see. Yet there were no hysterics, no denial of her abilities; instead, she was worried about *me*.

I slipped the .22 over my shoulder and turned away.

"Roland?"

"I have work to do, Lorraine. If I don't get it done, the healing part is just so much philosophy."

"Listen to me, you jerk. There's a cabin at the end of the road. If you can't make it out, go there and I'll send help."

I leaned over and kissed her. "My hero," I said.

It was very dark out there. The hills surrounding the pond were black shadows, only visible because they held no stars. Instead of pushing straight through the reeds, I worked back toward the pond, then began to crawl along the edge, where the reeds met deeper water. I wasn't heading for the hillside, as I'd told Lorraine. My view from the road would be extremely limited, blocked by the sharp angle of the surrounding hillside as well as the trees and shrubs. I needed open ground, and the beaver dam, while it wasn't exactly ground, was high enough to provide me with cover, yet low enough to give me a clean field of vision.

I pulled myself along the edge of the reeds, my feet trailing off into the cool water, congratulating myself on my hunting prowess and my rapid progress. The dam was in sight, now, odd black sticks poking out of a solid black mass. As I edged closer, looking for a rock to toss into the water once I was in position, I sensed movement ahead of me. For just a moment, I thought I heard the click of a released safety, thought I saw the barrel of a rifle coming up and around. Then a mass of white feathers exploded upward, clearing the cattails before the wings opened. It was a snowy egret, a very pissed-off snowy egret. His angry scream was echoed once, twice, three times as birds began to rise in front of me, pure white even in starlight. The only thing I could do was watch, open-mouthed, as they began to slowly beat their wings, slowly rise, thinking this was the most beautiful thing I'd ever seen.

Kennedy opened up with a tremendous barrage, pulling the trigger as fast as he could. As the rounds began to smack into the mud, birds rose from all parts of the marsh, a dozen quacking mallards, wings beating madly; a single panicked loon running across the water in search of altitude; two great blue herons, fully four feet tall, going almost straight up, then slowly turning away from the gunfire. The herons passed directly over me, flaunting seven-foot wingspans as they, too, screamed their annoyance and their fear.

I could hear bullets falling around me, but I never moved. Chalk it up to the fever, chalk it up to pure joy—the birds escaped and I would escape. It was inevitable.

But Kennedy wouldn't escape. I had him now, and the truth of it filled me with happiness, like a child granted one wish after a lifetime of deprivation. Or a sinner saved at the last possible moment. I began to laugh out loud, watching the AK47 spew orange flames as Kennedy, about two hundred yards away, worked through the clip. I put the nightscope to my eye, sighting in through the greenish glow. It would have been so easy to kill him; he was the kind of hunter who set baited traps, then came back to finish off his crippled prey. Never imagining his own leg in the jaws of the trap.

I waited for him to finish, kept the scope on him in case he decided to move his position. He didn't, of course. His arrogance wouldn't let him. He changed the clip, set the AK47 against a tree, lit a cigarette, settled back to await further developments. I moved to the edge of the bank, taking my time, then began to angle toward him.

My mind was clear and focused, but my body refused to follow suit. I recalled how I'd once trotted through the forest, moving from trail to trail with the relentless determination of a hungry coyote. Now my legs felt like tree trunks, rising and falling as if their only desire was to remain rooted to the earth. The rifle slung across my back weighed less than ten pounds, but it threatened to pull me over on the steeper slopes. After the first few minutes, my body was covered with sweat right down to my fingertips. I was going to be very cold as soon as that sweat saturated my clothing, and I knew it.

But I also knew that I had to accept the conditions. The worst thing I could do was push it, demand that my body perform the way it did in my workouts. Somehow, I settled on the belief that the whole thing had been scripted—me, Kennedy, Bouton, Lorraine . . . every bit of it, and the only thing that mattered was the play itself. As long as I pursued the part assigned to me, nothing could go wrong.

I moved from tree to tree, stopping every twenty-five yards or so to make sure Kennedy was still in place. Each time I looked, I found him leaning against the same tree, cigarette in hand. Once, I caught him peering through a huge pair of binoculars. I remember wondering what he expected to find. Enlarging a black hole doesn't make it visible.

When I was close enough to see the glow of Kennedy's cigarette, I eased my already snail-like pace. It was foolish, really. There was no wind, and the forest itself would muffle any sound. Even if I did make a noise he could hear, if I sent a rock tumbling down the slope or cracked a dried branch, he wouldn't be able to see me. The worst he could do was fire blindly into the trees, fire at what could easily be a raccoon or a skunk.

Nevertheless, I moved cautiously, letting the sole of my boot drift over the forest floor, listening to the messages it sent. Never letting my weight settle until I knew what was under my foot. When I was less than thirty yards away, I put the cross hairs in the center of his forehead, thought about ending it on the spot, then raised the scope three inches and blew a chunk of bark out of the tree he was leaning against.

The script—my script, anyway—called for him to make a stand, to set up behind a rock and return fire. That's not what he did. Instead, he screamed, the sound echoing behind the crack of the .22, and ran.

A good hunter must anticipate the reactions of his prey; this is a given. Animals live or die by habit, and Robert Kennedy was no exception. He lived by roads and houses and automobiles. The darkest thickets spelled terror for him, not safety. I was sure that his van was parked somewhere up on the mountain, maybe next to that cabin Lorraine told me about, and equally sure that he'd go for it. That's was why I'd kept between him and the narrow track he'd built. And why, slowed down as I was, I beat him to the road.

I had enough time to set up behind a tree, to listen to him stumble over the deadwood, falling, rising, unable to deal with a world that wasn't flat. When he appeared, rifle clutched in both hands, breath whistling in his smoker's lungs, I fired a round into bare rock just to see his reaction to the whine of a ricochet.

He reacted by going down on his face. Instead of bringing the AK47 to bear, he hugged it to his chest like it was a magic wand. Maybe it made him feel powerful. Or maybe he wasn't thinking at all. Maybe he was so frightened he couldn't do anything but lie there, a child surrounded by his deepest fears. After all, he couldn't see me, couldn't hear me, couldn't escape me.

"Are you gonna use that gun?" I called, surprised to find my voice little more than a hoarse squawk.

"Who are you?" His head lifted slightly, but the rest of his body remained on the ground.

"I don't know. Maybe I'm King Thong. Who do *you* think I am?"

I fired a round into the dirt about two inches from his nose, then began to move up the slope. He was going to have to fight soon (I could feel him working up the courage), and if I was in his line of fire, I'd have to kill him.

"Why are you doing this? Why don't you kill me? If you've got the guts." A long pause. "But you don't have the guts, do you? You're that Indian cop—I remember you—and cops aren't allowed to kill people. Are they?" Another pause. "Say something, you bastard. You half-breed cocksucker. Say *something*."

By the time he opened fire, I was already behind him. Knowing that he'd eventually run away from where he thought I was. That he'd come toward me. Still, I waited until I was sure, until he'd actually begun to climb, before I began to trudge up the mountain.

If I'd been tired before, I was exhausted now. Kennedy should have been able to catch me, to force my hand. Only his panic prevented a confrontation. I could hear him running toward me, hear his ragged breathing as he fought for oxygen. He couldn't seem to get more than twenty yards before stopping to catch his breath. Each time he paused, he'd fire half a dozen shots back down the mountain. Once, he screamed his defiance into the night, a long, eerie howl that raised the hair on the back of my neck.

I maintained a steady pace, picking them up and putting them down, just like I'd been taught in basic training. Remembering that night when Sergeant Belardi decided to teach us a lesson about limitations and how to overcome them. He woke us at midnight, loaded us up with full packs, then led us on a forced march. The march, Belardi explained, wouldn't be two or three or four hours long. No, we "assholes" were going to hike through those swamps until *he* decided to call it quits. If any of us "fairies" was stupid enough to collapse, the entire squad would pass the next two weeks doing close-order drill instead of eating breakfast.

Belardi had picked the perfect night for his lesson. The sky was overcast, and a misty rain locked our eyes onto the backs of the soldiers in front of us. We'd been forbidden to wear our watches, and with no visible moon, we couldn't know how long we'd been at it. An hour? Two? Ten? It seemed like we'd begun at the beginning of time and were expected to continue for all eternity.

Pick 'em up; put 'em down. Pick 'em up; put 'em down. Toward the end it was as if I'd run out of thoughts. I was no longer angry or resentful. The body marching under that gear had no more volition than a moving belt on an assembly line. It wouldn't stop until someone turned off the juice.

When I finally stepped into the little clearing around Lorraine Cho's prison, the moon, a sliver short of full, had climbed over the rim of the eastern ridges. It bathed the clearing in pale light, glinting in the windows of the tiny log cabin, flickering on the tumbling waters of a small stream. The glowing spring leaves of an enormous sugar maple seemed almost luminous, a reflection of the pure white starlight overhead.

I stood for a moment, open-mouthed, then had my first coherent thought in the last forty-five minutes. Water! I'd stopped sweating a long time ago. Not because my fever had dropped—if anything, it'd grown worse—but because I'd become thoroughly dehydrated. Nevertheless, I didn't cross that open, moonlit space; I stayed at the edge of the forest, concealing myself, as I'd done all my life, in the safety of shadows. When I reached the stream, I turned around to look for Kennedy, saw nothing, then buried my head in the water.

Kennedy was walking across the clearing when I raised my head. The noise of rushing water had covered the noise he made, just as the dark shadows had covered my own presence. He stopped near the van, then stared at the cabin as if he couldn't make up his mind whether to ambush me or flee while he had the chance. Either would have been better than what he actually did, which was turn to face in my direction. Without making any conscious decision to do so, I raised the rifle to my shoulder and shot him through the left kneecap.

He crashed to the ground, dropping the AK47 as he fell. I stood up, the .22 still against my shoulder, and began to walk toward him. He saw me, started to reach for his rifle, then looked back at me again.

"I don't think you want to do *that*," I said. "If you do *that*, I'll have to kill you."

He thought about it briefly, finally deciding that he didn't want to do *that*. What he wanted to do was grab his knee and howl in pain. Which he did.

I retrieved the AK47 and threw it into the woods.

"Take off your jacket and throw it to me. I'm cold."

"I'm bleeding," he screamed, "I'm bleeding and my leg is broke." His voice had the air of a petulant child. How could I do this to him? How could I be so cruel?

"If I was you, I'd take that jacket off right now. And I wouldn't put my hands in the pockets, either."

He managed to get the jacket off by rolling to his good side, then twisting out of it. When he tossed it to me, I put it on gratefully. My sweatshirt was soaked through, and I was very cold.

"Pull up your shirt and empty your pockets."

"Why don't you just put the cuffs on me? I'm unarmed and I'm not offering any resistance."

"You in a hurry to get to jail, Kennedy? You ready to start your book?"

I wanted to shoot him so bad, I could taste it. I wanted to smell the copper smell of his life's blood running out of his body, to see chunks of his brain glistening in the moonlight. I looked into his eyes and found them a faint gray-blue. So pale I could barely separate them from the surrounding whites.

"She's still alive, you know. Lorraine. Your wife is dead, but Lorraine is still alive."

I sat down on the damp grass, felt my legs almost groan with relief. Now that my adrenals had stopped pumping, I could feel the weariness begin to overtake my mind as it had already overtaken my body. I wasn't going to make it down that mountain. It wasn't in the script.

"I should have killed that bitch a long time ago."

"Which one?"

He didn't answer for a minute, then said, "I want a lawyer. I have a right to a lawyer."

I managed to stagger to my feet and walk over to the van. The door was unlocked, the keys in the ignition. I pulled the keys, stuck them in my pocket, then turned on the headlights.

"Perfect, don't you think? Bright lights are traditional for an interrogation." I stumbled back to him, sat down a few feet away. I could see his eyes, now. They were flat and merciless, showing no emotion deeper than wary calculation.

"You can't force me to confess. A coerced confession is useless in a courtroom. We're both cops and we both know that."

"Coerced? That's a big word for a hillbilly cop. You must have learned it while you were in Albany. Not that it matters. This isn't about a trial, Robert. You've already been convicted."

"What are you gonna do, kill me?" He said it with a sneer; then the truth hit him.

It was almost funny. First, he did a double take worthy of Larry, Curly, and Moe. Then his lips tightened and his nostrils flared; pure animal rage danced in those colorless eyes. The jaws of a trap or a bullet in the knee—it was all the same. He was helpless; he'd lost control. I think he would have preferred the fires of hell.

Then, with no transition, the rage disappeared as if someone had thrown a switch. "I wounded ya, didn't I? I knew I wounded ya. No way I could've missed. If you hadn't moved at the last second, you'd be rat food."

"Good for me; bad for you."

He shifted his weight slightly, then grabbed his knee. The bottom half of his trouser leg was soaked with blood.

"If you're gonna kill me, why don't you just do it?"

"I'm waiting for my cue."

"What?"

"Look around, Bobby. Quaint log cabin, babbling brook, moonlight on the maples—all ringed by the majesty of the Adirondack Mountains. What director could resist the location? For a final scene, of course. See, Bobby, it *has* to end here. There's no other way it can happen."

"Yeah, you're probably right. All the fuckin' noise we made, there's bound to be troopers waitin' down at the house. Most likely, they'll come in tomorrow on foot." He sighed, shook his head as though resigned to the inevitable. Only his eyes betrayed the truth. He was simply waiting for his chance. Killing time while he searched for an opening. "But I had a good run. All these years? I knew they had to get me sooner or later. I mean what're the odds of dyin' at home if you're in my line of work? I gotta admit, though, I wasn't expectin' no injun to track me down. It's like outta the wild, wild west or somethin'."

"Don't forget the nigger."

"Oh yeah, right. What's her name again?"

"Vanessa Bouton." The Anschutz felt like a bar of lead, as if I had ten-pound weights attached to my wrists. I wondered if Kennedy could read it. If he could *smell* it the way an animal smells weakness. He answered the question by leaning toward me, moving as slow and steady as a snake after a mouse. Too bad this mouse had a gun. I shot him in the left thigh, maybe six inches above his wounded knee.

He fell back, jerked himself, really, deliberately moving away from me. Looking for another few minutes of life, another chance to kill again. I listened to him yell, too far gone to feel much of anything. He thrashed on the ground, grunting, growling, screaming in a language beyond words. I'd once known a man who called himself a dog trainer. He'd start by visiting various dog pounds, looking for the biggest, meanest dogs he could find. Then he'd toss them in cages and poke at them with the end of a sharpened broomstick. Kennedy reminded me of one of those dogs, a huge shepherd-dane so lost in its hatred it saw the whole world as an opportunity for revenge.

"I won't kill you quickly," I said when he was calm enough to listen. "That's not a way out for you."

He pulled himself to a sitting position, fighting the pain. "What's the point of this? I don't get the fucking point." Then he grinned suddenly, showing small even teeth. The smile was feral. "You wanna show me that you're better, right? Better hunter; better killer. Right?"

I responded by changing the clip in the rifle. I did it carefully, partly because my hand was none too steady, and partly to show Kennedy that I wasn't terribly interested in his opinion of me.

"You're right and wrong, Robert. I'm the better hunter, but I knew that going in. You, on the other hand, are the better killer. How many did you get?"

"Thirty-one. Counting the faggots. I shouldn't count them really. They were for the money. You know how much my father's got socked away? Two million bucks. At least. Meanwhile I'm givin' out parkin' tickets on Main Street. It wasn't right."

"But you didn't kill your father, Robert. You killed your brother."

"I didn't *have* to kill my father. Cancer was doin' it for me. As for precious John-John. How does a cocksucker deserve to inherit a million dollars? Just tell me that." Despite the obvious pain, Kennedy seemed anxious to talk. Maybe he knew that I had to listen. That listening was in the script. "In a way, I enjoyed poppin' them homos. I mean about stalkin' 'em, gettin' 'em in the van without anybody seein' us. It was like a challenge, because what I was used to was workin' places where there was nobody to see what I was doin'. In New York, there's always some asshole walkin' down the street—you can't get no privacy—so what I had to do was snatch them faggets in a way that witnesses wouldn't remember it. Which I did and which makes me proud, but I also have to admit that the things I said to get the job done were purely disgusting.

"'Well, what'd you have in mind, honey? What do you like to do?'

"I'd have Becky lyin' there in a pair of goddamned split-crotch panties and I'd still have to spell out what I wanted to do. The poontang wasn't good enough.

"'What I wanna do, baby,' I'd say, 'is squeeze your pretty balls while you do her up. After that, we'll improvise.'

"Word of God, buddy, it was like the old days on the Albany Vice Squad. You're supposed to get them to make an explicit offer. Otherwise, it don't stand up in court. Meanwhile, the whores know this, so they're tryin' to get you to tell 'em exactly what you want before they name a price. I didn't mind playin' that game with the bitches. That was more like natural. But when it came to the homos, I used to just bust 'em and lie about it in court.

"That's where I fucked it up, right? The way I did the homos? I mean I read all the true crime books. About John Wayne Gacy and Henry Lee Lucas and the Green River Killer. I *knew* I should've fucked those faggots. Or at least jerk off on 'em or something. But I couldn't bring myself to do it. Bad enough I had'a let 'em screw my wife.

"Poor Becky. Started out a whore and ended up a whore. She didn't mind, though. Not for that kind of money. And it was Becky that really got me going, anyway. When I come back from Albany? Man, I knew I'd had me a real close shave. All I wanted to do was lay back and do my job. Only Becky was a bi-sexual woman. Understand? She liked girls. Now, where you gonna find a broad in Owl Creek willin' to sleep with a married woman and keep her mouth shut about it? Exactly nowhere. So why couldn't Becky see that? Why'd she keep naggin' at me? Tellin' me how good it could be?

"Truth, man, thinkin' about that stuff could get you real hot. *Real* hot. And I'd find myself thinkin' about it till I was near about to bust my britches. Tryin' to dream up a way we could do it and get away with it. I mean drivin' around in a cruiser, I seen plenty of times I could'a grabbed a broad off the road and done whatever I wanted. No, the grabbin' part would'a been no trouble at all, but what was I gonna do with 'em after I was finished? *That* was the problem.

"It was Becky said we should kill 'em. I swear it on the Bible. 'Why, Daddy,' she said, 'all we have to do is leave the bodies in a place where nobody will ever find them.'

"So that's how it started. Just practical, because there wasn't no other way to do it if you wanted to have the sex, and that's what we wanted. We'd find some lady broke down on the highway and I'd send Becky over to check it out. You know, see if she's got help comin' or if she's got some kinda way to fight back or if she's just too damn old and ugly . . . things like that. When Becky tossed me the high sign, I'd walk on over with my tool box, show 'em my badge, offer to give 'em a ride home. If they refused, why we'd just go on to the next one. Figurin' even if they were suspicious, what could they say? But if they took us up on our offer, I'd walk 'em to the van, bang 'em on the head and shove 'em inside. By the time they figured out what was happening, it was all over but the shoutin'.

"Now, let me tell you something about killin'. In case you don't already know it. Killin' is like dope. The more you do, the more you want. First off, they'd be beggin'. 'Please don't hurt me. Please don't hurt me.' Only thing was I *liked* hurtin' 'em, which was somethin' I didn't know when I started out. Later on they'd be sayin', 'Please don't kill me. Please don't kill me.' But, you know, I liked killin' 'em, too. I liked drawin' it out, takin' my time, doin' it *right*. Doin' it till they said the magic words. 'Kill me. Please kill me.'

"You know how many ways you could hurt a woman? How many ways you can think up if you put your mind to it? Afterwards, I'd be patrollin' Main Street, givin' out tickets, thinkin', Why didn't I do this; why didn't I try that. If I could'a got just a little more out of the bitch, it would'a been perfect."

He lapsed into silence, then. As if he'd exhausted himself in an attempt to impress me. His face sagged into a puzzled frown, but his eyes retained their intensity. I wondered what he hoped to accomplish. Was he, for instance, after one last chance to kill before he was locked up forever? Because he'd been right when he said he was finished. We'd made enough noise to alert the whole county. The cops may have arrived late in the afternoon, may have decided it was too dangerous to hike into those woods after a man armed with an assault rifle, but they'd still be out there. Especially with Bouton asking questions and Kennedy, who was supposed to be on duty, among the missing.

"Tell me something, Robert," I said. "When you do the book. Are you going to put in the part about killing your mother?"

"That was an accident."

"How about having sex with your brother?"

His face tightened, but he held his tongue.

"Maybe you can explain it by claiming he seduced you. After all, he was twelve years old and you were what . . . eighteen? What eighteen-year-old could refuse the charms of a twelve-year-old boy?"

"That's what he *liked* to do, all right? I was bein' *nice* to the little faggot."

"Save it for the book, Robert. Right now, we have a little game to play. You like games, don't you? Killing is a game for you, isn't it? Like cat and mouse?" I gave him a chance to answer, but he chose to remain silent. He may not have known what was coming, but he knew I was finally getting down to it. "The name of this game is 'You Bet Your Life.' No, wait a minute. It's called 'We Bet Our Lives.' We bet our lives that a blind woman named Lorraine Cho can make her way through a marsh, climb a steep hillside, find a road that's little more than a worn track, hike back through a stream to your house, avoid two vicious dogs, find help, and get back here before we die. How do you like the sound of it?"

"You're not gonna kill me, are you?"

"No, I'm not. But the rules of the game demand that I immobilize you. Turn around."

"What're you gonna do, cuff me?"

"I'm afraid I forgot to pack my handcuffs. I'm sure the captain'll be on my case about it."

"Look, I'm not . . . "

"If you don't turn around, I'm going to kill you very, very slowly."

He hesitated a moment, then read the signs correctly. Submit or die—it was a better choice than the one he'd given his thirty-three victims. What he'd told them was submit *and* die.

When he was fully turned, when his back was to me, I put the rifle up against my shoulder, took a deep breath, let it out and shot him right between the shoulder blades. I heard two distinct cracks, the first an exploding cartridge, the second an exploding spine. His legs collapsed under him and he fell forward onto the dirt, landing hard. I crawled over to him, wanting to be absolutely sure. The right side of his face lay flat and unmoving against the ground, but his left eye rolled in its socket, searching for me.

"I can't feel anything," he whispered. "I can't feel anything at all."

And neither could I.

THIRTY-TWO

It was early August when Mount Sinai Hospital in New York cut me loose. I came to Mount Sinai by way of Guardian Angel in Lake George, and to Guardian Angel by way of a police helicopter. (Which helicopter, by the way, I shared with a paralyzed Robert Kennedy and a possessive Lorraine Cho who hounded the working paramedics like an avenging angel looking for work.) Kennedy had caught me with two .00 shotgun pellets. The first had cracked a rib and stopped, but the second had found its way into my abdomen, where it nicked my colon, spewing bacteria-laden fecal matter into my abdominal cavity. My body had fought the massive infection that followed, an up-and-down battle that would have been lost (or so the doctors told me) if Lorraine hadn't made it down the mountain.

Or if Vanessa Bouton, Sheriff Pousson, and two dozen assorted deputies and state troopers hadn't been waiting at Kennedy's house. *With* a helicopter.

"A matter of hours," my surgeon later explained. "We saved your life."

What Dr. Manuel Ramirez meant was, "*I* saved your life." He was the most arrogant man I'd ever met, dispensing his talents with the diffidence of a British lord tossing loaves of bread to kneeling peasants. The fact that he was right—that he *had* saved my life—didn't make his attitude easier to swallow. Especially because, for a very long time, it didn't seem like much of a favor. I was delirious when they rushed me into surgery at Guardian Angel, and nobody stopped to explain the mechanics of colon repair. What Dr. Ramirez did was remove six inches of my colon, sew off the end where it turned into the rectum, then shove the other part like a hose through the outside of my abdomen, and cover it with a plastic bag.

Days later, when my fever dropped far enough for me to comprehend his royal proclamations, Dr. Ramirez paused at the foot of my bed. Trailed by eight or nine fawning residents, he peered at me over half-moon reading glasses before tossing me a few well-chosen words.

"A temporary colostomy. We reverse it later on."

Temporary? Later on? Did that mean an hour, a day, a week, a month, a year, a decade? Ramirez sauntered off, his white surgical gown swinging behind him like the robes of a high priest, before I could ask the obvious question.

I suppose he knew he could handle me. Not only was I running a fever, I was tied to the bed by two IV's and a sump pump. Lorraine, on the other hand, suffered from no such constraints. She cornered Ramirez near the elevator, endured his irritated sighs, and got the facts.

Temporary meant at least a month, assuming he managed to bring my infection under control.

It took him longer than he would have liked, too long for my taste, and I transferred myself to Mount Sinai in New York, where they'd practically invented bowel surgery. Unfortunately, Mount Sinai didn't have much better luck with the tenacious bacteria dining beneath my liver. All in all, it took six weeks before they put me back together. Six weeks of intermittent fever and IV needles that turned my veins as black as any junkie's.

Lorraine stayed with me for the first few days in Guardian Angel, then went back to her folks in New York. At the time, I figured that was the end of that. But when I arrived in New York, Lorraine was waiting beside my bed. Koocek was there as well, and the two women formed a curious relationship over the next three weeks. Koocek had never been much of a talker, but compared to Lorraine, she was a magpie. Lorraine went about her business with a furious concentration, bumping into things, stopping to fix them in her memory, going on to face the next obstacle. Koocek spent the hours in a plastic chair sketching the two people least able to complain—blind Lorraine Cho and delirious Roland Means.

When I finally came home, Lorraine and Marie came with me. Both stayed for the first few days, but then Koocek drifted back into her professional life, making the rounds of parties and openings as she pursued her own career path. Koocek had always been ambitious; she had to be. A painter may be able to finance her vision on the income derived from waiting tables. A monumental sculptor, on the other hand, has to have access to big bucks. For Koocek, those bucks came from grants, and the sources of those grants were often to be found at the parties and openings she religiously attended.

I assumed that Lorraine would follow Koocek's lead. I was weak but clear-headed, with no need for moment-to-moment care. Lorraine apparently had other ideas. She rarely left the apartment, insisting that her parents come to visit her, that she would not move in with them. At first, I put it to the fear all victims, even sighted victims, experience after a brutal assault. Later, I realized that a bond—always unspoken—had formed between us. I can't say that I understood that bond, or even that I spent much time analyzing it. Only that it was there and I didn't have any desire to break it.

It was nearly Labor Day when Vanessa Bouton, attaché case in hand, showed up with what she called "your options." Bouton had been to see me a number of times over the weeks. She'd accepted my official version of the events (that I was delirious most of the time, that Kennedy was going into the cabin for a weapon, that I shot him in the back in self-defense) without comment, submitting it to the prosecutors and the department brass who accepted it, also without comment. The issue became moot when Kennedy, perhaps fearing extradition to a death penalty state, decided to plead guilty to all the offenses surrounding his capture, including the premeditated murder of his wife.

Kennedy's admission paved the way for Bouton and myself to be

elevated to the status of NYPD heroes. The media had already can-
onized us, but the department, fearing embarrassment if we had to
testify at trial, kept its praise confined to a few clichés from the mouth
of a now obscure (and thoroughly expendable) Chief Bowman. Two
hours after Kennedy entered his guilty plea, however, the biggest big
monkey in the job, Commissioner Bernard Jackson, held a press conference on the steps of One Police Plaza. Bouton and I were to receive
the department Medal of Honor, a green breast bar dotted with gold
stars. In addition, I was to receive the Police Combat Cross and a
Silver Star.

Yay, team.

All this is a long way of explaining why I wasn't surprised
when Bouton turned up in the uniform of a full inspector. In
fact, what interested me as I stepped back to let her enter the
loft, was the fact that she'd shown up in uniform at all.
Whatever she'd come for had to be official.

"Means," she said, "how are you feeling."

"Good enough to know I'll get better."

Lorraine was over at my desk pounding away at an IBM
Selectric. She turned at the sound of Bouton's voice, waved
once, then went back to work.

"She writing a book?" Bouton asked, a frown of disapproval
pulling at her lips.

"All by herself."

The truth, which I didn't bother to tell Bouton, was that
Lorraine had been contacted by a dozen television talk-show
hosts and nearly every publisher in the country. The offers had
been monumental, beginning at six figures and spiraling out of
sight. She'd refused the TV shows, then negotiated through an
agent with the publishers, finally accepting the one offer that
would allow her to do the book on her own. The others, without
exception, had refused to part with the big bucks unless she
accepted a professional ghostwriter.

"Are you part of this, Means?" Bouton turned to face me, her new authority evident in her regal bearing. "You wouldn't be the coauthor?"

"More like the editor. But, don't worry, Cap . . . Inspector. The last thing I want is to be a celebrity. People look too hard at celebrities. You wanna sit down?"

She responded by crossing to the couch and taking a seat. Part of Lorraine's manuscript was lying on an end table. Bouton was presumptuous enough to pick it up, but couldn't bring herself to read it without permission.

"This the book?" She held it out to me.

"That's part of it." I accepted the pages, dropping them to my lap. "Lorraine's doing the last part first, which is kind of unusual. You want to hear some?"

"As long as I'm not in it."

"When she rose up and began to cross the marsh, Lorraine knew herself as Lazarus rising from the dead. She actually thought those words: I am Lazarus rising. And like Lazarus, she had to come forth by herself. She had to leave the tomb, to return to the warm flesh of the world, the babble of words, the rush of wind across her body.

"She stepped forward eagerly, knowing exactly where to put her feet, but there was a burden there as well. One she felt, but couldn't name. One that would become clear to her later on.

"She remembered reading a book about Lazarus. The title escaped her, but the author envisioned a Lazarus who never came back to the land of the living. A man who remained entombed even as he sat down to the evening meal. Even as he prayed to the man who'd pulled him from the grave.

"When she finally completed her journey, when she stumbled into a yard filled with the sharp bark of police radios, heard the excited voices, felt the solicitous hands on her arms, Lorraine knew that, like Lazarus, she would carry the burden of the tomb forever."

". . . Well, what do you think?"

"She's writing about herself as if she were someone else."

"True. I spoke to her about it, but she wasn't real interested in my opinion."

Bouton shifted her gaze to the back of Lorraine's bent head. "I think she's a victim. And I think she's lucky to be able to see it. Most victims try to resume their former lives before they're ready." She turned back to me, her eyes distant. "You put it to me pretty good, Means. That nightscope? I still can't accept what you did. You betrayed me at every turn."

I smiled, trying to make a joke of it (after all, what's done is done, right?), but she didn't smile back.

"You know, Inspector," I said, "between the two of us, we made a whole cop. All those contradictions you found in Thong's M.O.? I thought they were so much wishful thinking. I thought they'd jumped, full-blown, from the fountainhead of your ambition. But then, when Kennedy was right in our faces, when I could smell him, taste him on my tongue, you had all kinds of doubts. You wanted to wait for the pieces to fall into place."

Bouton shook her head in genuine disgust. "Forget the con game, Means. This was just another hunt for you. Bowman told me about your arrangement with Pucinski. You never play by the rules. Not for a minute."

"That's not entirely true, Inspector. I play by rules—tomb rules. It's not something you can understand." I gave her a minute to think about it. "But why don't you tell me what's on your mind? You didn't come here to talk about this."

"What makes you think so?"

"Because we both know there's nothing either one of us can do about it. Because we both know that you *should* have known what I was doing. Because while I may have lied about the particulars, I never denied what I was. And most of all, because you came to me with a promise you couldn't keep. You told me that, win or lose, I'd get out of ballistics, but what you were doing was gambling with both our careers. Besides, you got what you wanted, *Inspector* Bouton."

She leaned against the back of the sofa and peered at me

through half-closed eyes. I think she wanted me to add something, but I couldn't figure out what it was, so I held my peace and waited.

"You know, we found those trophies you were supposed to be looking for in Kennedy's house," she announced, changing the subject. "Anybody tell you about it?"

"Not a word."

"We found jewelery and personal effects, like we expected. But we also found a stack of letters. Letters from John to his brother describing the New York meat market. Everything, Means. What he did; who he did it with; where he did it. Maybe John didn't know it at the time, but his letters amounted to a manual on how to kill in New York City."

The last piece of the puzzle. All along, I'd wondered how an upstate cop had managed to negotiate New York's various strolls. Now I knew.

"Why'd he do it?" I asked. "The brothers hated each other. Why the letters?"

"I asked Robert Kennedy about that, and he told me that flaunting his sexual adventures was John's way of getting even."

We fell into a silence, then. I wasn't that long out of surgery, and my body was already looking forward to sliding between the sheets.

"We found Lydia Singleton," Bouton finally said.

"Where was she?" For once, I remembered that Lydia Singleton and Dolly Dope were the same person.

"She was in a vacant lot in the Bronx. Somebody beat her with a club, sliced her throat, covered her with garbage."

"You have a suspect?"

"Means, we don't have clue one. Not about Lydia Singleton or the six other women who've been killed in the same way."

I wanted to keep asking questions. (Were they looking for a demented john? Did the women know each other? Were the crime scenes clustered? Scattered?) But I could smell the bait. And the trap waiting for my inquisitive nose.

"I'm heading up the task force," Bouton said after a minute. "It won't be like Thong, of course. There are no advocacy groups for female prostitutes."

"Is that good or bad?"

"The advocacy groups?"

"The fact that it won't be like Thong."

She brought her finger up to her face, ran it down the side of her nose. "That's a very interesting question, Means. Nearly dying must have awakened your brain." She sat a little straighter, assuming her official prepared-to-lecture posture. "On balance, I'd say it's good. We won't have to deal with ten thousand hotline tips. They didn't help us with Kennedy, but they ate through our budget and manpower like ravenous wolves."

"What about the FBI? They working up a profile?"

"That's their job. Plus, the department has its own profiler now. A detective, second, named Roy Murtz. He spent a year training at Quantico."

"And now he's bucking for detective, first. Which he'll get if the profile is accurate." I pulled myself off the couch, limped to the refrigerator and retrieved a pitcher of iced tea. Bouton nodded her assent when I held it up for her inspection. "I suppose there's no doubt in your mind that the perpetrator's a psycho?"

"None."

"Have you checked with Miriam Brock?" I said it with a smile as I carried glasses of tea back to the couch.

"As a matter of fact, I have. She told me to ask you a question. Her exact words were, 'Ask him what he found out.'"

I managed a grin at that one. "Tell her I looked deep into my heart and discovered that I'm not Mr. Softie." I intended to leave it like that, but I couldn't. I rambled on, despite my best intentions. "Tell her you can't add by subtracting. You can't find out who you are by finding out who you're not."

Bouton sighed. "Enough with the bullshit. It's facts of life time. About a week ago, the New York Police Department, in all its majesty and wisdom, decided that you and it were quits forever. I spoke to the head of the unofficial committee that made this decision and persuaded him to let me offer you some options. Or, actually, two options. The first is a three-quarter disability pension. You won't have to see any doctors or submit to periodic reevaluation. Just take the money and run. The second option is to work directly under me on this task force. We'll be doing a lot of street work—setting up surveillance, running decoys through the various strolls, persuading prostitutes to trust us with information. It's right up your alley."

"Sorry to disappoint you, Inspector, but according to the surgeons, my alley doesn't go anywhere for the next five weeks."

"That's not a problem. This perp's not going to walk into a precinct and surrender. Plus, it'll take us nearly that long to set up the operation. In the meantime, I'll drop by from time and time, let you look at the paperwork, listen to what you have to say."

I couldn't read the expression on her face. There was eagerness to it, but something else as well. Maybe she thought she was doing me a favor. Or that she was still committed to saving me. Or that she knew she'd seriously lowered the testosterone level of the boys who run the NYPD by nabbing Thong on her own and she'd better not let this one get away.

"Sorry, Inspector, but I'll take door number one." I intended to let it go at that, but the crestfallen expression on her face was too genuine to ignore. "Don't take it personally. It's just that I've had enough. Something happened to me up on that mountain. I don't know exactly what it is, but I know I can't go back. I can't have the course of my life determined by a few elderly cops who haven't seen the streets in a decade. Besides, I don't need the money."

"What are you telling me, you're going to buy yourself a rocking chair? Maybe take up bingo? Learn to knit socks? You're a hunter, Means. There's no way you can stop."

"I didn't say I was going to stop, Inspector. I didn't say that at all."